Purple Springs

The third of Nellie McClung's four novels, *Purple Springs* (1921) completes the story of Pearlie Watson, the oldest child of shanty Irish immigrants settled in southwest Manitoba. Pearl – now a country schoolteacher – has learned that the pain and suffering of the world is ingrained in structures which are not easily or effectively swayed by 'the art of being kind.'

Purple Springs fictionally extends many of the arguments made by McClung in *In Times Like These* regarding 'male statecraft,' graphically illustrating the consequences through her characters. McClung skilfully weaves together these social critiques in a tale of love, vocation, and coming-of-age, which sees Pearl, as a prototypical McClung, take on the corrupt Conservative government of Manitoba – and win. McClung's own triumph in the 'Women's Parliament' held in Winnipeg's Walker Theatre in 1914 is here dramatically and delightfully recreated with Pearl Watson as the premier, in a speech taken virtually verbatim from McClung's own.

Purple Springs explores an important piece of Canadian social history. It invites its readers to enter imaginatively an earlier age when women were second-class citizens in law as well as custom, and gives at least one woman's view of what needed to be done to right that injustice.

RANDI R. WARNE is Program Director and Assistant Professor of Social Ethics at St Stephen's College, University of Alberta, where she also teaches women's studies. She has performed dramatic monologues in the role of Nellie McClung across Canada and on CBC radio.

PURPLE SPRINGS

Nellie L. McClung

With an introduction by
Randi R. Warne

UNIVERSITY OF TORONTO PRESS
TORONTO BUFFALO LONDON

© University of Toronto Press 1992
Toronto Buffalo London
Printed in Canada

ISBN 0-8020-5924-4 (cloth)
ISBN 0-8020-6864-2 (paper)

Purple Springs was first published in Toronto in 1921 by
Thomas Allen. That edition is reproduced following the
Introduction.

Printed on acid-free paper

Canadian Cataloguing in Publication Data

McClung, Nellie L., 1873–1951.
Purple springs
ISBN 0-8020-5924-4 (bound). – ISBN 0-8020-6864-2 (pbk.)
I. Warne, R.R. (Randi Ruth), 1952–
II. Title.

PS8525.C52P8 1992   C813'.52   C92-093588-5
PR9199.2.M33P8 1992

This book has been published with assistance from
the Canada Council and the Ontario Arts Council
under their block grant programs.

INTRODUCTION

Randi R. Warne

MANITOBA TORIES WORRIED OVER LADY ORATOR'S CAMPAIGN

MRS. NELLIE MCCLUNG, SPEAKING FOR ORGANIZATIONS IN PROVINCE, EXPOSES ROBLIN

Thousands Flock to Hear Her Addresses

On Eve of Elections Liberal Leader Predicts Victory
If Polls Are Protected

These excited headlines greeted readers of the *Montreal
Herald* on 9 July 1914.[1] Throughout the country, Canadians were being regaled with reports of the knock-down,
drag-out battle for the Manitoba legislature, led in large
measure by one of Canada's favourite novelists. Nellie
McClung's adversary in this great struggle was none other
than Sir Rodmond P. Roblin, Conservative premier, for
eight years the leader of a political 'machine' that had
run the province efficiently and, in the eyes of its critics,
in its own self-interest. Opposed to woman suffrage, re-

calcitrant on temperance legislation, Roblin's government presented itself as a bulwark of civilization, repulsing the anarchic waves of change threatening to consume the province. Despite repeated delegations and petitions from reform-minded citizens, Roblin stood firm. The last straw came on 27 January, when he informed a delegation organized by the Political Equality League of Manitoba – which included representatives from the Woman's Christian Temperance Union, the First Icelandic Women's Suffrage Association, the Women's Civic League, the Mothers' Association, the Manitoba Grain Growers' Association, and the Trades and Labour Council – that extending the franchise to women would 'ruin the home,' lead to divorce, and 'throw children into the arms of servant girls.'[2]

Sir Rodmond had done it. No sooner had the delegation left his office than plans were set in motion for a 'Woman's Parliament,' a play wherein roles were reversed so that men were disenfranchised and forced to beg for the privilege of the vote from an all-female legislature. The following night it was staged to a sell-out crowd at Winnipeg's Walker Theatre, with Nellie McClung as premier. Parodying Roblin's dismissive speech to the delegation perfectly, she brought down the house. As the *Montreal Herald* reported:

> The other evening Mrs. McClung spoke in Winnipeg in the Walker Theatre and long before the advertised hour of her address every seat in the large auditorium was filled. Last Thursday Sir Rodmond spoke here and on Monday his feminine tormentor made him look ridiculous. She has introduced into this campaign the most telling weapon with which the bombastic Premier of Manitoba could be at-

tacked and one which no person has even wielded against him before so poignantly and effectively. All Manitoba has been made to laugh at Sir Rodmond Roblin by Mrs. McClung.[3]

Purple Springs is McClung's fictional retelling of those heady days in Manitoba politics. Written six years after the battle itself, the novel was published in 1921, the year McClung was first elected as a Liberal member of the Alberta legislature. Her heroine is Pearl Watson, the cheerful yet formidable eldest daughter of shanty Irish immigrants, whose exploits had delighted readers of McClung's *Sowing Seeds in Danny* (1908) and *The Second Chance* (1910).[4] In these first two novels, Pearlie, as she was then called, energetically meets the challenge of helping her working-class parents care for their nine children, and uses her wit and ingenuous wisdom to help various folk in the community as well. The epigraph to *Sowing Seeds in Danny* expressed McClung's understanding of Pearlie's role, and what it took to build and mend community:

> So many faiths – so many creeds, –
> So many paths that wind and wind
> While just the art of being kind, –
> Is what the old world needs![5]

The decade of political struggle which intervened between McClung's first publications and *Purple Springs* marked McClung deeply, converting her hopeful confidence in individual transformation into a belief in the necessity of social and structural change. In *Purple Springs*,

Pearl has become McClung's fictional alter-ego, championing woman suffrage and rousting the corrupt Conservative government of a remarkably familiar-looking 'Premier Graham.' Indeed, the crowning point of the novel's action is Pearl's outrageously successful performance as premier in 'The Play,' a virtually verbatim account of the script McClung had herself performed in 1914.[6] *Purple Springs* is thus more than a dramatized account of an intriguing piece of social history; it also provides a record of the political development of one of Canada's most successful social activists.

In her own life, Nellie McClung was an internationally known author, speaker, and feminist reformer. She wrote sixteen books: four novels, two novellas, three short story collections, three volumes of wartime writing (ranging from speeches to inspirational stories to a ghostwritten tale of an escaping soldier), two volumes of selected newspaper columns, and a two-volume autobiography.[7] As well, her personal papers contain over four hundred articles, stories, and essays, published and unpublished, which she produced over a span of four decades. As a syndicated columnist in the thirties and forties she spoke out for the enfranchisement of Orientals in British Columbia and against the internment of the Japanese. In an era not known for its toleration, she called for Jewish immigration to Canada to escape Nazi persecution and argued vigorously for the many contributions Jews could make to Canadian culture.[8]

She was also an internationally known champion of women, formally challenging the innumerable barriers to their full social and political equality through her writing, speaking, and political campaigning. A lifelong member of the Woman's Christian Temperance Union and the Women's International League of Peace and Freedom, she also served as a Canadian delegate to the League of Nations in the 1930s. She advocated women's full equality in religious organizations and lobbied for almost two decades for the ordination of women in the Methodist, then United Church of Canada. For these and many other accomplishments, including her role as one of the 'Famous Five' in the Persons Case of 1929, in which women were declared legally 'persons' in the matter of 'rights and privileges' as well as in 'pains and penalties,' she became known across the country as 'Our Nell.'

It would seem reasonable to assume from these many accomplishments that McClung came from a background of wealth and education, but in fact her origins were not far removed from the Watson family's arduous life of rural subsistence described so vividly in her novels. She was born Nellie Mooney on 20 October, 1873 in a little Ontario farmhouse 'a mile from Chatsworth, on the Garafraxa Road, in a stony part of the county of Grey.'[9] Her Irish father, John Mooney, had emigrated with two older brothers from Nenagh in 1830 at the age of eighteen. After several dangerous years as a logger in Bytown (later Ottawa), he decided in 1841 to try his hand at farming in the Georgian Bay area, settling eventually in Sullivan Township. In 1858, some years after the death of his first wife, John Mooney married sixteen-year-old Letitia McCurdy, an immigrant from Dundee who had travelled to Canada only two years earlier with her mother and sister shortly after her father's death from cholera. The experiences and concerns of these two people – a laughter-loving Irish Methodist father and a dour but dedicated

Scottish Presbyterian mother – figure broadly throughout McClung's fiction. They are particularly evident in the characters of John and Mrs Watson of the Pearlie Watson trilogy. Their struggle to build a new life in a growing nation is highlighted in *Purple Springs*, driving home McClung's lifelong concern to make Canada into 'the land of the Second Chance' and 'the land of the Fair Deal.'[10]

The Mooneys and their seven children – Nellie being the youngest of the six still living – farmed the rough land of the Bruce Peninsula, a task both difficult and frustrating.[11] But word had begun to filter in about the endless opportunities in the great Northwest, firing the imaginations of many young men weary of the endless, back-breaking labour on stubborn and stony soil. Nellie Mooney's eldest brother Will was one of these, and in 1879 he travelled to the Red River country with the understanding that, if opportunities proved as promised, the Mooney clan would join him the following year. Thus it was that the Mooneys found themselves bound for the Souris River Valley in 1880. They departed from Owen Sound, travelling west by steamship, ox-cart, and on foot until they reached Millford, near the Tiger Hills of south-western Manitoba.

Nellie Mooney gloried in her new surroundings. She grew up a tomboy, ranging across the wide-open prairies she described so lovingly in her fiction. Like many of the children of settlers, she was educated intermittently, not learning to read until she was nine. Yet by sixteen she had attended Normal School in Winnipeg and was on her way to becoming a prairie schoolteacher. It was at her first teaching appointment in Manitou that she was to meet the person who would change the course of her life.

Nellie Mooney met Annie McClung in 1890 at a meeting of the Young Ladies Bible Class. The wife of the new Methodist minister, Mrs McClung impressed the younger woman to such a degree that she became, as McClung was later to write, 'the only woman I have ever seen whom I would like to have for a mother-in-law.'[12] She immediately set out to discover if there were any sons in the family, and when she was informed that the couple had only two young boys, aged fourteen and ten, she jauntily replied that it would make little difference when they were in their fifties. As fortune would have it, however, there was a third son, Wesley, who at eighteen was a pharmacist's assistant just back from the east. Determined to achieve her goal, she took her last three dollars to the pharmacy and bought a fountain pen she could ill afford and didn't need, thereby arranging to meet the red-headed young man who in 1896 would become her husband.[13]

Annie McClung proved to be an excellent choice as a mother-in-law. Not only had she raised her son to see women as equals, but also she was an ardent temperance and woman suffrage activist, lending considerable support and inspiration to her daughter-in-law. Further, she fully supported her literary aspirations. Nellie McClung had long wanted to be a writer, but the demands of being a wife and mother had left little time to do more than write advertisements for Wes's pharmacy, ads that none the less reveal her wit and lively sensibilities. One day in November 1902, however, Annie announced that Nel-

lie was to enter a short-story contest for *Collier's* magazine, leaving all of her domestic duties in her mother-in-
law's capable hands. Although she did not win the contest, the die was cast. The story later ended up in the
hands of E.S. Caswell, of the Wm. Briggs Publishing
Company, who encouraged McClung to expand her tale
of the Watson family to book length. After numerous
delays, including the loss and eventual recovery of the
manuscript, *Sowing Seeds in Danny* was published in 1908,
becoming the bestseller of the year and the Canadian
bestseller to date.[14]

The popularity of Nellie McClung's first novel was in
large measure due to the time in which she was writing.
The book appeared in a rapidly expanding literary market
in which an increasing number of female writers were
participating. Moreover, her skill at telling stories of the
'common people' was valued in an era when Canadians
were attempting to define a unique identity. Literature,
especially the kind that reproduced 'Canadian' experience, was highly regarded, not only for its artistic merits
but also for its role in nation-building.[15] McClung's witty,
authentic tales of frontier life served this purpose, making
the prairies come vividly alive for her readers. As a result,
she became one of the most well known and best loved
of Canadian writers. Tellingly, *Clearing in the West* (1935),
which recounts McClung's early days on the prairies, was
next only to *Sowing Seeds in Danny* in popularity during
McClung's lifetime.

In 1911 the McClung family moved to Winnipeg, leaving behind them the cosy rural life of Manitou which had
served as the backdrop for the tales of the Watson clan.
Much later, McClung recalled her anxiety about the move,

which had come about because of Wes's new position
with the Manufacturers' Life Insurance Company:

> I remember the day we left Manitou. I looked back from
> the window of the train as it made its labored way up the
> grade past Luke Armstrong's buildings and Elijah Harmer's
> big barn ... It was a bright June day, full of greenness and
> beauty, the air full of the scent of pea vines and wolf willow
> blossom. The hush of the noon-day lay on the fields for
> the workers had gone in for their mid-day meal. Peace and
> plenty lay over all and every building, grove of trees, every
> winding trail seemed like an old friend from whom we
> were parting. I knew one pleasant chapter of our lives was
> ending and a sudden fear gripped my heart – fear of the
> market place; fear of high places; fear of the strange coun-
> try. If I could have gone back to the safety of the known
> ways at that moment, I would have gone.[16]

McClung had reason to be concerned. In 1911 Winnipeg
was a city of 136,035 people, well over three times the
size of any other prairie community,[17] with a longstand-
ing reputation as a 'turbulent, rowdy and bawdy [town]
to which the homesteaders returned for boozy relaxation
and libidinous diversion.' Alcohol consumption was a
serious problem in the province, which that year saw over
a third of its total arrests (5,832 out of 13,413) made for
public drunkenness. In Winnipeg the situation was particularly acute. As James Gray has reported, 'The Winnipeg bars were designed for but a single purpose – for
stand-up drinking. Drinking was for the purpose of "getting drunk", almost never for relaxing conversation.' Nor
were residents safe beyond the infamous Main Street strip,

as liquor was also readily available at grocery stores. Women and children were regularly subjected to the rough and potentially dangerous behaviour of drinkers, who eventually carried their excesses into the home. As Gray explains so colourfully, '[m]any a father who went down to the corner for a bag of potatoes returned listing badly to starboard from the alcoholic ballast he had taken aboard at the store.'[18] Predictably, the results of such indulgence were not always benign; the violence perpetrated upon women and children by drunken men reached frightening proportions, making it one of the most serious social issues addressed by reformers.

An additional factor in Winnipeg life was the city's role as a major destination for immigrants. From 1901 to 1911 Winnipeg's population quadrupled.[19] Approximately one-third of the new arrivals spoke a language other than English, and many were illiterate. This rapid influx of ethnically diverse people contributed to a whole range of social problems such as poverty, violence, disease, 'white slavery' (prostitution), and exploitation of foreign workers in sweatshops. The increasing severity of these conditions alarmed social reformers such as J.S. Woodsworth, whose All People's Mission sought to improve the situation by helping immigrants establish themselves in their new country. While attending to material needs such as food and clothing, the mission also strongly supported educational efforts for both adults and children, and set up cultural activities such as 'Mothers' Meetings, Women's Councils, Girls' Clubs, sewing, cooking and fancy work classes, gymnasium classes and boys' clubs.' Writing in 1917 McClung concluded: 'All Peoples' Mission is not a charity – it is an institution which aims to making charity unnecessary, it teaches the people to help and respect themselves.'[20]

Woodsworth was a leading proponent of the widespread movement within Protestant Christianity known as the social gospel. Believing that Christianity was first and foremost a 'social religion,' which sought to 'build the Kingdom of God here on earth,' supporters worked tirelessly to transform conditions and to create a peaceful, egalitarian society. Social and political equality were thus religious issues; achieving those goals, a religious duty. While social gospel reformers held a range of views about proper strategies for social transformation,[21] all agreed that the end result should be the establishment of 'right relations between man and man.' Winnipeg proved to be a particularly fruitful ground for the practice of social Christianity: the city's numerous problems provided ample challenges for reformers such as Woodsworth and the radical professor Salem Bland, while at the same time its vitality and open-endedness as 'the Gateway to the West' rang true with the social gospel's essentially optimistic and progressive vision. At the fresh beginning of a new century – in Laurier's words, 'Canada's Century' – social gospellers were filled with a sense of endless possibility; they were convinced that the winds of change were blowing, and with the force of their efforts all serious social evils could indeed be abolished.

Purple Springs gives strong evidence of the impact of such thinking on Nellie McClung's view of the world. The novel expresses the conviction that fundamental social change, both in terms of cultural attitudes and specific political and legal structures, had to be brought about.[22] McClung was particularly aware of the back-breaking

work of those like her own family who were struggling
to build a new life on the frontier. She also recognized,
however, that many considered this labour demeaning,
a sign of inferior capacity or breeding. In the novel she
challenges that notion through an incident in which Pearl
is told that her family is 'socially impossible.' Pearl is first
troubled, then angry, for her parents' hard work has ben-
efited the entire community:

> ... many a thrill of pride had she experienced in thinking
> of her parents and their days of struggling. They had been
> and were, the real Empire-builders who subdued the soil
> and made it serve human needs, enduring hardships and
> hunger and cold and bitter discouragements, always with
> heroism and patience. The farm on which they now lived,
> had been abandoned, deserted, given up for a bad job, and
> her people had redeemed it, and were making it one of
> the best in the country! Every farm in the community was
> made more valuable because of their efforts ... But since
> she had been away, she learned to her surprise that the
> world does not give its crowns to those who serve it best
> – but to those who can make the most people serve them.
> (72–3)

Pearl's new understanding that such injustices needed to
be remedied comes to her in something very like a religious vision, as that 'which came to Elisha's servant at
Dothan when he saw the mountains were filled with the
horses and chariots of the Lord!' (74). No less than Pearl,
McClung understood the fight for 'the even chance for
everyone' as a kind of religious calling.

Equally essential to the vision was a re-evaluation of

women's status. In addition to the concern, shared with
male social gospellers, for just and safe working conditions in the public sphere ('right relations between man
and man'),[23] McClung asked a further question: what
would it take to establish right relations between men
and women? Clearly, for McClung, women would have
to have a say in the conditions under which they would
live, and that required a direct political voice.

By advocating that women should become active par-
ticipants in the political process, however, McClung was
flying in the face of a powerful and pervasive ideology.
The division of physical labour based on gender is ancient, but the doctrine of 'separate spheres' moved beyond the realm of work to invest sexual difference with
immense cultural and spiritual significance. The idea had
its origins in the Enlightment, and was fuelled by the
dualistic romanticism of the early nineteenth century, its
notion of a mystical, emotional 'feminine ideal' contrast-
ing sharply with the carnal, materialistic view of women
held in ages past. By the latter half of the century, as
sexual reproduction came to be seen as the cornerstone
of human progress, Darwinian theory gave further scientific justification for understanding men and women as
separate, even opposite, kinds of beings.

The doctrine of 'separate spheres' held that men and
women were destined biologically to perform very different functions in the world. Physical difference became
the hallmark by which human qualities were divided into
oppositional, polarized categories. Men were held to be
properly aggressive, 'rational,' and coolly logical, best
suited therefore to occupations such as business, politics,
and scientific inquiry, where determination and self-

affirming confidence would ensure success. In the public sphere their prowess was expressed through intense competition, where Darwin's doctrine of 'the survival of the fittest' held sway. It followed that only those capable of doing battle on such terms should enter the fray.[24]

The contrasts were sharp: women were seen to be soft where men were hard, emotional where men were rational and intellectual, spiritual where men were material. Too weak to withstand the pressures of the outside world, women found their proper sphere in the home, the safe womb from within which they could exercise their primary calling of 'moral motherhood.' That many, perhaps the majority, could not afford this luxury, being forced instead to labour for their bread both inside the home and out of it, proved nothing to those upholding such views. Darwin's theory of 'the specialization and differentiation of function' provided ample explanation of women's many and obvious capacities. The more a species evolved, the more specialized and unique its function became. Women who were solely concerned with 'moral motherhood' reflected this specialization and differentiation of function; women who laboured physically, worked outside the home, performed mathematical calculations, made public speeches, or learned Greek, did not. Rather than seeing these skills as accurate indicators of women's true abilities and potential, women who were competent in these ways were seen as abberations on the evolutionary scale.

Women were also solely responsible for the moral and spiritual education of their children. Properly raised, children would go forth from the home unsullied, capable of rising above all the dangers and difficulties of the out-

side world. It followed that any variation from this pattern on the children's part, any false step or falling into
temptation, was the result of 'poor home training.' In
other words, it was their mothers' fault. Women's high
status as the 'angels of the hearth' thus served to burden
them with an impossible responsibility for the lifelong
well-being of their children. Many began to feel this to
be keenly unjust, and by the latter half of the nineteenth
century women's groups were actively calling for more
direct control over the conditions into which their children were being born. They worked for temperance and
against prostitution, convinced that society itself should
benefit from 'moral mothering.'[25] The most immediate
means to this end was increasingly understood to be votes
for women.

Many women believed they had a right to suffrage
simply because they were citizens, a position stated plainly
in the Seneca Falls declaration of 1848 by Elizabeth Cady
Stanton and others. As early as 1852 Canadian women
were being sent to women's rights conventions in the
United States in support of the cause.[26] In McClung's
day, it was pointed out that women suffered, in effect,
from 'taxation without representation.' One suffragist's
response to the ubiquitous, if somewhat disingenuous,
question 'But who will mind the baby?' was that 'she
thought she could get the person that minded it when
she went to pay her taxes.'[27]

The argument for woman suffrage was therefore twofold. On the one hand, women claimed they should have
the vote because their unique moral nature would provide
a 'purifying' influence in the political realm; on the other,
women deserved the vote as tax-paying, responsible cit-

izens. Women could bring to the political process another point of view, by focusing on different issues from men or perhaps by seeing existing issues in a new light. The problem of 'white slavery' was a case in point: in the judgment of all-male legislators, theft from a railway station was a far more serious crime than the ruin of an underaged girl.[28] Activists like McClung were outraged at the low value placed on female lives, and worked vigorously to change the laws that reflected women's demeaned status. Obtaining the vote was seen as essential for lasting change, as well as a sign of cultural evolution.

In Manitoba, woman suffrage was a long-standing political issue. The first suffrage organization in western Canada was founded in the province by a group of Icelandic women who campaigned for a quarter century with petitions to the legislature and articles in the Icelandic press. The Woman's Christian Temperance Union, the first English-speaking organization to support the cause, in 1893 took a petition before the government which insisted that 'the rights of citizens not be denied on account of sex.'[29] One of the group's most active members was Dr Amelia Yeomans, who in 1885 became Winnipeg's first female physician. At her instigation, the WCTU staged a mock parliament in 1893 at the Bijou Theatre, twenty-one years before Nellie McClung's dramatic performance. It was a sober event, its appeal based on logic and justice. By the time McClung stepped onto the stage in 1914 it was evident that opposition to woman suffrage had less to do with logic than with prejudice, which, while noticeably impervious to argument, was handily dispatched with humour.[30]

Despite much effort, including the establishment of the Manitoba Equal Franchise Club in November 1894, the suffrage cause in Manitoba foundered, partly because sympathetic legislators twice backed down when their bills came up for second reading. Some progress was made in the closing decades of the century, when women property owners were given the right to vote in municipal elections in 1887, and in 1890 the school franchise, including the right to serve as trustees, was extended to women ratepayers.[31] But during the next twenty years the movement stagnated, achieving little more until a new generation of reformers breathed life into it once again.

In the interim, Manitoba politics came to be dominated by one of the most commanding political figures in the province's history. Sir Rodmond Palen Roblin had arrived 'a firm Ontario Liberal,' but before long the distinguished member for North Dufferin broke with his party over its management of railway interests in the province, and sat as an independent. His next foray into public prominence came the following year, when he became the only Protestant member of the legislature to speak out against the government on the question of separate schools for Roman Catholics. Defeated in 1892, Roblin turned to business, and soon amassed a significant fortune in the grain trade. He successfully re-entered politics in 1896, and was offered, and immediately accepted, leadership of the opposition. Two years later he relinquished the position to Hugh John Macdonald, son of Canada's first prime minister, on the grounds that the party required a leader with 'an established Conservative pedigree.' When Macdonald resigned to seek election to the House of Commons in 1900, the position of party leader came to rest once again on Roblin's shoulders.[32]

Throughout his tenure, Roblin was plagued by the temperance issue. As early as 1892 temperance supporters, mostly immigrants from Ontario, had sufficient strength to force a plebiscite on the question of prohibition of the provincial sale of liquor. Despite majority support, the Liberal government did not act, due to 'uncertainties as to its constitutional powers.' In 1899 an increasingly popular Conservative party, then led by Macdonald, offered an end to liquor sales as one of the key planks in its platform. Public opinion clearly supported the temperance cause, yet when Roblin resumed the leadership in 1900 he insisted on placing the issue once more before the people, claiming that sufficient doubt still remained about related issues such as the enforceability of any laws passed and the right of individuals to import liquor for private consumption. Temperance leaders were enraged, and urged the public to ignore the second plebiscite. As a result, the decision for prohibition was overturned, and the Roblin government held thereafter that it could do little but enforce the provincial Liquor Act as it existed.[33] Many Manitobans were suspicious that government inaction had little to do with uncertainty about public opinion or other logistical questions, and much to do with profits and the government's close ties with the 'liquor interests.'[34]

Charges of political corruption were first laid against Roblin during the provincial election of 1907, which swept the Conservatives to power. Yet as historian W.L. Morton has pointed out, 'The truth was that both parties practised flagrant electoral corruption, that all appointments to the Bench and civil service were political, and that Manitoban politics were the scene of an unresting struggle between the provincial political machine and its federal rival. And the fires of partisanship were fiercely fanned by the press.'[35] Vote-buying, ballot stuffing, and altered voters' lists were common practices during elections, as was the dispensing of political favours afterwards. Many Manitobans, McClung included, believed it was time for a change. They resented what they saw as a cynical manipulation of their concerns to support party interests, and felt that the introduction of women into the political process would be an effective way of dismantling the 'old boys' network' that had determined social and political realities for generations. 'The Machine,' the network of Conservative 'backroom boys' and party lackies, became one of McClung's chief targets in *Purple Springs*, and she dispatched characters like the pompous George Steadman and the dandyish Peter Neelands with a deft literary hand. Manitoba readers in particular could not miss Steadman's reference to the 'Good Roads Act' of 1914, or McClung's trenchant criticism of Conservative politics in Steadman's blatherings on temperance and woman suffrage in his introduction to Pearl's speech to the Chicken Hill school (90–5).

McClung became directly involved with the struggle to make the Roblin government act on pressing social concerns shortly after her arrival in Winnipeg in 1911. She began attending weekly meetings of the Canadian Women's Press Club, where 'great problems were discussed and the seed germ of the suffrage association was planted.'[36] In the early months of 1912 the Winnipeg

Political Equality League was founded, its members and officers including some of the most prominent local activists, both male and female.[37] The initial impetus for the organization's creation, however, was explained by journalist and WPEL member Lillian Beynon Thomas, as a 'direct outcome of the unsuccessful attempt of a small group of Winnipeg women to secure from the Roblin government laws to better the social and economic status of women.'[38] One episode, in which McClung and Mrs Claude Nash of the Local Council of Women escorted the premier into dank basement sweatshops with broken, overflowing plumbing and ill and injured workers to show him working conditions first-hand, left Sir Rodmond with no doubt that he faced a formidable opponent.[39]

Precisely how formidable Roblin was soon to find out. As Morton observed, much of the climate of Manitoba politics of the day, including its extreme partisanship, could be attributed to the attitude of the leaders of the Conservative administration: 'hard-headed, practical men who took life as they found it, were sceptical of reform and, with the possible exception of the Premier, indifferent to idealism.' Morton also noted their inability to 'fully respond to the new spirit of the times ... [s]uccess had made them arrogant.'[40] Roblin had reason to regret that arrogance, demonstrated repeatedly in his condescending dismissal of petitions and delegations from reform-minded citizens, as soon as the election of 1914 was called.

Nellie McClung was off and running. In short order she was stumping around the province in support of the Liberal party, which had promised woman suffrage if elected. She was already well known as an orator, having given readings from her novels and speeches on a range of social issues.[41] As her lifelong friend and fellow activist Lillian Beynon Thomas remarked: 'One of the most astonishing things about Mrs. McClung's campaign ... was that people paid for admission to her meetings to hear her talk politics. Most people, when talking politics, have felt honoured when people would attend their meetings, without any inducement but their address. But ... when Mrs. McClung began her political campaign, women's organizations all over the province begged her to go to them and give them an address ... when they were anxious to make some money ...'[42]

McClung's campaign against the Conservatives was wildly successful. She appeared to have the government in a panic, so much so that Conservatives burned her in effigy in Brandon.[43] Even the normally commanding premier was not safe. As one newspaper reported: 'Mrs. Nellie McClung, who ... has been following the premier steadily around the province was criticized by the premier in a manner which expressed intense regret that a lady should presume so much as to approach the public platform against him. "And I am told that she is coming here," he said [to one of his campaign audiences]. The intimation was no sooner given than there was a spontaneous outburst of applause which lasted for a full three minutes, while the premier was forced to stand glumly and wait for the storm to subside.'[44]

Given such evident political effectiveness, it is no surprise that McClung was described as 'the heroine of the campaign,' a 'great woman orator,' 'a power in the land,' a 'Canadian Joan of Arc,' and 'the most noted woman living in Canada.'[45] Reports of her quick wit and charismatic platform presence spread throughout the country and beyond, to the extent that she was received by the National American Woman Suffrage Association as a figure of equal importance with the famous British suffragist Emmeline Pankhurst. The NAWSA office in Nashville responded with typical gratitude: 'We feel that we can never thank you sufficiently for your inspired address on Thursday evening. ... enthusiastic admiration has been very widely expressed.'[46] One American newspaper commented that 'Mrs. McClung is considered one of the most forceful speakers in the cause that has ever visited Houston.'[47]

Despite all McClung's efforts, the Liberals did not win the Manitoba election of 1914. The Conservatives held a bare majority, winning by only four seats, although they were later able to add three northern seats where elections had been deferred. However, the tide had turned. The era of Roblinesque politics, of entrenched partisanship and party 'machines,' of patronage and paternalism, was widely seen as having run its course. Before long the opposition forced an inquiry into alleged government mishandling of funds in the construction of the new legislative buildings. A royal commission under Chief Justice T.A. Mathers of the Manitoba Court of King's Bench found sufficient evidence of fraud and political corruption to substantiate the charges, and on 12 May 1915 the Roblin government fell.[48]

Once in power the Liberals, under the leadership of T.C. Norris, made good their campaign promise of 1914. On 28 January 1916 Manitoba women became the first in Canada to be granted the provincial franchise.[49] Even so, the passage of Norris's bill, introduced on 10 January, was not without complications. One day before first reading Lillian Beynon Thomas was permitted to see a draft of the proposed bill and was 'chilled' to discover that it was framed in such a way that women could vote, but not run as candidates for the legislature. In an eleventh hour move she telephoned every member of the Political Equality League. She then contacted her well-known radical sister, newspaperwoman Frances Beynon, who was attending the Grain Growers' convention in Brandon. Fearing the consequences if the influential Grain Growers learned of the character of the bill, the government swiftly redrafted it. 'It was a long time before the Premier would speak to me,' Thomas noted.[50]

The excitement and challenge of those 'fighting days' are preserved in *Purple Springs*. Yet the novel is no didactic political lecture. McClung knew her audience well, and capitalized on the affection already established among her readers for the character of Pearlie Watson by framing her political commentary in conventional romantic melodrama.

As the novel opens, Pearl Watson, a girl of eighteen, had recently returned from Normal School in Winnipeg. Described in the previous novels as 'like the rugged little anemone, the wind flower that lifts its head from the cheerless prairie,'[51] Pearl has now matured into a lovely young woman: '... a well developed, tall, boyishly athletic girl, with a color in her cheeks like an Okanagon [*sic*] peach, hair of richest brown, with little gleams of gold, waving back naturally from a high forehead; a firm chin, with a dimple; and great brown eyes, full of lights, and with a dazzling brilliance that registered every thought of her brain and emotion of her heart' (3).

When last seen in *The Second Chance*, Pearlie had been promised by young doctor Horace Clay that after three years he would 'speak to her' of a matter of great importance. Three years having passed, Pearl is anxiously awaiting what she knows will be a proposal of marriage, and indeed for a brief time it seems it will come. But before he can commit himself Clay learns that he is suffering from an unnamed illness that could make him an invalid. Unwilling to burden Pearl with such responsibility, he explains, haltingly, that he is not good enough for her, and that she is too young to be 'induced' into marriage. Aware that he is concealing something, Pearl reluctantly but bravely agrees. The resulting twists and turns of romantic melodrama, combined with at least two complicating sub-plots, moves the story briskly along to its conclusion.

Freed from her anticipated marriage, Pearl finds herself involved in a number of unexpected situations. Her innocent report to the Chicken Hill school of her experiences of Winnipeg, including its politics, unwittingly draws her to the attention of the Conservative 'machine,' whose meddling attempts to counteract her influence provide much opportunity for humour as well as political commentary. Eventually she finds herself teaching in the community of Purple Springs, only to learn her reputation has preceded her. No one will board her but the isolated Annie Gray, ostracized by the community for her apparent 'immorality' of having a child but no husband. As the political campaign gathers momentum, these various strands (Clay, 'the machine,' and Annie Gray) are neatly woven together in a satisfying, broadly drawn resolution.

McClung's use of the traditional literary devices of romance allows her to lead her readers along less conventional political paths. Her skill with genre, as well as her keen ear for the rhythms and realities of small town rural life, enable her to paint convincing, familiar scenes which can then serve as the locus for treating the serious social issues of the day. In addition to the temperance and suffrage questions which were hotly debated in the Manitoba election of 1914, McClung used the novel to address two other impediments to women's social equality.

For at least a decade McClung had been advocating changes in the laws regarding married women's property rights.[52] In *Purple Springs* she states her case through a character named, appropriately, Mrs Paine, a thin, workworn but proud woman whose wealthy husband has kept her and their children on the brink of penury. Meanwhile, he has turned all of the farm's profits into a bank account amounting to $15,000, which he alone controls. She bears this burden with silent bitterness until informed that her husband intends to sell the farm and buy the hotel in Millford. To her dismay, she learns she has no legal rights in the property, or over her children. Although Pearl is able to help her in the end, McClung draws the readers' attention to several harsh points. First and foremost, a married woman was considered in law as 'one person' with her husband. Men thus controlled their wives' property; they also could not be sued for libel or slander. Nor could they be charged with rape, for rape could not be self-inflicted. Furthermore, couples were 'one purse,' with the husband being legally obligated only to provide sufficient support to offset utter destitution. Even if a wife earned money independently, as a farm woman might from selling butter and eggs, the fruits of her efforts still legally belonged to her husband. Although Manitoba's Married Woman's Protection Act of 1902 somewhat more liberally allowed women to leave the home if provoked by abuse, habitual drunkenness, or non-support, women like Mrs Paine remained essentially unprotected. Eventually, if slowly, the provinces worked to improve conditions, but the criminal code of Canada continued to consider husband and wife legally one person until 1975.[53]

The related issue of child custody is addressed in the novel through the story of Annie Gray. As McClung makes clear, the legal practice of allowing only unmarried women custody of their children could have terrible consequences, for a woman might be forced to choose between protecting her reputation and the safety of her child. She explores as well the potentially destructive power of social convention and a 'respectability' that could be unforgiving and judgmental rather than neighbourly. McClung uses her innate skill as a storyteller to illustrate precisely why women were arguing that they needed greater control over their own lives and the world into which they were bringing their children.

Underlying the entire novel is McClung's concern to establish right relations 'between man and man' in community, and specifically between men and women. In keeping with her belief that all human beings were basically good, she does not polarize her characters along gender lines. There are appealing characters of both sexes, and unpleasant and troublesome ones. She counters Mrs Paine's assertion that marriage means slavery for women, for example, by having Pearl reply: '... you are wrong in thinking that all men are mean and selfish. My father is not. We've been poor and all that, but we're happy. My father has never shirked his share of the work, and he has only one thought now, and that is to do well for us. There are plenty of happy marriages' (134).

(McClung was acutely aware of the social and political disadvantages in women's lives and the legal constraints under which they suffered. Yet at the same time her liberal optimism placed great faith in people's ability to change, once they are shown a better way. Mr Paine's conversion is a case in point; once made aware of his selfishness, and the reasons for his wife's aloofness, he is able to begin anew. McClung's message is twofold: the inequity of the law remains and hence must be changed, but individual lives can be improved in the meantime if problems are acknowledged and respect and communication restored.

McClung's understanding of the proper relationship of men and women is ultimately found in that between Pearl and Dr Clay. Great pain and unnecessary doubt are generated the one time he is dishonest; when straightforward and trusting of her judgment and her ability to know her own mind, everything works out well. His respect for her is undeniable throughout the novel. Though the plot is crafted along romantic lines, Pearl scarcely acts like a traditional heroine, for traditional heroines, when thwarted in love, rarely go out and bring down governments! Too, McClung is careful not to make Pearl choose between love and her career or calling. She rejects Mrs Paine's warning, and cries out instead, 'Don't ask me, Lord, I can't! ... but give me the desire of my heart, oh, Lord, and I will never tremble or turn back or be afraid. I will declare the truth before kings!' (137). For McClung, respectful loving relationships empower, rather than impede, social action in the service of justice. Through Pearl and Clay, readers are shown what men and women can be like, and that fairness and sensitivity do not make a man 'unmanly' any more than initiative and witty acuity make a woman less 'womanly.' A new model of life is possible, in which men and women can work together to build a better world.

The cornerstone of this creation, for McClung, is justice, and 'the even chance for everyone.' This passion for fairness made Sir Rodmond Roblin a particularly frustrating adversary, for as 'a gentleman of the old school' he assumed women – at least of a certain class – required special treatment and protection. Writing *Purple Springs* helped McClung reduce some of her exasperation through her gentle, yet firm, treatment of Premier Graham. It also allowed her the satisfaction of presenting the ultimate defeat of the Roblin government as a straightforward moral victory built on the inherent logic and rightness of her cause.

The reviews of *Purple Springs* were positive. A particularly appealing feature for many was the character of Pearl Watson, 'one of the most delightful women we have met in fiction in a long time,' said one reviewer. While many objected to the novel's 'excess of sentimentality,' it was generally conceded even by those critical of the book that 'its local setting and political scenes give it color and freshness.'[54] W.L. Morton described McClung's fiction as 'authentic, touched with genuine sentiment and lilting with Irish laughter.'[55] Though few contemporary reviews waxed so lyrical, her skill at rendering the characters and locale of southern Manitoba was undeniable, and a great source of her popularity.

Political content was another matter. Some reviewers ignored it altogether, or saw it as 'incidental to the main story.' At least one took exception to McClung's agenda, responding with the rather prickly comment that 'As a bit of fiction it will not attract, but as tractate on prohibition, suffragettism, [sic], and a third idea not noted yet, it will be read by seekers and believers. That third piece of propaganda relates to the absolute right of a woman to possession of her own child.'[56]

It is interesting to link this remark with observations by others that *Purple Springs* would be an ideal book to give to teenage girls. While there is no evidence that McClung intended to reach this audience (and, indeed, her readers were largely adults, both men and women), it would be difficult for adolescents to miss her concern for women's well-being, and the need to challenge convention to ensure that end. It may well have been that romance provided the necessary 'hook' for readers otherwise unwilling to listen to lectures on women's rights. Yet another reviewer tended to confirm this possibility, praising McClung's skill as a writer in the process: 'There is some good solid material for thought between the covers, too, but it is spiced with the piquant sauce of fine narration and one doesn't notice he has been reading serious stuff until he has digested it.'[57] Strong convictions, wit, and a gift for storytelling made for a potent political mix, and McClung's novels became yet another platform from which she could address the pressing social problems of her day.

The complexity of McClung's position as a public figure
no doubt contributed to the variety of opinions of her
work. As a writer she would never concentrate solely on
her art, believing that her gift for storytelling was also
invested with high moral purpose. Nor was she simply
a political figure who would fight a campaign and then
move on to the next. Nellie McClung had a vision of a
better world, and she sought to embody it in her life and
in her fiction. *Purple Springs* stands as her transformed
recollection of what was arguably the most vibrant, ex-
hilarating moment of her political career. It is little wonder that she would want to recreate it so that others could
share in it too.

NOTES

1 'Manitoba Tories Worried ...' McClung Papers, Provincial
   Archives of British Columbia, Add MSS 10, vol. 35
2 'Roblin Says Home Will Be Ruined by Votes for Women,'
   Manitoba Free Press, 28 Jan. 1914, pp 5 and 8
3 'Manitoba Tories Worried ...'
4 McClung, *Sowing Seeds in Danny* (Toronto: Wm. Briggs
   1908); *The Second Chance* (Toronto: The Ryerson Press
   1910)
5 The down-to-earth humour and intrinsic optimism which
   made Pearl such a favourite with readers is elsewhere revealed in an excerpt from Pearl's diary, in which she recounts one of the realities of rural life. *Sowing Seeds in
   Danny*, 221

            The little lams are beautiful,
            There cotes are soft and nice,

> The little calves have ringworm
> And the 2-year olds have lice!
>
> ...
>
> It must be very nasty,
> But to worrie, what's the use;
> Better be cam and cheerfull,
> And appli tobaka jooce.

For many struggling to make a life on the frontier, it was doubtless good advice to remain 'cam and cheerfull' while finding practical solutions to their inevitable problems.

6 The brilliant wit of McClung's imitation would not be lost on readers of the *Manitoba Free Press*, who on 28 January 1914 had been treated to Roblin's bombastic pronouncements ('Premier Roblin Says Home Will Be Ruined by Votes for Women') only to find them wickedly transformed the following day. 'Women Score in Drama and Debate.' McClung includes this article with another called 'Woman Suffragists Gambol at the Walker Theatre' in *The Stream Runs Fast: My Own Story* (Toronto: Thomas Allen 1945), 118–22.

7 These texts are, in order of publication, *Sowing Seeds in Danny* (1908); *The Second Chance* (1910); *The Black Creek Stopping House* (Toronto: Wm. Briggs 1912); *In Times Like These* (New York: D. Appleton and Company 1915); *The Next of Kin* (Toronto: Thomas Allen 1917); *Three Times and Out* (Boston: Houghton Mifflin 1918); *Purple Springs* (Thomas Allen 1921); *When Christmas Crossed 'The Peace'* (Thomas Allen 1923); *Painted Fires* (Thomas Allen 1925); *All We Like Sheep* (Thomas Allen 1926); *Be Good to Yourself* (Thomas Allen 1930); *Flowers for the Living* (Thomas Allen 1931); *Clearing in the West: My Own Story* (Thomas

Allen 1935); *Leaves from Lantern Lane* (Thomas Allen 1936); *More Leaves from Lantern Lane* (Thomas Allen 1937); *The Stream Runs Fast* (1945).

8 McClung wrote widely for publications as diverse as *Maclean's, Saturday Night, The War Cry,* and *The Grain Growers' Guide,* as well as for numerous religious magazines. Her columns, some dated and some not, are found in the McClung Papers, Add MSS 10, vol. 36. For example, on the Japanese, see 'What Did We Learn in 1941?' (3 Jan. 1942); on Jews in Canada, see 'Security Has Its Dangers Too,' 'What of Jews in Canada' (27 April 1940), and 'The Old Year Passes' (30 Dec. 1939).

9 McClung, *Clearing in the West* (1935; reprinted Toronto: Thomas Allen and Son 1965), 7. This first volume of autobiography tells the story of McClung's life up to her marriage to R.W. (Wes) McClung in 1896.

10 McClung, *In Times Like These* (1915; reprinted Toronto: University of Toronto Press 1972), 97

11 *Clearing in the West,* 26–37

12 McClung recounts this meeting in 'Can a Woman Raise a Family and Have a Career?' *Maclean's,* 15 Feb. 1928, p 10, and in *Clearing in the West,* 269. Discrepancies exist between the two versions, notably the person to whom McClung is speaking (Clara in the first case, Esther in the second) and in her age (almost sixteen or almost seventeen).

13 *Clearing in the West,* 274–5

14 *The Stream Runs Fast,* 76–7

15 Gordon Roper, 'New Forces: New Fiction (1880–1920),' in *Literary History of Canada,* ed. Carl Klinck (Toronto: University of Toronto Press 1965), 263

16 *The Stream Runs Fast,* 99

17 Ruben Bellan, *Winnipeg's First Century: An Economic History* (Winnipeg: Queenston House Publishing 1978), 114

18 James Gray, *Booze* (Scarborough: New American Library of Canada 1972), 3, 64, 13

19 Richard Allen, 'Introduction,' J.S. Woodsworth, *My Neighbor* (1911; reprinted Toronto: University of Toronto Press 1972), ix

20 McClung, in James Woodsworth, *Thirty Years in the Canadian North-West* (Toronto: McClelland and Stewart 1917), 257–8, 259

21 Richard Allen identifies three main types of social gospellers: 'The conservatives were the closest to traditional evangelicalism, emphasizing personal-ethical issues, tending to identify sin with individual acts, and taking as their social strategy legislative reform of the environment. The radicals viewed society in more organic terms. Evil was so endemic and persuasive in the social order that they concluded there could be no personal salvation without social salvation, [through] an immanent God working in the social process to bring his [*sic*] kingdom to birth ... Between conservatives and radicals was a broad centre party of progressives, holding the tension between the two extremes, endorsing in considerable measure the platforms of the other two, but transmuting them somewhat in a broad ameliorative programme of reform.' *The Social Passion: Religion and Social Reform in Canada 1914–28* (Toronto: University of Toronto Press 1973), 17

22 'To bring this about – the even chance for everyone – is the plain and simple meaning of life.' *In Times Like These*, 11

23 See Allen, *The Social Passion, passim.*

24 Modern readers may find such a conflictual, vicious construction of public life unusual. However, during Mc-
   Clung's lifetime the notion held sufficient sway that at
   least one leading scientist, the British pioneer immunolo-
   gist Sir Almroth Wright, was prepared to argue that the
   suffrage ought to be withheld from anyone who could
   not defend their views through physical struggle. As he
   states, 'Every one feels that public morality is affronted
   when senile, infirm, and bedridden men are brought to
   the poll.' Wright, *An Unexpurgated Case against Woman
   Suffrage* (New York: Hoeber Press 1913), 84–5. It followed
   for Wright that if women obtained the vote they should
   be prepared to be knocked down in the street, for they
   would be intentionally bringing down violence upon
   themselves. Wright was sufficiently well known in the
   debate over suffrage that McClung challenged him in
   In Times Like These, 70.
25 Hence the long-time motto of the Woman's Christian
   Temperance Union, 'To Make the World More Homelike.'
   Dolores Hayden explores the significant cultural challenge
   posed by this kind of activism in *The Grand Domestic Revolution* (Cambridge, Mass.: MIT Press 1981).
26 Catherine Cleverdon, *The Woman Suffrage Movement in
   Canada* (1950; reprinted Toronto: University of Toronto
   Press 1974), 16
27 *In Times Like These*, 51
28 Ibid., 76–7
29 Cleverdon, *Woman Suffrage Movement*, 49, 50
30 Regina Barreca has produced an excellent study of how
   humour functions in the social arena, and the effects of
   its use on women's status, in *They Used to Call Me Snow*

White ... But I Drifted: Women's Strategic Use of Humour (New York: Viking 1991).

31 Cleverdon, *Woman Suffrage Movement*, 51–3

32 W.L. Morton, *Manitoba: A History* (Toronto: University of Toronto Press 1957), 237, 249, 279, 282. The Manitoba School Question arose over the decision to abolish Manitoba's dual educational system in which French Catholic schools received public funding.

33 Ibid., 251, 282–3

34 As evidence of the fiscal appeal of provincial liquor sales, James Gray reports that in the years from 1925 to 1966 the population rose 50 per cent; provincial profits from liquor sales rose 1,800 per cent during the same period. Gray, *Booze*, 209

35 Morton, *Manitoba*, 294

36 *The Stream Runs Fast*, 101

37 Cleverdon, *Woman Suffrage Movement*, 55. The name was changed to the Manitoba Political Equality League in 1913 to indicate its provincial scope. Members included Vernon and Lillian Beynon Thomas, Dr Mary Crawford, labour activist Fred Dixon and his wife Winona Flett Dixon, agricultural expert E. Cora Hind, Frances Marion Beynon of the *Grain Growers' Guide*, and McClung.

38 Ibid.

39 Roblin's response, after demanding 'For God's sake, let me out of here! ... I'm choking! I never knew such hell holes existed!' was 'I still can't see why two women like you should ferret out such utterly disgusting things.' *The Stream Runs Fast*, 104–5. McClung calls the chapter 'A Gentleman of the Old School.'

40 Morton, *Manitoba*, 335

41 A number of these, including exceptionally witty pieces
   on temperance, women and war, and 'the new chivalry'
   are collected in *In Times Like These.*

42 Lillian Laurie (Lillian Thomas), 'What Nellie McClung
   Made,' newspaper report c. 1915, as cited in Candace
   Savage, *Our Nell: A Scrapbook Biography of Nellie L.
   McClung* (Saskatoon: Western Producer Prairie Books
   1979), 95.

43 Savage, *Our Nell*, 103

44 'Roblin Encounters Contrary Winds,' *Globe*, Toronto, 6
   July 1914, as cited in Savage, *Our Nell*, 96. Savage rightly
   notes the partisan character of newspapers at the time. In
   at least one Conservative paper, for example, McClung
   was referred to as 'a Liberal hack' whose services were
   necessary because 'The Liberals are sly. They know that
   whenever the devil cannot succeed a woman has to be
   employed.' Savage, 103

45 Ibid., 103

46 In 1917, McClung travelled extensively throughout the
   United States at the invitation of the National American
   Woman Suffrage Association. One itinerary had her travelling through New York, Wisconsin, Indiana, Kentucky,
   Tennessee, Alabama, Louisiana, Texas, Missouri, Nebras-
   ka, and Minnesota in the space of little more than a
   month. Her personal papers contain several telegrams insisting that her presence was essential if a particular state
   suffrage battle was to be won. McClung Papers, Add MSS
   10, vol. 11. The international dimensions of women's
   social activism at the turn of the century are only now
   being explored. See Judith Allen, 'Contextualizing Late-
   Nineteenth-Century Feminism: Problems and Compari-

sons,' *Journal of the Canadian Historical Association*, 1990 vol. 1, 17–36

47 'Women Ask Only Justice, Says Canadian Suffrage Lecturer: An Auditorium Rally Tonight,' McClung Papers, Add MSS 10

48 Morton, *Manitoba*, 337–43. Criminal charges were pressed against Roblin and three of his most prominent ministers, although these were dropped in 1917 due to Roblin's ill health. Despite the charges, there was never any suggestion that Roblin had personally profited from the malfeasance of the firm of Thomas Kelly and Sons, as McClung is careful to point out in *The Stream Runs Fast*, 102.

49 Women obtained the provincial franchise in Alberta and Saskatchewan in 1916, in Ontario and British Columbia in 1917, Nova Scotia in 1918, New Brunswick in 1919, Prince Edward Island in 1922, and Quebec in 1940. Newfoundland, not then part of Canada, gave women the vote in 1925.

50 Cleverdon, *Woman Suffrage Movement*, 63. Cleverdon's reading of this episode, and of the whole suffrage battle on the prairies, is benign to say the least, and underestimates the entrenched opposition to women's advancement prevalent at the time.

51 *Sowing Seeds in Danny*, 40

52 For example, see *In Times Like These*, 46–7.

53 Linda Silver Dranoff, *Women in Canadian Life: Law* (Toronto: Fitzhenry and Whiteside 1977), 23, 27

54 *Literary Review*, 11 March 1922, p 494, McClung Papers, Add. MSS 10, vol. 28; *Boston Transcript*, 18 March 1922, p 6; *Book Review Digest*, 15 April 1922, McClung Papers.

55 Morton, *Manitoba*, 319

56 Unidentified clipping, McClung Papers; 'Canadian Suffragettes,' 2 April 1922, McClung Papers
57 Unidentified clipping, McClung Papers

PURPLE SPRINGS

CONTENTS

PURPLE SPRINGS

:-:

CHAPTER I

THE DAY BEFORE

IT was the last day of February, the extra day, dead
still, and biting cold, with thick, lead-colored skies
shading down to inky blue at the western horizon.
In the ravine below John Watson's house trees
cracked ominously in the frost, and not even a
rabbit was stirring. The hens had not come out,
though an open door had extended an invitation, and
the tamworths had burrowed deeper into the stack
of oat straw. The cattle had taken refuge in the
big shed, and even old Nap, in spite of his thick
coat, had whimpered at the door to be let in.

Looking out of the western window, Pearl Watson,
with a faint wrinkle between her eyebrows, admitted
to herself that it was not a cheerful day. And Pearl
had her own reasons for wanting fine weather,
for tomorrow was the first of March, and the day
to which she had been looking forward for three
years to make a momentous decision.

The thought of this day had gone with her in the
three years that had passed, like a radiant gleam,
a glorious presence that brightened and idealized
every experience of life, a rainbow that glorified every
black cloud, and there had been some clouds in her

life black enough to bring out the rainbows' colors
too; as when her mother's serious illness had called
her back from the city, where she was attending
school. But each day had brought her one day
nearer the great day, which now she could call
"Tomorrow."

It had never occurred to Pearl to doubt the young
doctor's sincerity, when, three years before, he had
said he would wait until she was eighteen years old
before he asked her something.

"And it will depend on your answer," he had said,
"what sort of a day it is. It may be a dark, cold,
horrible day, with cruel, biting wind, or it may be a
glorious day, all sunshine and blue sky—that will all
depend on your answer." And she had told him,
honestly and truthfully, not being skilled in the
art of coquetry, that "it generally was fine on the
first of March."

That the young doctor might have forgotten all
about the incident never crossed her mind in the
years that followed. She did not know that there
was witchery in her brown eyes and her radiant
young beauty that would stir any young man's
heart and loosen his tongue, causing him to say
what in his sober moments he would regard as foolishness.

Pearl did not know this; she only knew that a
great radiance had come to her that day, three
years before, a radiance whose glory had not dimmed.
Every thought and action of her life had been in-
fluenced by it, and she had developed like a fine
young tree on which the spring sunshine had per-

petually fallen, a fine young tree that had been
sheltered from every cold blast, watered by the rains
and bathed in perpetual sunshine, for Pearl's young
heart was fed from the hidden springs of love and
romance. For her the darkest night was lighted
by stars; for her the birds sang of love and hope and
happiness; for her the commonest flower was rich
in beauty and perfume; and so the end of the three
years found her a well developed, tall, boyishly
athletic girl, with a color in her cheeks like an
Okanagon peach, hair of richest brown, with little
gleams of gold, waving back naturally from a high
forehead; a firm chin, with a dimple; and great brown
eyes, full of lights, and with a dazzling brilliance that
registered every thought of her brain and emotion of
her heart.

From the time when she was twelve years old the
young doctor, who had then just come to Millford,
had been her hero—worshipped afar, and in great
secrecy.

Many a time when the family lived in the village,
and Pearl was left to mind the swarm of boys while
her mother was out working, she had raced to the
window just to see him drive by, and, having seen
him and perhaps caught a smile or nod, if he noticed
her, she would go back to her strenuous task of
keeping her young brothers clothed and happy and
out of the wealth of a quickened imagination she
would tell them more and more wonderful tales
of the glorious world into which their young feet
had strayed.

When the doctor had time and inclination to talk

to her, Pearl's young heart swam in a crimson sea of delight, but if by any chance he hurried by, his mind filled with other things, she suffered for a brief season all the pangs of unrequited affection, and looked anxiously in the glass many times to see if her face showed signs of early decay.

But the mood soon passed and optimism again reigned. During the times of depression many a sunflower had its yellow petals torn away, as she sought to wring from it definite information regarding the state of his affections. If the sunflower brought in an adverse decision, without a moment's hesitation Pearl began upon another, and continued until a real, honest, authentic flower declared in her favor. But that she did not really trust the oracles was shown by the great frequency with which she consulted them!

As she grew older, Pearl would have liked to talk to some one about her dreams, but it was hard to begin. There was really nothing to tell. She might as well try to explain the sparkle of the sunshine, or the joyousness of the meadowlark's song in the spring, as to try to analyze the luminous wonder that had come into her own heart that day when the purple mist lay on the Tiger Hills, and the snowdrifts were beginning to sink and sag and break into little streams. It could not be done.

But still she wondered what experiences other people had had, and wished that someone would talk to her about it. At the Normal the girls had talked about "crushes" and "mashes" and people having a "bad case," and she knew that the one

qualification they demanded in matters of the heart
was that the young man should have the means and
inclination to "show a girl a good time." She could
not talk to them—there did not seem to be any
point of contact. And when the subject of love
and marriage was discussed around the family
circle, her mother's dictum was always brief and
concise:

"You'll get who's for ye—and you'll have your
number. There's lots of trouble for them that don't
marry, and there's lots more for them that do. But
there's no use in advisin' or warnin'; it's like the pigs
and the hot swill—one will stick in his nose and run
away squalin'; the next one will do the same, and
the next and the next. They never take warnin's;
it's the way of the world!"

But nothing dimmed the glory of Pearl's rainbow
dream or stilled the happy songs her heart sang day
and night. She had often pictured the day the
Doctor would come and tell her that the three years
were past. He would drive out with his team, for the
snow would be too deep for his car, and she would
first hear the sleigh-bells, even before old Nap
would begin to bark, and he would come in with his
cheeks all red and glowing, with snow on his beaver
coat; and he would tell her it was too fine to stay in,
and wouldn't she come for a ride?

So sure was she that he would come that she
had laid out on her bed, in the little room under the
rafters, her heavy coat, overshoes and scarf, and had
spent some time deciding whether her red tam or the
brown velvet hat was the most becoming, and

finally favored the tam, because she had once heard
the Doctor say that red was the color for winter, and
besides, the brown hat had a sharp rim that might
give a person a nasty poke in the eye . . . in case . . .

She made all her preparations on the day before,
because, she told herself, a doctor's time was so
uncertain that he might, remembering this, be
afraid of being called away on The Day, and so come
a day sooner.

Pearl thought of all this as she stood at the
window and looked out on the bare farm yard,
swept clean of beast or fowl by the bitter cold which
had driven them all indoors.   A bright fire burned in
the Klondike heater, and from the kitchen came the
cheerful song of a canary.   The house was in a state
of great tidiness, with its home-made lounge in
front of the fire, piled high with gaily flowered cushions, and the brightly striped rag carpet which was
the culmination of the united efforts of the family
the winter before, and before the fire a tiger-striped
cat with her paws stretched out to the heat.

Pearl was alone in the room, for all the children
were at school, her father and Teddy out, and her
mother in the kitchen making the last of the mince-
meat into pies, which sent out a real baking odor of
cinnamon and cloves; a roast of pork that had been
"doing too fast," was now sitting on the top of the
high oven, its angry, sparking, sizzling trailing off
into a throaty guttering.   Some sound or smell of it
seemed to have penetrated Nap's dreams, for he
wakened suddenly and sat up, licking his lips and
pounding the floor with his tail.

Suddenly the telephone rang, the three short and one long, which indicated that it was the Watson family who were wanted. Pearl's heart thrilled with expectation. Of course he would phone before he came to make sure she was at home. The receiver was in her hands in a moment.

"Hello!" she called, almost choking with excitement.

"Will you tell your father," called back a man's voice at the end of the wire, "that the cattle are coming home from the range. Last night's snow was too much for them, and Jim Fidler has just phoned through to warn us. They're comin' on mad for feed, tramplin' and bawlin', and they'll hit your place first—mos' likely—tho' they may turn south at Beckers'—better phone Beckers and see."

"All right!" said Pearl, in a steady voice, "all right, and thank you."

Pearl hastily put on a coat and went to the barn to give the unwelcome news to her father and Teddy, who were busy fanning out the weed seeds from the seed grain.

"They're comin' airly," said John Watson, slowly, as he shook down the bag of seed wheat that he had just filled; "but I guess they are the best judge of whether they can make a livin' outside any longer. Well, what we have we'll share, anyway. There's no use in contradictin' a bunch of hungry steers. Keep a watch on the phone, Pearlie dear, and find out which way they turn at Beckers'. We'll open up an oat stack for them, anyway—so if they come rampin' in in the middle of the night there'll be something ready."

Pearl ran back across the wind-swept yard to the
house, for the one thought in her mind was that a
message might come over the phone for her! Ordinarily the home-coming of the hungry cattle would
have been an event of such importance that it would
have driven out all others; but there was only one
consuming thought in her mind to-day.

When she came in the phone was ringing, and her
mother, with her hands in the pie-crust, said:
"Pearlie, dear, run in to the phone—that's twice it's
rung since you were out, and sure I couldn't go—and
me this way."

Pearl took the receiver down and found a conversation in progress. She had no thought of
listening in—for at once she surmised it might be a
message regarding the cattle going to one of the
other houses. The first sentence, however, held her
in its grip, and all thought of what she was doing
was driven from her mind.

"They are going to offer the doctor the nomination tomorrow—he'll make the best run of any one
in these parts."

It was a man's voice, far away and indistinct.

"That will please Miss Morrison—she always
wanted to get into politics;" it was a woman who
replied—"but I'm not so sure she has any chance, the
doctor is a pretty cautious chap. I often think he
has a girl somewhere—he goes to Hampton pretty
often."

"He's not worried over women, believe me," the
man's voice cut in. "I think he likes that young
Watson girl as well as any one, and she has them all

skinned for looks—and brains too, I guess.

The woman's voice came perceptibly nearer, and seemed to almost hiss in her ear—unconsciously she felt the antagonism. "That's absurd," she said, with sudden animation; "why, these people are nobody, the mother used to wash for me a few years ago. They are the very commonest sort—the father was only a section man. The doctor enjoys her cute speeches, that's all, but there's absolutely nothing in it—he as much as told me so."

Pearl hung up the receiver with a click, and, pressing her lips together, walked over to the window with two crimson spots burning like danger signals on her cheeks. When Pearl's soul was burdened she always wanted to get outside, where the sky and the wind and the big blue distance would help her to think. But the day was too cold for that, so instinctively she walked to the window, where the short afternoon sun was making a pale glow on the heavy clouds.

Old Nap came from his place behind the table and shoved his cold nose into her hand, with a gentle wagging of his tail, reminding her that all was not lost while she still had him.

Dropping down on her knees beside him, Pearl buried her face in his glistening white collar, and for one perilous moment was threatened with tears. But pride, which has so often come to our rescue just in time, stepped into her quivering young heart, she stood up and shook her head like an angry young heifer.

" 'Common,' are they?" she said, with eyes that

darted fire; "not half common enough—decent people
that do their work and mind their own business,—
helpin' a friend in need and hurtin' no wan—it would
be a better world if people like them were commoner!
'And the mother washed for ye, did she, you dirty
trollop? Well, it was a God's mercy that some one
washed for you, and it was good clane washin' she did,
I'll bet—and blamed little she got for it, too, while
you lay in your bed with your dandruffy hair in a
greasy boudoir cap, and had her climb the stairs
with your breakfast. And you'd fault her for
washin' for you—and cleanin' your house—you'd
fault her for it! I know the kind of ye—you'd rather
powder ye'r neck than wash it, any day!"

No one would recognize the young Normalite
who two weeks before had taken the highest marks
in English, and had read her essay at the closing
exercises, and afterwards had it printed, at the
editor's request, in the *Evening Echo,* for Pearl's
fierce anger had brought her back again to the
language of her childhood.

"And he as much as told you, did he?" she
whispered, turning around to glare in stormy wrath
at the unoffending telephone—"he as much as told
you there was nothing in it?"

Pearl puckered her lips and shut one eye in a
mighty mental effort to imagine what he would say,
but in trying to hear his words she could only see
his glowing face, the rumpled hair she loved so well,
and then his voice came back like a perfect phonograph record, that strong, mellow, big voice which
had always set her heart tingling and drove away

every fear. She couldn't make him say anything else but the old sweet words that had lived with her for the last three years.

The storm faded from her eyes in a moment, and in the rush of joy that broke over her, she threw herself down beside old Nap and kissed the shiny top of his smooth black head. Then going over to the telephone, she shook her fist at it.

"Did my mother wash for you, ma'am? She did—and you never had better washin' done! Are we common people?—we are, and we're not ashamed. We're doin' fine, thank you—all the children are at school but me, and I've gone thro' the public school and Normal too. The crops are good—we have thirty head of cattle and six horses, sound in wind and limb. Some day we'll have a fine new house, and we'll live all over it too. John Watson did work on the section, and they'd be fine and glad to get him back. He owes no man a dollar, and bears no man a grudge. I wouldn't change him for the Governor-General for me dad—and now listen— I'm tellin' ye something, I'm goin' to marry the doctor—if he wants me—and if you don't like it there's a place you can go to. I'll not be namin' it in the presence of Nap here, for he's a good Christian.

"And you, sir,"—she addressed the telephone again,—"I thank you for your kind words regarding brains and looks. I hope it is a true word you speak, for I may need both before I'm done."

The home-coming of the cows at eventime has

been sung about, written about, talked about,
painted, and always it has had in it the restfulness of
evening,—the drowsy whirr of insects' wings, the
benediction of the sunset, the welcoming gladness of
a happy family. But these pictures have not been
painted by those of us who have seen the hungry
cattle come in from the range when the snow covers
the grass, or the springs dry up, and under the influence of fear they drive madly on.

All day long the range cattle, about three hundred
in number had searched the river bottom for the
grass which the heavy snowfall of the night before
had covered; searched eagerly, nervously all the
while, bawling, ill-naturedly pushing and horning,
blaming each other in a perfectly human way. Disconsolately they wandered over the river to the other
bank feeling sure they would find grass there, only
to find the snow over everything, and not even a
little rosebush showing its head.

Then it was that the old cow, an acknowledged
leader of the herd, who bore the name of the "Broncho," on account of her wildness, her glaring red
eyes and her branching horns, with an angry toss of
her head to shake the water from her eyes, lifted her
voice in one long, angry, rolling bellow that seemed
to startle the whole herd. It had in it defiance, and
determination. Like the leading spirit among the
leprous men who sat at the gate of Samaria, the
"Broncho" gathered up the feeling of the meeting
in one long soul-stirring, racuous bawl, which,
interpreted, meant, "Why sit we here until we
die?"

The primitive law of self-preservation was at work—even a cow will not starve quietly. The grass had been scarce for days, and she had lain down hungry each night for a week; and now, when the grass had gone entirely, the old cow had taken her determination; she would go home and demand her right to live. This thought surging through her soul, gave decision to her movements. Whether the other cattle came or not did not matter in the least—she knew what she was going to do. The strong northwest wind which began to whip the fresh snow into loose waves, turned the cattle to face the southeast, in which direction the settlement lay. Miserable cattle, like miserable people, are easily led. It is only the well-fed and comfortable who are not willing to change their condition, and so when the others saw the "Broncho" forging up the hill, the whole herd, as if at a word of command, lurched forward up the bank.

They surged onward, bawling, crowding, trampling, hooking without mercy. Companions they had been for months before, eating together, sleeping together, warming each other, playing together sometimes when the sun was bright. That was all forgotten now, for the hunger-rage was on them, and they were brutes, plain brutes, with every kind instinct dead in their shivering breasts. They knew but one law, the law of the strongest, as they drove onward, stumbling and crowding, with the cold wind stinging them like a lash.

The night closed in, dark and cheerless, closed in early, under the dull gray, unrelenting skies, and al-

though lights blinked out cheerfully from uncur
tained windows, and willow plumes of smoke spread
themselves on the cold night air above all the farm-
houses, the hearts of the people were apprehensive.

It was the last day of February—green grass was
still far away—and the cattle, hungry, red-eyed and
clamorous, were coming home!

CHAPTER II

THE DAY !

"When time lets slip one little perfect day,
  O take it—for it may not come again."

WHEN Pearl woke on the morning of March 1st, it
was with a heart so light and happy it brought back
the many Christmas mornings that lay scattered behind her like so many crimson roses, spilling their
perfume on the shining road which led back to childhood. The sunshine that sifted through the white
muslin curtains of the one small window, was rich
and warm, as if summer had already come, and
Pearl suddenly remembered that the sky had been
overcast and heavy the day before, and the air stinging cold.

She went to the window, and looking out saw that
the clouds had all gone, leaving no trace in the un-
scarred sky. The sun was throwing long blue shadows over the fields, brightening the trees on the river
bank, with a thin rinse of pale gold. Down in the
ravine, the purple blue of the morning twilight was
still hanging on the trees. The house was very quiet
—there did not seem to be anyone stirring, either inside or out.

Pearl dressed herself hastily, humming a tune in
happy excitement. Her whole being was charged
with happiness—for the great day had come.

Coming down stairs on light feet, she threw a red
sweater around her shoulders and went out the front
door. In her great moments, Pearl craved the open

sky and great blue distances, and on this day of all
days, she wanted to breathe deep of its golden air.
Somewhere she had read about air that tasted like
old wine! And as she stood facing the early sun that
had come up in a cloudless sky of deepest blue, she
knew what was meant.

From the dull tomb of yesterday, with its cavern-
like coldness and gloom, had come the resurrection of
a new day, bright, blue, sparkling, cloudless; for
March had slipped in quietly in the night, with a
gentle breeze of wonderful softness, a quiet breeze,
but one that knew its business, and long before daylight it had licked the hard edges of the drifts into
icy blisters, and had purred its way into all sorts of
forgotten corners where the snow lay thickest.

It went past Pearl's face now with velvety smoothness—patting her cheeks with a careless hand, like
a loving friend who hurries by with no time for anything but this swift re-assurance. But Pearl knew
that the wind and the sun and the crisp white snow,
on which the sunbeams danced and sparkled, were her
friends, and were throbbing with joy this morning,
because it was her great day.

She went in at last, remembering that the children
must be washed and fed for school, and found Danny's garter for him just in time to save him from the
gulf of despair which threatened him. She made up
the two tin pails of lunch with which her young
brothers would beguile the noontide hour. She put
a button on Mary's spat, in response to her request
of "Aw, say Pearl, you do this—I can't eat and sew."
The sudden change in the weather forced a change in

the boys' foot-gear, and so there had to be a frenzied hunt for rubbers and boots to replace the frost-repelling but pervious moccasin.

One by one, as the boys were ready, fed, clothed and rubbered, they were started on their two-mile journey over the sunny, snowy road, Danny being the first to so emerge, for with his short, fat legs, he could not make the distance in as short a time as the others.

"Mr. Donald wants you to come over on Friday, Pearl—I almost forgot to tell you—he wants you to talk to us about the city, and the schools you were in—and all that. I told him you would!"

This was from Jimmy, the biggest of the Watson boys now attending school.

"All right," said Pearl, "sure I will."

There was more to the story, though, and Jimmy went on,—

"And the Tuckers said they bet you thought yourself pretty smart since you'd been to the city. . . .

"And then what happened," asked Pearl, when he paused.

"He went home—it wouldn't stop bleedin'! but Mr. Donald says a good nose-bleed wouldn't hurt him—though of course it was wrong to fight—but it was no fight—you know what they're like—one good thump—and they're done!"

"Good for you, Jimmy" said his sister approvingly, "never pick a quarrel or hit harder than you need, that's all!—but if trouble comes—be facing the right way!"

"You bet," said Jimmy, as he closed the door behind him and the stillness which comes after the children have gone fell on the Watson home.

"Sure and ain't the house quiet when they're gone," said Mrs. Watson, looking out of the window across the gleaming landscape, dotted in six places by her generous contribution to the Chicken Hill school.

"And it won't be long until they're gone—for good."

"Cheer up," honest woman," cried Pearl gaily, "you hav'nt even lost either Teddy or me, and we're the eldest. It looks to me as if you will have a noisy house for quite a while yet, and I would'nt begin to worry over anything so far away—in fact, ma, it's a good rule not to worry till you have to, and don't do it then!"

Pearl was bringing back "the room" to the state of tidiness it enjoyed during school hours, moving about with joyous haste, yet with strict attention to every detail, which did not escape her mother's eye.

"It's grand to be as light of heart as you are, Pearlie child," she said, "I'm often afraid for you—when I think of all the sad things in life and you so sure that everything will happen right. It is to them that the world is brightest that the darkest days can come, and the lightest heart sometimes has heaviest mournin'."

A little wither of disappointment went over Pearl's bright face, but she shook it off impatiently. She wished her mother would not talk like this on this day—of all days.

"Don't spoil a good day, ma, with sad talk. Look

out at the Spring sun there, and the cattle, even the wild ones from the range, with their sides steaming and then nosing around so happy now, forgetting all about the bad times they had even as late as last evening. There's no use telling them there's cold days coming—they wouldn't believe now—and anyway they'll know soon enough. Isn't it best to let every one have their sunny day—without a cloud on it."

Before her mother could form an answer, the three short and one long ring came on the phone. Pearl's heart turned over in its bounding joy. It had come —she knew it had come.

She took down the receiver:

"Hello," she said, in a thin voice.

"Pearl," said the voice, deep, mellow, eager. She thought she had remembered what his voice was like, but she hadn't. It was a hundred times sweeter than it had been in her memory.

"Yes," she said, holding the receiver so tightly her knuckles went white with the pressure.

"What day is it, Pearl," he said, with the laugh in his voice, the bantering laugh that made his patients love him.

"O I know" she said—"I know."

"You havn't forgotten what we said?"

"Not a word of it."

His voice came nearer, though he spoke lower.

"The train is not in yet, it is stuck out in the hills, but likely to get out any minute. Dr. Brander is on it, coming out from the city to operate for me in a

very serious case, I'm not sure when I can get out
—but you'll wait for me—won't you, Pearl?"

She put her red young lips close to the transmitter.

"For a thousand years!" she said.

"Well, it won't be that long," he said, with his
happy laugh.

Pearl knew exactly how his brows were lifted, and
his eyes wide opened,

"But it's great to have as good a margin, Pearl—
and listen"—his voice fell again until it seemed to
whisper in her ear—"did you happen to notice what
sort of a day it is?"

"Well," said Pearl, "I am not surprised. Didn't I
tell you it would be?"

"You told me!" he said.

Then it was that from Pearlie Watson's young
heart there opened up a shining path straight up into
heaven, and every inch of that radiant highway was
bright with the gleam of angel's wings, and as she
stood there leaning against the wall, her eyes dazzled
with the glory of it, it seemed as if all the sweet songs
that lovers have ever sung, and all the tender words
they have ever spoken came marching, gaily marching
down the shining highway, right into her heart.

Outside the sun gleamed and beat on the melting
snow, which sent back quivery vibrations that smote
the eyeballs like fire. The cattle shook the water
from their sun-dazzled eyes, and turned their heads
away from it, but it climbed steadily higher until it
stood right over them, and blazing down upon the
snowy world, defied old man Winter to his face.

Pearl was never quite sure about it in after years.

But that day she did not doubt her eyes, that star dust danced in the waves of sunshine; that the gray snow birds played crack the whip outside the window; that the willow hedge, palpitating in the sunshine, beat time with its silvery branches to the music that lilted through her heart; that the blue in the sky was bluer than it had been, and the sunshine more golden than it ever was in the highest noon in highest June.

She was quite sure it was so, for every spot of color within doors was glorified too. The roses in the cushions on the lounge glowed like a fire in the heart of a green wood; the cat's eyes gleamed like olivines, but of course Pearl knew from the way he rubbed his head against her shoulder as she sat on the lounge beside him, and from the way he blinked at her—he knew, having no doubt in some occult cat-way, listened in on the phone! There was no mis-taking his swaggering air of importance—he was in on it, and gave much credit to himself for having brought it all about.

The old dog, being just a plain, honest-hearted, loving dog, only knew that Pearl was very happy over something. He did not probe the cause—if it pleased her—it was enough.

At four o'clock there came another message—which set Pearl's heart dancing, and spotted her cheeks with a glowing color—the operation was over—apparently successful—and they were driving back to town. The other train might be late too, so it would be impossible for him to come out—but would she still wait? Did the thousand year limit still hold?

There was just a hint of fatigue in his voice, which awakened all the maternal instincts in Pearl, and made her heart very tender to him.

"I will wait—forever," said Pearl.

"Just until tomorrow," came back the voice—"just till tomorrow—and it will be fine tomorrow—won't it, Pearl? Say it will be fine."

"Finer still," she replied, with her cheeks like the early roses in June.

The day went by on satin wings—with each minute so charged with happiness that Pearl could well believe that heaven had slipped down to earth, and that she was walking the streets of the new Jerusalem. She sang as she worked in the house, her sweet, ribbony voice filling the room with a gladness and rapture that made her mother, with her mystical Celtic temperament almost apprehensive.

"She's a queer girl, is Pearlie," she said that night, when Pearl had gone upstairs to arbitrate a quarrel which had broken out between Bugsey and Danny as to whose turn it was to split the kindling wood. "Day about" it had been until Bugsey had urged that it be changed to "week about," and the delicate matter in dispute now was as to the day on which the week expired. Danny, who had been doing the kindling, was certain that the date of expiry had arrived, but Bugsey's calendar set the day one day later, and the battle raged, with both sides ably argued, but unfortunately not listened to by the opposing forces.

"She's a queer child, is Pearlie," said Mrs. Watson, as she beat up the bread-batter downstairs, "she's that light-hearted and free from care, and her eighteen years old. She's like somethin' that don't belong on earth, with her two big eyes shinin' like lamps, and the way she sings through the house, settin' the table or scourin' the milk pails or mendin' a coat for the boys—it don't seem natural. She's too happy, whatever it's about, and it makes me afraid for her. She's the kind that sees nothin' wrong, and won't see trouble comin' till it's too late. I often feel afraid she's too good and happy for this world. She's always been the same, liltin' and singin' and makin' everyone happy around her."

Jimmy was washing his face in the enamel basin which stood on a box below the mirror, and looking around with a dripping wet face, felt with a wildly swinging motion of his arms for the towel. When he had secured it, and all danger of soapsuds getting into his eyes was removed, he joined the conversation.

"Gosh, Ma!" he said, "you don't know Pearl, she's not the saint you take her for. I'll bet the Tucker kids don't think she's too good to live. Not much! They know she can hold up her end of a row as well as any one. When she found out they had killed the cat they got from us, and tanned the skin to make a rim on a cap, you should have seen Pearl. She just cut loose on the two of them, and chased them through the sloughs and up the road clear home —larrupin' them with a binder whip, as fast as she could swing it—the yowls out of them would have done your heart good!"

Mrs. Watson stopped her work, with her floury hands raised in consternation.

"God's mercy," she cried, "did Pearl do that—
and both of them bigger'n her. Ain't it a wonder
they did not turn on her?"

"Turn"—Jimmy cried scornfully, "Turn—is it?
They were too busy runnin'. Gosh—they would'a
flew if they knew how. Served them right—they
knew blame well they deserved it, for Pearl would
never have given them the cat if they hadn't worked
it so smooth. They told her they wanted a strain of
Tiger in their cats, for all of theirs were black—and
Pearl gave them our fine young Tom—and they
promised all sorts to be good to him—and when
Pearl saw his skin on their caps, and put it to them,
they said they hadn't said it was a 'strain of tiger for
their cats' they wanted, but a 'strand of tiger for
their caps'—that's what made Pearl so mad. Mr.
Donald said Pearl did quite right, and he told the
Tuckers they were the making of great politicians
—they were so smart at getting out of things. But
Gosh, you should have seen Pearl! She finished the
job off right, too, you bet, and made them put up a
slab at the school and did the printin' on it in red ink.
You can see it there,—they have·had to print it over
once or twice. We all know the words off by heart:

'Young Tom,
Tiger cat,
Owned by P. Watson,
Given away in good faith April 1st,
Wickedly killed to make a cap, April 15th,
Avenged by former owner, May 1st.
T. Tucker.   S. Tucker.'

"People all look at it when they come to the church, and I guess the Tuckers feel pretty small. Pearl says if they are really sorry, it is all right, and young Tom has not died in vain. Every cat has to die sometime, and if he had softened the Tuckers' hearts —it is all right. Pearl said she wasn't real sure about them, and I guess if they kill another cat, she'll kill them sure—she said that's the way to do with people like them. Make them repentant—or dead!"

"God save us all," cried Mrs. Watson, in real distress, "whatever will happen to her when she goes out into the world. That's awful talk for a girl especially. Whatever will become of her when she leaves home. She'll be in hot water all the time."

"No fear of Pearlie!" said her father proudly—as he opened the end door of the stove and picked up a coal for his pipe, placing it without undue haste in the bowl, and carefully pressing it down with his thumb. Leaning back in the chintz-covered rocking chair, he spread his feet out to the heat which came from the oven door, and repeated, "No fear of Pearlie— there ain't a girl in the country better able to do for herself. Faith—and she's no fool—and never was— I ain't worrying about Pearlie wherever she goes— or whatever she meets—I ain't worrying."

"You don't worry about anything, John," said Mrs. Watson, in reproof, as she covered the bread with many wrappings and fixed two chairs to hold it behind the stove for the night; "you didn't even worry the night the crop froze, sleepin' and snorin' the whole night through, with me up every half hour watching the thermometer, and it slippin' lower and

lower, and the pan o'water on the woodpile gettin' its
little slivers of ice around the edge, and when the
thermometer went to thirty, I knew it was all up
with the wheat, but do you think I could wake you
—you rolled over with a grunt, leavin' me alone to
think of the two hundred acres gone in the night,
after all our hard work. . . and then to have you
come down in the mornin', stretchin' and yawnin',
after a good night's sleep, and says you, as cheerful
as could be, "Cold mornin', Ma!"

John Watson took his pipe from his mouth, and
laughed quietly.

"And what was wrong with that, Ma—sure now
it was cold—you said yourself it was," he said
gently.

The boys joined in the laugh, but Mrs. Watson repeated her point.

"Cold it was, sure enough, but think o' me up
frettin' and fumin', and you come down as cheerful
as if starvation wasn't starin' us in the face."

"But we didn't starve, Ma," said Billy, coming to
his father's defense, "the crop was all right for feed,
and we did well after all. You had all your frettin'
for nothing."

"It's that way mostly," said John Watson, "I
never saw any good yet in frettin'. Anyway, Ma
does enough of it for all of us, so that lets me out.
There's the two kinds of Irish—them that don't fret
over anything—and them that frets over everything
—that's me and you, Ma—and it works out fine—it
runs about even. You've always been so sure that
things were goin' wrong, I've just had to be a little

surer that they weren't. And then of course I knew that night that you would watch the frost—if there was any watchin' to it."

"John, it is well for you that you have some one to do your watchin'," said Mrs. Watson. "You're an easy goin' man, John, but I'll say this for you, that a better natured man never lived."

When all the family had gone to bed, and the last sound had died out in the house, Pearl stood long at the window and looked out at the moonlit valley. The warm day had melted the frost from the window, and when she put out the lamp, the moonlight seemed almost as clear as day. Silvery-mauve and blue it lay on the quiet, snowy fields, with a deeper color on the trees, as if they had wound yards and yards of the gauzy stuff around their bare shoulders, for the night was chilly. To Pearl it was even more beautiful than the sunshine of the day, for in its silvery stillness, she could think and dream without interruption.

The night was too beautiful to sleep, and the riot of joy in her heart made her forget that any one ever grew weary or tired. She was part of the moonlight, with its glistening witchery, part of the overarching sky, with its wealth of glittering stars, part of the velvety night wind that caressed the trees in its gentle passing. Her young soul was in tune with them all, for the greatest thing in life had come to her in those few common-place words that had come to her over the telephone. He had not forgotten—he was coming tomorrow!

The tired note in his voice had awakened an entirely new chord in the song her heart sang. He needed her. He needed some one to look after him, care for him, watch him, save him from the hundred little worrying things that were sapping his energy. People did not understand that he ever got tired—he was so strong, so buoyant, so ready to do things for them. Well, there will be some one now, thought Pearl, with a glow that surged through her veins and made her cheeks flame, to take care of him.

"Is the doctor in, Mrs. Clay?"

"He is—but he's sleeping—maybe I can tell you what you want to know—step in here—so he won't hear us—he was out all night—and he must not be wakened. . . . .

And when he had to go—she would harness the team and drive him, so he could sleep all the way, and when the roads were fit for it, she would drive the car—and soon she would be able to set bones and do common things like that. He would show her —and then they would go to New York—in two or three years maybe—he had told her once he wanted to do this—for a post-graduate course—and they would have a little suite, and she would study, too.

And always, always, always they would be together—and no matter how many people there were praising him and wanting him—he would just be her man—and at night, when he was tired—and all the noise of the day was over and everyone was gone, she would have him all to herself.

Pearl's head sank on the window sill, while an ecstasy of joy swept over her—happy tears filled her eyes—life was so sweet—so rich—so full. . . . .

CHAPTER III

WHEN the operation was over, the two doctors drove back to Millford, the younger man so deeply engrossed in his own thoughts he hardly heard the older doctor's incessant conversation. But that did not in anywise discourage Dr. Brander, for to him, talking was much like breathing, it went on easily, unconsciously, and without the necessity of a listener.

On Dr. Clay there had fallen the pleasant, drowsy feeling of one whose work is done for the day, and a hard day it had been, with its uncertainty of the delayed train, and his patient's condition. But all had gone well, and his patient's reaction had been satisfactory. More than that, the older doctor had concurred in all that he had done, and commended his treatment of the case from the beginning.

So, comfortably seated in the cutter, with a brown bear robe over their knees, and the mate of it over the seat, the two doctors drove home in the purple-blue twilight, seated side by side, but with minds far removed from each other.

The doctor's horses knew every road that led home, and trotted on without any guidance or word from him—they were a fine team of glossy chestnuts of whom the young doctor was extremely proud. But tonight, a strange lassitude of spirit was upon him and he only wanted to relax his weary brain and dream away the snowy miles to the rhythmic beat of the horses' hoofs.

He had never been more contented in his life.

His work was going well—that day the Liberals had offered him the nomination for the coming provincial election. It was an honor which he appreciated, though he had no desire to enter politics. He loved his work—the people he served were devoted to him —he could read it in their faces and their stammering words. He knew what they wanted to say, even though it was conveyed in a few halting fragments of sentences—"You're all right—Doc—sure—glad you got here—we knew you'd make it—somehow—you and them high steppers of yours can get through the snow—if any one can."

Slowly, for a great weariness was on him, he began to think of Pearl, the red-cheeked shining-eyed Pearl, who had singled him out for her favor ever since he came to the village six years ago; Pearl, with her contagious optimism and quaint ways, who had the good gift of putting every one in good humor. He smiled to himself when he thought of how often he had made it convenient to pass the school just at four o'clock, and give Pearl and the rest of them a ride home, and the delight he had always had in her fresh young face, so full of lights and shadows.

"Robbing the cradle, eh, Doc?" Sam Motherwell had once said, in his clumsy way, when he met them on the road—"Nothin' like pickin' them out young and trainin' them up the way you want them."

He had made no answer to this, but he still felt the wave of anger that swept over him at the blundering words. "All the same, I wish Pearl were older"— he had admitted to himself that day. "If she keeps her wise little ways and her clever tongue, she'll be a great woman—she has a way with her."

At the rink, he had always looked forward to a skate with her—it was really a dull night for him if she were not there, and now he wondered just what it was that attracted him so. There was a welcoming gladness in her eyes that flattered him, a comradeship in her conversation that drew him on to talk with more ease and freedom; there was a wholesome friendliness in what she said, which always left him a sense of physical and mental well-being.

"What a nurse she would make," he thought, "what a great nurse;" "I wish she were older. . . . eighteen is too young for a girl to marry—I wouldn't allow it at all—if I didn't know who she is getting —that makes all the difference in the world. . . . . of course her father and mother may object, but I believe what Pearl says, goes—what Pearl says will go—with all of us! The Parker house can be bought—and fixed up. . . . we'll have a fireplace put in, and waterworks—I wish I did not feel so tough and tired. . . . but she said she'd wait a thousand years!"

Suddenly the voice of Dr. Brander rasped through his brain, and brought him to attention:

"Clay, you're in love, or something—I don't believe you've heard a word I said, you young scamp, in the last six miles—and you've missed a fine exposition on cancers—causes and cure."

"I beg your pardon, Dr. Brander," he apologized, "I believe I was almost asleep. I get into a drowsy habit on my long drives—especially when I am

coming home—when the day's work is over—it
seems good to stretch out—but I do apologize:
What were you saying?"

"O, I'm done now," said his companion, not in the
least disturbed; "I want you to tell me about yourself and your work here. You know you interest me,
Clay. You are a sort of popular idol with all these
people, and I have been wondering how you do it.
A man must give freely of himself to be as popular as
you are, Clay—do you ever find yourself giving out
under the strain, and in need of a rest?"

"Just a little tired, sometimes," the young man
confessed, "but it's nothing—at all."

The old man watched him narrowly, taking careful
note that the pallor of his face had suddenly changed
to a heightened color. "When we get supper, Clay,
I want to have a serious talk with you. You may remember that I approached this subject the last
time you were in the city. I want to give you the
report on the examination I gave you at that
time." There was a quality in his voice which gave
the young man a momentary sense of dread, not un-
mixed with a certain impatience. He was too tired
to be bothered. He wanted nothing but a chance
to think his own thoughts, as the sorrel team struck
off the miles with their tireless feet.

When they had had supper at the Chinese restaurant, they went to the doctor's office. The sun,
though long since set, still threw spikes of light upon
the western sky and caught the under side of one
ragged cloud which seemed to have been forgotten
in an otherwise clear sky.

In the office, a cheerful coal fire glowed through its mica windows, and in front of the doctor's leather chair, were his slippers, and over it was thrown a brightly colored house coat.

A gasoline lamp threw a strong white light on the comfortable room, and the city papers lay, still unfolded, on the table beside a pile of letters.

The old doctor exclaimed with delight:

"Who fixes you up so fine, Clay—surely there's a woman around this place?"

"My landlady"—said the young doctor, "looks after me."

"I know, I know," said the older man, "I know the kind of fellow you are—the kind women love to fuss around. I'll bet you get dozens of bedroom slippers and ties and mufflers at Christmas. Women are like cats—they love to rub their heads against any one that will stroke them and say 'poor pussy'—they're all the same."

The old doctor seated himself in the big chair and warmed his hands before the glowing coals.

"And now, Clay, I want to talk to you. There are certain facts that must be told. I have been interested in your case ever since I met you. You are a distinct type, with your impulsive temperament, clear skin and tapering fingers. But what I have to say to you would have been said easier if I did not know you so well—and if I had not been here and seen you in your native setting—as it were. . . . Being a medical man yourself, Clay, you know the difficulties of the situation."

The young doctor sat down suddenly, and smiled wanly.

"There need be no difficulty, Dr. Brander", he said, "I am ready to hear. . . " he left the sentence unfinished.

The old doctor went on:

"There is no immediate cause for alarm," he said, speaking slowly, "people live for years with it, as you know—a cracked plate sometimes outlasts the good one—and as a matter of fact none of us are entirely free from it."

The old doctor was swaying backwards as he spoke, and his voice rose and fell with the motion, as the tone of a phonograph when the door is opened or shut.

"You will have to be more careful, though, Clay, you will have to call a halt on your activities—there must be no more of the all night sessions of yours—and those fifty mile drives—it is just like this—you are carrying a mortgage on your business—a heavy mortgage—and yet one that the business can carry—with care, great care. Many a good business man carries a heavy mortgage and pays well too, but of course it cannot stand financial strain or stress like the business which is clear of debt. With great care, you should be good for many years—but you must not draw on your reserves—you must never spend your capital—you must never be tired, or excited, or hurried, or worried."

And this climate is a bit strenuous in winter—you must get out before another one comes, and live some place that is easier. This country keeps a man on his toes all the time, with its brilliant sunshine, its strong winds, its bracing air. You need a softer air, a duller atmosphere, a sleepier environment that will make you never do today what you can put off till tomorrow, and never put off till tomorrow what you might as well put off till the day after tomorrow."

"What a life!" broke from the young man's lips.

"A very fascinating life, my dear sir," said the old doctor, intoning his words like a very young clergyman—"a fascinating life, and one that I would enjoy. Here we hurry up in the morning and hurry to bed at night so we can hurry to get up again in the morning—we chase ourselves around like a cat in the ancient pursuit of its own tail, and with about the same results. The Western mind is in a panic all the time—losing time by the fear of losing time. The delights of meditation are not ours—we are pursued, even as we pursue; we are the chasers and the chased; the hunter and the hunted; we are spending and are spent; we are borrowed and lent—and what is the good of it all? I have always wanted to be an Oriental, dreaming in the shade of a palm tree, letting the sun and the wind ripen my fruits and my brain, while I sat—with never a care—king of the earth—and the air—O, take it from me, young fellow, there are wonderful delights in contemplation, delights of which we are as ignorant as the color blind are of the changing hues of the Autumn woods, or the deaf man is of music. We are deaf, blind and dumb about the things of the soul! We think activity is the only form of growth."

The young doctor, whose handsome face had grown pale, watched him with a sort of fascination. The words seemed to roll from his lips without the

slightest effort, and apparently without causing his
heart one emotion. If the young doctor had not
known him so well, he would have thought him entirely unconcerned.

"We are cursed, you and I, and all of us," he
resumed, "with too much activity. We are obsessed
with a passion for material achievement." We are
hand-worshippers — leg-worshippers — speed-wor-
shippers. We mistake activity for progress."

"But it is progress," burst from the young man,
"activity does bring achievement—development."

The door of the office opened suddenly, and two
young fellows rushed in.

"Are you coming to the lacrosse meeting, Doc,—
we are going to organize, and we want you for President again, of course."

Then, seeing the city doctor, whom they recognized,—

"Excuse the interruption, but we can't get on without Dr. Clay, he's the whole works of the lacrosse
team."

"I will not be able to go over tonight, boys," said
the Doctor, "but you'll get on all right. You are
getting to work pretty early—this is the first fine
day."

When the lacrosse boys had gone, Dr. Clay finished
his argument:

"These fellows prove what I was saying. When
I came here six years ago, there was not even a baseball team in the place—the young fellows gathered on
street corners in summer, loafing and idling, revell-
ing in crazy, foolish degrading stories—absolute

degenerations—now see them—on the tail of a
blizzard, they dig out their lacrosse sticks and start
the game on the second fine day. From the time the
hockey is over now, until hockey time again—these
fellows talk and dream lacrosse, and a decenter,
cleaner lot of lads you won't find anywhere. Activity
has saved them—activity *is* growth, it is life—
it is everything!"

The old man shook his head slowly:

"They are not saved, my dear boy—none of us
are—who depend on outward things for your happiness. Outward things change—vanish. 'As a man
thinketh in his heart—so is he!'—that is the secret
of triumphant living. As a man thinketh. These
fellows of yours—for I know this lacrosse team has
been one of the many ways you took of sapping your
energy—do not think. They play, run, scrap, cheer,
but there's no meditation—no turning inward of the
thoughts, no mental progress.

"It would not be natural for growing boys, alive
to their fingertips, to sit yapping like lazy collie
dogs, just thinking," said the young doctor heatedly
"They want avenues of self-expression, and in
lacrosse and hockey they find it."

"Artifical aids to happiness—every one of them—
crutches for lame souls—the Kingdom of Heaven
is within you," the old doctor rambled on, "but it
is all a part of this great new country—this big west
is new and crude and distinct—only the primary
colors are used in the picture, there are no half tones,
no shadows, and above all—or perhaps I should say
behind all—no background. A thing is good or bad—

black or white—blue or red.   We are mostly posters
here in this great big, dazzling country."

In the silence that fell on them, the young man's
mind went limping back to the old doctor's first
words—the dreadful, fateful, significant words. He
had said it—said the thing that if it were true would
exile him from the world he loved! On him the ban
had fallen!

"I suppose," said he, standing behind his chair,
whose back he held with nervous fingers, "there is no
chance that you might be mistaken. It is hard for me
to believe this. I am so strong—so well—so much
alive, except my cough—I am as well as ever I was,
and the cough is a simple thing—this seems impossible to me!"

The old doctor had gone to the window to watch
the throng of boys and girls who raced past on their
way to the hill for an evening's sleigh-ride.

"It always seems impossible," he said, with the
air of a man who is totally disassociated from human
affairs, and is simply stating an interesting fact,
"that is part of the disease, and a very attractive
part too.   The people who have it, never think they
have—even to the last they are hopeful—and sure
they will be better tomorrow. No, I am afraid I
am not mistaken. You know yourself the theory
Clay, of the two sets of microbes, the builders and
the destroyers. Just at the present moment, the
destroyers have the best of it—they have put one
over on the builders—but that does not say that the
good microbes are not working—and may yet win.
You are young, buoyant, happy, hopeful, temper-

ate in your habits—all of which gives you a better chance—if you will throw the weight of your influence on the side of the builders—there is a good chance of winning—I should think with your Irish blood you would enjoy the fight, Clay."

The young doctor turned around suddenly and threw back his head, with an impatient gesture.

"I love a fight, Dr. Brander, but it has to be for something worth while. I have fought for the life of a man, a woman, a child, and I have fought joyfully —for life is sweet, and I desired it for these people, believing it to be a good gift. But in the fight you outline for me, I see nothing to fire man's heart. I won't fight for life if it means just breathing and scraping along at a poor, dying rate, cheating the undertaker of a nice little piece of legitimate business —I can't grow enthusiastic over the prospect of always thinking about myself—and my rest—and my sleep—or my clothes—always looking for a draught or fleeing from the night air or a thunderstorm—never able to do a man's job or a day's work. I can't do it, Dr. Brander, and you couldn't do it. It's a poor, miserable, dull existence, unhappy for me, and no service to any one."

Two red spots burned in his cheeks, and the old doctor, noticing them, wished again that he had come to see him sooner.

"See here, Clay," he said, sitting down again, with his hands spread out on his knees, "you exaggerate this thing. You do not think you are working unless you are slaving and owling around all hours of the night, setting bones and pulling teeth, or ushering

into this wicked world sundry squalling babies who
never asked to come, and do not like it now they are
here. You have been as strong as an ox, and keen as
a race-horse, now you have to slow up—you have to
get out of this country before another winter, and
when you come back in Spring you can go on with
your patients—always with care."

The young doctor surveyed him with curling lip.

"Resume my practice," he said, "how simple.
Send word ahead, I suppose, by circular letter—
'Dear Friends, I will be with you May 1st, to attend
to your medical needs. Save your appendicitis and
neuralgia and broken bones for me. Medical season
opens for business May 1st, every one welcome'.
Something like that ought to be sufficient to hold my
practice. It has always seemed to me very incon-
siderate for people to get sick in the winter, and certainly it is no time for infants to begin their career.
. . . . . . Now, see here, Dr. Brander, I appreciate
all you say. I know why you are talking this way
to me. It is out of the kindness of your heart—for
you have a soft old heart behind all that professional-
ism. But it does not look reasonable to me that a
man who has really lived, can ever drag along like
you say. Who wants to live, anyway, beyond the time
of usefulness? I don't. I want to pass out like old
Prince—you remember my good old roan pacer, do
you?

"That red-eyed old anarchist of yours that no one
could harness but you?"

"That's the one—as good a horse as ever breathed
—misunderstood, that was all—well, he passed on,

as the scientists say, last Fall, passed on in a blaze of glory too, but just how glorious his death was, I don't believe I realized until tonight."

"How did it happen?"

"I had a thirty mile drive to see Mrs. Porter, at Pigeon Lake—and just as I was about to start, another message came that it was very urgent if her life was to be saved. Old Prince would not drive double—and my team was tired out. So I started with him alone. The snow came on when I was half way there, and that made the going bad—to add to the difficulties, a strong wind drove the blinding snow in our faces. But the old boy ploughed on like a wrecking engine—going out in a storm to clear the track. He knew all about it, I never had to urge him. The last mile was the worst—he fell once, but staggered to his feet and went on, on three legs. . . . When we got to the house, I knew it was all up with old Prince—he had made his last journey."

"But he was still living when I came out to see him four hours later. The men had put him in a box stall, and had done all they could, but his eyes were rolling, and his heart missed every fourth beat."

"The two little girls came out and cried over him, and told him he had saved their mother's life, and tried to get him to eat sugar lumps. . . . and—right to the last there was the same proud look in his red eyes, and he gave me a sort of wink which let me know it was all right—he didn't blame me or any one—and so I kissed him once, on the white star on his honest forehead, and I put my left arm around his head so he couldn't see what was coming, and sent a bullet through his brain."

"We buried him on the hillside overlooking the lake, and the little girls put a slab up over him, which says:

> "Prince of the house of Clay
>   Who saved our mother's life,
>   Lies here in peace, and lives
>   In grateful memory in our hearts."

There was a silence, in which each man's mind went back to the one overwhelming thought—that bound them so close together.

Then the young doctor said slowly: "If what you say is true, I envy Prince—and would gadly change places with him."

The old man recovered himself in a moment: "You take things too seriously, Clay," he said quickly: "be glad you are not married. A wife and children clutter up a man's affairs at a time like this —you are quite free from family ties, I believe?"

"Quite free," the young man replied, "all my relatives live in the East, all able to look after themselves. I have no person depending on me—financially, I mean."

"Marriage," began the old doctor, in his most professional tone, as one who reads from a manuscript, "is one-fourth joy and three-fourths disappointment. There is no love strong enough to stand the grind of domestic life. Marriage would be highly successful were it not for the fearful bore of living together. Two houses, and a complete set of servants would make marriage practically free from disappointments. I think Saint Paul was right when he ad-

vised men to remain single if they had serious work
to do. Women, the best of them, grow tiresome and
double-chinned in time."

The young doctor laughed his own big, hearty
laugh, the laugh which his devoted patients said did
them more good than his medicine.

"I like that," he said, "a man with a forty-two
waist measure, wearing an eighteen inch collar, finding fault with a woman's double chin. You are not
such a raving beauty yourself."

The old man interrupted him:

"I do not need to be. I am a doctor, a prescriber of
pills, a mender of bones, a plumber of pipes. . . . .
my work does not call for beauty. Beauty is an embarrassment to a doctor. You would be happier,
young fellow, without that wavy brown hair and
those big eyes of yours, with their long lashes. A
man is built for work, like a truck. Gold and
leather upholstering do not belong there. Women
are different; it is their place in life to be beautiful,
and when they fail in that, they fail entirely. They
have no license to be fat, flabby double-chinned,
flat-footed. It is not seemly, and of course you cannot tell how any of them may turn out. They are all
pretty at sixteen. That is what makes marriage such
a lottery."

"I don't agree with you at all," said his companion,
"it is absurd to expect a woman of fifty to have the
slim grace of a girl of eighteen. My mother was a
big woman, and I always thought her very beautiful.
I think you have a pagan way of looking at marriage.
Marriage is a mutual agreement, for mutual benefit

and comfort, for sympathy and companionship.
Family life develops the better side of human nature,
and casts out selfishness. Many a man has found
himself when he gets a wife, and in the caring for his
children has thrown off the shackles of selfishness.
People only live when they can forget themselves,
for selfishness is death. You're a great doctor, Dr.
Brander, but a poor philosopher."

The older man smiled grimly.

"See here, Clay," he said, "did you ever think of
how nature fools us poor dupes? Nature, old Dame
Nature, has one object, and that is to people the
earth—and to this end she shapes all her plans.
She makes women beautiful, graceful, attractive and
gives them the instinct to dress in a way that
will attract men. Makes them smaller and weaker
than men, too, which also makes its appeal. Why,
if I hadn't watched my step, I'd been married a
dozen times. These little frilled and powdered vixens
have nearly got me. . . . . . If nature used half as
much care in keeping people healthy and free from
accidents, as she does in getting them here—it would
be a happier world. But that is not nature's concern
—She leaves that to the doctors!"

"Well, how does the time go? Isn't that the
train whistle?"

"No hurry," said Dr. Clay, rising, "it stops at
the water-tank, and that whistle is for the hill."

They walked over to the station in silence, and
stood watching the red eye that came gliding
through the moonlit valley. The train seemed to be
slipping in to the station without a sound, in the

hope that no one would notice how late it was.

"Come up and see me, Clay," said the old man kindly. "I want to give you a thorough examination —and I will expect you in a week—we'll talk things over, and see what is best. You have my bag, don't bother coming on—all right then—here's a double seat—so I can stretch out—though it's hardly worth while for an hour. Goodbye, Clay, remember all I told you!"

When the doctor went back to his office, he sat long in his chair in front of the fire, and thought. The place was the same—the cheerful fire—the rows of books—the Fathers of Confederation picture on the wall—and his college group. Everything was the same as it had been—only himself. Everything in the room was strong, durable, almost everlasting, able to resist time and wear. He was the only perishable thing, it seemed.

He wondered how people act when confronted by the ruin of their hopes. Do they rave and curse and cry aloud? He could not think clearly—his mind seemed to avoid the real issue and refuse to strike on the sore place, and he thought of all sorts of other things.

The permanence—the dreadful permanence of everything in the room seemed to oppress him. "Man is mortal," he said, "his possessions outlive him every last one of these things is more durable than I am". The gray wall of the office—so strong and lasting—what chance had an army of microbes against it—the heavy front door, with its cherry panels and brass fittings, had no fear of draughts or

cold. It had limitless resistance. The stocky
stove, on its four squat legs, could hold its own and
snap its fingers at time. They were all so arrogantly
indestructible, so fearfully permanent—they had no
sympathy, no common meeting ground with him.

A knock sounded on the door, and when he opened
it, the station agent was there, with a long box in
his hand.

'It's marked 'Rush', so I thought I had better
shoot it over to you, Doc," he said.

"Thanks, old man," the Doctor said mechanically,
and put the box down on the table. On a white label,
in bright red letters, stood out the word 'Perishable."

The word struck him like a blow between the eyes.
"Perishable!" Then here was something to which he
might feel akin. He opened the box, with detached
interest. A sweet breath of roses proclaimed the
contents. He had forgotten about sending for them
until now—Pearl's roses for this day—nineteen
American Beauties!

He carefully unpacked the wrapping, and held up
the sheaf of loveliness, and just for one moment had
the thrill of joy that beauty had always brought to
him. Pearl's roses! The roses, with which he had
hoped to say what was in his heart—here they
were, in all their exquisite loveliness, and ready
to carry the words of love and hope and tenderness
—but now . . . . he had nothing to say . . . . . .
love and marriage were not for him!

He sat down heavily, beside the table over which
the roses lay scattered, spilling their perfume in the
room.

He fingered them lovingly, smoothing their velvety petals with a tender hand, while his mind sought in vain to readjust itself to the change the last two hours had brought.

He turned again to the fire, which glowed with blue and purple lights behind the windows of isinglass, curling and flaming and twisting, with fascinating brilliance. Long he sat, watching it, while the sounds outside in the street grew less and less, and at last when he went to the window, he found the street in darkness and in silence. The moon had set, and his watch told him it was two o'clock.

The wind whimpered in the chimney like a lonesome puppy, rising and falling, cying out and swelling with eerie rythm; a soft spring wind, he knew it was, that seemed to catch its breath like a thing in pain.

Looking again at the roses, he noticed that the leaves were drooping. He hastily went into the dispensary and brought out two graduates filled with water to put them in; but when he lifted them—he saw, with poignant pain—they were gone past helping—they were frost-bitten.

Then it was that he gathered them in his arms, with sudden passion, and as he sat through the long night, he held them closely to him, for kin of his they surely were—these frosted roses, on whose fragrant young hearts the blight had so prematurely fallen!

CHAPTER IV

AT daybreak, when the light from the eastern
sky came in blue at the window blind, and the gasoline lamp grew sickly and pale, the doctor went to
bed. He had thought it all out and outlined his
course of action.

He did not doubt the old doctor's word; his own
knowledge gave corroborative evidence that it was
quite true, and he wondered he had not thought of it.
Still, there was something left for him to do. He
would play up and play the game, even if it were a
losing fight. His own house had fallen, but it would
be his part now to see that the minimum amount of
pain would come to Pearl over it. She was young,
and had all the world before her—she would forget.
He had a curious shrinking from having her know
that he had the disease, for like most doctors, he
loathed the thought of disease, and had often quoted
to his patients in urging them to obey the laws of
physiological righteousness, the words of Elbert
Hubbard that "The time would come when people
would feel more disgrace at being found in a hospital
than in a jail, for jails were for those who broke
men's laws, but those in the hospital had broken
the laws of God!"

He shuddered now when he thought of it, it all
seemed so unnecessary—so wantonly cruel—so
inexplicable.

Above all, Pearl must not know, for instinctively

he felt that if she knew he was a sick man, she would
marry him straight away—she would be so sweet
about it all, and so hopeful and sure he would get
well, and such a wonderfully skilful and tender nurse,
that he would surely get well. For one blissful but
weak moment, which while it thrilled it frightened
him still more—he allowed himself to think it would
be best to tell her. Just for one weak moment the
thought came—to be banished forever from his
mind. No! No! No! Disaster had come to him, but
Pearl would not be made to suffer, she would not
be involved in any way.

But just what attitude to take, perplexed him.
Those big, soft brown eyes of hers would see through
any lie he tried to invent, and he was but a poor liar
anyway. What could he tell Pearl? He would tem-
porize—he would stall for time. She was too young
—she had seen so little of the world—it would be
hard to wait—he believed he could take that line
with her—he would try it.

When he awakened, the sun was shining in the
room, with a real spring warmth that just for a
minute filled him with gladness and a sense of well-
being. Then he remembered, and a groan burst
from his lips.

The telephone rang:

Reaching out, he seized it and answered.

"It's me," said a voice, "It's Pearl! I am coming
in—I know you're tired after yesterday, and you
need a long sleep—so don't disturb yourself—I'll

be in about two o'clock—just when the sun is brightest—didn't I tell you it would be finer still today?"

"You surely did, Pearl," he answered, "however
you knew."

"I'm not coming just to see you—ma wants a new
strainer, and Bugsey needs boots, and Mary has to
have another hank of yarn to finish the sweater
she's knitting—these are all very urgent, and I'll
get them attended to first, and then:

She paused:

"Then you'll come and see me, Pearl"—he finished,
"and we'll have the meeting which we adjourned
three years ago—to meet yesterday."

"That's it," she said, "and goodbye until then."

He looked at his watch, it was just ten—there was
yet time.

Reaching for the telephone, he called long distance, Brandon. "Give me Orchard's greenhouses,"
he said.

After a pause he got the wire:

"Send me a dozen and a half—no, nineteen—
American Beauty roses on today's train, without
fail. This is Dr. Clay of Millford talking."

He put back the telephone, and lay back with a
whimsical smile, twisting his mouth. "The frosted
ones are mine," he said to himself, "there will be
no blight or spot or blemish on Pearl's roses."

It was quite like Pearl to walk into the doctor's
office without embarrassment. It was also like her
to come at the exact hour she had stated in her telephone message—and to the man who sat waiting for
her, with a heart of lead, she seemed to bring the
whole sunshine of Spring with her.

Ordinarily, Dr. Clay did not notice what women wore, they all looked about the same to him—but he noticed that Pearl's gray coat and furs just needed the touch of crimson which her tam o'shanter and gloves supplied, and which seemed to carry out the color in her glowing cheeks. She looked like a red apple in her wholesomeness.

He had tried to get the grittiness of the sleepless night out of his eyes, and had shaved and dressed himself with the greatest care, telling himself it did not matter—but the good habit was deeply fastened on him and could not be set aside.

There was nothing about the well-dressed young man, with his carefully brushed hair and splendid color, to suggest disease. Pearl's eyes approved of each detail, from the way his hair waved and parted back; the dull gold and purple tie, which seemed to bring out the bronze tones in his hair and the steely gray of his eyes; the well-cut business suit of rough brown tweed, with glints of green and bronze, down to the dark brown, well-polished boots.

Pearl was always proud of him; it glowed in her eyes again to-day, and again he felt it, warming his heart and giving him the sense of well-being which Pearl's presence always brought. All at once he felt rested and full of energy.

When the first greetings were over, and Pearl had seated herself, at his invitation, in the big chair, he said, laughing:

" 'Tis a fine day, Miss Watson."

"It is that!" said Pearl, with her richest brogue, which he had often told her he hoped she would never lose.

"And you are eighteen years old now," he said, in the same tone.

"Eighteen, going on nineteen," she corrected gaily.

"All right, eighteen—going on—nineteen. Three years ago there was a little bargain made between us —without witnesses, that we would defer all that was in our minds for three years—we'd give the matter a three years' hoist—and then take it up just where we left it!"

She nodded, without speaking.

"Now I have thought about it a lot," he went on, "indeed I do not think a day has gone by without my thinking of it, and incidentally, I have thought of myself and my belongings. I wish to draw your attention to them—I am twenty-nine years old— I've got a ten years' start of you, and I will always expect to be treated with respect on account of my years—that's clearly understood, is it?"

He was struggling to get himself in hand.

"Clearly understood," she repeated, with her eyes on him in unmistakable adoration.

"Six years ago," he seemed to begin all over gain— "I came out of college, with all sorts of fine theories, just bubbling over with enthusiasm, much the same as you are now, fresh from Normal, but somehow they have mostly flattened out, and now I find myself settling down to the prosy life of a country doctor, who feeds his own horses and blackens his own boots, and discusses politics with the retired farmers who gather in the hardware store. I catch myself at it quite often. Old Bob Johnson and I are quite decided there will be a war with Germany before many years. We don't stop at Canadian affairs—the world is not too wide for us! Yes, Pearl, here I am, a country doctor, with an office in need of paint—a very good medical library—in need of reading—a very common-place, second-rate doctor—who will never be a great success, who will just continue to grub along. With you, Pearl, it is different. You have ambition, brains—and something about you that will carry you far—I always knew it—and am so glad that at the Normal they recognized your ability."

A puzzled look dimmed the brightness of her eyes just for a moment, and the doctor stumbled on.

"I am all right, as far as I go—but there's not enough of me—I'm not big enough for you, Pearl."

Pearl's eyes danced again, as she looked him up and down, and he laughed in spite of himself.

"For goodness sake, girl," he cried, "don't look at me, you make me forget what I was saying—I can't think, when you train those eyes of yours on me."

Pearl obediently turned her head away, but he could still see the dimple in her cheeks.

"I have had a long fight with myself, Pearl," and now that he was back to the truth, his voice had its old mellowness that swept her heart with tenderness —"a long fight—and it is not over yet. I'm selfish enough to want you—that is about 99.9% of me is selfish, the other infinitesimal part cries out for me to play the man—and do the square thing—I am making a bad job of this, but maybe you understand."

He came over and turned her head around until she
faced him.

"I have begun at the wrong end of this, dear, I
talk as if you had said—you cared—I have no right
to think you do. I should remember you are only
a child—and haven't thought about—things like
this!"

"O, haven't I, though," she cried eagerly. "I've
been thinking—all the time—I've never stopped
thinking—I've had the loveliest time thinking."

The doctor went on in a measured tone, as one
who must say the words he hates to utter. All the
color had gone from his voice, all the flexibility.
It was as hard as steel now, and as colorless as a dusty
road.

"Pearl, I am going to say what I should say, not
what I want to say. . . . Supposing I did induce you
to marry me now. Suppose I could . . . in ten
years from now, when you are a woman grown, you
might hate me for taking advantage of your youth,
your inexperience, your childish fancy for me—I am
not prepared to take that risk—it would be a criminal
thing to run any chances of spoiling a life like yours."

Her eyes looked straight into his, and there was a
little muttered cry in them that smote his heart
with pity. He had seen it in the faces of little
children, his patients, who, though hurt, would not
cry.

"And I am selfish enough to hope that in a few
years, when you are old enough to choose, you will
think of what I am doing now, and know the sacrifice
I am making, and come to me of your own free will—

no, I did not intend to say that—I do not mean what I said—the world is yours, Pearl, to choose as you will—I have no claim on you! You start fair."

Pearl's cheeks had lost a little of their rosy glow, and her face had taken on a cream whiteness. She stood up and looked at him, with widely opened eyes. A girl of smaller soul might have misunderstood him, and attributed to him some other motive. Though Pearl did not agree with him, she believed every word he had said.

"Supposing," she said eagerly, "that I do not want to start fair—and don't want to be free to choose—supposing I have made my choice—supposing I understand you better than you do yourself, and tell you now that you are not a second-hand doctor—that you are a sun and a shield to this little town and country, just as you have been to me—you bring health and courage by your presence—the people love and trust you—suppose I remind you that you are not only a doctor, but the one that settles their quarrels and puts terror into the evil-doer. Who was it that put the fear into Bill Plunkett when he blackened his wife's eyes, and who was it that brought in the two children from the Settlement, that were abused by their step-father, and took the old ruffian's guns away from him and marched him in too! That's a job for a second-rate doctor, isn't it? I hear the people talking about you, and I have to turn my back for fear they hear my eyes shouting out, 'That's my man you're praising' and here he is, telling me he is a second-rate doctor! Is that what you were when the fever was so bad, and all the Clarkes had it at once, and you nursed six of them through it? Mrs. Clarke says the only undressing you did was to loosen your shoe-laces!"

"Don't. you see—I know you better than you do yourself. You don't see how big your work is. Is it a small thing to live six years in a place and have every one depending on you, praising you—loving you—and being able to advise them and lead the young fellows any way you like—making men of them, instead of street loafers—and their mothers so thankful they can hardly speak of it."

"You evidently don't know what we think of you, any of us—and here I am—I don't know when it began with me—the first day I saw you—I think, when I was twelve—I've been worshipping you and treasuring up every word you ever said to me. I don't know whether it is love or not, it's something very sweet. It has made me ambitious to look my best, do my best and be my best. I want to make you proud of me—I will make you proud of me— see if I don't—I want to be with you, to help you, look after you—grow up with you—I don't know whether it is love or not—it—is something! There is nothing too hard for me to do, if it is for you— everything—anything would be sweet to me—if you were with me. Is that love?

She was standing before him, holding his hand in both of hers, and her eyes had the light in them, the tender, glowing light that seemed to flame blue at the edges, like the coal fire he had watched the night before.

Impulsively he drew her to him, and for a moment

buried his face in her warm, white neck, kissing the curling strands of her brown hair.

"O Pearl," he cried, drawing away from her, "O Pearl—you're a hard girl to give up—you make me forget all my good resolutions. I don't want to do what I ought to do. I just want you."

There was a smothered cry in his voice that smote on Pearl's heart with a sudden fear. Mothers know the different notes in their children's cries—and in Pearl, the maternal instinct was strong.

She suddenly understood. He was suffering, there was a bar between them—for some reason, he could not marry her!

She grew years older, it seemed, in a moment, and the thought that came into her brain, clamoring to be heard, exultantly, insistently knocking for admission, was this—her mother's pessimistic way of looking at life was right—there were things too good to be true—she had been too sure of her happiness. The thought, like cold steel, lay against her heart and dulled its beating. But the pain in his eyes must be comforted. She stood up, and gravely took the hand he held out to her.

"Doctor," she said steadily, "you are right, quite right, about this—a girl of eighteen does not know her own mind—it is too serious a matter—life is too long—I—I think I love you—I mean I thought I did—I know I like to be with you—and—all that—but I'm too young to be sure—and I'll get over this all right. You're right in all you say—and it's a good thing you are so wise about this—we might have made a bad mistake—that would have brought us unhappiness. But it has been sweet all the time, and I'm not sorry—we'll just say no more about it now and don't let it worry you—I can stand anything —if you're not worried."

He looked at her in amazement—and not being as quick as she, her words deceived him, and there was not a quiver on her lips, as she said:

"I'll go now, doctor, and we'll just forget what we were saying—they were foolish words. I'm thinking of going North to teach—one of the inspectors wrote me about a school there. I just got his letter today, and he asked me to wire him—I'll be back at the holidays."

She put the red tam on her brown hair, tucking up the loose strands, in front of the glass, as she spoke. Manlike, he did not see that her hands trembled, and her face had gone white. He sat looking at her in deep admiration.

"What a woman you are, Pearl," broke from his lips.

She could not trust herself to shake hands, or even look at him. Her one hope was to get away before her mask of unconcern broke into a thousand pieces by the pounding of her heart, which urged her to throw her arms around him and beg him to tell her what was really wrong—oh, why wouldn't he tell her!

"You'll think of this, dear," he said, "in a few years when you are, I hope, happily married to the man of your choice, and you will have a kindly thought for me, and know I was not a bad sort—you'll remember every word of this Pearl, and you will understand that what is strange to you now—and you will perhaps think of me—and if not with pleasure, it will at least be without pain."

He wanted to give her the roses, which had come just a few moments before she came in, but somehow he could not frame a casual word of greeting. He would send them to her.

She was going now.

"Pearl, dearest Pearl," he cried "I cannot let you go like this—and yet—it's best for both of us."

"Sure it is," she said, smiling tightly, to keep her lips from quivering. "I'm feeling fine over it all." The pain in his voice made her play up to her part.

"I can't even kiss you, dear,'" he said. "I don't want you to have one bitter memory of this. I want you to know I was square—and loved you too well to take the kiss, which in after life might sting your face when you thought that I took advantage of your youth. A young girl's first kiss is too sacred a thing."

Suddenly Pearl's resolution broke down. It was the drawn look in his face, and its strange pallor.

She reached up and kissed his cheek.

"A little dab of a kiss like that won't leave a sting on anyone's face," she said.

She was gone!

CHAPTER V

MRS. CROCKS THREW THE SWITCH

When Pearl came out of the doctor's office into the sunshine of the village street, she had but one thought — one overwhelming desire, expressed in the way she held her head, and the firm beat of her low-heeled shoes on the sidewalk—she must get away where she would not see him or the people she knew. She realized that whatever it was that had come between them was painful to him, and that he really cared for her. To see her, would be hard on him, embarrassing to them both, and she would do her share by going away—and she remembered, with a fresh pang—that when she had spoken of this, he had made no objection, thus confirming her decision that for her to go would be the best way.

The three glorious years, so full of hopes and dreams, were over! Pearl's house of hopes had fallen! All was over! And it was not his fault—he was not to blame. Instinctively, Pearl defended him in her mind against a clamorous sense of injustice which told her that she had not had a square deal! The pity of it all was what choked her and threatened to storm her well-guarded magazine of self-control! It was all so sudden, so mysterious and queer, and yet, she instinctively felt, so inexorable!

Pearl had always been scornful of the tears of love-lorn maidens, and when in one of her literature lessons at the Normal, the sad journey of the lily-maid on her barge of black samite, floating down the river, so dead and beautiful, with the smile on her face and the lily in her hand, reduced form A to a common denominator of tears, and made the whole room look like a Chautauqua salute, Pearl had stoutly declared that if Elaine had played basket-ball or hockey instead of sitting humped up on a pile of cushions in her eastern tower, broidering the sleeve of pearls so many hours a day, she wouldn't have died so easily nor have found so much pleasure in arranging her own funeral.

But on this bright March day, the village street seemed strangely dull and dead to her, with an empty sound like a phone that has lost its connection. Something had gone from her little world, leaving it motionless, weary and old! A row of icicles hung from the roof of the corner store, irregular and stained from the shingles above, like an ugly set of ill-kept teeth, dripping disconsolately on the sidewalk below, and making there a bumpy blotch of unsightly ice!

In front of the store stood the delivery sleigh, receiving its load of parcels, which were thrown in with an air of unconcern by a blocky young man with bare red hands. The horse stood without being tied, in an apparently listless and melancholy dream. A red and white cow came out of the lane and attempted to cross the slippery sidewalk, sprawling helplessly for a moment, and then with a great effort recovered herself and went back the way she came, limping painfully, the blocky young man hastening her movements by throwing at her a piece of box lid, with the remark that "that would learn her."

The sunshine so brilliant and keen, had a cold and merciless tang in it, and a busy-body look about it, as if it delighted in shining into forbidden corners and tearing away the covers that people put on their sorrows, calling all the world to come and see! Pearl shuddered with the sudden realization that the sun could shine and the wind could blow bright and gay as ever, though hearts were writhing in agony!

She hoped she would not see any of the people she knew, for the pain that lay like a band of ice around her heart might be showing in her face—and Pearl knew that the one thing she could not stand was a word of sympathy. That would be fatal. So she hurried on. She would send a wire of acceptance to her inspector friend, and then go over to the stable for her horse, and be on her way home.

But there is something whimsical about fate. It takes a hand in our affairs without apology, and throws a switch at the last moment. If Pearl had not met Mrs. Crocks at the corner, just before she took the street to the station, this would have been a different story. But who knows? We never get a chance to try the other way, and it is best and wisest and easiest of comprehension to believe that whatever is, is best!

Mrs. Crocks was easily the best informed person regarding local happenings, in the small town of Millford. She really knew. Every community has its unlicensed and unauthorized gossips, who think they know what their nieghbors are thinking and doing, but who more often than not get their data wrong, and are always careless of detail. Mrs. Crocks was not one of these.

When Bill Cavers got drunk, and spent in one grand, roaring spree all the money which he and his wife and Libby Anne had saved for their trip to Ontario, there were those who said that he went through six hundred dollars that one night, making a rough guess at the amount. Mrs. Crocks did not use any such amateur and unsatisfactory way of arriving at conclusions. She did not need to—there was a way of finding out! To the elevator she went, and looked at the books under cover of looking up a wheat ticket which her husband had cashed and found that Bill Cavers had marketed seventeen hundred and eight dollars worth of wheat. From this he had paid his store bill, and the blacksmith's bill, which when deducted, left him eight hundred and fourteen dollars—she did not bother with the cents. The deductions were easily verified—both the storekeeper and the blacksmith were married men!

This was the method she followed in all her research—careful, laborious and accurate at all costs, with a fine contempt for her less scientific contemporaries. The really high spots in her life had been when she was able to cover her competitors with confusion by showing that their facts were all wrong, which process she referred to as "showing up these idle gossips."

James Crocks, her husband, had chosen for himself a gentler avocation than his wife's, and one which brought him greater peace of mind—proprietor of the big red stable which spread itself over half a block, he had unconsciously defined himself, as well

as his place of business, by having printed in huge
white letters with black edging across the shingled
roof, the words:

"HORSE REPOSITORY" PROP. J. CROCKS.

Here the tired horses could forget the long trail
and the heavy loads, in the comfortable stalls, with
their deep bedding of clean straw; and here also,
James Crocks himself was able to find the cheerful
company, who ate their meals in quietude of heart,
asking no questions, imputing no motives, knowing
nothing of human intrigue, and above all, never,
never insisting that he tell them what he thought
about anything! Most of his waking hours were
spent here, where he found the gentle sounds of
feeding horses, the honest smell of prairie hay and
the blessed absence of human chatter very soothing
and restful.

As time went on, and James Crocks grew more and
more averse to human speech—having seen it cause
so much trouble one way'n another, Mrs. Crocks
found it was an economy of effort to board one of the
stable boys, and that is how it came about that Mr.
Bertie Peters found himself called from the hay-mow
above the stable, to his proprietors' guest chamber,
and all the comforts of a home, including nightly
portions of raisin pie—and best of all, an interested
and appreciative audience who liked to hear him talk.
Mrs. Crocks as usual had made a good choice, for as
Bertie talked all the time, he was sure to say something once in a while. A cynical teacher had once
said of Bertie, that he never had an "unuttered
thought."

But even though the livery stable happenings as related by Bertie gave Mrs. Crocks many avenues of information, all of her prescience could not be explained through that or any other human agency. The young doctor declared she had the gift or divination, was a mind reader, and could see in the dark! Many a time when he had gone quietly to the stable and taken out his team without as much as causing a dog to bark, removing his sleigh bells to further cover his movements, and stealing out of town like an absconding bank-teller, to make a call, returning the same way, still under cover of night, and flattering himself that he had fooled her this time, she would be waiting for him, and timed her call to the exact minute. Just as he got in to his room after putting his team away, his phone would ring and Mrs. Crocks would ask him about the patient he had been to see. She did not always call him, of course, but he felt she knew where he had been. There was no explanation—it was a gift!

Pearl had been rather a favorite with Mrs. Crocks when the Watson family lived in Millford, but since they had gone to the farm and prosperity had come to them as evidenced by their better clothes, their enlarged house, their happier faces, and more particularly Pearl's success in her school work in the city, all of which had appeared in the local paper, for the editor was enthusiastic for his own town— Mrs. Crock's friendly attitude had suffered a change. She could put up with almost anything in her friends, but success!

But when she met Pearl on the street that day, her manner was friendly.

"Hello stranger," she said, "I hear you have been
doing big things down there in the city, winnin'
debates and makin' speeches. Good for you, Pearl—
I always said you were a smart girl, even when your
people were as poor as get-out—I could see it in you
—but don't let it spoil you, Pearl—and don't ever
forget you are just a country girl. But I am certainly
glad you did so well—for your mother's sake—many a
time I was dead sorry for her having to work so hard!
It's a comfort to her now to see you doin' so well.
Where have you been now? I saw you comin' out
of the doctor's office just now—anybody sick? You're
not looking as pert as usual yourself—you haven't
been powderin' your face, I hope! No one sick, eh?
Just a friendly call then, was it? See here, Pearl—
when I was young, girls did not do the chasin', we let
the men do that, and I'm here to tell you it's the best
way. And look here, there's enough girls after Doctor
Clay without you—there was a man from the city
telling Bertie at the stable that he seen our doctor
in a box at the Opera with the Senator's daughter
two weeks ago, and that she is fair dippy about him,
and now that he is thinking of goin' into politics, it
would be a great chance for him. The other side are
determined to make him run for them against old
Steadman, and the old lady is that mad she won't
let his name be mentioned in the house. She says
the country owes it to Mr. Steadman to put him in
by acclamation! And the doctor hasn't accepted it
yet. The committee went to see him yesterday and
he turned them down but they won't take no for an
answer, and they asked him to think it over—I

suppose he told you all about it——"

For the first time Mrs. Crocks stopped for breath. Her beady eyes were glistening with excitement. Here was a scoop—if Pearl would only tell her. She would be able to anticipate the doctor's answer.

"What is he goin' to do, Pearl, I know he would tell you; I have always said that doctor thinks more of you than he does of any of the other girls! What did he say about it, will he take it?"

Pearl was quite herself now—composed, on her guard, even smiling.

"I think the doctor would prefer to make his own announcement," she said, "and he will make it to the committee."

Mrs. Crocks' eyes narrowed darkly, and she breathed heavily in her excitement. Did Pearl Watson mean to tell her in as many words, to mind her own business. But in Pearl's face there was no guile, and she was going on her way.

"Don't be in a hurry, Pearl," said Mrs. Crocks, "can't you wait a minute and talk to an old friend? I am sure I do not care a pin whether the doctor runs or not. I never was one to think that women should concern themselves with politics—that surely belongs to the men. I have been a home body all my life, as you know, and of course I should have known that the doctor would not discuss his business with a little chit like you—but dear, me, he is one terrible flirt, he cannot pass a pretty face. Of course now he will settle down no doubt, every one thinks he will anyway, and marry Miss Keith of Hampton—the Keith's have plenty of money, though I don't believe

that counts as much with the doctor as family,
and of course they have the blue blood too, and
her father being the Senator will help. What! must
you go—you're not half as sociable as you used to
be when you brought the milk every morning to the
back door—you sure could talk then, and tell some
of the weirdest things. I always knew you would be
something, but if you freeze up like a clam when you
meet old friends—it does not seem as if education has
improved you. Can't you stay and talk a minute?"

"I could stay," said Pearl, "and I can still talk, but
I have not been able to talk to you. You see I do not
like to interrupt any one so much older than myself!"

When Pearl walked away, Mrs. Crocks looked after
her with a look of uncertainty on her face. Pearl's
words rang in her ears!

"She's smart, that kid—she's smart—I'll say that
for her. There is not a man in town who dare look
me in the eye and take a rise like that out of me, but
she did it without a flicker. So I know I had her mad
or she wouldn't have said it, but wasn't she smooth
about it?"

Then her professional pride asserted itself, reminding her that a slight had been put upon her, and her
mood changed.

"Of all the saucy little jades," she said to herself
"with the air of a duchess, and the fine clothes of
her! And to think that her mother washed for me
not so long ago, and that girl came for the clothes
and brought them back again! And now listen to her!
You put your foot in it, Pearl my young lady, when
you rubbed Jane Crocks the wrong way, for people

cannot do that and get away with it! And remember
I am telling you."

When Pearl left Mrs. Crocks standing on the street
she walked quickly to the station, but arriving there
with the yellow blank in her hand, she found her
intention of accepting a school in the North had grown
weak. She did not want to go to the North, or
any place. She suddenly wanted to stay. She would
take a school some place near—and see what was
going to happen; and besides—she suddenly thought
of this—she must not decide on anything until she
saw Mr. Donald, her old teacher, and got his advice.
It would not be courteous to do anything until she
saw him, and tomorrow was the day he wanted her to
go to the school to speak to the children. Why, of
course, she could not go—and so Pearl reasoned in
that well-known human way of backing herself up
in the thing she wanted to do! So she tore off a
couple of blank forms and put them in her purse, and
asked the agent if he knew how the train from the
East was, and he gave her the assurance that it had
left the city on time and was whoopin' it along through
the hills at Cardinal when last heard from—and stood
a good chance of getting in before night.

All the way home, Pearl tried to solve the tangle
of thoughts that presented themselves to her, but
the unknown quantity, the "X" in this human
equation, had given her so little to work on, that it
seemed as though she must mark it "insufficient
data" and let it go! But unfortunately for Pearl's
peace of mind it could not be dismissed in that way.

One thing was evident—it was some sudden hap-

pening or suggestion that had changed his attitude
towards her, for there was no mistaking the tenderness in his messages over the phone the day before
—and why did he remember the day at all, if it
were only to tell her that she was too young to
really know her own mind. The change—whatever
it was—had taken place in the interval of his phon-
ing, and her visit, and Mrs. Crocks had said that a
committee had gone to see him and offer him the
nomination! What difference would that make?
The subtle suggestion of the senator's daughter
came back to her mind! Was it possible—that the
Watson family were——what she had once read of
in an English story —— 'socially impossible.' Pearl
remembered the phrase. The thought struck her
with such an impact that she pulled her horse up
with a jerk, and stood on the road in deep abstraction.

She remembered the quarrel she had once had with
a girl at school. It all came back in a flash of rage that
lit up this forgotten corner of her memory! The
cause of the quarrel did not appear in the record,
but that the girl had flung it at her that her people
were nothing and nobody—her mother a washer-
woman and her father a section hand—now stood out
in letters of flame! Pearl had not been angry at the
time—and she remembered that her only reason for
taking out the miserable little shrimp and washing
her face in the snow was that she knew the girl had
said this to be very mean, and with the pretty certain
hope that it would cut deep! She was a sorrel-topped,
anæmic, scrawny little thing, who ate slate-pencils
and chewed paper, and she had gone crying to the

teacher with the story of Pearl's violence against her.

Mr. Donald had found out the cause, and had spoken so nicely to Pearl about it, that her heart was greatly lifted as a result, and the incident became a pleasant recollection, with only the delightful part remaining, until this moment. Mr. Donald had said that Pearl was surely a lucky girl, when the worst thing that could be said to her was that her two parents had been engaged in useful and honorable work—and he had made this the topic for a lesson that afternoon in showing how all work is necessary and all honorable. Out of the lesson had grown a game which they often played on Friday afternoons, when a familiar object was selected and all the pupils required to write down the names of all the workers who had been needed to bring it to perfection.

And the next day when lunch time came, Mr. Donald told them he had been thinking about the incident, and how all that we enjoy in life comes to us from our fellow-workers, and he was going to have a new grace, giving the thanks to where it belonged. He said God was not the kind of a Creator who wanted all the glory of the whole world—for he knew that every man and woman or boy or girl that worked, was entitled to praise, and he liked to see them thanked as they deserved.

A new grace was written on the board, and each day it was repeated by all the pupils. Pearl remembered that to her it had seemed very grand and stately and majestic, with the dignity and thrill of a pipe-organ:

"Give us to know, O God, that the blessings we are

about to enjoy have come to us through the labors
of others. Strengthen the ties of brotherhood and
grant that each of us may do our share of the
world's work."

But the æsthetic emotions which it sent through
her young soul the first time she said it, did not in any
way interfere with the sweet satisfaction she had in
leaning across the aisle and wrinkling up her nose
at her former adversary!

She began to wonder now if Mr. Donald had been
right in his idealistic way of looking at life and
labor. She had always thought so until this minute,
and many a thrill of pride had she experienced in
thinking of her parents and their days of struggling.
They had been and were, the real Empire-builders
who subdued the soil and made it serve human needs,
enduring hardships and hunger and cold and bitter
discouragements, always with heroism and patience.
The farm on which they now lived, had been aban-
doned, deserted, given up for a bad job, and her
people had redeemed it, and were making it one of
the best in the country! Every farm in the community was made more valuable because of their efforts.
It had seemed to Pearl a real source of proper pride
—that her people had begun with nothing, and were
now making a comfortable living, educating their
children and making improvements each year in their
way of living and in the farm itself! It seemed that
she ought to be proud of them, and she was!

But since she had been away, she learned to her
surprise that the world does not give its crowns to
those who serve it best—but to those who can make

the most people serve them, and she found that many people think of work as a disagreeable thing, which if patiently endured for a while may be evaded ever afterwards, and indeed her mother had often said that she was determined to give her children an education, so they would not need to work as hard as she and their father had. Education then seemed to be a way of escape.

Senator Keith, of Hampton, with his forty sections all rented out, did not work. Miss Keith, his daughter, did not work. They did not need to work— they had escaped!

It was quite a new thought to Pearl, and she pondered it deeply. The charge against her family —the slur which could be thrown on them was not that of dishonor, dishonesty, immorality or intemperance—none of these—but that they had worked at poorly paid, hard jobs, thereby giving evidence that they were not capable of getting easier ones. Hard work might not be in itself dishonorable—but it was a confession.

Something in Pearl's heart cried out at the injustice of this. It was not fair! All at once she wanted to talk about it to—some one, to everybody. It was a mistaken way of looking at life, she thought; the world, as God made it, was a great, beautiful place, with enough of everything to go around. There is enough land—enough coal—enough oil. Enough pleasure and beauty, enough music and fun and good times! What had happened was that some had taken more than their share, and that was why others had to go short, and the strange part of it all was that the hoggish ones were the exalted ones, to whom many bowed, and they—some of them—were scornful of the people who were still working—though if every one stopped working, the world would soon be starving.

"It is a good world—just the same," said Pearl, as she looked away to her left, where the Hampton Hills shoved one big blue shoulder into the sky-line. "People do not mean to be hard and cruel to each other—they do not understand, that's all—they have not thought—they do not see."

From the farm-houses set back in the snowy fields, came the cheerful Spring sounds of scolding hens and gabbling ducks, with the occasional bark of a dog. The sunshine had in it now no tang of cold or bitterness, for in Pearl's heart there had come a new sense of power—an exaltation of spirit that almost choked her with happiness. Her eyes flashed—her hands tingled—her feet were light as air. Out of the crushing of her hopes, the falling of her house of dreams, had come this inexplicable intoxication, which swept her heart with its baptism of joy.

She threw back her head and looked with rapture into the limitless blue above her, with something of the vision which came to Elisha's servant at Dothan when he saw the mountains were filled with the horses and the chariots of the Lord!

"It is a good world," she whispered, "God made it, Christ lived in it—and when He went away, He left His Spirit. It can't go wrong and stay wrong. The only thing that is wrong with it is in people's hearts, and hearts can be changed by the Grace of God.

A sudden feeling of haste came over her—a new sense of responsibility—there were so many things to be done. She roused the fat pony from his pleasant dream, to a quicker gait, and drove home with the strange glamour on her soul.

CHAPTER VI.

RED ROSES

When Pearl rode into the farmyard, she saw her brother Tommy coming in great haste across the fields, waving his arms to her with every evidence of strong excitement. The other children were on their way home, too, but it was evident that Thomas had far outrun them. Tommy had a tale to tell.

"There is going to be real 'doin's' at the school on Friday," he cried, as soon as he was within calling distance of her. "Mr. Donald has asked all the big people, too, and the people from Purple Springs, and the women are going to bring pies and things, and there will be eats, and you are to make the speech, and then maybe there will be a football match, and you can talk as long as you like, and we are all to clap our hands when your name is mentioned and then again when you get up to speak—and it's to be Friday."

Tommy told his story all in one breath, and without waiting to get a reply, he made his way hurriedly to the barn where his father and Teddy were working. There he again told it, with a few trifling variations. "You are all to come, and there will be a letter to-morrow telling you all about it, but it is a real big day that is going to be at school, and all the big people, too, and it is to hear Pearl talk about what she saw and heard in the city, and there will be cakes and stuff to eat and the Tuckers said they would not come and

Jimmy said 'Dare you to stay away' and they did not take his dare."

Teddy, in true brotherly fashion, professed some doubts of the success of the undertaking.

"Pearl is all right to talk around home, but gee whiz, I don't believe she can stand right up and talk like a preacher, she'll forget what she was goin' to say, I couldn't say two words before all those people."

John Watson went on with the fanning of the wheat. He had stopped the mill only long enough to hear Tommy's message, and Teddy's brotherly apprehensions, he made no comment. But a close observer would have noticed that he worked a little faster, and perhaps held his shoulders a little straighter—they had grown stooped in the long days when he worked on the section. Although his shoulders had sagged in the long hard struggle, there had always burned in his heart the hope that better days would come—and now the better days were here. The farm was doing well—every year they were able to see that they were making progress. The children were all at school, and today—today Pearlie was asked to speak to all the people in the neighborhood. Pearlie had made a name for herself when she got the chance to get out with other boys and girls. It was a proud day for John Watson, and his honest heart did not dissemble the pride he felt in his girl.

Pearl herself had a momentary feeling of fear when she heard the plans that were being made. The people she knew would be harder to speak to than strangers. But the exaltation that had come to her heart was still with her, and impelled her to speak.

There were things which should be said—great matters were before the country. Pearl had attended many political meetings in the city, and also as many sessions of the Legislature as she could, and so she knew the Provincial political situation, and it was one of great interest.

The government had been in power for many years and had built up a political machine which they believed to be invincible. They had the country by the throat, and ruled autocratically, scorning the feeble protests of the Opposition, who were few in number and weak in debate. Many a time as Pearl sat in the Ladies' Gallery and listened to the flood of invective with which the cabinet ministers smothered any attempt at criticism which the Opposition might make, she had longed for a chance to reply. They were so boastful, so overbearing, so childishly important, it seemed to her that it would be easy to make them look ridiculous, and she often found herself framing replies for the Opposition. But of course there was a wide gulf between the pompous gentlemen who lolled and smoked their black cigars in the mahogany chairs on the red-carpeted floor of the House, and the bright-eyed little girl who sat on the edge of her seat in the gallery and looked down upon them.

She had been in the gallery the day that a great temperance delegation had come and asked that the bar might be abolished, and she had listened to every word that had been said. The case against the bar had been so well argued, that it seemed to Pearl that the law-makers must be moved to put it away forever. She did not know, of course, that the liquor interests of the province were the strong supporters of the Government, and the source of the major portion of their campaign funds; that the bars were the rallying places for the political activities of the party, and that to do away with the bars would be a blow to the Government, and, as the Premier himself had once said, "No Government is going to commit suicide," the chances for the success of the delegation were very remote. Pearl did not know this, and so she was not prepared for it when the Premier and one of his Ministers stoutly defended the bar-room as a social gathering place where men might meet and enjoy an innocent and profitable hour.

"It is one of our social institutions that you are asking us to destroy," cried the Minister of Education, "and I tell you frankly that we will not do it. The social instincts distinguish man from the brute, and they must be cherished and encouraged. Your request is not in the best interests of our people, and as their faithful representatives who seek to safeguard their interests and their highest welfare, we must refuse."

And the Government desks were pounded in wild enthusiasm! And Pearl had come away with a rage in her heart, the wordless rage of the helpless. After that she attended every meeting of the Suffrage Society, and her deep interest and devotion to the cause won for her many friends among the suffrage women.

The news of the proposed meeting in the school

brought out many and varied comments, when it was
received in the homes of the district. Mr. Donald
sent to each home a letter in which he invited all the
members of each family to be present to "do honor to
one who has brought honor to our school and
district."

Mrs. Eben Snider, sister of Mrs. Crocks, a wizened
little pod of a woman with a face like parchment,
dismally prophesied that "Pearl Watson would be
clean spoiled with so much notice being taken of
her. 'Put a beggar on horseback,'" she cried,
when she read the invitation, "and you know where
he will ride to!" "The Watsons are doing too well
—everything John Watson touches turns to money
since he went on that farm, and this last splurge for
Pearl is just too much. I won't be a party to it!
It is too much like makin' flesh of one and fowl of
the other. Mr. Donald always did make too much
of a pet of that girl, and then all those pieces in the
paper, they will spoil her, no girl of her age can
stand it—it is only puttin' notions in her head, and
from what I can hear, there's too much of that now
among women. I never had no time to be goin'
round makin' speeches and winnin' debates, and
neither has any other decent woman. It would suit
Pearl better to stay at home and help her mother;
they say she goes around town with her head dressed
up like a queen, and Jane says she's as stiff as pork
when a person speaks to her. I'll tell Mr. Donald
what I think of it."

At the Steadman home, the news of the meeting
had a happier reception, for Mr. Steadman, who was

the local member of Parliament, was asked to preside,
and as the elections were likely to take place before
the year was out, he was glad of this chance to address
a few remarks to the electors. He had been seriously
upset ever since he heard that the young doctor
was to be offered the nomination for the Liberals.
That would complicate matters for him, and make
it imperative that he should lose no opportunity of
making himself agreeable to his constituents.

Before the news of the meeting was an hour old,
Mr. Steadman had begun to arrange his speech,
and determined that he would merely make a few
happy random extempore remarks, dashed off in
that light, easy way which careful preparation can
alone insure; and Mrs. Steadman had decided that
she would wear her purple silk with the gold embroidery, and make a Prince of Wales cake and a
batch of lemon cookies—some of them put together
with a date paste, and the rest of them just loose,
with maybe a date or a raisin in the middle.

Mrs. Watson was in a state of nerves bordering
on stage fright, from the time that Tommy brought
home the news, a condition which Pearl did her best
to relieve by assuming a nonchalance which she did
not feel, regarding the proposed speech.

"What ever will you talk about, Pearlie, dear,"
her mother cried in vague alarm; "and to all them
people. I don't think the teacher should have
asked ye, you could do all right with just the scholars,
for any bit of nonsense would ha' done for them,
but you will have to mind what you are sayin'
before all the grown people!"

Pearl soaked the beans for tomorrow's cooking, with an air of unconcern.

"Making a speech is nothing, Ma," she said, "when a person knows how. I have listened to the cabinet ministers lots of times, and there's nothing to it. It is just having a good beginning and a fine flourish at the end, with a verse of poetry and the like of that—it does not matter what you say in between. I have heard the Premier speak lots of times, and they go crazy over him and think he is a wonderful speaker. He tells how he was once a farmer's boy and wandered happily over the pasture fields in his bare feet, and then how he climbed the ladder of fame, rung by rung—that is fine stuff, every one likes that; and whenever he got stuck he told about the flag of empire that waves proudly in the breeze and has never known defeat, and the destiny of this Canada of ours, and the strangers within our gates who have come here to carve out their destiny in this limitless land, and when he thought it best to make them sniffle a little he told about the sacred name of mother, and how the tear-drop starts at mention of that dear name, and that always went big, and when he began to run down a little, he just spoke all the louder, and waved his arms around, and the people did not notice there was nothing coming; we used to go over and listen to the speeches and then make them when the teachers were not in the room— it was lots of fun. I know lots of the Premier's speeches right off. There is nothing to it, Ma, so don't you be frightened."

"Pearl, you take things too light," said her mother severely, "a person never knows when you are in earnest, and I am frightened about you. You should not feel so careless about makin' speeches, it is nothing to joke about. I wish you would be for writin' out what you are goin' to say, and then we could hear you go over it, and some one could hold the paper for you and give you the word if you forget— it would be the safest way!"

"All right, Ma," said Pearl, "I'll be making it up now while I peel the potatoes."

While they were talking there came a knock at the door, and when it was opened, there stood Bertie from the livery stable, with a long green-wrapped box in his hand, which he gave to Mrs. Watson, volunteering without delay, all the information he had regarding it. Bertie never failed to reveal all the truth as he knew it—so, keeping nothing back, he gave the history of the box so far as he had been able to gather it.

"It's for Pearl—and the doctor sent it out. I don't know why he didn't give it to her when she was in, for she was in his office—it's flowers, for it is marked on it—and they came from Hampton.

Bertie would have stayed to see the flowers opened, for he knew that Mrs. Crocks would be much interested to know just what they were, and what Pearl said, and what her mother said—and if there was a note inside—and all the other good stuff he would be able to gather, but Pearl took them, with an air of unconcern, and thanking Bertie, said quite carelessly:

"Don't wait for an answer, Bertie, I can phone if there is any need, and I know you are in a hurry— we must not keep you."

And before Bertie knew what had happened, he found himself walking away from the door.

When the roses had been put in water, and each of the children had been given a smell and a feel of the velvety petals, and Mrs. Watson had partially recovered from the shock that the sight of flowers in the winter, always gave her for they reminded her so of her father's funeral, and the broken pillar which the Oddfellows sent; Pearl read the card:

"To Pearl—eighteen-going-on-nineteen,
Hoping that the years will bring her nothing
but joy."

It was written on one of the doctor's professional cards, and that was all. But looking again into the envelope there was a folded note which she did not read to the assembled and greatly interested group. When she was alone in the little beamed room upstairs, she read it:

"Dear Pearl:—I forgot to give you the roses when you were in this afternoon. Accept them now with my deep affection. You have been a bright spot in my life, and you will always be that—like a red rose in a dull room. Your success will always be very dear to me, and my prophecy is that you will go far. I will always think of you with deepest admiration and pride. Ever yours,

HORACE CLAY."

Pearl read it twice; then impulsively pressed it to her cheek.

"It sounds like good-bye," she said, with her lips trembling, "it sounds like the last of something.

Why won't he tell me? It is not like him."

A wither of loneliness went over her face as she clasped the note between her hands.

"I don't believe it is that," she said fiercely. "I won't believe it!" Mrs. Crocks' words were taunting her; "'the doctor thinks more of blue blood than he does of money, and if he goes into politics it will mean a lot to him to be related to the senator.'"

An overwhelming rage was in Pearl's heart, in spite of her determination not to believe the suggestion; a blind, choking rage—it was all so unfair.

"My dad is more of a man than Senator Keith," she said to herself, "for all his fine clothes and his big house. He was nothing but a heeler for the party, and was made Senator because there was no dirty job that he would not do to get votes for them. I know how he bought liquor for the Galicians and brought them in by the car-load to vote, like cattle, and that's blue blood, is it? Sure it is—you can see it in his shot-silk face and his two bad old eyes swollen like oysters! If the doctor wants him he can have him, and it's blamed little frettin' I'll do! . . . . . My dad eats with his knife, does he? All right, he bought the knife with honest money, and he earned what's on it too. All the dirty money they have would not buy him, or make him do a mean trick to any one. I am not ashamed of him—he suits me, and he can go on eating with his knife and wearing his overalls and doing anything he wants to do. He suits me!"

When Pearl went back to the kitchen, her father was taking off his smock. Supper was ready, and

he and Teddy had just come in. The dust of the
fanning-mill was on his face and his clothes. His
unmittened hands were red and rough, and bore
traces of the work he had been doing. In his hair
were some of the seeds and straws blown out by the
mill. There was nothing very attractive about
John Watson, unless it was his kindly blue eyes
and the humorous twist of his mouth, but in Pearl's
heart there was a fierce tenderness for her father,
a protective love which glorified him in her eyes.

"Did you hear the news, pa," she cried, as she
impulsively threw her arms around his neck. "Did
you know that I am going to speak in the school, and
they are all coming out to hear me. Are you glad,
Pa, and do you think I can do it?"

Her burning cheek was laid close to his, and he
patted her shoulder lovingly

"Do I think you can do it, Pearlie, that I do— you
can do whatever you go at—I always knew that."

"Pearl, child," cried her mother,"don't be hugging
your Pa like that, and you with your good dress on;
don't you see the dust and dirt on him—you will ruin
your clothes, child."

Pearl kissed him again, and gave him one more
hug, before she said, "It is clean dirt, Ma, and it will
brush off, and I just couldn't wait; but sure and it's
clean dirt anyway."

"It is gettin' colder," said John Watson, as he
hung up his smock behind the door, "our Spring is
over for awhile, I think. I saw two geese leggin'
it back as fast as they could go, and each one scoldin'
the other one—we'll have a good spell of winter yet,

I am afraid, in spite of our two warm days and all the signs of Spring."

"Weather like yon is too good to last," said Mrs. Watson complacently, "I knew it wasn't the Spring, it was too good to last."

Pearl went to the window and looked out—already there was a threat of snow in the whining wind, and as she watched, a stray flake struck the window in front of her.

"It was too good to last," she said with a sigh which broke into a sob in the middle, "It was too good to be true!"

CHAPTER VII

THE INNOCENT DISTURBER

IF there was any lack of enthusiasm among the parents it had no reflection in the children's minds, for the Chicken Hill School, after the great announcement, simply pulsated with excitement. Country children have capabilities for enjoyment that the city child knows nothing about, and to the boys and girls at Chicken Hill the prospect of a program, a speech from Pearl Watson, and a supper—was most alluring. Preparations were carried on with vigor. Seats were scrubbed by owners, and many an ancient landmark of ink was lost forever. Frayed window blinds that had sagged and drooped, and refused to go up or down, were taken down and rolled and put back neat and even, and the scholars warned not to touch them; the stove got a rubbing with old newspapers; mousey corners of desks were cleaned out— and objectionable slate rags discarded. Blackboards were cleaned and decorated with an elaborate maple leaf stencil in green and brown, and a heroic battle cry of "O Canada, we stand on guard for thee" executed in flowing letters, in the middle. Mary Watson was the artist, and spared no chalk in her undertaking, for each capital ended in an arrow, and had a blanket of dots which in some cases nearly obliterated its identity. But the general effect was powerful.

The day before, every little girl had her hair in

tight braids securely knotted with woollen yarn.
Boudoir caps were unknown in the Chicken Hill
School, so the bare truth of these preparations were
to be seen and known of all. Maudie Steadman
had her four curls set in long rags, fastened up with
pins, Mrs. Steadman having devised a new, original
way of making Maudie's hair into large, loose
"natural" curls, which were very handsome, and not
until this day did Mrs. Steadman show to the public
the method of "setting."

Mr. Donald had placed all details of the entertain-
ment in the hands of Mary Watson and Maudie
Steadman, and no two members of a House-Committee ever worked harder, or took more pleasure
in making arrangements.

"Let's not ask the Pipers—they're dirt poor,"
said Maudie, when they sat down at noon to make
out the list of providers.

"Indeed, we will," said Mary, whose knowledge
of the human heart was most profound. "If people
are poor, that's all the more reason why they would
be easily hurt, and it's not nice for us to even know
that they are poor. We'll ask them, you bet—
and Mrs. Piper will bring something. Besides—
if we didn't ask them to bake, they wouldn't come
—and that's the way rows start in a neighborhood.
We'll manage it all right—and if there are any sand-
wiches left over—we'll send them to the smaller
children, and the Pipers will come in on that. It
ain't so bad to be poor," concluded Mary, out of
her large experience, "but it hurts to have people
know it!"

When Pearl, with her father and mother arrived at

the school on the afternoon of the meeting, it came
to her with a shock, how small the school was, and
how dreary. Surely it had not been so mouse-gray and
shabby as this when she had been there. The paint
was worn from the floor, the ceiling was smoked
and dirty, the desks were rickety and uneven—the
blackboards gray. The same old map of North
America hung tipsily between the blackboards. It
had been crooked so long that it seemed to be
the correct position, and so had escaped the eye of
the House-Committee, who had made many improvements for this occasion.

In the tiny porch, there were many mysterious baskets and boxes and tin pails of varying sizes, and within doors a long table at the back of the room had on
it many cups and saucers, with a pile of tissue paper
napkins. A delightful smell of coffee hung on the
air.

Pearl wore her best brown silk dress, with a lace
collar and cuff set contributed the Christmas before
by her Aunt Kate from Ontario, and at her waist, one
of the doctor's roses. The others had been brought
over by Mary, and were in a glass jar on the tidy
desk, where they attracted much attention and specu-
lation as to where they had come from. They
seemed to redeem the bare school-room from utter
dreariness, and Pearl found herself repeating the
phrase in the doctor's letter, "Like a rose in a dark
room."

The children were hilariously glad to see Pearl,
and her lightness of heart came back to her, when a
group of them gathered around her to receive her

admiration and praise for their beautifully curled
hair, good clothes and hair ribbons. Bits of family
history were freely given to her too, such as Betty
Freeman's confidential report on her mother's absence, that she dyed her silk waist, and it streaked,
and she dyed it again—and just as soon as she could
get it dry, she would come—streaks or no streaks—
and would Pearl please not be in a hurry to begin.

Then the meeting was called to order, and the
smaller children were set like a row of gaily colored
birds around the edge of the patform, so their elders
could sit on their little desks in front, and the school-
room was filled to its last foot of space.   There were
about a dozen chairs for the older people.

Pearl had gone to the back of the room to speak
to the old gardener from Steadman's farm, a shy old
man, who just naturally sought the most remote corner for his own. Her affectionate greeting brought a
glow into his face that set Pearl's heart throbbing
with jo

"It's good to see you, Pearl," he said, "you look
like a rose to me, and you don't forget an old friend."

Pearl held the hard old gnarled hand in her own,
and her heart was full of joy. The exaltation of
the day she rode home was coming to her. Love
was the power that could transform the world.
People everywhere, all sorts of people, craved love
and would respond to it. "If I can cheer up poor old
Bill Murray, and make him look like this, with a
glisten in his eyes, I'm satisfied," she thought.

To Mr. Donald Pearl looked like a rose, too, a rose
of his own growing, and his voice trembled a little

when he called the meeting to order and in his stately
way bade everyone welcome.

"I am going to hand over the meeting to Mr.
Steadman in a moment," he said, "but before I do
I wish to say that the Chicken Hill School is very
proud today to welcome one of its former pupils,
Miss Pearl Watson."

At this the gaily colored company who bordered the
platform, burst into ecstatic hand clapping, in which
the older members joined rather shamefacedly.
Demonstrations come hard to prairie people.

"The years she spent in this school were delightful
years to me," went on Mr. Donald. "She helped me
with the younger children—she helped me to keep
up enthusiasm for the work—she helped me to make
life pleasant for all of us—she did more—she helped
me to believe that life is worth the struggle—she
helped me to believe in myself. I was not surprised
that Pearl made a record in her work in the city;
she could not fail to do that. She is in love with life
—to me, she is the embodiment of youth, with all
its charms and all its promise."

"I have wanted to hear her impressions of the
city. Nothing, to her, is common-place—she sees
life through a golden mist that softens its sharp
outlines. I am glad that every one could come
today and give a welcome home to our first graduate from Chicken Hill School!"

This threatened to dislodge the seating arrangement on the platform, for in their enthusiastic applause, the Blackburn twins on account of the shortness of their legs and the vigor of their applause, lost

their balance and fell. But they bore it well, and were restored without tears! The excitement was so great that no one of the young row would have known it if they had broken a bone!

"And now I will ask our local member, Mr. Steadman, to take charge of the meeting, and give the neighborhood's welcome to our first graduate!"

Then Mr. Steadman arose! He was a stout man, with a square face, and small, beady black eyes and an aggressive manner; a man who felt sure of himself; who knew he was the centre of his own circle. There was a well-fed, complacent look about him too which left no doubt that he was satisfied with things as they were—and would be deeply resentful of change. There was still in his countenance some trace of his ancestor's belief in the Divine right of kings! It showed in his narrow, thought-proof forehead, and a certain indescribable attitude which he held toward others, and which separated him from his neighbors. Instinctively, the people who met him, knew he lacked human sympathy and understanding, but he had a hold on the people of his constituency, for through his hands went all the Government favors and patronage. Anyone who wanted a telephone, had to "see Mr. Steadman." The young people who went to the city to find employment, were wise to see Mr. Steadman before they went. So although he was not liked, he had a prestige which was undeniable.

Mr. Steadman began his remarks by saying how glad he was to be offered the chair on this glad occasion. He always liked to encourage the young, and he believed it our duty to be very tolerant and encouraging to youth.

The boundaries of the platform began to wriggle. They had heard Mr. Steadman before—he often came in and made speeches—but he never brought any oranges—or peanuts or even "Farmers' Mixed."

"Youth is a time of deep impressions," went on the chairman; "wax to receive—granite to retain." Youth was the time of learning, and he hoped every boy and girl in his presence would earnestly apply himself and herself to their books, for only through much study could success be attained. That is what put him where he was today.

More wriggles, and some discussion at his feet!

He was glad to know that one of Mr. Donald's pupils had been able to do so well in the city. Three cheers for the country! He had always believed it was the best place to be brought up—and was glad to say that he too, had spent his youth on a farm. Most of the successful men of the world came from the farms.

He believed absolutely in education for women, education of a suitable kind, and believed there was a definite place for women in the world—a place which only women could fill. That place was the home—the quiet precincts of home—not the hurly-burly of politics—that was man's sphere—and a hard sphere it was, as he knew well. He didn't wish to see any woman in such a hard life, with its bitter criticism and abuse. He was sorry to notice that there was a new agitation among women in the city —it had come up in the session just closed—that women wanted to vote.

Mr. Steadman threw out his hands with a gesture of unconcern:

"Well," I say, "let them vote—if they want to—let them run the whole country; we'll stay at home. It's time we had a rest, anyway!"

A little dry cackle of laughter went over the room at this, in which Mr. Donald did not join—so it got no support from the pupils of Chicken Hill, who faithfully followed their teacher's lead.

Mr. Steadman went on blithely:

"I am old fashioned enough to want my wife to stay at home. I like to find her there when I come home. I don't want her to sit in Parliament; she hasn't time—for one thing."

Mrs. Steadman sat in front, with the purple plume in her hat nodding its approval:

"And I say it in all kindness to all women—they haven't the ability. They have ability of their own, but not that kind. Parliaments are concerned with serious, big things. This year, the program before our Provincial Parliament, is 'Good Roads.' We want every part of this Province to enjoy the blessing of of good roads, over which they can bring their produce to market, binding neighborhoods together in the ties of friendship. Good roads for everyone is our policy."

"Now what do women know about making roads? They are all right to go visiting over the roads after they are built, but how much good would they be in building them?"

This was greeted with another scattered rattle of laughter, followed by a silence, which indicated intense listening. Even the restless edging of the platform knew something was happening, and listened.

"Our Opposition is coming forward with a foolish program of fads and fancies. They want the women to have the vote; they want to banish the bar! They want direct legislation. These are all radical measures, new, untried and dangerous. With women voting, I have no sympathy, as I said. They are not fitted for it. It is not that I do not love women—I do—I love them too well—most of them."

He paused a moment here—but no one laughed. The audience did not believe him.

"There are some women in the city whom I would gladly send to jail. They are upsetting women's minds, and hurting the homes. Don't let us take any chances on destroying the home, which is the bulwark of the nation. What sight is more beautiful then to see a mother, queen of the home, gathering her children around her. She can influence her husband's vote—her son's vote—she has a wider and stronger influence than if she had the vote herself. Her very helplessness is her strength. And besides, I know that the best women, the very best women do not want to sit in Parliament. My wife does not want to—neither did my mother—no true woman wants to, only a few rattle-brained, mentally unbalanced freaks—who do not know what they want."

Pearl smiled at this. She had heard this many times.

"Now, as to banishing the bar, you all know I am

not a drinker. I can take it—or leave it—but I am broad minded enough to let other people have the same privilege that I ask for myself. Men like to gather in a friendly way, chat over old times or discuss politics, and have a glass, for the sake of good fellowship, and there's no harm done. There are some, of course, who go too far—I am not denying that. But why do they do it? They did not get the right home training—that is why. In the sacred precincts of home, the child can be taught anything —that's the mother's part, and it is a more honorable part than trying to ape men—and wear the pants."

This brought a decided laugh—though if Mr. Steadman had been sensible to thought currents, he would have felt twinges in his joints, indicating that a storm was brewing. But he was having what the preachers call a "good time," and went merrily on.

"Direct legislation is a dangerous thing, which would upset representative government. It is nothing less than rabble rule, letting the ignorant rabble say what we are to do. Our vote is too wide now, as you know, when every Tom, Dick and Harry has a vote, whether they own an inch of ground or not. Your hired man can kill your vote, though you own a township of land. Do you want to give him more power? I think not! Well if the opposition ever get in power, the women and the hired men, and even the foreigners will run the country, and it will not be fit to live in. We're doing all right now, our public buildings, our institutions are the best in Canada. We have put the flag on every schoolhouse in the country—we have good, sane, steady govern-

ment, let us stick to it. I believe that the next
election will see the good ship come safely into port
with the same old skipper on the bridge, and the
flag of empire proudly furling its folds in the breeze.
We have no fears of the fads and fancies put forward
by short-haired women and long-haired men."

That being the end of his speech, the place where
his superior always sat down, amidst thunderous
applause. Mr. Steadman sat down, too, forgetting
that he had been asked to be the Chairman, and
introduce Pearl.

The applause which followed his remarks, was not
so vociferous as he had expected, partly because there
were no "Especially instructed clappers." No one
was very enthusiastic, except Mrs. Steadman, who
apparently agreed with all he said.

Rising to his feet again he said: "The good ladies
have bountifully provided for our needs today—
what would we do without the ladies? but before
we come to that very interesting item on our program, we are going to hear from Pearl Watson. Pearl
Watson is one of the girls who has taken full advantage of our splendid educational system, than which
there is none better in Canada—or in the world.
As a member of the Legislature, I am justly proud
of our Department of Education, and today we will
be entertained by one of our own products, Pearl
Watson, on whom we might well hang the label
"Made in Canada." I do not know whether she
intends to say a piece—or what, but bespeak for her
a respectful and courteous hearing."

Mr. Steadman sat down, adjusting his gold and

blue tie, and removed his glasses, which he put away
in a large leather case that closed with a snap. His
attitude indicated that the real business of the day
was over, now that he had spoken.

Pearl came forward and stepped to the platform,
displacing temporarily one of the twins, to make a
space where she might step. Having restored him
safely, she turned to the people. There was a smile
in her eyes that was contagious. The whole roomful
of people smiled back at her, and in that moment
she established friendly relations with her audience.

"It has been a real surprise to me," she began, in a
conversational tone, "to hear Mr. Steadman make a
speech. I am sure his colleagues in the House would
have been surprised to have heard him today. He
is a very quiet man there—he never speaks. The
first night I went to the House with a crowd of
Normalites, I pointed out our member, to let those
city girls see what we could raise in the country—but
it seems the speeches are all made by half a dozen,
the others just say "Aye" when they're told. All
on one side of the House say "Aye;" the other side
say "No." I have heard Mr. Steadman say "Aye,"
lots of times—but nothing more. The Premier, or
one of the Cabinet Ministers tells them when to say
it—it all looks very easy to me. I would have thought
even a woman could do it. The girls used to tease me
about how quiet my representative was. He sat
so still that it just seemed as if he might be asleep,
and one girl said she believed he was dead. But
one day, a window was left open behind him—and
he sneezed, and then he got right up and shut it—

Do you remember that day, Mr. Steadman?"

He shook his head impatiently, and the expression of his face was not pleasant. Still, no one would attribute anything but the friendliest motive to Pearl's innocent words.

"My! I was glad that day," she said, "when you sneezed, it was a quick stop to the rumor—I tell you—and I never heard any more about it. I am sorry Mr. Steadman is not in favor of women voting, or going to Parliament, and thinks it too hard for them. It does not look hard to me. Most of the members just sit and smoke all the time, and read the papers, and call the pages. I have seen women do far harder work than this. But of course what Mr. Steadman says about building roads all over the country, is a new one on me. I did not know that the members were thinking of doing the work! But I guess they would be glad to get out and do something after sitting there all cramped up with their feet asleep for the whole winter."

"Still, I remember when Mr. Steadman was Councillor here, and there was a bridge built over Pine Creek—he only let the contract—he did not build it —it was his brother who built it!"

There was a queer thrill in the audience at this, for Bill Steadman had got the contract, in spite of the fact that he was the poorest builder in the country —and the bridge had collapsed inside of two years. George Steadman winced at her words.

But Pearl, apparently innocent of all this, went on in her guileless way:

"I think Mr. Steadman is mistaken about women

not wanting to sit in Parliament. He perhaps does not know what it feels like to stand over a wash-tub —or an ironing board—or cook over a hot stove. Women who have been doing these things long would be glad to sit anywhere!"

There was a laugh at this, in which Mr. Steadman made a heroic attempt to join, shaking his head as he did so, to counteract any evil effect which the laugh might cause.

"But I did not intend to speak of politics," said Pearl, "I intended to tell you how glad I am to be back to Chicken Hill School, and how good home looks to me. No one knows how to appreciate their home until they have left it—and gone away where no one cares particularly whether you are sick or well —happy or miserable. Do you boys find it pretty hard to wash your necks—and you wish your mother hadn't such a sharp eye on you—be glad you have some one who thinks enough of you to want your neck to be clean. You hate to fill the wood-box, do you? O, I know what a bottomless pit it is—and how the old stove just loves to burn wood to spite you. But listen! By having to do what you do not want to do, you are strengthening the muscles of your soul—and getting ready for a big job.

"Having to do things is what makes us able to do more. Did you ever wonder why you cannot walk on water. It is because water is so agreeable—it won't resist you. It lets you have your own way.

"The teachers at the Normal talked to us every Friday afternoon, about our social duties, and rural leadership and community spirit and lots of things.

They told us not to spend our time out of school tatting and making eyelet embroidery, when there were neighborhoods to be awakened and citizens to be made. That suits me fine, for I can't tat anyway. One of the girls tried to show me, but gave it up after three or four tries. She said some could learn, and some couldn't. It was heredity—or something."

"Anyway, Dr. McLean said teachers were people who got special training for their work, and it was up to them to work at it, in school and out. He said that when we went out to teach, we could be a sort of social cement, binding together all the different units into one coherent community, for that's what was needed in Canada, with its varied population. One third of the people in Canada do not speak English, and that's a bad barrier—and can only be overcome by kindness. We must make our foreign people want to learn our language, and they won't want to, unless they like us.

"He said Canada was like a great sand-pile, each little grain of sand, beautiful in its own way, but needing cement to bind it to other grains,and it was for us to say whether we would be content to be only a sand pile, or would we make ourselves a beautiful temple.

"I wish I could give it all to you—it was great to hear him. He said no matter how fine we were as individuals, or how well we did our work, unless we had it in our hearts to work with others, and for others—it was no good. If we lacked social consciousness, our work would not amount to much. I thought of our old crumply horn cow. She always gave a big pail of milk—but if she was in bad humor, she would quite likely kick it over, just as the pail was full. I used to think maybe a fly had stung her, but I guess what was really wrong was that she lacked social consciousness. She did not see that we were depending on her.

"That's why the liquor traffic is such a bad thing, and should be outlawed. Individuals may be able to drink, and get away with it, but some go under, some homes are made very unhappy over it. If we have this social consciousness, we will see very clearly that the liquor traffic must go! No matter how much some people will miss it. If it isn't safe for everybody, it isn't safe for anybody. I used to wish Dr. McLean could talk to the members of Parliament.

"He told us one of the reasons that the world had so many sore spots in it was because women had kept too close at home, they were beginning to see that in order to keep their houses clean, they would have to clean up the streets, and it was this social consciousness working in them, that made them ask for the vote. They want to do their share, outside as well as in.

"There was a woman who came and talked to us one day at the Normal. She is the editor of the Women's section of one of the papers, and she put it up to us strong, that there was work for each of us. We had to make a report of her address, and so I remember most of it.

"She said that Canada is like a great big, beautiful

house that has been given to us to finish. It is just
far enough on so that you can see how fine it is going
to be—but the windows are not in—the doors are
not hung—the cornices are not put on. It needs
polishing, scraping, finishing. That is our work.
Every tree we plant, every flower we grow, every
clean field we cultivate, every good cow or hog we
raise, we are helping to finish and furnish the house
and make it fit to live in. Every kind word we say
or even think, every gracious deed, if it is only
thinking to bring out the neighbor's mail from town,
helps to add those little touches which distinguish a
house from a barn."

"We have many foreign people in this country,
lonesome, homesick people—sometimes we complain
that they are not loyal to us—and that is true. It
is also true that they have no great reason to be loyal
to us. We are not even polite to them, to say nothing of being kind. Loyalty cannot be rammed down
anyone's throat with a flag-pole."

Mr. Steadman cleared his throat at this—and
seemed about to speak—but she went on without
noticing:

"Loyalty is a gentle growth, which springs in the
heart. The seeds are in your hands and mine; the
heart of our foreign people is the soil—the time of
planting is now—and the man or woman who by
their kindness, their hospitality, their fair dealing,
honesty, neighborliness, makes one of the least of
these think well of Canada, is a Master Builder in
this Empire.

"If we do not set ourselves to finish the house, you

know what will happen to it. I remembered this part of her speech because it made me think about our school-house the year before Mr. Donald came —when we could not get a teacher. Do you remember? Windows were broken mysteriously—the rain beat in and warped and drenched and spoiled the floors. The chimney fell. Destruction always comes to the empty house, she said—the unfinished house is a mark for the wantonly mischievous. To keep what we have, we must improve it from year to year. And to that end we must work together—fighting not with each other—but with conditions, discouragements, ignorance, prejudice, narrowness—we must be ready to serve, not thinking of what we can get from our country, but what we can give to it."

In the silence that fell, the people sat motionless. They did not notice that Pearl was done speaking— for their thoughts went on—she had given them a new view of the service they might give.

Mrs. Piper, on whose heart, Pearl's words had fallen like a benediction, saw that in making her rag-carpet, over which she had worked so hard—she was helping to furnish one little corner of her country, for it would make her front room a brighter place, and there her children, and the boys and girls of the neighborhood would have good times and pleasant memories. She had thought of it in a vague way before, but Pearl had put it into words for her— and her heart was filled with a new rapture. It was worth while to work and struggle and try her best to make a pleasant home. There was a purpose in it all —a plan—a pattern.

Even Mrs. Thompson had a glimmering of a
thought regarding her precious flowers, the slips of
which she never gave away. With them she could
gladden the hearts of some of her neighbors, and
Noah Thompson, her husband, who made it his boast
that he never borrowed or lent, became suddenly
sorry he had refused a neck yoke to his Russian
neighbor.

George Steadman, too, found his soul adrift on a
wide sea, torn away from the harbor that had seemed
so safe and land-locked, so unassailable; and on
that wider sea there came the glimpses of a sunrise,
of a new day. It puzzled him, frightened him,
angered him. In the newness of it all, he detected danger. It blew across his sheltered soul like a draught,
an uncomfortable, cold-producing draught—and
when he found himself applauding with the others,
he knew that something dangerous, radical, subtle
and evil had been let loose—the girl would have to be
watched. She was a fire-brand, an incendiary—she
would put notions in people's heads. It was well
he had heard her and could sound the warning.
But he must be politic—he would not show his hand.

The children were singing, and every one had
risen. Never before had he heard the Chicken Hill
people sing like this:

"O Canada, our home, our native land,
    True, patriot love, in all our sons command;
    With glowing hearts we see thee rise,
    Thou true land, strong and free,
    And stand on guard, O Canada
    We stand on guard for thee."

The children began the second verse, the people following lamely, for they did not know the words; but the children, proud of their superior knowledge, and with a glow in their impressionable little hearts, sang exultantly—this song of home and country.

CHAPTER VIII

THE POWER OF INK

THE Chicken Hill correspondent of the Millford "Mercury" described the meeting in the school as follows:

"The Chicken Hill School was the scene of a happy gathering on Friday afternoon last, when the neighbors and friends gathered to welcome home Pearl Watson, who has just completed a successful First Class Teacher's Normal course in Winnipeg. Pearl is a great favorite, and certainly disappointed no one, for she gave an address on present day questions which will not soon be forgotten. Pearl is an out and out believer in temperance and woman suffrage, and before she was through, she had every one with her—as one man put it, he'd like to see the women vote, if for nothing else than to get Pearl Watson into Parliament, for there would sure be hides on the barn door if she ever got there, and a rustling of dry bones."

"After Pearl's address, the ladies of the district served resfreshments, and a good time was spent. Pearl's arm must have ached, shaking hands, and if she could be spoiled with praise, she would be spoiled for sure, but Pearl is not that kind. It is rumored that she will be offered the Purple Springs school, and if she accepts, we congratulate Purple Springs."

When George Steadman read the Chicken Hill

news, his face became a yellowish gray color—much like the hue of badly laundered clothes. His skin prickled, as if with an electric current, for hot rage ate into his soul. His name was not even mentioned. He wasn't there at all—and he was the member for Millford. Of all the silly rot—well, he'd see about it.

On Monday morning, with the offending sheet in his hand, Mr. Steadman made his way to the "Mercury" office, a dingy, little flat-roofed building, plastered with old circus posters outside, and filled with every sort of junk inside. At an unpainted desk piled high with papers, sat the editor. His hair stood up like a freshly laundered, dustless mop; his shirt was dirty; his pipe hung listlessly in his mouth—upside down, and a three days' crop of black beard peppered his face. He looked like a man who in early youth had slept on newspapers and drank ink, and who now would put his feet on the table if there had been room, but there was scarcely room for them on the floor, for it was under the table that he kept his exchanges. There were shelves around the walls, but they were filled with rubber boots, guns, baskets of letters, a few books, miscellaneous articles of clothing and some empty tobacco jars.

So on account of the congested condition on and under the table, Mr. Driggs was forced to sit in an uncomfortable position, with his legs and those of the table artistically entwined.

Mr. Steadman began, without replying to the editor's friendly greeting:

"Who writes this balderdash from our district," he asked harshly.

"Professional secret," replied Mr. Driggs, speaking through his shut teeth, for he did not wish to dislodge his pipe; the last time he let it out of his mouth he had had no end of a time finding it. "Never give away names of contributors, not etiquette."

"I don't care a hang for your etiquette—I want to know." The member for Millford was not in a trifling mood.

"Sorry," said Mr. Driggs, holding his pipe still closer.

"See here, Driggs," said Mr. Steadman haughtily, "do you know who you're talking to—I have it in my power to throw you a good deal of business one way'n another—I've thrown you a good deal of business. There's an election coming on—there will be bills, cards, streamers, what not; good money in printing for the Government—do you savvy?"

"I savvy," said Mr. Driggs cheerfully.

"Well then"—George Steadman was sure now he was going to get the information—"who writes this stuff from Chicken Hill?"

"I don't know," said the editor calmly, "honest, I don't. This was a new one—strange writing—and all that. I called up Pearl Watson to see if there had been a meeting, and she verified it, but didn't tell me anything. She said you presided. Then I ran the item—I thought it was very good—what's wrong with it? It seemed like real good country correspondence to me—with that bucolic freshness which we expect to find in country contributors, perhaps not the literary polish found in Stoddarts' lectures, but rattling good stuff just the same."

"See here Driggs," the other man interrupted, "listen to me. There's an election coming on—you've always been with us—I don't know what you think—and it don't matter. This girl Watson is against us—and she's as smart as they make them, and has plenty of nerve. Now I don't want to see that girl's name in the paper again. A few more spreads like this—and every district in the country will want her. She don't know her place—she's got nerve enough to speak anywhere. She spits out things, hardly knowing what she means—she's dangerous, I tell you. If the other side got hold of her and primed her what to say, she could do us a lot of harm—here, for mind you, she's got a way with her. We don't want any trouble. There's a little talk of runnin' Doc. Clay, but I believe he's got more sense than to try it. The last man that ran against me lost his deposit. But, understand, Driggs, no mention of this girl, cut out her name."

Then Mr. Driggs slowly took his pipe from his mouth, and laid it carefully on the lowest pile of papers. It's position did not entirely suit him, and he moved it to another resting place. But the effect was not pleasing even then—so he placed it in his pocket, taking a red handkerchief from his other pocket, and laying it carefully over the elusive pipe, to anchor it—if that were possible.

"Mr. Steadman," he said, in his gentlest manner, "sit down."

Removing an armful of sale bills from the other chair, he shoved it over to his visitor, who ignored the invitation.

"You must not attempt to muzzle the press, or take
away our blood-bought liberties. Blood-bought liberties is good! It's a serious matter to come to a natural
born, heaven inspired Editor, and tell him to curb
his news instinct. Pearl Watson is a particular friend
of mine. Pearl's sayings and doings are of interest to
me as a citizen, therefore, I reason they are of interest to all citizens. She is a young lady of great charm,
who does honor to our little town. I stand absolutely
for home boosting. Shop at home—shop early—
sell your hammer and buy a horn—my motto!
Pearl Watson—one of the best ads we have—I'm for
her."

"All right," said Mr. Steadman harshly, "you defy
me then, and when you defy me, you defy the Government of the Province, the arm of the Government
reaches far—Driggs, and you know that before you
are done, I'll put you out of business before two
weeks have gone by. You owe every one—you owe
the paper people—you owe on your printing press.
Your creditors are all friends of the Government.
All I have to do is to say the word and they'll close
you out. The Government will put a man in here
who has sense enough to do as he is told."

Mr. Driggs' faced showed more concern than he
had exhibited before. There were certain bills he
owed—forgotten to be sure in normal times—but
now they came up blinking to the light, rudely dis-
interred by Mr. Steadman's hard words. They
had grown, too, since their last appearance, both in
size and numbers—and for a moment a shade of
annoyance went over his face. Details of business
always did annoy him!

But an inner voice cautioned him to be discreet. There was always a way around a difficulty. Mr. Driggs believed in the switch system which prevails in our railroading. When two trains run towards each other on a track one must go off on a switch, to avoid a collision. It does not take long and when the other train has gone roaring past, the switched train can back up and get on the track and go serenely on—he resolved to be tactful.

"Mr. Steadman," he said, "I am surprised at all this. Pearl is only a slip of a girl. What harm can she do you? You are absolutely solid in this neighborhood. The government has this country by the throat—the old machine works perfectly. What are you afraid of?"

"We're not afraid—what have we to be afraid of? We have only sixteen opposition members in the House—and they're poor fish. We're solid enough —only we don't want trouble. The women are getting all stirred up and full of big notions. We can hold them down all right—for they can't get the vote until we give it to them—that's the beauty of it. The Old Man certainly talked plain when they came there askin' for the vote. He just laid them out. But I can see this girl has been at their meetings— and women are queer. My woman, even, thought there was a lot of truth in what the Watson girl said. So there was—but we're not dealing with truth just now—politics is not a matter of truth. We want to get this election over without trouble. We want no grief over this, mind you—everything quiet—and sure. So you got your orders right now. Take them

or leave them. But you know where your bread is
buttered, I guess."

Mr. Steadman went out of the office, shutting the
door with a strong hand. The editor buried his face
in his hands and gently massaged his temples with
his long ink-stained fingers, and to all appearance, his
soul was grieved within him. It seemed as though
his proud spirit was chafing at the bonds which the
iniquitous patronage system had laid on him.

For a brief period he sat thus, but when he raised
his head, which he did suddenly, there was a gleam
in his eye and a smile on his face which spread and
widened until it burst into a a laugh which threatened
to dislodge the contents of the table. He threw himself back in his swing chair and piled both feet on
the table, even if there was no room for them—if
ever there had come a time in his history when he was
in the mood to put his feet on the table, that time
was now.

He addressed his remarks to his late guest:

"You fragrant old he-goat, you will give orders to
me, will you—you are sure some diplomat—you
poor old moth-eaten gander, with your cow-like
duplicity."

Mr. Driggs could not find the figure of speech
which just suited the case, but he was still trying.

"You poor old wall-eyed ostrich, with your head in
the sand, thinking no one can see you, you forget that
there is a portion of your anatomy admirably placed
—indeed in my mind's eye I can see the sign upon it.
It reads 'Kick me.' It is an invitation I will not
decline. He thinks he can wipe our good friend

Pearlie off the map by having her name dropped from the Millford "Mercury," forgetting that there are other ways of reaching the public eye. There are other publications, perhaps not in the class with the Millford "Mercury," but worthy little sheets too. There is the "Evening Echo," struggling along with a circulation of a quarter of a million—it will answer our purpose admirably. I will write the lead today while the lamp of inspiration burns, and I will hear Pearl speak, and then oh, beloved, I will roll up my sleeves and spit on my hands and do a sketch of the New Woman—Pearlie, my child—this way lies fame."

CHAPTER IX

THE DOCTOR'S DECISION

WHEN Pearl left him so abruptly, Dr. Clay found himself battling with many emotions. His first impulse was to call her back—tell her everything. Pearl was not a child—she would know what was best. It was not fair to deceive her, and that was just what he had done, with the best intentions.

But something held him back. The very heart of him was sick and full of bitterness at the sudden slap which fate had given him. His soul was still stinging with the pain of it. Everything was distorted and queer, and in the confusion of sensations the outstanding one was the instinct to hide all knowledge of his condition. No one must know. He would go to see the old doctor and swear him to secrecy. After all, his life was his own—he was under obligation to no one to stretch it out miserably and uselessly.

He would go on as long as he could, and live it out triumphantly. He would go out like Old Prince. He thought of the hymn which gives thanks to God, "Who kindly lengthens out our days," and the thought of it was mingled with something like scorn. He did not want any lengthening out of his time if there could not be real power, real service in each day. He would live while he lived, and die when he had to, and with that resolution he tried to get back his calmness of spirit.

Looking at himself in the glass, he had to admit his face was haggard, and thinner than it had been, and he knew he had lost weight. Still, that could be recovered—he was not going to worry or think about himself. He had always contended that disease was ninety per cent. imagination and ten per cent. reality, and now he was going to see. Every one is under the death sentence; the day is set for each man. "I am no worse off," he thought, "than I was before—if I could only see it that way—and I will—I am going to be the Captain of my soul—even though it may be for a very short cruise —no disease or whimpering weakness will usurp my place—'Gladly I lived—gladly I died, and I laid me down with a will,' he quoted, but his mouth twisted a little on the words. Life was too sweet. He loved it too well to lay it down gladly. O no, there could be no pretence of gladness.

He found himself thinking of Pearl, and the tender, loving, caressing light in her eyes, her impulsive kiss—her honest words of heavenly sweetness; what a girl she was! He had watched her grow from a little bright-eyed thing, who always interested him with her wisdom, her cheerfulness, her devotion to her family, until now, when she had grown to be a serious-minded, beautiful girl, with a manner full of repose, dignity, grace—a wonderfully attractive girl—who looked honestly into his eyes and told him she loved him, and he had had to turn away from his happiness and tell her it could not be. And he had seen the dimming of those shining eyes and the tightening of her lips.

He had had to hurt Pearl, and that was the bitterest thought of all.

Again the temptation came to tell her! But the stern voice of conscience cried out to him that if she knew she would consider herself bound to him, and would not take her liberty, and the finest years of her young life would be spent in anxiety and care.

"I might live to be an old man," he said bitterly. "If I were sure I could drop out soon, it would not matter so much. Pearl would still have her life ahead of her, and I would come to be but a memory, but as it is—there's but one straight and honorable course—and I will take it."

Then he thought of the roses, and wrote a card and a note, and called Bertie at the Livery Stable to come to the office. When Bertie arrived, much out of breath, the doctor charged him to be quick in his errand of delivering them. Bertie was anxious to talk, and volunteered the information that Pearl Watson was an awful pretty girl, but Mrs. Crocks had just met her on the street and been talkin' to her a little while, and she thought Pearl was gettin' pretty stuck up.

"Bertie, dear," the doctor said, not unkindly, "did any one ever tell you that you talk too easy?"

"Sure they did," said Bertie honestly, "but Mrs. Crocks likes me to talk."

"O well," the doctor smiled, "you and Mrs. Crocks are not really dangerous—but Bertie, remember this, silence does not often get any one into trouble, and if you are ever in doubt about whether to tell things or not—don't tell them! It's the best way—now, will you try to remember?"

"Yes, sir," said Bertie pleasantly.

All of which Bertie carefully hid in his heart, but
his object in so doing was not to attain the scrip-
tural sequence—"that he sin not with his mouth."
It was that he might rehearse it accurately to Mrs,
Crocks!

The doctor had forgotten all about the committee
who were going to wait on him that evening to
receive his decision regarding the coming election.
His mind had been too full of his own affairs. But
promptly at eight o'clock, his office bell rang, and
the gentlemen came in.

It seemed years to the doctor since he had seen
them. Life had so changed for him in the interval.
The committee had come back with greater enthusiasm than ever. Corroborative evidence had been
pouring in; the doctor was the only man who could
defeat the present member.

"Doctor, it is sure up to you," said the President,
a stocky man, whose face had a patchy beard resembling a buffalo-robe on which the moths had
played their funny tricks, "and I'll tell you why.
The women are beginning to raise hell all over the
country. They have societies now, and they're
holding debates, and getting up plays—and all that.
They have the Government scared. My stars, I
remember the time women didn't bother no more
about politics than a yellow dog does about religion.
But that good day is gone. They're up and comin'
now, and comin' with a whoop. Now, that's why
we want you,—at least it's one reason—the women

like you—you have a way with them—you listen
to them—and feel sorry over their aches and pains—
cure them—if you can—but the big thing is—you
feel sorry. Now, if you will run, the women will
try to make their men vote for you—I don't think
any one of the women will go against you. The men
here are mostly for the Government, and this year
they have the bridge at Purple Springs for a bait.
It's goin' on for sure—work for every one—that
votes right. The Government has been in so long,
you've just had to be on their side to hold your job—
they have their fingers on everything. You know
our candidate has lost his deposit for three elections
—but there's a chance this year—if you'll run."

Then the field organizer took up the argument.
He was a young man sent out from the city office
to rally the faithful and if possible see that the best
candidates were selected. He was a shop-worn
young man, without illusions. He knew life from
every angle, and it was a dull affair in his eyes.

"Politics is a game of wits," he said; "the smartest
one wins, and gets in and divides the slush money.
The other side howl—because they didn't get any.
We're sore now because we haven't had a look-in
for fourteen years—we're thirsty and dry—and we
long for the water-brooks—which is, government
jobs. There's just one distinction between the parties," he said, "one is in and one is out! That's
all. Both parties have the same platform too, there
is only one principle involved, that is the principle
of re-election. But it really seems as if our time is
coming."

Young Mr. Sommersad lighted a cigarette and blew billows of smoke at the ceiling. His whole bearing was that of a man who had drunk the cup of life to the very dregs and found even the dregs tasteless and pale.

"You are pessimistic," said the doctor, "you surely take a materialistic view of the case. Is it really only a matter of getting into the public treasury? That hardly seems worth a man's effort; it looks more like a burglar's job."

"I mean, Clay," said the organizer, with slightly more animation, "the political game is not a game of sentiment or of high resolves. One man cannot do much to change the sentiment of a whole province; we must take things as we find them. People get as good government as they deserve—always. This year the advantage comes to us. 'It is time for a change' is always a good rallying cry, and will help us more than anything."

"What is the opposition platform this year," said the doctor, "what would I have to believe? Haven't you decided on a program, some sort of course of action?"

"O sure," replied the other, "we have a great platform—woman suffrage—banish the bar—direct legislation—we have a radical platform—just the very thing to catch the people. I tell you everything is in our favor, and with your popularity here, it should be a cinch."

The doctor looked at him, without enthusiasm.

"But the platform needn't worry you," he hastened to explain, "it's not necessarily important—

it's a darn good thing to get in on—but after that—"

"It can be laid away," said the doctor, "for
another election. Well now, as I understand it,
the case against the present Government is just
that. They promised prohibition years ago, and
got in on that promise—but broke it joyously,
and canned the one man who wanted to stand
for it—that's why they deserve defeat and have
deserved it all these years. But if the Opposition
have the same ethics, what's the use of changing.
Better keep the robbers in we know, than fly to
others that we know not of."

While the organizer had been speaking, the
remainder of the committee were vaguely uncomfortable. He was not getting anywhere; he was
spoiling everything. They knew the doctor better
than he did.

The doctor stood up, and there was something
about the action which announced the adjourn-
ment of the meeting.

"It does not appeal to me," he said, "not as
outlined by you. It's too sodden, too deeply selfish.
I see no reason for any man who has a fairly decent,
self-respecting job, to give it up and devote his time
to politics, if you have given me a correct picture
of it."

The organizer became deeply in earnest:—

"Look here, Clay," he said, "don't be hasty.
I'm telling you the truth about things, that's all.
You can be as full of moral passion as you like—
the fuller the better. The Opposition can always
be the Simon-pure reformers. I'm not discouraging

you—in fact, we want you to be that."

The doctor interrupted him, impatiently:—

"But I must not expect anything to come of it. Moral reform—and all that—is fine for election dope, but governments have no concern with it, these promises would not be carried out."

"I am not saying what we mean," said Mr. Summersad, with abundant caution; "I say we want to defeat the Government—that's our business. We want to get in—further than that we have no concern. The new Premier will set our policy. But if you ask me my opinion, I do not mind telling you that I don't think any government of men are very keen on letting the women vote—why should they be? But there's always a way out. What will happen is this—if our fellows get in, they will grant a plebiscite, men only voting of course, and it will go strong against the women—but that will let us out."

The doctor's eyes snapped:—

"That's surely a coward's way out," he said, "and why should any woman have to ask for what is her right. Women, although they are not so strong as men, do more than half the work, and bear children besides, and yet men have been mean enough to snatch the power away from them and keep it. Well, you have certainly been frank, Mr. Sommersad, I must thank you for that. I will be equally frank. I do not see that there is anything to choose between the two parties. If your presentation of the case is correct, the country is in a bad way, and the political life is a re-incarnation

of that fine old game of 'pussy wants a corner!'
I never did see much in it, so I will decline the
nomination. I am sorry, Mr. Gilchrist," he said
to the local President. His words had a ring of
finality.

When the committee were leaving they met Miss
Keith, of Hampton, on the street. Miss Keith
was worth looking at, with her white fox furs,
high-heeled shoes and long black ear-rings. Miss
Keith carried a muff as big as a sheaf of wheat,
and a sparkling bead-bag dangled from her wrist.
Miss Keith's complexion left nothing to be desired.
When she passed the committee there came to
them the odor of wood violets. The committee
were sufficiently interested to break into a group
on the corner and so be able to turn around and
watch her, without appearing to stop for that
purpose

She went into the doctor's office.

"By gum," said the President, looking at the
door through which she had disappeared, "don't
these women beat all? They go where they like—
they do as they like—they wear what they like—
they don't care what men think, any more. They're
bold—that's what they are! and I don't know as
I believe in lettin' them vote—By Gosh!"

The organizer raised his hand in warning, and
spoke sternly.

"Hold your tongue," he said, "they're a long
way from votin'. Believe what you like—no one
cares what you believe—but sit tight on it! I
talked too much just now. Let's learn our lesson."

Bertie, whose other name was now lost in oblivion, and who was known as "Bertie Crocks" for purposes of identification, standing at the corner of the "Horse Repository," saw Miss Keith entering the doctor's office, and wondered again how any one ever thought a small town dull.

CHAPTER X

The turning of a key, the opening of a door, are commonplace sounds to most of us; but to a prisoner, weary of his cell, they are sounds of unspeakable rapture. The dripping of a tap, may have in it the element of annoyance—if we have to get up and shut it off before we can get to sleep, but a thirsty traveller on the burning sands of the desert, would be wild with joy to hear it. All which is another way of saying that everything in life is relative.

On the day that Pearl spoke in the school-house, there sat in one of the seats listening to her, a sombre-faced woman, who rarely came to any of the neighborhood gatherings. The women of the neighborhood, having only the primary hypothesis of human conduct, said she was "proud." She did not join heartily in their conversations when they met her, and had an aloofness about her which could only be explained that way. She had a certain daintiness about her, too, in her way of dressing—even in the way she did her hair— and in her walk, which made the women say with certain resentment, that Mrs. Paine would like to be "dressy."

But if Mrs. Paine had any such ambitions, they were not likely to be achieved, for although she and her husband had lived for years in this favored

district, and had had good crops, Sylvester Paine
was known all over the country as a hard man.
The women would have liked Mrs. Paine much
better if she had talked more, and complained
about him—she was too close-mouthed they said.
They freely told each other, and told her, of their
hopes, fears, trials and triumphs—but Mrs. Paine's
communications were yea and nay when the conversation was on personal matters, and she had a
way of closing her lips which somehow prevented
questions.

But on the day when Pearl spoke in the school
Mrs. Paine's face underwent a change which would
have interested a student of human nature. Something which had been long dead, came to life again
that day; fluttering, trembling, shrinking. In her
eyes there came again the dead hopes of the years,
and it made her face almost pitiful in its trembling
eagerness. There was a dull red rage in her eyes
too that day, that was not good to see, and she
was determined that it should not be seen, and for
that reason, she slipped away when Pearl was
through, leaving some excuse about having the
chores to do. She could not bear to speak to the
women and have them read her face; she knew it
would tell too much. But she must talk to Pearl.
There were things that Pearl could tell her.

That night she called Pearl on the phone. The
other receivers came down quickly, and various
homely household sounds mingled in her ears—
a sewing-machine's soft purring in one house—a
child's cry in another—the musical whine of a

cream separator in a third. She knew they were
all listening, but she did not care. Even if she could
not control her face, she could control her voice.

When Pearl came to the phone, Mrs. Paine invited
her to come over for supper the next night, to which
Pearl gave ready acceptance—and that was all.
The interested listeners were disappointed with
the brevity of the conversation, and spoke guard-
edly and in cipher to each other after Pearl and
Mrs. Paine had gone: "Somebody is away, see!
That's why! Gee! some life—never any one asked
over only at such times—Gee! How'd you like
to be bossed around like that?"

"She did not begin right—too mealy-mouthed.
Did you hear what he's going to buy? No! I'll
tell you when I see you—we've too big an audience
right now. Don't it beat all, the time some people
have to listen in—"

"O well, I don't care! Anything I say I'm ready
to back up. I don't pretend I forget or try to
twist out of things."

One receiver went up here, and the sound of
the sewing-machine went with it.

Then the conversation drifted pleasantly to a
new and quicker way of making bread that had
just come out in the "Western Home Monthly."

The next evening Pearl walked over the Plover
Slough to see Mrs. Paine. She noticed the quantity
of machinery which stood in the yard, some under
cover of the big shingled shed, and some of it sitting out in the snow, gray and weather-beaten.
The yard was littered, untidy, prodigal, wasteful—

every sort of machine had evidently been bought and used for a while, then discarded. But within doors there was a bareness that struck Pearl's heart with pity. The entrance at the front of the house was banked high with snow, and evidently had not been used all winter, and indeed there seemed no good reason for its ever being used, for the front part of the house, consisting of hall, front room opening into a bed-room, were unfurnished and unheated.

Mrs. Paine was genuinely, eagerly glad to see Pearl, and there was a tense look in her eyes, an underglow of excitement, a trembling of her hands, as she set the table, that did not escape Pearl.

But nothing was said until the children had gone to bed, and then Mrs. Paine departed from her life-long habit of silence, and revealed to Pearl the burdens that were crushing her.

She was a thin woman, with a transparency about her that gave her the appearance of being brittle. Her auburn hair curled over her white forehead, and snakily twisted around her ivory white ears. Her eyes were amber-brown, with queer yellow lights that rose and fell as she talked, and in some strange way reminded Pearl of a piece of bird's-eye maple. She was dressed in the style of twenty years before, with her linen collar inside the high collar of her dress, which was fastened with a bar pin, straight and plain like herself. In the centre of the pin was a cairn-gorm, which reflected the slumbering, yellow light in her eyes. The color of her face was creamy white, like fine stationery.

"I thought all my hopes were dead, Pearl," she said with dry lips, "until you spoke, and then I saw myself years ago, when I came out of school. Life was as rosy and promising, and the future as bright to me then as it is to you now. But I got married young—we were brought up to think if we did not get married—we were rather disgraced, and in our little town in Ontario, men were scarce—they had all come West. So when I got a chance, I took it."

Pearl could see what a beautiful young girl she must have been, when the fires of youth burned in her eye—with her brilliant coloring and her graceful ways. But now her face had something dead about it, something missing—like a beautifully-tiled fireplace with its polished brass fittings, on whose grate lie only the embers of a fire long dead.

Pearl thought of this as she watched her. Mrs. Paine, in her agitation, pleated her muslin apron into a fan.

The tea-kettle on the stove bubbled drowsily, and there was no sound in the house but the purring of the big cat that lay on Pearl's knee.

"Life is a funny proposition, Pearl," continued Mrs. Paine, "I often think it is a conspiracy against women. We are weaker, smaller than men—we have all the weaknesses and diseases they have—and then some of our own. Marriage is a form of bondage—long-term slavery—for women."

Pearl regarded her hostess with astonished eyes. She had always known that Mrs. Paine did not look happy; but such words as these came as a shock to her romantic young heart.

"It isn't the hard work—or the pain—it isn't that—it's the uselessness of it all. Nature is so cruel, and careless. See how many seeds die— nature does not care—some will grow—the others do not matter!"

"O you're wrong, Mrs. Paine," Pearl cried eagerly; "it is not true that even a sparrow can fall to the ground and God not know it."

Mrs. Paine seemed about to speak, but checked her words. Pearl's bright face, her hopefulness, her youth, her unshaken faith in God and the world, restrained her. Let the child keep her faith!

"There is something I want to ask you, Pearl," she said, after a long pause. "You know the laws of this Province are different from what they are in Ontario."

Her voice fell, and the light in her eyes seemed to burn low, like a night-light, turned down.

"He says," she did not call her husband by name, but Pearl knew who was meant, "he says that a man can sell all his property here without his wife's signature, and do what he likes with the money. He wants to sell the farm and buy the hotel at Millford. I won't consent, but he tells me he can take the children away from me, and I would have to go with him then. He says this is a man's country, and men can do as they like. I wonder if you know what the law is?"

"I'm not sure," said Pearl. "I've heard the women talking about it, but I will find out. I will write to them. If that is the law it will be changed— any one could see that it is not fair. Lots of these

old laws get written down and no one bothers
about them—and they just stay there, forgotten—
but any one would see that was not fair. Men
would not be as unjust as that."

"You don't know them," said Mrs. Paine; "I
have no faith in men. They've made the world,
and they've made it to suit themselves. My husband takes his family cares as lightly as a tomcat.
The children annoy him."

She spoke in jerky sentences, often moistening
her dry lips, and there was something in her eyes
which made Pearl afraid—the very air of the room
seemed charged with discords. Pearl struggled to
free her heart from the depressing influence.

"All men are not selfish," she said, "and I guess
God has done the best He could to be fair to every
one. It's some job to make millions of people and
satisfy them all."

"Well, the Creator should take some responsibility," Mrs. Paine interrupted, "none of us asked
to be born—I'm not God, but I take responsibility
for my children. I did not want them, but now they
are here I'll stand by them. That's why I've stayed
as long as this. But God does not stand by me."

Her voice was colorless and limp like a washed
ribbon. It had in it no anger, just a settled conviction.

"See here, Mrs. Paine," began Pearl, "you've
been too long alone in the house. You begin to
imagine things. You work too hard, and never
go out, and that would make an archangel cross.
You've just got to mix up more with the rest of

us. Things are not half so black as they look to you."

"I could stand it all—until he said he could take away my home," the words seemed to come painfully. "I worked for this," she said, "and though it's small and mean—it's home. Every bit of furniture in this house I bought with my butter money. The only trees we have I planted. I sowed the flowers and dug the place to put them. While he is away buying cattle and shipping them, and making plenty of money—all for himself—I stay here and run the farm. I milk, and churn, and cook for hired men, and manage the whole place, and I've made it pay too, but he has everything in his own name. Now he says he can sell it and take the money. . . . Even a cat will fight and scratch for its hay-loft."

"Oh well," said Pearl, "I hope you won't have to fight. Fighting is bad work. It's a last resort when everything else fails. Mr. Paine can be persuaded out of the hotel business if you go at it right. He does not understand, that's all. That's what causes all the misery and trouble in life—it is lack of understanding."

Mrs. Paine smiled grimly: "It's good to be young, Pearl," she said.

After a while she spoke again: "I did not ask you over entirely for selfish reasons. I wanted to talk to you about yourself; I wanted to warn you, Pearl."

"What about!" Pearl exclaimed.

"Don't get married," she said; "Oh don't, Pearl,

I can't bear to think of you being tied down with children and hard work. It's too big a risk, Pearl, don't do it. We need you to help the rest of us. When I listened to you the other day I came nearer praying than I have for many years. I said, 'Oh, Lord, save Pearl,' and what I meant was that He should save you from marriage. You'll have lots of offers."

"None so far," laughed Pearl, "not a sign of one."

"Well, you'll get plenty—but don't do it, Pearl. We need you to talk for us."

"Well, couldn't I talk if I were married?" asked Pearl, "I have heard married women talk."

"Not the same; they haven't the heart. People cannot talk if their own hearts are sore. That's why we want to keep you light-hearted and care-free. I wish you would promise me, Pearl, that you won't marry."

Pearl hesitated, hardly knowing how to meet this.

"That's asking a lot, Mrs. Paine. Every girl hopes to marry some time," she said at last, and if the light had been better Mrs. Paine would have seen the color rising in Pearl's cheeks; "And you are wrong in thinking that all men are mean and selfish. My father is not. We've been poor and all that, but we're happy. My father has never shirked his share of the work, and he has only one thought now, and that is to do well for us. There are plenty of happy marriages. I — can't promise not to but there's no danger yet — I have no notion of it."

"All right, Pearl," said Mrs. Paine, "keep away

from it. Some way I can't bear to think of you tied down with a bunch of kids, and all your bright ways dulled with hard work and worry. Well, anyway, you'll talk about it—about the vote I mean."

"All the time," Pearl laughingly responded. "Wherever two or three gather Pearl Watson will rise and make a few remarks unless some one forcibly restrains her. I will promise that—that's easy."

When Pearl walked home that night the moon was trying to shine through a gray rag of a cloud that was wrapped around its face. The snow on the road caught the muffled rays of light, and she could see her way quite well after her eyes grew accustomed to the darkness. There was a close, protecting feeling about the gray darkness that suited her mood. It was a comfortable, companionable night, with a soft air full of pleasant sounds of dogs barking, and sleigh-bells, and with the lights in the neighbors' houses for company. Pearl was not conscious of fear. All her life she had gone about in the night as fearlessly as by day.

Mrs. Paine's words troubled her. Was it possible life could be as dull and drab a thing as it seemed to her. Perhaps, though, she had never been in love! She had married because she did not want to be an old maid. Only love can redeem life from its common-place monotony. Maybe that was why things had gone wrong.

She thought about Mrs. Paine's words about being tied down with children and hard work, and how she had pleaded with her to be warned! Pearl tried

to make the warning real and effective—tried to
harden her heart and fill it with ambitions, in
which love and marriage had no place. She tried
to tell herself it was her duty to never marry;
she would be free to work for other women. She
tried to think of a future apart from marriage,
apart from the hopes and dreams that had been
so dear and sweet. Could it be that she was being
called of God to be a leader in a new crusade against
injustice? Was it her part to speak for other women?
Since the day she spoke in the school there had
been a glowing wonder in her heart which told
her she could move people to higher thinking and
nobler action. She had seen it in their eyes that
day. She had seen the high resolve in their faces,
seen it, and been glad and fearful too. Was it
possible that God was calling her to declare a
message to the people, and could it be that it was
for this reason her sweet dreams had been so suddenly broken?

Pearl stopped in the road in her agitation of
spirit, as the possibility of this surged over her.
Every sound seemed to have died away, not a
dog barked or a tree creaked in the gray darkness
which shrouded the world. Even the lights in
the houses seemed to hold a steady gleam, without
as much as winking an eye—waiting for her answer.

The whole world seemed to be holding its breath
expectantly, in a waiting, quivering silence. It
was as if her name had been called; the curtain had
rolled up, and a great audience waited.

A sudden, helpless feeling set her heart beating

painfully into her throat, a smothering sense of fear, quite new to her, who had never known fear.

"I can't do it!" broke from her, in a cry; "Don't ask me, Lord, I can't! I can't do it alone—but give me the desire of my heart, oh, Lord, and I will never tremble or turn back or be afraid. I will declare the truth before kings!"

CHAPTER XI

ENGAGED

THE trustees of Purple Springs School had reached the climax of their professional duties. They were about to appoint a teacher, and being conscientious men, anxious to drive a good bargain for the people, they were proceeding with deep caution to "look around."

Looking at the modest equipment of Purple Springs School, the observer would wonder why such stress was laid on the teacher's qualifications. The school-house was a bleak little structure of wood, from whose walls the winds and rain had taken the paint. It was set in an arid field, that knew no tree or flower. Its three uncurtained windows threw a merciless light on the gray floor and smoked walls.

Former teachers had tried to stir the community to beautify the grounds and make the inside more homelike, but their efforts had been fitful and without result. Trees died, seeds remained in the ground, and gray monotony reigned at Purple Springs. Still, the three trustees believed it was an enviable position they had in their hands to bestow, and were determined that it should not be given lightly.

Just at the time that they were hard engaged in "lookin' 'round," the secretary's wife came back from a visit to Chicken Hill, and told about

Pearl Watson, who had been to the city and come back "quite a girl," able to talk, and just as nice and friendly as ever. Mrs. Cowan was not well read in the political situation of the day, and so did not know that Pearl had been guilty of heretical utterances against the Government.

If this had been known to the trustees her candidature would not have been considered, for all of the trustees were supporters and believers in the Government—and with reason. Mr. Cowan had a telephone line built expressly for him; Mr. Brownlees had been given a ditch—just where he wanted it, digging it himself, and been paid for it by the Government; the third trustee had been made game warden, at a monthly salary and no duties; so naturally they would like not to hear their friends criticized. Mrs. Cowan only read newspapers to see the bargains, crotchet patterns, and murders, and after that, she believed their only use was to be put on pantry shelves. So her account of Pearl's address was entirely without political bias.

"She's a fine looking girl," said Mrs. Cowan, "and it's nice to hear her talk, even if she isn't saying anything. She's brown-eyed, tall, and speaks out plain so every one can hear, and what she says is not too deep—and you'd never know she was educated, to hear her talk."

The three trustees resolved to look into the case. Being masters of duplicity, they decided to call on Miss Watson at her home, and to go in the early morning hours, believing that the misty light of

8 a.m. will reveal many things which the glare
of high noon might hide. They would see first
would she be up? They had once had a teacher
who lay in bed the whole day on Saturday. Would
she have her hair combed? They were not keen
on artistic effects in the school buildings, but were
a unit on wanting a tastefully dressed teacher.
It was decided that the call would be early and
unannounced.

They found Pearl in a pink and white checked
gingham house dress, with her brown hair done
up in the style known as a French roll, sewing
at a machine in the front room, and at once Mr.
Cowan, who was the dominant spirit of the party
signalled to the others—"So far so good." Miss
Watson, even though the hour was early, was up,
dressed neatly—and at work. All of this was
in the glance which Mr. Cowan shot over to his
colleagues.

Investigating still further, for Mr. Cowan knew
the value of detail in estimating human character;
the general arrangement of the room won his approval. It was comfortable, settled, serene—it
looked like home—it invited the visitor to come
in and be at rest. A fire burned in the heater, a
bird sang in the kitchen, a cat lay on the lounge
and did not move when he sat down beside it,
showing that its right of way had not been dis-
puted. Mr. Cowan saw it all.

After the introductions were over, Mr. Cowan
put forth some questions about her qualifications,
and at each answer, his colleagues were given to

understand by a faint twitter of his eyes that Miss Watson was still doing well.

"You're young, of course," said Mr. Cowan, with the air of a man who faces facts—but his natural generosity of spirit prompted him to add "but you'll get over that, and anyway a girl is older in her ways than a boy."

"We measure time by heart-beats," said Pearl, as she handed him a flowered cushion to put behind his head, "not by figures on a dial."

She tossed it off easily, as if poetry were the language of every day life to her.

Mr. Cowan shut one eye for the briefest space of time, and across the room his two friends knew Miss Watson's chances were growing brighter every minute. "My wife happened to be down at Chicken Hill the day you spoke, and she said you sure did speak well, for a girl, and she was hopin' you'd speak at our school some night—and we could get a phonograph to liven things up a bit—I guess we're broad-minded enough to listen to a woman."

Mr. Cowan's confidence in his companions was amply justified. They nodded their heads approvingly, like men who are willing to try anything once.

"Well, you see," Mr. Cowan went on, "we have a nice district, Miss Watson. We're farmer people, of course, with the exception of the few who live at the station; we're farmers but we're decent people—and we're pretty well-to-do farmers—we have only one woman in the district—that we sort of wish wasn't there."

"Why?" asked Pearl quickly.

"Well you see, she got in first, so to speak. She bought the farm beside the river, and it was her that called the place 'Purple Springs.' It's an outlandish name, but it seems to kind a' stick. There's no springs at all, and they are certainly not purple. But she made the words out of peeled poplar poles, with her axe, and put them up at the front of her house, facin' the track, and the blamed words stick. Mind you, she must have spent months twistin' and turnin' them poles to suit her and get the letters right, and she made a rustic fence to put them on. They're so foolish you can't forget them. She's queer, that's all—and she won't tell who she is, nor where she came from—and she seems to have money."

Pearl looked at him inquiringly. There must be more than that to the story, she thought.

"The women will tell you more about her—that's sure. They gabble a lot among themselves about her—I don't know—we think it best to leave her alone. No woman has any right to live alone the way she does—it don't look well."

"Well, anyway," Mr. Cowan spoke hurriedly, as one who has been betrayed into trifling feminine matters, and is anxious to get back to man's domain, "we'll take you—at seventy-five dollars a month, and I guess you can get board at Mrs. Zinc's here at about fifteen. That ain't bad wages for a girl your age. You can stay at Mrs. Zinc's anyway till you look around—Mrs. Zinc don't want a boarder. Girls can fit in any place—that's one reason in our neighborhood we like a girl better

—there's no trouble about boardin' them. They can always manage somehow. Even if things ain't very good—it don't seem to phaze them—same as a man. We had a man once, and we had to pay him twenty-five dollars a month extra, and gosh— the airs of him—wanted a bed to himself and a hot dinner sent to the school. By Gum! and got it! We'll be lookin' for you at the middle of the month, and you can stay at Mrs. Zinc's and look around."

When the delegation had departed, Pearl acquainted her mother with the result of their visit. Mrs. Watson had retired to the kitchen, all of a flutter, as soon as the visitors came.

"I'm going to Purple Springs, Ma," she said, "to take the school, and they'll give me seventy-five dollars a month."

Mrs. Watson sat down, dramatically, and applied her print apron to her eyes—an occasion had come, and Mrs. Watson, true to tradition, would make the most of it. Her mother had cried when she left home—it was a girl's birthright to be well cried over—Pearlie Watson would not go forth unwept!

"Cheer up, Ma," said Pearl kindly, "I'm not going to jail, and I'm not taking the veil or going across the sea. I can call you up for fifteen cents, and I'll be bringing you home my washing every two weeks—so I will not be lost entirely."

Mrs. Watson rocked herself disconsolately back and forth in her chair, and the sound of her sobs filled the kitchen. Mrs. Watson was having a good time, although appearances would not bear out the statement.

"It's the first break, Pearlie, that's what I'm thinkin'—and every night when I lock the door, I'll be lockin' you out—not knowin' where ye are. When a family once breaks you never can tell if they'll ever all be together again—that's what frightens me. It was bad enough when you went to the city—and I never slept a wink for two nights after you'd gone. But this is worse, for now you're doin' for yourself and away from us that way."

"Gosh, Ma," spoke up Mary, "you sure cry easy, and for queer things. I think it's grand that Pearl can get out and earn money, and then when I get my entrance, I'll go to the city and be a teacher too. You're going to get back what you've spent on us, ma, and you ought to be in great humor. I'm just as proud of Pearl as I can hold, and I'll be tellin' the kids at school about my sister who is Principal of the Purple Springs School."

"Principal, Assistant and Janitor," laughed Pearl, "that gives a person some scope—to be sure."

Mrs. Watson hurriedly put up the ironing-board, and set to work. She would get Pearl ready, though she did it with a heavy heart.

Pearl finished her sewing and then went upstairs to make her small wardrobe ready for her departure, and although she stepped quickly and in a determined fashion, there was a pain, a lonely ache in her heart which would not cease, a crying out for the love which she had hoped would be hers.

"I wonder if I will ever get to be like ma," she thought, as she lined the bottom of her little trunk with brown paper, and stuffed tissue paper into

the sleeves of her "good dress," "I wonder! Well,
I hope I will be like her in some ways, but not in
this mournful stuff—I won't either. I'll sing when
I feel it coming on me—I will not go mourning all
my days—not for any one!"

She began to sing:—

"Forgotten you? Yes, if forgetting
 Is thinking all the day
How the long days pass without you.
Days seem years with you away!"

Pearl's voice had a reedy mellowness, and an
appeal which sent the words straight into Mary's
practical heart. Mary, washing dishes below,
stopped, with a saucer in her hand, and listened
open-mouthed:—

"If the warm wish to see you and hear you,
And hold you in my arms again,
If that be forgetting—you're right, dear,
And I have forgotten you then!"

Her voice trailed away on the last line into a sob'
and Mary, listening below, dropped a tear into
the dish-water. Then racing up the stairs, she
burst into Pearl's room and said admiringly:

"Pearl, you're a wonder. It's an actress you ought
to be. You got me blubbering, mind you. It's
so sad about you and your beau that's had a row,
and both of you actin' so pale and proud, you
made me see it all. Sing it again! Well, for the
love of Pete—if you ain't ready to blubber too.
That's good actin', Pearl—let me tell you—how
can you do it?"

Pearl brushed away the tears, and laughed: "I just hit on the wrong song—that one always makes me cry, I can see them, too, going their own ways and feeling so bad, and moping around instead of cutting out the whole thing the way they should. People are foolish to mope!" Pearl spoke sternly.

"I think you sing just lovely," said Mary, "now go on, and I'll get back to the dishes. Sing 'Casey Jones'—that's the best one to wash dishes to. It's sad, too, but it's funny."

Mrs. Watson held the iron to her cheek to test its heat, and listened—too—as Pearl sang:—

> "Casey Jones—mounted to the cabin,
> Casey Jones—with the orders in his hand,
> Casey Jones—mounted to the cabin
> And took his farewell tri-ip—to the prom-
> ised land!"

"It's well for them that can be so light-hearted," she said, "and leave all belonging to them—as easy as Pearl. Children do not know, and never will know what it means, until one of their own ups and leaves them! It's the way of the world, one day they're babies, and the next thing you know they're gone! It's the way of the world, but it's hard on the mother."

Pearl came down the stairs, stepping in time with Casey Jones's spectacular home-leaving:—

> "The caller called Casey, at—a half-past-four,
> He kissed his wife at the station door."

"How goes the ironing, honest woman," she said, as she lovingly patted her mother's shoulder. "It's a proud old bird you ought to be getting one of your young robins pushed out of the nest—instead of standing here with a sadness on your face."

The mother tried to smile through her tears.

"Pearlie, my dear, you're a queer girl—you never seem to think of what might happen. It may be six weeks before you can get home—with the roads breaking up—and a lot can happen in that time. Sure—I might not be here myself," she said, with a fresh burst of tears.

"Ma, you're funny," laughed Pearl, "I wish you could see how funny you are. Every Christmas ever since I can remember, that's what you said—you might never live to see another, and it used to nearly break my heart when I was little, and until I made up my mind that you were a poor guesser. You said it last Christmas just the same, and here you are with your ears back and your neck bowed, heading up well for another year. You're quite right in saying you may not be here, but if you are not you'll be in a better place. Sure, things may happen, but it's better to have things happen than to be scared all the time that they may happen. The young lads may take the measles and then the mumps, and the whooping-cough to finish up on—and the rosey-posey is going around too. But even if they do—it's most likely they will get over it—they always have. Up to the present, the past has taken care of the future. Maybe it always will."

"O yes, I know there's always a chance things

will go wrong—I know it, Ma—" Pearl's eyes
dimmed a little, and she held her lips tighter;
"there's always a chance. The cows may all choke
to death seeing which of them can swallow the
biggest turnip—the cats may all have fits—the
chickens may break into the hen-house and steal
a bag of salt, eat it and die. But I don't believe
they will. You just have to trust them—and you'll
have to trust me the same way. Just look, Ma—"

She took a five-dollar bill from her purse and
spread it on the ironing-board before her mother.
Fifteen o' them every month! See the pictures
that's on it, of the two grand old men. See the
fine chin-whiskers on His Nibs here! Ain't it a
pity he can't write his name, Ma, and him President of the Bank, and just has to make a bluff at
it like this. Sure, and isn't that enough to drive
any girl out to teach school, to see to it that bank
presidents get a chance to learn to write. Bank
presidents always come from the country; I'll
be having a row of them at Purple Springs—I'm
sure. They will be able to tell in after years at
Rotary Club luncheons how they ran barefooted
in November, and made wheat gum—and chewed
strings together. They just like to tell about their
chilblains and their stone-bruises."

Her mother looked at her wonderingly: "You
think of queer things, Pearl—I don't know where
you get it—I can't make you out—and there's
another thing troubling me, Pearl. You are goin'
away—I don't suppose you will be livin' much
at home now. You'll be makin' your own way."

She paused, and Pearl knew her mother was laboring under heavy emotion. She knew she was struggling to say what was difficult for her to get into words.

"When you've been away for a while and then come back to us, maybe you'll find our ways strange to you, for you're quick in the pick-up, Pearl, and we're only plain workin' people, and never had a chance at learnin'. There may come a time when you're far above us, Pearl, and our ways will seem strange to you. I get worried about it, Pearl, for I know if that time ever comes, it will worry you too, for you're not the kind that can hurt your own and not feel it."

Pearl looked at her mother almost with alarm in her face, and the fears that had been assailing her that her family were beyond the social pale came back for a moment. But with the fear came a fierce tenderness for all of them. She saw in a flash of her quick imagination the tragedy of it from her mother's side, and in her heart there was just one big, burning, resolute desire, that pain from this source might never smite her mother's loving heart. The hard hands, the sunburnt face, the thin hair that she had not taken time to care for, the hard-working shoulders, slightly stooped, the scrawny neck, with its tell-tale lines of age, were eloquent in their appeal. Pearl saw the contrast of her mother's life and what her own promised to be, and her tender heart responded, and when she spoke, it was in an altered tone. All the fun had gone from it now, and it was not a child's voice, nor a girl's voice, but a woman's, with all a woman's gentleness and understanding that spoke.

"Mother," she said, "I know what is in your heart, and I will tell you how I feel about it. You're afraid your ways may seem strange to me. Some of them are strange to me now. I often wonder how any one can be as unselfish as you are and keep it up day in and day out, working for other people. Most of us can make a good stab at it, and keep it up for a day or so, but to hit the steady pace, never looking back and never being cross or ugly about it—that's great!"

"And about the other . . . If ever there comes a time when an honest heart and a brave spirit in a woman seems strange to me, and I get feeling myself above them—if I ever get thinking light of honesty and kindness and patience and hard work, and get thinking myself above them—then your ways will be strange to me, but not until then!"

Mrs. Watson's face cleared, and a look of pride shone in her eyes. Her face seemed to lose some of its lines, and to reflect some of the lavish beauty of her daughter.

"You've comforted me, Pearl," she said simply, "and it's not the first time. Whatever comes or goes, Pearl, you'll know we are proud of you, and will stand back of you. Your outspoken ways may get you into trouble, but we'll always believe you were right. We haven't much to give you—only this."

"Sure and what more would any one want, leavin'

home," Pearl was back to the speech of her childhood now. "That's better than a fur coat to keep out the cold, and the thought of my own folks makes me strong to face the world, knowin' I can always come home even if everything else is closed. That's good enough!"

Pearl kissed her mother affectionately, and went back to her work upstairs, and soon Mary and her mother heard her singing. Mary stopped scrubbing the kitchen floor, and Mrs. Watson left the iron so long on Teddy's shirt that it left a mark:

"Say Au Revoir," sang Pearl, "but not goodbye,
The past is dead—love cannot die,
T'were better far—had we not met,
I loved you then—I love you yet."

There was something in her voice that made her mother say, "Poor child, I wonder what's ahead of her."

CHAPTER XII

THE MACHINE

SEATED in one of the billowy tapestry chairs of the Maple Leaf Club, with a mahogany ash-stand at his elbow and the morning paper in his hand, the Cabinet Minister gave an exclamation which began far down in the throat, tore upward past his immaculate collar, and came forth as a full-sized round word of great emphasis and carrying power.

It brought to him at once Peter Neelands, one of the ambitious young lawyers of the city, who was just coming into prominence in political circles.

"What did you say, sir?" Peter asked politely.

The Cabinet Minister controlled his indignation admirably, and with his pudgy knuckles rapped the offending newspaper, with the motion used by a carpenter when trying to locate the joist in a plastered wall, as he said:—

"Here is absolutely the most damnably mischievous thing I have seen for years, and this abominable sheet is featuring it on the Women's Page. They will all read it—and be infected. Women are such utterly unreasonable creatures. This is criminal."

"What is it, sir?" Peter asked deferentially.

The older man handed him the paper, and sat back in his chair, with his fat hands clasped over his rotund person, and an expression of deep disgust in his heavy gray eyes.

"Anything!—anything!—" he cried, "to gain a political advantage. They will even play up this poor little uneducated, and no doubt, mentally unfit country girl, and put in her picture and quotations from her hysterical speeches. They never think—or care—for the effect this will have on her, filling her head with all sorts of notions. This paper is absolutely without a soul, and seems determined to corrupt the country. And on the Women's Page, too, where they will all read it!"

"By Jove! that was good"—exclaimed the young man, as he read.

"What was good—are you reading what I gave you to read?" came from the older man.

"Yes, about this girl at Millford, it says: 'In the discussion that followed, the local member heatedly opposed the speaker's arguments favoring the sending of women to Parliament, and said when women sat in Parliament, he would retire—to which the speaker replied that this was just another proof of the purifying effect women would have on politics. This retort naturally brought down the house, and the local member was not heard from again'—terribly cheeky, of course, but rather neat, sir, don't you think?"

The Cabinet Minister took a thick cigar from his vest pocket, without replying.

"Who is the member from Millford?" he demanded.

"George Steadman, sir, a big, heavy-set chap—very faithful in his attendance, sir, absolutely reliable—never talks, but votes right."

"I don't recall him," said the great man, after
a pause, "but your description shows he's the sort
we must retain."

He lit his cigar, and when it was drawing nicely,
removed it from his mouth, and looked carefully
at it, as if he expected to find authentic information in it regarding private members. Failing this,
he put it back in his mouth, and between puffs
went on:—

"Let me see—they are wanting a bridge near
there, aren't they? on the Souris?"

"Yes sir, at Purple Springs."

"All right—we ought to be able to hold the fort
there with the bridge—but the trouble is, this thing
will spread, and when the campaign warms up,
this girl will be in demand."

He lapsed into silence again.

Peter, still holding the paper, volunteered:—

"She seems to be one of those infant prodigies
who could sing 'The Dying Nun,' and recite 'Curfew
Shall Not Ring Tonight,' before she could talk
plainly."

The Cabinet Minister gave no sign that he was
listening—mental agitation was written on his face.

"But we must head her off some way, I'll admit—
I don't mind saying it—though of course it must
not be repeated—these damnable women are making
me nervous. I know how to fight men—I've been
fighting them all my life—with some success."

"With wonderful success, sir!" burst in Peter.

The older man threw out his hands in a way that
registered modesty. It had in it the whole scrip-

tural injunction of "Let another praise thee—and not thine own mouth."

"With some success," he repeated sternly, "but I cannot fight women. You cannot tell what they will do; they are absolutely unreliable; they are ungrateful, too. Many of these women who form the cursed Women's Club, are women I have been on friendly terms with; so has the Chief. We have granted them interviews; we have listened to their suggestions; always with courtesy, always with patience. We have asked them to come back. In certain matters we have acceded to their requests— in some unimportant matters—" he added quickly. "But what is the result? Is there any gratitude? Absolutely none. Give them an inch—they will take a mile. Women are good servants, but bad masters."

"Don't you think, sir," said Peter, much flattered by being talked to in this friendly way by the great man, "don't you think it is these militant suffragettes in England who are causing the trouble? Before they began their depredations, women did not think of the vote. It is the power of suggestion, don't you think, and all that sort of thing?"

They were interrupted just then by the arrival of Mr. Banks, one of the Government organizers, who, ignoring Peter's presence, addressed himself to the Cabinet Minister. His manner was full of importance. Mr. Banks had a position in the Public Works Department, and occasionally might be found there. Sometimes he went in for his mail, and stayed perhaps half an hour.

He addressed the Cabinet Minister boldly:—

"Did you see this? Looks like trouble, don't it? What do you suggest?"

Mr. Banks did not remove either his hat or his cigar. Cabinet Ministers had no terror for him— he had made cabinet ministers. If Mr. Banks had lived in the time of Warwick that gentleman might not have had the title of "King-Maker."

"What do you think yourself," asked the Cabinet Minister deferentially, "you know the temper of the country perhaps better than any of us; shall we notice this girl or just let her go?"

Mr. Banks laughed harshly.

"We can't stop her, as a matter of fact—she isn't the kind that can be shut up. There's nothing to her—I've made inquiries. The people have known her since she was born, and ran the country barefooted—so we can't send her a 'Fly—all is discovered' postcard. It won't work. People all honest—can't get any of them into trouble—and then let them off—and win her gratitude. This is a difficult case, and the other side will play it up, you bet. The girl has both looks and brains, and a certain style. She went to the Normal with my girl. My kid's crazy about her."

"Do her people need money?" asked Peter; he was learning the inner side of politics.

His suggestion was ignored until the pause became painful—then the organizer said severely:—

"Nobody needs money, but every one can use it. But money is of no use in this case. This has to be arranged by tact. Tact is what few members of the party have; their methods are raw."

"But there is no harm done yet," said Peter hopefully, "a few country people in a bally little school-house, and the girl gets up and harangues. She's been to the city, and knows a few catch phrases. There's nothing to it. We wouldn't have known of it—only for the enthusiastic friend who pours his drivel into this paper."

Mr. Banks looked at Peter in deep contempt.

"Whoever wrote this does not write drivel, Peter," he said, with a note of fatigue in his voice. "He has made out a good case for this girl. Every one who reads this wants to see her. I want to see her, you want to see her—that's the deuce of it."

"Well, why don't you go," said Peter, "or send me? I'd like to go. Perhaps it would be better to send a young man. I often think—"

Mr. Banks looked at him with so much surprise in his usually heavy countenance that Peter paused in confusion.

"I often think," he braved the disgust he had evoked, and spoke hurriedly to get it said before the other man had withered him with his eyes; "I often think a young man can get along some-times—girls will tell him more, feeling more companionable as it were—" He paused, feeling for a convincing climax.

But in spite of Mr. Banks' scorn of Peter Neeland's efforts at solving their new difficulty, he soon began to think of it more favorably, coming to this by a process known as elimination. No one else wanted to go; he could not think of anything else. Peter

would not do any harm—he was as guileless as a
blue-eyed Angora kitten, and above all, he was willing
and anxious to get into the game. This would give
him an opportunity. So Mr. Banks suddenly made
up his mind that he would authorize a cheque to be
drawn on the "Funds." It could easily be entered
under "Inspection of Public Bridges," or any old
thing—that was a mere detail.

The Cabinet Minister, who was later acquainted
with the plan, and had by that time recovered his
mental composure, almost spoiled everything by
declaring it was a most unwise move, and absolutely unnecessary.

"Leave her alone," he declared, as he sipped his
whiskey and soda—"people like that hang themselves
if they get enough rope. What is she anyway—but
an unlearned, ignorant country girl, who has been in
the city and gathered a few silly notions, and when
she goes home she shows off before her rustic friends.
"My dear boy," he addressed Peter now, from an
immeasurable distance, "the secret of England's
greatness consists of letting every damn fool say
what he likes, they feel better, and it does no harm.
We must expect criticism and censure—we are well
able to bear it, and with our men in every district,
there is little to fear. We'll offset any effect there
may be from this girl's ravings by sending the Chief
out for one speech."

The Minister of Public Works lapsed into meditation and drummed pleasantly with his plump, shining
hand on the table beside him. The sweet mellowness
which had been Mr. Walker's aim for years, lay on

his soul. The world grew more misty and golden
every moment, and in this sunkissed, nebulous haze,
his fancy roamed free, released from sordid cares—
by Mr. Walker's potent spell. It was a good world
—a good world of true friends, no enemies, no contra-
diction of sinners or other disagreeable people,
nothing but ease, praise, power, success, glorious old
world, without any hereafter, or any day of account-
ing. Tears of enthusiasm made dewy his eyes—
he loved everybody.

"The old Chief has a hold on the people that cannot be equalled. I thought it was wonderful last
night at the banquet, the tribute he paid to his
mother. It reveals such a tender side of him, even
though he has received the highest honor the people
can give him, yet he remembers so tenderly the old
home and its associations. That's his great secret
of success—he's so human—with faults like other
men, but they only make him all the more beloved.
He is so tolerant of all. When that poor simpleton
stuffed the ballot-box—out somewhere in the Blue
Mountains, a really clever piece of work too, wonderfully well done—with the false bottom—I don't
see how they ever discovered it—but it is hard to
deceive the enemy—there's no piece of crooked work
they are not familiar with. He was nearly crazy when
they caught him at it—thought he could be put in
jail—he forgot, the poor boob . . . . who he was working for . . . . I'll never forget how fine the old Chief
allayed his fears—"All for a good cause, my boy," he
said, in that jovial way of his, "I have no fear—the
Lord will look after His own." No wonder he can

get people to work for him. It is that hearty good
nature of his, and he never preaches to any one, or
scolds. He was just as kindly to the poor fellow as
if he had succeeded. It was wonderful."

"Great old boy, all right," Peter agreed heartily.

That afternoon Mr. Banks arranged with one of
the partners of the law firm to which Peter was at-
tached to release him for an indefinite period, and his
salary could be charged to the Government under
"Professional Services, Mr. P. J. Neelands," and
being a fair-minded man, and persuaded that a labor-
er was worthy of his hire, he suggested a substantial
increase in salary for Mr. Neelands, considering the
delicate nature of the task he was undertaking, and
who was paying for it.

The spring, notwithstanding its early March
smiles, delayed its coming that year, and the grim
facts of the scarcity of feed faced the thriftiest
farmers. The hungry cattle grew hungrier than
ever, and with threatening bellows and eyes of
flame pushed and crowded around the diminishing
stacks. The cattle market went so low that it did
not pay to ship them to the city, though humane
instincts prompted many a farmer to do this to
save their stock from a lingering death, and their
own eyes from the agony of seeing them suffer.

On April the first came the big storm, which
settled forever the feed problem for so many hungry
animals. It was a deliberate storm, a carefully
planned storm, beginning the day before with a
warm, soft air, languorous, spring-like, with a

pale yellow sun, with a cap of silver haze around its
head, which seemed to smile upon the earth with
fairest promises of an early spring. The cattle
wandered far from home, lured by the gentle air
and the mellow sunshine.

It was on this fair day that Mr. P. J. Neelands
took his journey to the country to do it a service,
and it is but fair to say that Mr. Neelands had
undertaken his new work with something related
to enthusiasm. It savored of mystery, diplomacy,
intrigue, and there was a thrill in his heart as he
sat in the green plush-covered seat, and leaning
back, with his daintily shod feet on the opposite
seat, surveyed himself in the long mirror which
filled the door at the end of the stateroom. It
was a very smartly dressed young man he saw,
smiling back engagingly, and the picture pleased
him. Expenses and salary paid, with a very delightful piece of work before him, which, if handled
tactfully and successfully, would bring him what
he craved—political promotion in the Young Men's
Club. The face in the glass smiled again. "Diplomacy is the thing," said Peter to himself. "It
carries a man farther than anything—and I'm glad
my first case has a woman in it."

He buffed his nails on the palm of his other
hand, and, looking at them critically, decided
to go over them again.

"There's nothing like personal neatness to impress
a girl; and this one, from her picture, will see everything at a glance."

Crossing the river at Poplar Ridge, he looked

out of the window at the pleasant farmyard of
one of the old settlers on the Assiniboine; a fine
brick house, with wide verandahs, an automobile
before the door, a barnyard full of cackling hens,
with a company of fine fat steers in an enclosure—
a pleasing picture of farm life, which filled his
imagination.

"What a country of opportunity," thought Peter,
"a chance for every one, and for women especially.
Everything in life is done for them. This house
was built for some woman, no doubt. I hope she
appreciates it, and is contented and happy in it.
Women were made to charm us—inspire us—cheer
us, but certainly not to rival us!"

Peter, with his hands on the knees of his well-
creased trousers, hitched them slightly, just enough
to reveal a glimpse of his lavender socks.

"Perhaps this girl needs only an interest—a love
interest—" Peter blushed as he thought it—"to
quiet her. If her affection were captured, localized,
centralized, she would not be clamoring to take a
man's place. She might be quite willing to enter
politics, indirectly, and be the power behind a
man of power.

He looked again at the newspaper picture of
Pearl Watson, and again at his own reflection in
the long glass.

"And a girl like this," Peter meditated, "would
be a help, too. She is evidently magnetic and convincing." His mind drifted pleasantly into the
purple hills and valleys of the future, and in a
delightfully vague way plans began to form for

future campaigns, where a brilliant young lawyer became at once the delight of his friends and the despair of his enemies, by his scathing sarcasm, his quick repartee, and still more by his piercing and inescapable logic. Never had the Conservative banner been more proudly borne to victory. Older men wept tears of joy as they listened and murmured, "The country is safe—thank God!"

Ably assisting him, though she deferred charmingly to him, in all things, was his charming young wife, herself an able speaker and debater who had once considered herself a suffragette, but who was now entirely absorbed in her beautiful home and her brilliant husband.

Peter flicked the dust from his tan shoes with a polka-dotted handkerchief, while rosy dreams, full of ambition and success filled his impressionable mind.

Through the snowy hills the train made its way cautiously, making long and apparently purposeless stops between stations, as if haunted by the fear of arriving too early. At such times Peter had leisure to carefully study the monotonous landscape, and he could not help but notice that the disparity in the size of the barn and that of the house in many cases was very great. A huge red barn, with white trimmings, surmounted by windmills, often stood towering over a tiny little weather-beaten, miserable house, which across a mile or two of snow, looked about the size of a child's block.

But small houses can be made very cosy, thought Peter complacently, for the glamor of adventure was on him, and no shade of sadness could assail his high spirits.

Some of the women who came to the train were disappointing in appearance. They were both shabby and sad, he thought, and he wondered why but looking closely at them he thought, with the fallacy of youth, that they must be very old.

Peter tried to outline his course of action. He would take a room at the hotel, making that his headquarters, and go out into the country—and stop at the Watson home, to ask directions or on some trivial errand, and meet her that way. But the thought would come back with tiresome regularity —suppose the first person who came to the door, gave him the directions he wanted—and shut the door. Well, of course he could ask for a drink, ... but even that might fail. Perhaps he should have brought an egg-beater—or a self-wringing mop to demonstrate, or some of the other things his friends had suggested. However, that did not need to be decided at once. Peter prided himself on his ability to leave tomorrow alone! So he made his way to the hotel on the corner, facing the station, untroubled by what the morrow might bring forth, and registered his name in the large book which the clerk swung around in front of him, and quietly asked for a room with a bath.

The clerk bit through the toothpick he had in his mouth, so great was his surprise, but he answered steadily:

"All rooms with bath are taken—only rooms with bed left."

"Room with bed, then," said Peter, and he was given the key of No. 17, and pointed to the black and red carpeted stairway.

CHAPTER XIII

THE STORM

I⊤ was a morning of ominous calm, with an hour of bright sun, gradually softening into a white shadow, as a fleecy cloud of fairy whiteness rolled over the sun's face, giving a light on the earth like the garish light in a tent at high noon, a light of blinding whiteness that hurts the eyes, although the sun is hidden. It was as innocent a looking morning as any one would wish to see, still, warm, bright, with a heavy brooding air which deadens sound and makes sleighs draw hard and horses come out in foam.

James Crocks, of the Horse Repository, sniffed the air apprehensively, bit a semi-circle out of a plug of tobacco, and gave orders that no horse was to leave the barn that day, for "he might be mistaken, and he might not," but he thought "we were in for it."

Other people seemed to think the same, for no teams could be seen on any of the roads leading to the village. It was the kind of morning on which the old timers say, "Stay where you are, wherever it is—if there's a roof over you!"

Wakening from a troubled dream of fighting gophers that turned to wild-cats, Mr. Neelands, in No. 17, made a hurried toilet, on account of the temperature of the room, for although the morning was warm, No. 17 still retained some of last week's temperature, and to Mr. Neelands, accustomed to the steam heat of Mrs. Marlowe's "Select Boarding

House—young men a specialty"—it felt very chilly,
indeed.   But Mr. Neelands had his mind made up
to be unmoved by trifles.

After a good breakfast in the dining room, Mr.
Neelands walked out to see the little town—and to
see what information he could gather. The well-
dressed young man, with the pale gray spats, who
carried a cane on his arm and wore a belted coat,
attracted many eyes as he swung out gaily across
the street toward the livery stable.

His plans were still indefinite. Bertie, who was
in charge of the stable, gazed spell-bound on the
vision of fashion which stood at the door, asking
about a team. Bertie, for once, was speechless
—he seemed to be gazing on his own better self—the
vision he would like to see when he sought his mirror.

"I would like to get a team for a short run," said
Mr. Neelands politely.

"Where you goin'," asked Bertie.

Mr. Neelands hesitated, and became tactful.

"I am calling on teachers," he said, on a matter of
business, "introducing a new set of books for school
libraries."

It was the first thing Mr. Neelands could think of,
and he was quite pleased with it when he said it.
It had a professional, business-like ring, which
pleased him.

"A very excellent set of books, which the Department of Education desire to see in every school,"
Mr. Neelands elaborated.

Then Bertie, always anxious to be helpful and to
do a good deed, leapt to the door, almost upsetting

Mr. Neelands in his haste. Bertie had an idea! Mr. Neelands did not connect his sudden departure with his recent scheme of enriching the life of the country districts with the set of books just mentioned, and therefore waited rather impatiently for the stableboy's return.

Bertie burst in, with the same enthusiasm.

"See, Mister, here's the teacher you want; I got her for you—she was just going to school."

Bertie's face bore the same glad rapture that veils the countenance of a cat when she throws a mouse at your feet with a casual "How's that."

Mr. Neelands found himself facing a brown-eyed, well-dressed young lady, with big question marks in both eyes, question marks which in a very dignified way demanded to know what it was all about.

In his confusion, Mr. Neelands, new in the art of diplomacy, blundered:

"Is this Miss Watson?" he stammered.

The reply was definite.

"It is not, and why did you call me."

Icicles began to hang from the roof. Mr. Neelands would have been well pleased if they had fallen on him, or a horse had kicked him—or anything.

He blushed a ripe tomato red. Bertie, deeply grieved, reviewed the situation.

"He said he wanted to see the teachers, and I just went and got you—that's all—you were the nearest teacher."

"Awfully sorry," began Mr. Neelands, "I did not know anything about it. I am just a stranger, you see.

There was something in Miss Morrison's eye which simply froze the library proposition. He could not frame the words.

"If you have any business with me you may make an appointment at the school. People who have business with the teachers generally do come to the school—not to the livery stable," she added, in exactly the tone in which she would have said "All who have failed to get fifty per cent. in arithmetic will remain after four," a tone which would be described as stern, but just.

Mr. Neelands leaned against a box-stall as Miss Morrison passed out. He wiped his face with the polka-dot handkerchief, and the word which the Cabinet Minister had used came easily to his lips.

"Why didn't you speak to her when you got a chance?" asked Bertie, anxious to divert the blame and meet railing with railing. He was always getting in wrong just trying to help people. Darn it all! Mr. Neelands could still think of no word but the one.

"I wish it had been Pearl," said Bertie, "Gee! she wouldn't ha' been so sore; she'd just laughed and jollied about it."

"So you know Pearl, do you?" Mr. Neelands could feel a revival of interest in life; also the stiffness began to leave his lips, and his tongue felt less like tissue paper.

"I guess everyone knows Pearl," said Bertie, with a consciousness of superiority on at least one point. Whereupon he again fulfilled the promises of youth, the leadings of his birth star and the

promptings of his spirit guides, and told all he
knew about the whole Watson family, not forgetting the roses he had taken to her, and Mrs.
Crocks' diagnosis of it all.

He had an interested listener to it all, and under
the inspiration which a sympathetic hearing gives
he grew eloquent, and touched with his fine fancy
the romantic part of it.

"Mrs. Crocks says she believes Pearl is pretty
sweet on the Doctor. Pearl is one swell girl, and
all that, but Mrs. Crocks says the Doctor will
likely marry the Senator's daughter. Gee! I
wouldn't if I was him. She hasn't got the style
that Pearl has—she rides a lot and has nerve—
and all that, but she's bow-legged!" His tone was
indescribably scornful.

Mr. Neelands gasped.

"Yep," went on Bertie complacently, "we see
a lot here at the stable and get to know a lot—
one way'n another—we can't help it. They come
and go, you know."

"The doctor won't run for Parliament — he
turned it down. Mrs. Crocks thinks the Senator
maybe persuaded him not to—the Senator is for
the Government, of course, and it is the other side
wanted the doctor; anyway, that suits old Steadman; he'll likely go in again on account of the
bridge at Purple Springs. Every one wants to
get work on it with the Spring hangin' back the
way it is."

"How about a horse? I want to take a drive
into the country," said Mr. Neelands.

"No horse can go out of here today," answered

Bertie. "Mr. Crocks says there'll be a storm, an he won't take no chances on his horses. He says people can judge for themselves and run risks if they want to, he'll decide for the horses—and they can't go."

"O, all right," said Mr. Neelands. "How far is it to the Watson farm?"

"Are you going out?" asked Bertie. "Better phone and see if she's at home. Here's the phone— I'll get her."

Mr. Neelands laid a restraining hand on Bertie's arm. "Easy there, my friend," he said, his tone resembling Miss Morrison's in its commanding chilliness, "How far is it to the Watson farm?"

"Five miles in summer, four in winter," Bertie answered a little sulkily.

"You would call this winter, I suppose," said the traveller, looking out at the darkening street.

"I'd call it—oh, well, never mind what I'd call it—I'm always talking too much—call it anything you like." Bertie grew dignified and reserved. "Call it the first of July if you like! I don't care."

That is how it came that Mr. Neelands took the out-trail when all the signs were against travelling, but to his unaccustomed eye there was nothing to fear in the woolly grayness of the sky, nor in the occasional snowflake that came riding on the wind. The roads were hard-packed and swept clean by the wind, and the sensation of space and freedom most enjoyable.

Mr. Neelands as he walked filed away tidily in his mind the information received. There were

valuable clues contained in the stable-boy's chatter,
which he would tabulate, regarding the lady of his
quest. She was popular, approachable, gifted with
a sense of humor, and perhaps disappointed in love.
No clue was too small to be overlooked—and so,
feeling himself one of the most deadly of sleuths,
Mr. Neelands walked joyously on, while behind
him there gathered one of the worst blizzards that
the Souris Valley had known.

The storm began with great blobbery flakes of
snow, which came elbowing each other down the
wind, crossing and re-crossing, circling, drifting,
whirling, fluttering, so dense and thick that the
whole air darkened ominously, and the sun seemed
to withdraw from the world, leaving the wind and
the storm to their own evil ways.

The wind at once began its circling motions,
whipping the snow into the traveller's face, blinding and choking him, lashing him mercilessly and
with a sudden impish delight, as if all the evil
spirits of the air had declared war upon him.

He turned to look back, but the storm had closed
behind him, having come down from the north-
west and overtaken him as he walked. His only
hope was to go with it, for to face it was impossible,
and yet it seemed to have no direction, for it blew
up in his face; it fell on him; it slapped him, jostled
him, pushed him, roared in his ears, smothering
him, drowning his cries with malicious joy. No
cat ever worried or harrassed a mouse with greater
glee than the storm fiends that frolicked through
the valley that day, took their revenge on the city

man, with his pointed boots, his silk-lined gloves, his belted coat and gray fedora, as he struggled on, slipping, choking, falling and rising. It seemed to him like a terrible nightmare, in its sudden, gripping fury.

It pounded on his eyeballs until he was not sure but his eyes were gone; it filled his mouth and ears, and cold water trickled down his back. His gloves were wet through, and freezing, for the air grew colder every minute, and the terror of the drowning man came to him. He struggled on madly, like a steer that feels the muskeg closing around him. He did not think; he fought, with the same instinct that drives the cattle blindly, madly on towards shelter and food, when the storm lashes them and the hunger rage drives them on.

Sylvester Paine, shaking the snow from his clothes like a water spaniel, and stamping all over the kitchen, was followed by his wife, who vainly tried to sweep it up as fast as it fell. She made no remonstrance, but merely swept, having long since learned that her liege lord was never turned aside from his purpose by any word of hers.

When he was quite done, and the snow was melting in pools on the floor, he delivered his opinion of the country and the weather: "This is sure a hell of a country," he said, "that can throw a storm like this at the end of March."

She made no reply—she had not made either the country or the weather, and would not take responsibility for them. She went on wiping up the water from the floor, with rebellion, slumbering, hidden rebellion in every movement, and the look in her eyes when she turned to the window, was a strange blending of rage and fear.

"Why don't you answer me," he said, turning around quickly, "Darn you, why can't you speak when you're spoken to?"

"You did not speak to me," she said. "There was nothing for me to say."

He looked at her for a moment—her silence exasperated him. She seemed to be keeping something back—something sinister and unknown.

"Well, I can tell you one thing," he went on, in a voice that seemed to be made of iron filings, "you may not answer when I speak to you—you'll do what you're told. I'm not going to slave my life out on this farm when there's easier money to be made. Why should you set yourself above me, and say you won't go into a hotel? I have the right to decide, anyway. Better people than you have kept hotels, for all your airs. Are you any better than I am?"

"I hope so," she said, without raising her eyes from the floor. She rose quietly and washed out her floorcloth, and stood drying her hands on the roller towel which hung on the kitchen door. There was an air of composure about her that enraged him. He could not make it out. The quality which made the women call her proud kindled his anger now.

The storm tore past the house, shaking it in

its grip like a terrier shaking a rat. It seemed to
mock at their trivial disputes, and seek to settle
them by drowning the sound of them.

His voice rang above the storm:—

"I'll sell the farm," he shouted. "I'll sell every
cow and horse on it. I'll sell the bed from under
you—I'll break you and your stuck-up ways, and
you'll not get a cent of money from me—not if
your tongue was hanging out."

The children shrank into corners and pitifully
tried to efface themselves. The dog, with drooping
tail, sought shelter under the table.

Sylvester Paine thought he saw a shrinking in
her face, and followed up his advantage with a
fresh outpouring of abuse.

"There's no one to help you—or be sorry for
you—you haven't a friend in this neighborhood,
with your stuck-up way. The women are sore on
you—none of them ever come to see you or even
phone you. Don't you think I see it! You've no
one to turn to, so you might as well know it—
I've got you!"

His last words were almost screamed at her, as
he strove to make his voice sound above the storm,
and in a sudden lull of the storm, they rang through
the house.

At the same moment there was a sound of something falling against the door and the dog, with
bristling hair, ran out from his place of shelter.

Mrs. Paine turned quickly to the door and opened
it, letting in a gust of blinding snow, which eddied
in the room and melted on the hot stove.

A man, covered with snow, lay where he had fallen, exhausted on the doorstep.

"What's this," cried Paine, in a loud voice, as he ran forward; "where did this fellow come from?"

In his excitement he asked it over and over again, as if Mrs. Paine should know. She ventured no opinion, but busied herself in getting the snow from the clothes of her visitor and placing him in the rocking chair beside the fire. He soon recovered the power of speech, and thanked her gaspingly, but with deep sincerity.

"This is a deuce of a day for any one to be out," began the man of the house. "Any fool could have told it was going to storm; what drove you out? Where did you come from, anyway?"

Mrs. Paine looked appealingly at him:—

"Let him get his breath, can't you, see, he is all in," she said quietly, "he'll tell you, when he can speak."

In a couple of hours, Peter Neelands, draped in a gray blanket, sat beside the fire, while his clothes were being dried, and rejoiced over the fact that he was alive. The near tragedy of the bright young lawyer found dead in the snow still thrilled him. It had been a close squeak, he told himself, and a drowsy sense of physical well-being made him almost unconscious of his surroundings. It was enough for him to be alive and warm.

Mrs. Paine moved about the house quietly, and did all she could with her crude means to make her guest comfortable, and to assure him of her hospitality. She pressed his clothes into shape again, and gave him a well-cooked dinner, as well served as her scanty supplies would allow, asking no questions, but with a quiet dignity making him feel that she was glad to serve him. There was something in her manner which made a strong appeal to the chivalrous heart of the young man. He wanted to help her—do something for her—make things easier for her.

The afternoon wore on, with no loosening of the grip of the storm, and Peter began to realize that he was a prisoner. He could have been quite happy with Mrs. Paine and the children, even though the floor of the kitchen was draughty and cold, the walls smoked, the place desolate and poor; but the presence of his host, with his insulting manners, soon grew unbearable. Mr. Paine sat in front of the stove, smoking and spitting, abusing the country, the weather, the Government, the church. Nothing escaped him, and everything was wrong.

A certain form of conceit shone through his words too, which increased his listener's contempt. He had made many sharp deals in his time, of which he was inordinately proud. Now he gloated over them. Fifteen thousand dollars of horse notes were safely discounted in the bank, so he did not care, he said, whether spring came or not. He had his money. The bank could collect the notes.

Peter looked at him to see if he were joking. Surely no man with so much money would live so poorly and have his wife and children so shabbily dressed. Something of this must have shown in his face

"I've made money," cried Sylvester Paine, spitting at the leg of the stove; "and I've kept it—or spent it, just as I saw fit, and I did not waste it on a fancy house. What's a house, anyway, but a place to eat and sleep. I ain't goin' to put notions into my woman's head, with any big house—she knows better than to ask it now. If she don't like the house—the door is open—let her get out—I say. She can't take the kids—and she won't go far without them."

He laughed unpleasantly: "That's the way to have them, and by gosh! there's one place I admired the old Premier—in the way he roasted those freaks of women who came askin' for the vote. I don't think much of the Government, but I'm with them on that—in keepin' the women where they belong."

"But why," interrupted Peter, with a very uneasy mind, "why shouldn't women have something to say?"

"Are you married?" demanded his host.

"No, not yet," said Peter blushing.

"Well, when you're married—will you let your wife decide where you will live? How you earn your living—and all that? No sir, I'll bet you won't—you'll be boss, won't you? I guess so. Well, every man has that right, absolutely. Here am I—I'm goin' to sell out here and buy a hotel—there's good money in it, easy livin'. She—" there was an unutterable scorn in his voice, "says she won't go—says it ain't right to sell liquor. I say she'll come with me or get out. She might be able

to earn her own livin', but she can't take the kids.
Accordin' to law, children belong to the father—
ain't that right? There's a man comin' to buy
the farm—I guess he would have been out today,
only for the storm. We have the bargain made—
all but the signin' up.

Mrs. Paine stood still in the middle of the floor,
and listened in terror. "A man coming to buy
the farm!" Every trace of color left her face!
Maybe it was not true.

He saw the terror in her face, and followed up his
advantage.

"People have to learn to do as they're told when
I'm round. No one can defy me—I'll tell you that.
Every one knows me—I can be led, but I can't
be driven."

Peter Neelands had the most uncomfortable
feeling he had ever known. He was not sure whether
it was his utter aversion to the man who sat in
front of the stove, boasting of his sharp dealing, or
a physical illness which affected him, but a horrible
nausea came over him. His head swam—his ear-
drums seemed like to burst—every bone began to
ache.

The three days that followed were like a nightmare, which even time could never efface or rob
of its horror. The fight with the storm had proven
such a shock to him that for three days a burning
fever, alternating with chills, held him in its clutches,
and even when the storm subsided kept him a prisoner sorely against his will.

In these three days, at close range, he saw some-

thing of a phase of life he had never even guessed
at. He did not know that human beings could
live in such crude conditions, without comforts,
without even necessities. It was like a bad
dream—confused, humiliating, horrible—and when
on the third day he was able to get into his
clothes his one desire was to get away—and yet,
to leave his kind hostess who had so gently nursed
him and cared for him, seemed like an act of
desertion.

However, when he was on his feet, though feeling
much shaken, and still a bit weak, his courage
came back. Something surely could be done to
relieve conditions like this.

The snow was piled fantastically in huge mounds
over the fields, and the railway cuts would be
drifted full, so no train would run for days. But
Peter felt that he could walk the distance back
to town.

His host made no objection, and no offer to drive
him.

In the tiny bedroom off the kitchen, which Mrs.
Paine had given him, as he shiveringly made his
preparations for leaving, he heard a strange voice
in the other room, a girl's voice, cheery, pleasant.

"I just came in to see how you are, Mrs. Paine.
No thank you, I won't put the team in the stable—
I ran them into the shed. I am on my way home from
driving the children to school. Some storm, wasn't
it? The snow is ribbed like a washboard, but it is
hard enough to carry the horses."

Peter came out, with his coat and his hat in his

hand, and was introduced. His first thought was
one of extreme mortification—three days' beard
was on his face. His toilet activities had been
limited in number. He knew he felt wretched,
seedy, groggy—and looked it. Something in Pearl's
manner re-assured him.

"Going to town?" said she kindly, "rather too
far for you to walk when you are feeling tough.
Come home with me if you are not in a hurry, and
I will drive you in this afternoon."

Peter accepted gladly.

He hardly looked at her, holding to some faint
hope that if he did not look at her she would not
be able to see him either, and at this moment
Peter's one desire was not to be seen, at least by
this girl.

In a man's coonskin coat she stood at the door,
with her face rosy with the cold. She brought an
element of hope and youth, a new spirit of adventure into the drab room, with its sodden, common-
place dreariness. Peter's spirits began to rise.

Outside the dogs began to bark, and a cutter
went quickly past the window.

Mrs. Paine, looking out, gave a cry of alarm.

"Wait, Pearl! Oh, don't go!" she cried, "stay
with me. It's the man who is going to buy the
farm. He said he was coming, but I didn't believe
him;" her hands were locking and unlocking.

Without a word, Pearl slipped off her coat and
waited. She seemed to know the whole situation,
and instinctively Peter began to feel easier. There
was something about this handsome girl, with the

firmly-set and dimpled chin, which gave him confidence.

In a few moments Sylvester Paine and his caller
came in from the barn. Pearl stood beside Mrs.
Paine, protectingly. Her face had grown serious;
she knew the fight was on.

Sylvester Paine nodded to her curtly, and introduced his guest to every one at once.

"This is Mr. Gilchrist," he said, "and now we'll
get to business. Get the deeds." he said, to his
wife shortly.

Mrs. Paine went upstairs.

"Who did you say the young lady is?" asked Mr.
Gilchrist, who thought he recognized Pearl, but
not expecting to see her here, wished to be sure.
Mr. Gilchrist, as President of the Political Association, had heard about Pearl, and hoped she might
be an able ally in the coming election.

"This is Pearl Watson," said Mr. Paine, rather
grudgingly. "This is the girl that's working up
the women to thinking that they ought to vote.
Her father and mother are good neighbors of mine,
and Pearl was a nice kid, too, until she went to
the city and got a lot of fool notions."

"I'm a nice kid yet," said Pearl, smiling at him,
and compelling him to meet her eye, "and I am a
good neighbor of yours too, Mr. Paine, for I am
going to do something for you today that no one
has ever done. I'm going to tell you something."

She walked over to the table and motioned to
the two men to sit down, though she remained
standing. Sylvester Paine stared at her uncom-

prehendingly. The girl's composure was discon-
certing. Her voice had a vibrant passion in it
that made Peter's heart begin to beat. It was like
watching a play that approaches its climax.

"Mr. Gilchrist probably does not understand
that there is a small tragedy going on here today.
Maybe he does not know the part he is playing
in it. It is often so in life, that people do not know
the part they played until it is too late to change.
You've come here today to buy the farm."

Mr. Gilchrist nodded.

"Ten years ago this farm was idle land. Mr. and
Mrs. Paine homesteaded it, and have made it one
of the best in the country. It has been hard work,
but they have succeeded. For the last five years
Mr. Paine has not been much at home—he has
bought cattle and horses and shipped them to the
city, and has done very well, and now has nearly
fifteen thousand dollars in the bank. There is
no cleverer man in the country than Mr. Paine
in making a bargain, and he is considered one of
the best horsemen in the Province. He pays his
debts, keeps his word, and there is no better neighbor in this district."

Sylvester Paine watched her open-mouthed—
amazed. How did she know all this? It made
strange music in his ears, for, in spite of all his
bluster, he hungered for praise; for applause. Pearl's
words fell like a shower on a thirsty field.

"Meanwhile," Pearl went on, "Mrs. Paine runs
the farm, and makes it pay, too. Although Mrs.
Paine works the hardest of the two, Mr. Paine

handles all the money, and everything is in his name. He has not noticed just how old and worn her clothes are. Being away so much, the manner of living does not mean so much to him as to her, for she is always here. Mrs. Paine is not the sort of woman who talks. She never complains to the other women, and they call her proud. I think Mrs. Paine has been to blame in not telling Mr. Paine just how badly she needs new clothes. He always looks very well himself, and I am sure he would like to see her well dressed, and the children too. But she will not ask him for money, and just grubs along on what she can get with the butter money. She is too proud to go out poorly dressed, and so does not leave home for months at a time, and of course, that's bad for her spirits, and Mr. Paine gets many a cross look from her when he comes home. It makes him very angry when she will not speak—he does not understand."

"Mr. Paine's intention now is to sell the farm and buy the hotel in Millford. He will still go on buying cattle, and his wife will run the hotel. She does not want to do this. She says she will not do it—it is not a proper place in which to raise her children. She hates the liquor business. This is her home, for which she has worked."

"It is not much of a home; it's cold in winter and hot in summer. You would never think a man with fifteen thousand dollars in the bank would let his wife and children live like this, without even the common decencies of life. That's why Mrs. Paine has never had any of her own people

come to visit her, she is ashamed for them to see
how badly off she is. No, it is not much of a home,
but she clings to it. It is strange how women and
animals cling to their homes. You remember
the old home on the road to Hampton your people
had, Mr. Gilchrist, the fine old house with the
white veranda and the big red barn? It was the
best house on the road. It burned afterwards—
about three years ago."

Mr. Gilchrist nodded.

"Well, we bought, when we came to our farm
here, one of your father's horses, the old Polly
mare—do you remember Polly?"

"I broke her in," he said, "when she was three."

"Well, Polly had been away a long time from
her old home, but last summer when we drove
to Hampton, Polly turned in to the old place and
went straight to the place where the stable had
stood. There was nothing there—even the ruins
are overgrown with lamb's quarters—but Polly
went straight to the spot. It had been home to
her."

A silence fell on the room.

"There is no law to protect Mrs. Paine," Pearl
went on, after a long pause. "The law is on your
side, Mr. Gilchrist. If you want the place there
is no law to save Mrs. Paine. Mr. Paine is quite
right in saying he can take the children, so she
will have to follow. Mrs. Paine is not the sort of
woman to desert her children. She would live
even in a hotel rather than desert her children.
The law is on your side, gentlemen—you have the

legal right to go on with the transaction."

"What law is this?" said Mr. Gilchrist.

"The law of this Province," said Pearl.

"Do you mean to say," said Mr. Gilchrist hotly, "that Mrs. Paine cannot claim any part of the price of this farm as her own—or does not need to sign the agreement of sale, has she no claim at all?"

"She has none," said Pearl, "she has no more claim on this farm than the dog has!"

"By Gosh! I never knew that," he cried. "We'll see a lawyer in town before we do anything. That's news to me."

"Are you sure of it, Pearl?" Mrs. Paine whispered. "Maybe there's something I can do. This young man is a lawyer—maybe he could tell us."

Sylvester Paine was trying to recover his point of view.

"Can you tell us," Pearl asked Peter, who sat in a corner. intensely listening, "what the law says?"

"The law," said Peter miserably—as one who hates the word he is about to utter— "gives a married woman no rights. She has no claim on her home, nor on her children. A man can sell or will away his property from his wife. A man can will away his unborn child—and it's a hell of a law," he added fiercely.

Pearl turned to Robert Gilchrist, saying, "Mr. Gilchrist, the law is with you. The woman and the three children have no protection. Mr. Paine is willing that they should be turned out. It is up to you."

Mrs. Paine, who had come down the stairs with the deed in her hand, laid it on the table and waited. For some time no one spoke.

Sylvester Paine looked at the floor. He was a heavy-set man, with a huge head, bare-faced and rather a high forehead. He did not seem to be able to lift his eyes.

"I suppose," continued Pearl, "the people who made the laws did not think it would ever come to a show-down like this. They thought that when a man promised to love and cherish a woman— he would look after her and make her happy, and see to it that she had clothes to wear and a decent way of living—if he could. Of course, there are plenty of men who would gladly give their wives everything in life, but they can't, poor fellows— for they are poor; but Mr. Paine is one of the best off men in the district. He could have a beautiful home if he liked, and his wife could be the hand- somest woman in the neighborhood. She is the sort of woman who would show off good clothes too. I suppose her love of pretty things has made her all the sorer, because she has not had them. I just wanted to tell you, Mr. Gilchrist, before you closed the deal. Mrs. Paine would never tell you, and naturally enough Mr. Paine wouldn't. In fact he does not know just how things stand. But I feel that you should know just what you are doing if you take this farm. Of course, it is hardly fair to expect you to protect this woman's home and her children, and save her from being turned out, if her husband won't—you are under no obli-

gation to protect her. She made her choice years
ago—with her eyes open—when she married Sylvester Paine. It seems . . . she guessed wrong
. . . and now . . . she must pay!"

Mrs. Paine sank into a chair with a sob that
seemed to tear her heart out. The auburn hair
fell across her face, her lovely curly hair, from
which in her excitement she had pulled the pins.
It lay on the table in ringlets of gold, which seemed
to writhe, as if they too were suffering. Her breath
came sobbing, like a dog's dream.

Sylvester Paine was the first to speak.

"Pearl, you're wrong in one place," he said,
"just one—you had everything else straight. But
you were wrong in one place."

He went around the table and laid his hand on
his wife's head.

"Millie," he said, gently.

She looked up at him tearfully.

"Millie!"

He stood awkwardly beside her, struggling to
control himself. All the swagger had gone from
him, all the bluster. When he spoke his voice was
husky.

"Pearl has got it all straight, except in one place."
he said. "She's wrong in one place. She says you
guessed wrong when you married me, Millie."

His voice was thick, and the words came with
difficulty.

"Pearl has done fine, and sized the case up well
. . . but she's wrong there. It looks bad just
now, Millie—but you didn't make such a rotten

guess, after all. I'm not just sayin' what I'll do
but—"

"The deal is off, Bob," he said to Mr. Gilchrist,
"until Mrs. Paine and I talk things over."

And then Pearl quietly slipped into her coat
and, motioning to Peter, who gladly followed her,
went out.

CHAPTER XIV

THE big storm had demoralized the long-distance telephone service, so, that it was by night letter-gram that George Steadman was commissioned by the official organizer of the Government to find P. J. Neelands, who had not been heard of since the morning of the storm. Mr. Steadman was somewhat at a loss to know how to proceed.

He was very sorry about Mr. Neelands and his reported disappearance. Mr. Neelands was one of the friendliest and most approachable of the young political set, and Mr. Steadman had often listened to his speeches, and always with apprecia-tion. He wondered why Mr. Neelands had come to Millford now without telling him.

At the hotel, nothing was known of the young, man, only that he had taken a room, registered, slept one night, and gone, leaving all his things. Mr. Steadman was conducted to Number 17, and shown the meagre details of the young man's brief stay. His toilet articles, of sterling silver with his monogram, lay on the turkish towel, which at once concealed and protected the elm top of the bureau; his two bags, open and partly unpacked, took up most of the floor space in the room. His dressing-gown was hung on one of the two hooks on the back of the door, suspended by one shoulder, which gave it a weary, drunken

look.   There   was   something   melancholy   and
tragic about it all.

"In the midst of life we are in death," said George
Steadman   to   himself   piously,   and   shuddered.   "It
looks bad. Poor young fellow—cut off in his prime—
he did not even have a fur coat, and went out
never thinking."

He examined the telegram again— "On business
for the Government, it said, "of a private nature.
See 'Evening Echo' March 21st, Page 23." What
could that mean?

George   Steadman   did   not   take   the   "Evening
Echo." He hated the very sight of it. The "Morning Sun" was good enough for him. He remembered
the thrill of pride he had felt when his Chief had
said one day in debate, that he wanted nothing
better than the "Sun" and the Bible.   It was an
able utterance, he thought, reminding one of the
good old Queen's reply to the Ethiopian Prince,
and should have made its appeal even to the Opposition; but the leader had said, in commenting
on it, that he was glad to know his honorable friend
was broad-minded enough to read both sides!

And now he was told to look up the Opposition
paper, and the very page was given. His first thought
was that it was a personal attack upon himself.
But how could that be?   He never opened his
mouth in the house—he never even expressed an
opinion, and as the campaign had not yet begun—
he had not done anything.

He read the telegram again.   In desperation he
went back to the long distance booth, but found

the line still out of order, and a wire had come giving the details of the damage done by the storm. It would be several days before communication could be established. There was no help coming from headquarters, and from the wording of the telegram there seemed to be a reason for their not giving clear details. He must get a copy of the paper.

Reluctantly he went to the printing office and made known his errand. Mr. Driggs was delighted to give him the paper—he had it some place, though he very seldom opened any of his exchanges. He evidently bore Mr. Steadman no ill-will for his plain talk two weeks ago. With some difficulty he found it, with its wrapper still intact. It was a loose wrapper, which slipped off and on easily. Mr. Steadman remarked carelessly that there was an editorial in it to which his attention had been drawn, on hearing which Mr. Driggs turned his head and winked at an imaginary accomplice.

Mr. Steadman went over to the livery stable to find a quiet, clover-scented corner in which he might peruse his paper. An intuitive feeling cautioned him to be alone when he read it.

In the office, Mr. Steadman found a chair, and opened his paper. Bertie, ever on the alert for human interest stories, watched from a point of vantage. He told Mrs. Crocks afterwards about it.

"The paper seemed to tangle up at first and stick to his fingers. He wrastled it round and round and blew on it, and turned over pages and folded it back—Gee, there was a lot of it. It filled the

whole table, and pieces dropped on the floor. He
put his foot on them, like as if he was afraid they'd
get away. At last he found something, and he
just snorted—I got as close as I could, but I couldn't
see what it was. There was a picture of a girl—
and he read on and on, and snorted out three times,
and the sweat stood out on his face. Twice he
cleared up his throat like your clock does when it
gets ready to strike, and then he tore out a page
of the paper and put it in his pocket, and he gathered up the rest of it and burned it, all but one
sheet that was under the table, and I got it here."

Bertie brought home the news at six o'clock.
Mrs. Crocks had a copy of the paper in her hands
at six-fifteen.

Meanwhile, George Steadman, was feeling the
need of counsel. His head swam, and a cruel sense of
injustice ate into his heart. He was a quiet man—
he did not deserve this. All his life he had side-
stepped trouble—and here it was staring him in
the face. In desperation he went to Driggs, the
editor. He was a shrewd fellow—he would know
what was best to be done.

He found Mr. Driggs still in a sympathetic
mood. He threw back his long black hair and read
the article, with many exclamations of surprise.
In places he smiled—once he laughed.

"How can any one answer this, Driggs?" asked
Mr. Steadman in alarm. "What can be done about
it? I wish you would write something about it.
I can't think who would do this. There were no
strangers that day at the school—not that I noticed.

None of our people would do it. What do you think about it, Driggs? Would the girl write it herself?"

"No," replied the editor honestly, "I am quite sure Pearl did not do this."

Suddenly Mr. Steadman thought of the telegram and the missing man. He resolved to take Driggs into his confidence.

Driggs was as quick to see the import of it as King James was to smell gunpowder on that fateful November day when the warning letter was read in Parliament.

"The Government have sent him out to investigate this in your behalf," he said.

"But where is he?" asked Mr. Steadman.

Mr. Driggs' bushy brows drew down over his eyes.

"There's one person can help us," he said. He threw on his jute-colored waterproof and his faded felt hat. Mr. Steadman followed him as he went quickly to the Horse Repository.

Bertie was hastily consulted, and Bertie as usual ran true.

"Sure I saw him," said Bertie. "Ain't he back yet? Gee! I'll bet he's froze! He'll be dead by now for sure. He had on awful nice clothes, but thin toes on his boots, sharp as needles, and gray socks with dots on them, and a waist on his coat like as if he wore corsets, and gray gloves—and a cane, Swell! He was some fine looker, you bet, but he wouldn't last long in that storm."

"Where did he go, Bertie?" asked Mr. Steadman,

trying to hold his voice to a tone of unconcern.

"He asked about teachers, and about how far it was to Watson's."

Mr. Driggs and Mr. Steadman's eyes met.

"If he's any place," said Bertie cheerfully, "he'll be there."

To the Watson's Mr. Steadman and Mr. Driggs determined to go, although, by this time the evening was well advanced.

The storm had piled the snow into huge drifts which completely filled the railway cuts, but fortunately for those who travelled the sleigh roads, the snow was packed so hard that horses could walk safely over it. Bridges over ravines were completely covered, people made tunnels to the doors of their stables, and in some cases had to dig the snow away from their windows to let the light in. But the sun had come out warm, and the weather prophets said it was the last storm of the season.

When Mr. Steadman and Mr. Driggs approached the Watson home, they found every window lighted and several sleighs in the yard. From the house came sounds of laughter and many voices.

"There is no funeral here," said Mr. Driggs lightly.

George Steadman shuddered, "he may never have reached here," he said in a voice of awe.

They knocked at the woodshed door, but no one heard them. Then they went quietly in, and finding the kitchen door open, went in.

Mr. Watson, who stood at the door of the "room," shook hands with them quietly, and said in a whisper:—

"They're acting tableaux now, just step up to the door and see them. The children are having a party. Pearl will explain it in a minute. Just step in and watch; you're just in time—they're just goin' to do King Canute."

The two men looked in. About a dozen young people were in the room, which was well lighted by a gasoline hanging-lamp. The furniture was pushed into a corner to leave a good floor space. A curtain was suspended from one of the beams, and behind it there seemed to be great activity and whispered directions. Every one was so intently waiting, they did not notice that the audience had been augmented by the two men at the door.

In front of the curtain came Pearl to announce the next tableaux:—

Ladies and gentlemen," she said solemnly, although her audience began to laugh expectantly, "we will now present to you a historical tableaux, a living picture of a foolish old king, who thought he could command the waves to stand still. Seated in his arm-chair on the shore you will see King Canute. Behind him are the rugged hills of the Saxon coast. Before him the sea tosses angrily. The tide is rolling in. Each wave is a little bigger than the last, the seventh wave being the largest of all. This tableaux, ladies and gentlemen, in the production of which we have spared no trouble and expense, teaches the vanity of human greatness. Careful attention has been given to detail, as you will observe."

She disappeared behind the curtain for a moment, and when it was pulled back by invisible hands—(broom wire handled by Mary) she was discovered sitting robed in purple (one of the girls had brought her mother's Japanese dressing-gown) with a home-made but very effective crown on her head. Her throne was an arm-chair, raised on blocks of wood. As King Canute, Pearl's eyes were eagle-like and keen, her whole bearing full of arrogance and pride. Dramatically she waved her right arm towards the sea, and in bitter words chided it for its restless tossing, and commanded it to hear the words of the ALL HIGH, Great and Powerful King, and stay—just—where—it—was!

But even as she spoke, a small wave came rolling in, gently lapping the shore. It was Danny Watson, with a small white apron tied around his person, which at each revolution, made a white crest of breaking foam.

The King re-doubled his imprecations, and commands, tearing his hair and threatening to rend his garments, but wave after wave came rythmically to shore, growing in size and speed, until the seventh wave, crested with foam—a pillow-case torn across and fastened with safety-pins—came crashing to her feet, amid thunderous applause.

When the company, with the king at one end and the first and smallest wave at the other, stood up to take their applause, and respond to curtain calls, next to Pearl stood the seventh wave—crested with foam, dishevelled of hair—a four days' growth of whiskers on his face—but a happy-looking wave —nevertheless.

Mr. Steadman grabbed hold of his friend hysterically. He could not speak.

"Well, thank God, he's not dead anyway," he gasped at last.

"But I fancy," murmured Mr. Driggs, "that he is dead—to the cause!"

"Make a speech, Pearl," cried one of the company. "Mr. Neelands would like to hear you do that one of the Premier's, when he laid the cornerstone, about 'the generations yet unborn.' Go on, Pearl, that's a good one!"

"Don't forget 'the waves of emigration breaking at our feet'!" said Mary, handing Pearl one of Teddy's coats.

Pearl slipped on the coat, carefully adjusting the collar. Then fingering an imaginary watch-chain, she began. Her face grew grave—her neck seemed to thicken. Her voice was a throaty contralto.

"We are gathered here to-day." she declaimed, "to take part in a ceremonial, whose import we cannot even remotely guess! Whose full significance will be revealed, not in your time or mine, but to the generations yet unborn!"

Peter Neelands gave a shout of recognition! Mr. Driggs felt a strong hand on his arm. George Steadman whispered hoarsely. Come away, Driggs. That girl frightens me. This is no place for us!"

CHAPTER XV

THE Spring was late, cruelly late, so late indeed that if it had been anything else but a season, it would have found itself in serious trouble—with the door locked and a note pinned on the outside telling it if it could not come in time it need not come at all. But the Spring has to be taken in, whenever it comes —and be forgiven too, and even if there were no note on the door, there were other intimations of like effect, which no intelligent young Spring could fail to understand. Dead cattle lay on the river bank, looking sightlessly up to the sky. They had waited, and waited, and hung on to life just as long as they could, but they had to give in at last.

Spring came at last, brimful of excitement and apologies. It was a full-hearted, impulsive and repentant young Spring, and lavished all its gifts with a prodigal hand; its breezes were as coaxing as June; its head burned like the first of July; its sunshine was as rich and mellow as the sunshine of August. Spring had acknowledged its debt and the overdue interest, and hoped to prevent any unpleasantness by paying all arrears and a lump sum in advance; and doing it all with such a flourish of good fellowship that the memory of its past delinquency would be entirely swept away!

The old Earth, frozen-hearted and bleached by wind and cold, and saddened by many a blighted hope, lay still and unresponsive under the coaxing breezes and the sunshine's many promises. The Earth knew what it knew, and if it were likely to forget, the red and white cattle on the hillside would remind it. The Earth knew that these same warm breezes had coaxed it into life many times before, and it had burst into bud and flowers and fruit, forgetting and forgiving the past with its cold and darkness, and the earth remembered that the flowers had withered and the fruit had fallen, and dark days had come when it had no pleasure in them, and so although the sun was shining and the warm winds blowing—the earth lay as unresponsive as the pulseless cattle on its cold flat breast.

But the sun poured down its heat, and the warm breezes frolicked into the out-of-the-way places, where old snowdrifts were hiding their black faces, and gradually their hard hearts broke and ran away in creeping streams, and the earth returned to the earth that gave it; a mist too, arose from the earth, and softened its bare outlines, and soon the first anemone pushed its furry nose through the mat of gray grass, and scored another victory on the robin; the white poplar blushed green at its roots; the willows at the edge of the river reddened higher and higher, as the sap mounted; beadings of mouse-ears soon began to show on their branches—a green, glow came over the prairie, and in the ponds, millions of frogs, at the signal from an unknown conductor, burst into song.

Then it was that the tired old Earth stopped thinking and began to feel—a thrill—a throb—a pulsing of new life—the stirring of new hopes which mocked its fears of cold or frost or sorrow or death.

The Souris Valley opened forgiving arms to the repentant young Spring, and put forth leaves in gayest fashion. The white bones, fantastically sticking through faded red hides, were charitably hidden by the grass, so that the awakened conscience of the tender young Spring might not be unduly reminded of its cruelty and neglect.

The woman who lived alone at Purple Springs always expected great things of the Spring. She could not grow accustomed to the coldness of her neighbors, or believe that they had really cut her off from any communication, and all through the winter which had just gone she had kept on telling herself that everything would be different in the Spring. Looking day after day into the white valley, piled high with snow, she had said to herself over and over again: "There shall be no more snow—there shall be no more snow"—until the words began to mock her and taunt her, and at last lost their meaning altogether like an elastic band that has stretched too far. If she had been as close a student of the Bible as her mother, back in Argylshire, she would have known that her impatience with the snow, which all winter long had threatened and menaced her, and peered at her with its thousand eyes, was just the same feeling that prompted John on the Isle of Patmos, wearied by the eternal breaking of the waves on his island prison, to set down as the first condition in the heavenly city: "There shall be no sea."

Three years before, Mrs. Gray had come to the
Souris Valley, and settled on the hill farm. It had
been owned by a prospector, who once in a while lived
on it, but went away for long periods, when it was
believed he had gone north into that great unknown
land of fabled riches. He had not been heard from
for several years, and the people of the neighborhood
had often wondered what would be done with the
quarter-section, which was one of the best in the
district, in case he never came back. The Cowans,
who lived nearest, had planted one of the fields,
and used the land for the last two seasons. The
Zink's had run their cattle in the pasture, and two
of the other neighbors were preparing to use the
remaining portions of the farm, when there arrived
Mrs. Gray and her seven-year-old son to take
possession.

It was Mr. Cowan who demanded to know by
what right she came, and when she had convinced him by showing him the deed of the farm, she
came back at him by demanding that he pay her
the rent for the acres he had used, which he did
with a bad grace.

She had not been long in the neighborhood when
there came to demonstrate a new sewing machine
a drooping-eyed, bewhiskered man, in a slim buggy,
drawn by a team of sorrel ponies. He claimed to
have known Mrs. Gray in that delightfully vague
spot known as "down East," and when he found
how eagerly any information regarding her was received, he grew eloquent.

Mrs. Cowan departed from her hard and fast

rule, and the rule of her mother before her, and asked him to stay for dinner, and being an honest man, in small matters at least, the agent did his best to pay for his victuals. He told her all he knew—and then some, prefacing and foot-noting his story with the saving clause "Now this may be only talk—but, anyway, it is what they said about her." He was not a malicious man—he bore the woman, who was a stranger to him, no grudge; but that day as he sat at dinner in the Cowan's big, bare kitchen, he sent out the words which made life hard for the woman at Purple Springs.

So much for the chivalry of the world and the kindly protection it extends to women.

Vague rumors were circulated about her, veiled, indefinite insinuations. The Ladies' Aid decided they would not ask her to join, at least not until they saw how things were going. She might be all right, but they said a church society must be careful.

The woman watched each other to see who would go to see her first. She came to church with her boy, to the little church on the river flat, and the minister shook hands with her and told her he was glad to see her. But the next week his wife, spending the afternoon at Mrs. Cowan's, "heard something," and the next Sunday, although he shook hands with her and began to say he was glad to see her, catching Mrs. Cowan's eye on him, he changed his sentence and said he was glad to see so many out.

All summer long the woman at Purple Springs

held to the hope that someone would come to see her. At first she could not believe they were wilfully slighting her. It was just their way, she thought. They were busy women; she often saw them out in their gardens, and at such times it was hard for her to keep from waving to them.

The woman who lived the nearest to her, geographically, was Mrs. Cowan, and one day—the first summer—she saw Mrs. Cowan beating rugs on the line, and as the day was breezy, it seemed as if she waved her apron. Mrs. Gray waved back, in an ecstacy of joy and expectation—but there came no response from her neighbor—no answering signal, and as the lonely woman watched, hoping, looking, praying—there rolled over her with crushing sadness the conviction that all her hopes of friendliness were in vain. The neighborhood would not receive her—she was an outcast. They were condemning her without a hearing—they were hurling against her the thunders of silence! The injustice of it ate deeply into her soul.

Then it was that she began to make the name "Purple Springs" out of the willow withes which grew below the house. She made the letters large, and with a flourish, and dyed them the most brilliant purple they would take, and set them on a wire foundation above her gate. The work of doing it gave solace to her heart, and when the words were set in place—it seemed to her that she had declared her independence, and besides, they reminded her of something very sweet and re-assuring —something which helped her to hold her head up against the current of ill thoughts her neighbors were directing toward her.

That was the year the school was built, and no other name for it but "Purple Springs" was even mentioned, and when the track was extended from Millford west, and a mahogany-red station built, with a tiny freight shed of the same color, the name of Purple Springs in white letters was put on each end of the station. So, although the neighbors would not receive the woman, they took the name she brought.

Her son Jim, a handsome lad of seven, went to school the first day it was opened. Her mother heart was fearful for the reception he might get, and yet she tried to tell herself that children were more just than their elders. They would surely be fair to Jim, and when she had him ready, with his leather book-bag, his neat blue serge knickerbocker suit, his white collar and well-polished boots, she thought, with a swelling of pride, that there would not be a handsomer child in the school, nor one that was better cared for.

Down the hill went Jim Gray, without a shadow on his young heart. So long as he had his mother, and his mother smiled at him, life was all sunshine.

He gave his name to the teacher, and answered all her questions readily, and was duly enrolled as a pupil in Grade I, along with Bennie Cowan, Edgar Zink and Bessie Brownlees, and set at work to make figures. He wondered what the teacher wanted with so many figures, but decided he would humor her, and made page after page of them for

her. By noon the teacher decided, on further
investigation, to put Master James Gray in Grade
II, and by four o'clock he was a member in good
standing of Grade III.

That night there was much talk of James Gray,
his good clothes, and his general proficiency, around
the firesides of the Purple Springs district.

The next day Bennie Cowan, who was left behind
in Grade I, although a year older than Jim Gray,
made the startling announcement:

"Jim Gray has no father."

He sang the words, gently intoning, as if he
took no responsibility of them any more than if
they were the words of a song, for Bennie was a
cautious child, and while he did not see that the
absence of a father was anything to worry over,
still, from the general context of the conversation
he had heard, he believed it was something of a
handicap.

The person concerned in his announcement,
being busy with a game of marbles, did not notice.
So quite emboldened, Bennie sang again, "Jim
Gray has no father—and never had one.

The marble game came to an end.

"Do you mean me asked Jim, with a puzzled
look.

The others stopped playing, too. It was a fear-
some moment. Jim Gray was the most unconcerned
of the group.

"That's all you know about it," he said carelessly,
as he shut one eye and took steady aim at the
"dib" in the ring, "I've had two."

"Nobody can have two fathers—on earth," said Bessie Brownlees piously—"we have one father on earth and one in heaven."

"Mine ain't on earth," said Jimmy, "mine are both in heaven."

That was a poser.

"I'll bet they're not," said Bennie, feeling emboldened by Jim's admission of a slight irregularity in his paternal arrangements.

"How do you know?" asked Jim, still puzzled. It did not occur to him that there was anything unfriendly in the conversation—"You never saw them!"

"Well," said Bennie, crowded now to play his highest card, "anyway, your mother is a bad woman.'

Jim looked at him in blank astonishment. His mother a bad woman, his dear mother! The whole world turned suddenly red to Jim Gray—he did not need any one to tell him that the time had come to fight.

The cries of Bennie Cowan brought the teacher flying. Bennie, with bleeding lip and blackened eyes, was rescued, and a tribunal sat forthwith on the case.

James Gray refused to tell what Bennie Cowan had said. His tongue could not form the words of blasphemy. The other children, all of whom had heard his history unfavorably discussed at home, did not help him, and the case went against the boy who had no friends. Exaggerated tales were told of his violence. By the end of the week he had struck Bennie Cowan with a knife. A few days later it was told that he had kicked the teacher. Nervous mothers were afraid to have their children exposed to the danger of playing with such a vicious child.

One day a note was given to him to take home. It was from the trustees, asking Mrs. Gray if she would kindly keep her son James at home, for his ungovernable temper made it unsafe for other children to play with him.

That was three years ago. Annie Gray and her son were as much a mystery as ever. She looked well, dressed well, rode astride, wore bloomers, and used a rifle, and seemed able to live without either the consent or good-will of the neighborhood.

In harvest time she still further outraged public opinion by keeping a hired man, who, being a virtuous man, who had respect for public opinion, even if she hadn't, claimed fifteen dollars a month extra for a sort of moral insurance against loss of reputation. She paid the money so cheerfully that the virtuous man was sorry he had not made it twenty!

It was to this district, with its under-current of human passions, mystery and misunderstanding, that Pearl Watson came. The miracle of Spring was going on—bare trees budding, dead flowers springing; the river which had been a prisoner all winter, running brimming full, its ice all gone, and only little white cakes of foam riding on its current. Over all was the pervading Spring smell of fresh earth, and the distant smoulder of prairie fires.

CHAPTER XVI

PRINCE OF THE HOUSE OF CLAY

WHEN the train came in from the west, Dr. Clay stepped off and walked quickly to his office. He called at the drug store before going to his private office, and inquired of the clerk:

"Any one wanting me, Tommy?"

"Sure—two or three—but nothing serious. Bill Snedden wanted you to come out and see his horse."

"See his horse!" exclaimed the doctor in surprise.

"Yes, Democracy hasn't been feeling well. Just sort of mopin' around the stall. Not sick—just out of sorts, you know, down-hearted like."

"Well, why doesn't he get Dr. Moody? Horses are not my line."

"O but he says this is different. Democracy is more like a human being than a horse, and Dr. Moody don't know much about a horse's higher nature. He says he's scared to have Dr. Moody come out anyway—every time he comes, a horse dies, and he's gettin' superstitious about it. T'aint that he has anything against Dr. Moody. He spoke well of him and said he was nice to have around in time of trouble, he's so sympathetic and all that, but he don't want to take any chances with Democracy. He would have liked awful well to see you, doctor. I told him you'd be home tonight, and he'll give you a ring. No, there was nothing serious. There was a young fellow here from the city came out to see Pearl Watson, they said, about some set of books or something. He got lost in the storm, and frozen pretty badly. He's out at Watsons yet, I think. But they didn't phone, or anything —at least, I didn't get it. I just heard about it."

"All right, Tommy," said the doctor, and went on.

In his own apartment he found everything in order. Telephone messages were laid beside his mail. His slippers and house-coat were laid out. The coal fire gleamed its welcome.

The doctor's heart was lighter than it had been. His interview with the old doctor had been very encouraging.

"You are looking better, Clay," the old man had said. "Have you gained in weight? I thought so. You are going a little easier, and sleeping out— that's right. And you see you can save yourself in lots of ways—don't you? Good! I'm pleased with you. I hear they are after you to run against the Government. You won't touch it, of course. No good for a man in your condition. Anyway, a doctor has his own work—and if you keep your head down, and get away every winter, you'll live to be an old man yet."

The doctor sat down to read his mail. There were the usual letters from old patients, prospective patients, people who had wonderful remedies and had been cruelly snubbed by the medical profession. He glanced through them casually, but with an absent-mindedness which did not escape his housekeeper when she came in.

Mrs. Burns was determined to tell him some-

thing, so determined, that as soon as she entered,
he felt it coming. He knew that was why she came.
The bluff of asking him if he got his telephone
messages was too simple.

Mrs. Burns was a sad looking woman, with a
tired voice. It was not that Mrs. Burns was tired
or sad, but in that part of the East from which
she had come, all the better people spoke in weary
voices of ladylike weakness.

"Well, Mrs. Burns," the doctor said, "what has
happened today?" He knew he was going to get
it anyway—so he might as well ask for it.

"George Steadman was in an awful state about
the young fellow who came out from the city to
see Pearl Watson. He got lost in the storm, and
stayed three days at Paines, and then Pearl came
over and took him home with her. Some say the
Government sent him about the piece in the paper,
and some say he's her beau. I don't know. Mrs.
Crocks saw Pearl when she brought him in, and she
could get nothing out of her. He's at the hotel still,
though nobody seems to know what his business is."

"O well," laughed the doctor, "we'll just have
to watch him. Don't leave washings on the line,
and lock our doors—he can't scare us."

Mrs. Burns afterwards told Mrs. Crocks that
"Doctor Clay can be very light at times, and it
seems hardly the thing, considering his profession."

Mrs. Burns could never quite forgive herself for
leaving so early that night, and almost lost her
religion, because no still, small voice prompted her
to stay. Just as she left the office, the young man,

the mysterious stranger, came to the door, and Mrs. Burns knew there was no use going back through the drug store and listening at the door. The doctor had heavy curtains at each door in his office, and had a way of leaving the key in the door, that cut off the last hope. So she went home in great heaviness of spirit.

P. J. Neelands presented his card, and was given a leather chair beside the fire. He asked the doctor if he might smoke, and was given permission.

"I am going to talk to you in confidence, Doctor Clay," he said, nervously. "I guess you're used to that."

The doctor nodded encouragingly: "That's what doctors are for. Go right on, Mr. Neelands."

"The fact of the matter is—I'm in love," said Peter, taking the head plunge first.

"O that's nothing," said the doctor. "I mean—that's nothing to worry about."

"But she does not care a hang for me. In fact, she laughs at me."

Peter's face was clouded in perlpexity

"But I'll begin at the beginning: I belong to the Young Men's Political Club in the city, and I was sent out here—at least, I mean I asked to come on a delicate mission. I'm speaking to you confidentially, of course."

"Of course," said the doctor, "have no fears."

"Well, perhaps you saw this." He produced the article that had caused the fluttering in the Governmental nest.

The doctor suddenly came to attention.

"Do you know who wrote it? No! Well anyway, I came out to see about it—to investigate—look over the ground. But, doctor, I got the surprise of my life. This girl is a wonder."

"Well," the doctor's sympathetic manner had gone. He was sitting up very straight in his chair now, and his eyes were snapping with suppressed excitement. "What did you think you could do about it? Did you think you could stop her—hush her up—or scare her—or bribe her—or what?"

"I did not know," said Peter honestly. "But I want to tell you what happened. I was three days at Paine's—caught by the storm—do you know them? Well, it's a good place to go to see what women are up against. I was mad enough to throw old Paine out of his own house, and I found out he was going to sell the farm over her head, and By Jove! I see now why the women want to vote, don't you?"

"I've always seen why," replied the doctor. "I thought every one with any intelligence could see the justice of it." The doctor's manner was losing its friendliness, but Peter, intent on his own problems, did not resent it.

"Well, just when this man Gilchrist came to sign the papers, the morning I left, she came in—Pearl Watson, I mean—and Doctor, I never heard anything like it. Talk about pleading a case! She did not plead—she just reviewed the case—she put it up to Gilchrist—it was marvellous! If she had asked me to shoot the two of them, I would have done it. She had me—she has me yet—she's the most charming, sweet-souled and wonderful girl I ever saw."

The doctor endeavored to speak calmly:

"Well, what about it?" he said. "I agree with you—she is all of that."

"I am going back to resign from the party. I am going to throw my weight on the other side," Peter spoke with all the seriousness of youth. "The girl has shown me what a beastly, selfish lot the politicians are, and I am going back to denounce them, if they won't change. But I want to ask you something, Doctor—you won't think I am cheeky, will you? She gave me absolutely no hope— but girls sometimes change their minds. I would wait for years for her. I simply can't live without her. I thought from the way she spoke there was some one else—if there is—I will just crawl away and die—I can't live without her!"

"O shut up," said the doctor impatiently. "Better men than you have to live without—the women they love—that's foolish talk."

"Well, tell me, doctor," cried Peter desperately, "I just have to know. Is there any reason why I can't hope to win her? Do you know of any reason —you know Pearl well. Is there any reason that you know of? Has any one any right—to stop me from trying?"

The doctor considered. Here was just the situation he had told Pearl he hoped would arise. This young fellow was clean, honest, and there was no doubt of his deep sincerity. He had told Pearl she

must forget him. He had tried to mean it, and
here it was—here was the very situation he said
he hoped for. He would play up—he could make
himself do what was right, no matter how he felt.

He heard himself say mechanically:

"There is no reason, Mr. Neelands; Pearl is free
to decide. No one has the smallest claim on her."

Peter sprang up and caught his hand, wondering
why it should be so cold. He also wondered at the
flush which burned on the doctor's cheeks.

"Thanks, old man," he cried impulsively, "I
cannot tell you how I thank you. You have rolled
a house off me—and now, tell me you wish me well—
I want your good word."

The doctor took his outstretched hand, with
an effort.

"I wish you well," he said slowly, in a voice
that was like a shadow of his own.

When Peter had gone, the doctor rose and paced
the floor.

"I'm a liar and a hypocrite," he said bitterly.
"I don't wish him well. I said what was not so
when I said I hoped to see her married to some
one else—I don't — I want her myself. I can't
give her up! I won't give her up!"

The next morning, before the doctor started to
make his calls, Robert Gilchrist, President of the
Political Club, came to see him, again.

"I am not satisfied with that interview we had
with you, doctor," he said, "the day the organizer
was here. That fellow made a mess of everything,

and I don't blame you for turning it down. But I tell you, there's more in it than this fellow thinks. There is a real moral issue to be decided, and I am here to admit I've had a new look at things in the last few days. I am going into the city to see our leader, and I want to see how he feels. But, doctor, some of our laws are simply disgraceful; they've got to be changed."

He went on to tell the doctor of the day he went to buy Sylvester Paine's farm.

"I never felt any meaner than when Pearl told me what it meant, and what I was doing. Doctor, if you had seen the look in Mrs. Paine's face when Pearl was putting it up to me; Lord, it was tragic. It was as if her hope of Heaven was in dispute, and didn't Pearl put it to me? Say, doctor, that girl can swing an election. No one can resist her arguments—she's so fair about everything—no one can get away from her arguments. The reason these laws have been left the way they are, is that no one knows about them. Did you know that a man can sell everything, and do what he likes with the money, no matter what his wife says—and did you know a man can take his children away from the mother—Did you know about these?"

"I did," said the doctor, "in a vague way. Fortunately they do not often come up—men are better than the laws—and they would need to be."

"Well, doctor, I'll tell you what I want to say. I believe it is your duty to run. The women need a few members there to stick up for them. Pearl thinks our party is all right too—she says they'll grant the vote—if they get in—and she was at the big meeting where the women asked them to make it a plank in their platform. She says some of the old hide-bound politicians gagged a little, but they swallowed it—they had to. I wish you could hear Pearl talk, doctor. She seemed disappointed when I told her you weren't going to run."

"You haven't thought of any one else, Bob?" the doctor asked, after a pause. "You wouldn't consider it yourself?"

"Any one else but you will surely lose his deposit. The bridge at Purple Springs will hold them over there, and they have taken off a slice on the east of the riding and put it in Victoria—where it is sure to go against the Government anyway. No, this will go to Steadman by acclamation, unless you let us nominate you."

"Well, I'll reconsider," said the doctor, "and phone you inside of twenty-four hours."

When Mr. Gilchrist had gone, the doctor sat with his hands behind his head. His eyes were very bright, and a flush mantled his cheek. His heart thumped so hard, he could hear it.

"Keep away from excitement, Clay," he could hear the old doctor saying, "excitement eats up your energy and does not give the builders a chance. With care, and patience, you may win—but if you will not save yourself, and nurse yourself, and go slow—you are a dead man!"

He pressed his hands tightly to his head.

"Pearl had been disappointed," Bob had said.

It would be a disgrace to let this riding go by default. There was the liquor question which had hung fire for fourteen years, while the Government had simply played with it, and laughed at the temperance people. If women had the vote, what a power Pearl would be!

Still, one vote in Parliament was nothing—one man could do but little—and besides, the old doctor had found him improved—he might be able to beat out the disease yet—by being careful. A campaign would mean late hours, long drives, meeting people — making speeches — which he hated — the worst kind of excitement—to move a vote of thanks tired him more than a week's work.

Still, Pearl would be pleased—he hadn't done much for Pearl. He had won her love—and then had to turn it away—and had seen those eyes of her's cloud in disappointment. It had been a raw deal.

Looking through the window, he saw Bertie, with his team, waiting outside the door. He was letting Bertie take full care of his horses now, and saving himself in that way.

The sorrel horse on the side next him tossed his head, and chewed the bit, with a defiant air that set waves of memory in motion. He had bought this fine four-year-old, because he had reminded him of old Prince—the same color—the same markings, and the same hard mouth and defiant red eye.

Usually, he did not keep Bertie waiting—but this morning it did not matter—there were other things to be decided. The sorrel horse seemed to be looking at him through the office window.

"There was another sorrel horse to take your place, Prince," said the doctor, looking at the big sorrel, but thinking of his predecessor; "although that did not influence you in any way—you left that to me to find out—you considered that my business. I believe I will be safe in leaving it to some one higher up to get another doctor to take my place—doctors—and sorrel horses—there are plenty of them. You had the right philosophy, Prince. No one else could have saved the woman's life—so you did that—and let me rustle for another horse. I'll do the same—after all—it is not individuals who count—it is the race. We do our bit—and pass on. Straight ahead of me seems to be a piece of work I can do—and if I have to pay for the privilege of doing it—I'll pay—without regrets."

He reached for the telephone, and called Mr. Gilchrist.

"Hello Bob," he said steadily, "I've reached a decision No, it didn't take me long. Yes, I will. I'll accept the nomination. All right Bob — I hope so. Thank you for your good opinion—All right."

CHAPTER XVII

WHEN Peter J. Neelands returned to the city, he sought an interview with his Chief. It was a bold stroke, Mr. Neelands knew, but the circumstances warranted it. He must lay the matter before his superior officer; as a loyal member of the party, he must bring in a warning. He must make the Government understand.

The old leader was one of the most approachable of men, genial, kindly and friendly. The interview was arranged without difficulty, and Peter, with his heart beating uncomfortably, was shown by the old retainer who kept guard in the outside office, through the blue velvet hangings, into the Chief's private office.

At a long oaken table, on which were scattered a few trade journals and newspapers, he found the great man. An unlighted cigar was in his mouth, and he sat leaning back in a revolving chair.

"Well, Peter, my son—how are you?" he said gaily, extending his hand. "And so you feel you must see the old man on business of importance, vital importance to our country's welfare. That's good; glad to see you, take a chair beside me and tell uncle who hit you."

The Chief was a man of perhaps sixty years of age, of florid countenance, red mustache, turning gray, splendidly developed forehead, dark gray

eyes with wire-like wrinkles radiating from them,
which seemed to have been caused more by laughter
than worry; a big, friendly voice of great carrying
power, and a certain bluff, good fellowship about
him which marked him as a man who was born to
rule his fellowmen, but to do it very pleasantly.

Peter was complimented to be received so cor-
dially. He was sure he could make this genial,
courteous, kindly old gentleman see certain questions from a new view-point. He must see it.

"Perhaps you have heard of a girl at Millford
who is making somewhat of a stir along the lines
of the Woman Suffrage question," Peter began.

The great man nodded, and having begun to nod,
absent-mindedly continued, much to Peter's dis-
comfiture. Peter hastily reviewed the case, though
he could see his listener was bored exceedingly.

"Now, what I want you to do, sir," he said
earnestly, "is this. Let this girl come and address
the members of the Government and the Legislature—I mean our members—privately, of course.
Let her show you the woman's side of the question.
I know, sir, you turned them down when the delegation came, but a man can always change his
mind. The thing is inevitable; the vote is coming.
If this Government does not give it—the Government will go down to defeat."

The Chief stopped nodding, and the amiability of
his face began to cloud over. He sat up very suddenly and spread his plump hands on the table.

"The Opposition have endorsed Woman Suffrage,
sir," said Peter earnestly. "They are making it a
plank in their platform."

"Sure they have," cried the Premier, with a laugh, "sure they have. They are big enough fools to endorse anything! What do we care what they endorse?"

"But I want to get this over to you, Mr. Graham, that we are losing our opportunity to do a big thing, something that will live in history, if we fail to give women the vote. Women are human, they have a right to a voice in their own government, and if you would just let this girl come out and talk to you—and the members."

"Look here, Peter," said the great man tolerantly, "I like enthusiasm—the world is built on it. But I'm an old man now, and have been a long time dealing with the public and with politics. Politics is a dirty mess—it's no place for women, and I certainly do not need to be instructed by any eighteen-year-old girl, pleasant as the process might be. I believe all you say about her—and her charm. You had better go and marry her—if you want to."

Peter's face colored. "I would be very happy to do so, but she turned me down, sir."

"Don't be discouraged, lad; a woman's 'no' generally means 'yes'," said his Chief. "Now, even if she could talk like the Angel Gabriel, I won't let her at the members of this Government—I'll tell you why. I have these fellows trotting easy. They're good boys—they do as they're told. Now what's the use of getting them excited and confused. Peter, you know how it is with the Indians—in their wild state, eating rabbits and digging roots—they're happy, aren't they? Sure they are. If you

bring them into town, show them street-cars and
shop windows and take them to theatres, you excite
them and upset them, that's all. O no, Peter, I'll
take no chances on spoiling my simple-hearted
country members by turning loose this orb-eyed
young charmer who has thrown you clean off your
trolley."

"But, sir, consider the case .yourself; won't you
admit, sir, that the laws are fearfully unjust to
women?" Peter began to explain, but the Premier
interrupted:

"Peter, the world is very old; certain things are
established by usage, and the very fact that this
is so argues that it should be so. Women are weaker
than men—I did not make them so—God made
them so. He intended them to be subject to men.
Don't get excited over it. It sounds well to talk
about equality—but there's no such thing. It did not
exist in God's mind, so why should we try to bring
it about? No, no, Peter, women are subject to
men, and always will be. It would not do to make
them independent in the eyes of the law, independent economically. If they were they would not
marry. Look at the women in the States—where
in some places they vote—look at the type that
develops. What does it bring?—race-suicide, divorce
—free love. I'm an old-fashioned man, Peter, I
believe in the home."

"So do I," said Peter, "with all my heart."

The great man began to show signs of impatience.

"Before I go," said Peter earnestly, "let me make
one more appeal to you. This is a live issue. It

cannot be dismissed by a wave of the hand. Will
you listen to a debate on it—will you let it be discussed in your hearing?"

The old man considered a moment—then he said:
"This will wear off you, Peter. I, too, have been
young. I understand. Forget it, boy, and get
back to normal. No, I will not hear it discussed.
I know all about it—all I want to know. I don't
know why I am wasting so much time on you and
your particular type of foolishness, Peter. I have
people like you seeing me every day. Usually they
are dealt with by Mr. Price, in the outer office.
He has orders to put the can on them and open the
door. O no, Peter, there will be no radical measures
while I sit at the helm—I am too old to change my
mind."

Peter began to put on his gloves The older man
held out his hand.

"Well, good-bye, Peter," he said kindly, "come
again—come any time—always glad to see you."

"I will not be back," said Peter quietly, "this
is good-bye. If I cannot show you that you are
wrong, I will go out and help the women to show
the people that you are wrong. Pearl says if the
Premier is too old to change his mind we will do
the next best thing."

"And what is that?"

"Change the Premier," Peter replied, steadily.

The old man laughed, with uproarious mirth.

"Peter, you're funny all right, you're rich; I
always did enjoy the prattle of children, but I can't
fool away any more time on you—so run along
and sell your papers."

Peter went through the blue velvet hangings, past the worthy henchman, who sat dozing in his chair, and made his way to the front door. The mural decorations in the corridor caught his eye— the covered wagon, drawn by oxen plodding patiently into the sunset—the incoming settlers of the pioneer days.

"I wonder if the women did not do their full share of that," he thought. "They worked, suffered, hoped, endured—and made the country what it is. I wonder how any man has the nerve to deny them a voice in their own affairs."

While Peter was taking his departure, and before he had reached the front gate, one of the many bells which flanked the Premier's table was wildly rung.

"Send Banks to me," he said crisply, to the lackey who appeared.

The genial mood had gone; his brows were clamped low over his eyes. He had chewed the end off his cigar.

"Every time the women raise ructions it sets me thinking of her. I wonder what became of her," he murmured. "The ground seems to have swallowed her. She might have known I did not mean it; but women don't reason—they just feel."

The news of P. J. Neelands' resignation from the Young Men's Political Club made a ripple of excitement in Government circles, and brought forth diverse comments.

"There's a girl in it, I hear," said one of the

loungers at the Maple Leaf Club; "some pretty little suffragette has won over our Peter."

"He does not deny it," said another, "he'll tell you the whole story—and believe me, Peter is an enthusiastic supporter of the women's cause now. I see in this morning's paper he made a speech for them last night called 'The Chivalry of the Law.' Peter has the blood of the martyrs in him for sure—for he was in a straight line for the nomination here in 'Centre.' "

"Peter Neelands makes me tired," said a third gloomily. "Why does he need to get all fussed up over the laws relating to women—they have too much liberty now—they can swear away a man's character—that's one thing I'd like to see changed. It's dangerous, I tell you."

The first man finished the discussion:

"I always liked Peter, and am sorry he's quit us. He'll have a following, too, just because he does believe in himself."

Though the loungers at the Maple Leaf Club took the news of Peter Neelands' secession with composure, mingled with amusement, the chief organizer, Mr. Banks, viewed it with alarm, and voiced his fears to the head of his department, who sat in his accustomed chair, with a bottle of the best beside him. The Honorable member listened, but refused to be alarmed. It was past the third hour of the afternoon, and the rainbow haze was over everything.

"I tell you," said Mr. Banks, "something is going to break if we can't ge· this thing stopped. The

women are gaining every day. Their meetings
are getting bigger, and now look at Peter Neelands.
This Watson girl has got to be canned—got rid of—
if we have to send her to do immigration work in
London, England."

The honorable member did his best to hold his
head steady.

"Do what you like, Banks," he said thickly,
"only save the country. My country if she's right;
my country if she's wrong; but always my country!
'Lives there a man with soul so dead,' eh, Banks?
That's the dope—what? Damn the women—but
save the home—we gotta save the home."

Oliver Banks looked at him in deep contempt,
and shook his head. "These birds make things
hard for us," he murmured. "He looks like a
Minister of the Crown now, doesn't he? Lord!
wouldn't he make a sight for the women! I'd like
to hear their description of him just as he sits now."

The minister sat with his pudgy hands spread out
on the arms of his chair. His head rolled uncertainly, like a wilting sunflower on a broken stalk. His
under lip was too full to fit his face. If he had
been a teething infant one would have been justified in saying he was drooling.

The organizer called a waiter and instructed him
to phone to the gentleman's house and speak to his
chauffeur.

"Tell him to take the old man home," he said
briefly, "he seems to be—overtaken."

"Very good, sir," said the waiter, without a
flicker of an eyelash.

Then the organizer went to a telephone booth and called George Steadman, of Millford, requesting him to come at once to the city on important business.

CHAPTER XVIII

NONE of us has lived long without discovering that everything he has he pays for; that every gain has a corresponding loss; that a development even of one of our own faculties, is at the expense of the others. The wild wheat is small and dwarfed in size in its native state, but very hardy. Under persistent cultivation it grows bigger and more productive, but, unfortunately, susceptible to the frost. The wild rabbit when domesticated grows bigger and more beautiful, but loses his speed and cleverness. So it is all through life—it all comes in the bill—we cannot escape the day of reckoning.

If Pearl Watson had not had a taste for political speeches and debates; if she had read the crochet patterns in the paper instead of the editorials, and had spent her leisure moments making butterfly medallions for her camisoles, or in some other lady-like pursuit, instead of leaning over the well-worn railing around the gallery of the LegislativeAssembly, in between classes at the Normal, she would have missed much; but she would have gained something too.

For one thing, she would have had an easier time getting a boarding-house in the Purple Springs District, and would not be standing looking disconlately out at the Spring sunshine, one day at the end of April, wondering, with a very sore heart, why nobody wanted to give her board and shelter. It was a new and painful sensation for Pearl, and it cut deeply.

Mrs. Zinc could not keep her beyond May the first, for relatives were coming from the East. Mrs. Cowan could not take her, for she had too much to do as it was—and could not get help that wasn't more trouble than it was worth. They would waste more than their wages, and what they did not waste they would steal. Mrs. Cowan's tongue was unloosed by the memory of her wrongs, and it was half an hour before Pearl could get away. Mrs. Cowan had surely suffered many things at the hands of help of all nationalities. She had got them from employment bureaus, government and private; from the Salvation Army and from private friends in the old country. Her help had come from everywhere except from the Lord! No indeed, she couldn't take any one to board.

A careful canvass of the neighborhood had resulted in disappointment; not one home was available. Embarrassment had sat on the faces of many of the women when they talked with her about it, and Pearl was quick to see that there was something back of it all, and the antagonism of the unknown lay heavily on her heart.

The yellow Spring sun, like liquid honey, fell in benediction on the leafless trees, big with buds, and on the tawny mat of grass through which the blue noses of anemones were sticking. Cattle eagerly cropped the dead grass and found it good, and men were at work in the fields. They all had

homes and beds, Pearl thought, with a fresh burst
of homelessness.

She had prepared her blackboards for the next
day, and made her desk tidy, and was just about
to leave for the day and walk the mile to Mrs.
Howser's to see if she could make it her abiding
place, when Bessie Cowan came running with a
letter.

"Please, teacher," said Bessie, out of breath
from running, "Ma thought this might be an important letter, and you should have it right away.
It came in our mail."

Pearl took it, wonderingly. It bore the official
seal of the Department of Education. Only once
had she received such a letter, and that was when
she received permission to attend the Normal. When
she opened it, she read:

"Dear Madam:—You have been recommended
to us by the Principal of the Normal School for
special work required by this Department, and we
will be pleased to have you come to our office inside
of the next week for instructions. We will pay
you a salary of one hundred dollars a month, and
travelling expenses, and we believe you will find
the work congenial. Kindly reply as soon as possible."

Pearl's heart was throbbing with excitement.
Here was a way of escape from surroundings which,
for some unknown reason, were uncomfortable and
unfriendly.

Bessie Cowan watched her closely, but said not

a word. Bessie was a fair-skinned little girl, with eyes far apart, and a development of forehead which made her profile resemble a rabbit's.

"Thank you, Bessie" said Pearl, "I am glad to have this." She sat at her desk and began to write. Bessie ran home eagerly to tell her mother how the letter had been received.

Pearl decided to write an acceptance, and to 'phone home to her mother before sending it.

When the letter was written she sat in a pleasant dream, thinking of the new world that had opened before her. "Travelling expenses," had a sweet sound in her young ears—she would go from place to place, meet new people, and all the time be learning something—learning something—and forgetting.

Pearl winced a little when she recalled Mrs Crocks' words when she came through Millford on her way to Purple Springs:

"The doctor should be the candidate, but I guess Miss Keith won't let him. They say he's holdin' off to run for the Dominion House next Fall. You maybe could coax him to run, Pearl. Have you seen him lately? Miss Keith was down twice last week, and he went up for Sunday. It looks as if they were keepin' close company—oh well, he's old enough to know his own mind, and it will be nice to have the Senator's daughter livin' here. It would give a little style to the place, and that's what we're short of. But it's nothing to me—I don't care who he marries!"

Pearl had hurried away without answering. Mrs. Crocks' words seemed to darken the sun, and put the bite of sharp ice in the gentle spring breeze. Instead of forgetting him, every day of silence seemed to lie heavier on her heart; but one thing Pearl had promised herself—she would not mope—she would never cry over it!

She read the letter over and tried to picture what it would mean. A glow of gratitude warmed her heart when she thought of the Normal School Principal and his kindness in recommending her. She would fulfil his hopes of her, too. She would do her work well. She would lose herself in her work, and forget all that had made her lonely and miserable. It was a way of escape—the Lord was going to let her down over the wall in a basket.

There was a very small noise behind her, a faint movement as if a mouse had crossed the threshold.

She turned quickly, and gave a cry of surprise and delight.

At the door, shyly looking in at her, was a little boy of perhaps ten years of age, with starry eyes of such brilliance and beauty she could see no other feature. He looked like a little furry squirrel, who would be frightened by the slightest sound.

For a moment they looked at each other; then from the boy, in a trembling voice, clear and high pitched, came the words:

"Please, teacher!"

The tremble in his voice went straight to Pearl's heart.

"Yes, dear," she said, "come right in—I want you —I'm lonesome—and I like little boys like you."

His eyes seemed to grow more luminous and wistful.

"I can't come in," he said. "I can't come into
the school at all—not the least little bit—I have
an 'ungovernable' temper."

"I'm not afraid," said Pearl gravely, "I am very
brave that way, and don't mind at all. Who says
you have?"

"The trustees," he said and his voice began to
quiver. "They sent mother a letter about me."

"O, I know you now, James," said Pearl, "come
in—I want to talk to you. I was going to see you
just as soon as I got settled."

Cautiously he entered; the out-door wildness was
in his graceful movements. He stopped a few feet
away from her and said again:

"Please, teacher."

Pearl smiled back, reassuringly, and his eyes
responded.

"Did you get a place yet?" he asked eagerly

"No, I didn't," she answered. She was going to
tell him that she would not need a place, for she
was going away, but something stopped her. Somehow she could not dim the radiance of those eager
eyes.

"Teacher!" he cried coming nearer, "would you
come and live with us? My mother is just sweet,
and she would like to have you. She is away today,
to Millford, and won't be home till eight o'clock.
I stayed at home because I wanted to see you.
My mother watched you going to the houses—
we can see all of them from our house—and every
time you came away from them—she was glad.
We have a spy-glass, and we could see—that's

how we knew how nice you were, teacher"—he was almost near enough to touch her now. "You can have my bed if you will come."

Pearl wanted to draw him to her and kiss the fear forever from his face, but she was still afraid he might vanish if she touched him.

"My mother thinks you are nice," he said softly. "We saw you patting Cowan's dog and walking home with the children. One day we saw you walking home with Edgar Zinc. He held your hand—and my mother got to thinking that it might have been me that you had by the hand, and she cried that day, and couldn't tell why. It wasn't because she was lonely—because she never is lonely. How could she be when she has me? She tells me every day she is not lonely But we'd like fine to have you live with us, teacher, because you're nice."

Pearl's arm was around him now, and he let her draw him over to her.

"Tell me all about yourself," she said, with a curious tugging at her heart.

"We're orphans," he said simply, "mother and I—that means our people are dead. We had no people, only just our daddy. We didn't need any people only him, and he's dead And then we had Mr. Bowen—and he's dead. Don't it beat all how people die? Are you an orphan?"

Pearl shook her head.

James continued: "We're waiting here until I get bigger and mother gets enough money—and then we're going back. It's lovely to be going back. This isn't the real Purple Springs—we

just called it that for fun, and because we love
the name. It makes us happier when we say it.
It reminds us. Mother will tell you if you live
with us."

"At night we light the fire and watch it crackling,
and I sit on mother's knee. Ain't I a big boy to sit
on a lady's knee?—and she tells me. At Purple
Springs there's pansies as big as plates—mother
will draw them for you—and the rocks are always
warm, and the streams are boiling hot, and nobody
is ever sick there or tired. Daddy wouldn't have
died if we'd stayed there. But there's things in
life no one understands. We'll never leave when we
go back."

The boy rambled on, his eyes shining with a great
excitement. Pearl thought she was listening to the
fanciful tales with which a lonely woman beguiled
the weary hours for her little son   It was a weirdly
extravagant fairy story, and yet it fascinated Pearl
in spite of it's unlikeness to truth. It had all the
phantasy of a midsummer night's dream.

The boy seemed to answer her thoughts.

"Ain't it great to have something lovely to
dream over, teacher? I bet you've got sweet dreams,
too. Mother says that what kills people's souls is
when they have no purple springs in their lives.
She says she's sorry for lots of people   They live
and walk around, but their souls are dead, because
their springs have dried up."

Pearl drew him closer to her. He was so young—
and yet so old—so happy, and yet so lonely. She
wanted to give him back a careless, happy, irrespon-

sible childhood, full of frolicking fun and mischief,
without care or serious thought. She longed to see
him grubby-fisted, bare-footed, tousle-haired, shouting and wrestling with her young tykes of brothers.
It was not natural or happy to see a child so elfin,
so remote, so conscious of the world's sorrows.

"Will you come with me now, teacher?" he asked
eagerly.

Pearl could not resist the appeal. The sun hung
low in an amber haze as they left the school and
took the unfrequented road to the brown house
on the hill—the house of mystery.

The air was full of the drowsy sounds of evening;
cattle returning after their day's freedom in the
fields, cow-bells tinkling contentedly. Somewhere
in the distance a dog barked; and on the gentle
breeze came the song of a hermit thrush, with an
undertone of cooing pigeons. The acrid smell of
burning leaves was in the air.

The river valley ran into the sunset with its
bold scrub-covered banks, on the high shoulder of
which the railway cut made a deep welt, purple now
with evening. Every day the westbound train, with
its gray smoke spume laid back on its neck like a
mane, slid swiftly around the base of the hill until
the turn in the river made it appear to go into a
tunnel, for the opposite bank obscured it from view.
It re-appeared again, a mile farther west, and its
smoke could be followed by the eye for many miles
as it made its way to the city. This year it was the
Government's promise that the river would be
bridged at Purple Springs and the road made more
direct.

"Mother says no one could be lonely when they
can see the trains," said James Gray. "Mother
just loves the trains—they whistle to us every day.
They would stop and talk to us only they're in such
a hurry."

When her young escort led Pearl Watson into
the living-room she gave an exclamation of delight.
A low ceiling, with weathered beams; a floor covered with bright-colored, hand-made rugs, book-
cases filled with books, a few pictures on the wall,
and many pieces of artistically constructed furniture.

"Mother makes these in the winter, she and I.
We work all evening, and then we make toast at
the fire-place and play the phonograph and pretend
we have visitors. Ever since we knew you were
coming you've been our visitor, and now tonight
I'll hide you, and mother will think I'm just pretending, and then you'll come out, and mother
will think she's dreaming again."

Pearl helped her young friend to milk the two
fine cows that came up to the bars expectantly,
after which the evening meal was prepared, and
Pearl was amazed at the deft manner in which the
boy set about his work. He told her more about
calories and food values and balanced meals than
the Domestic Science Department at the Normal
School had taught her.

"How do you know all this?" she asked him in
surprise.

"Mother reads it in books and tells me. Mother
learns everything first, and tells me—she is determined," said the boy gravely, "that I will have

just as good a chance as other children. She says
if she ever did anything that wasn't right, and
which made it hard for me—she'll make it up.
Mother says God is often up against it with people,
too. He has to let things happen to them—bad
things—but He can always make it up to them—
and He will! Do you think that too, teacher?"

"I am sure of it," said Pearl, with a catch in her
throat and a sudden chill of doubt. Were there
some things which even God could not make up
to us?

The fireplace was laid with red willow wood, and
when everything was ready, and the hour had come
when Mrs. Gray was expected home, Pearl and
James waited in the big chair before the fire, which
darted tongues of purple flame and gave a grateful
heat, for the evening was chilly. They did not light
the lamp at all, for the light from the fire threw a
warm glow over the room.

A great peace seemed to have come to Pearl's
heart. The neighbors of Purple Springs, with their
inhospitable hearts, seemed far away and unreal.
That thought in some occult way came to her
with comforting power from the spirit which dwelt
in this home.

For three years no friendly foot had come to this
threshold, no one had directed a friendly thought
to the woman who lived here, nor to the child;
yet woman and child had lived on happily in spite
of this, and now to Pearl, on whom the taboo of
the neighborhood had also fallen, there came the
peace of mind which could set quietly at defiance

the opinion of the little world which surrounded her.

So intent were Pearl and James on the story that Pearl was telling they did not hear the buggy, which drove up to the house. Mrs. Gray got out and took out her parcels at the front door. The leaping flames from the fire-place in the pretty room, made a picture she loved well. It was so significant of home—and it is those who have not always had a home who love it best. She stopped to watch the light as it danced on the shelves of books and the brightly colored hangings and rugs.

Seeing Pearl in the big chair, with her arm around the boy, Annie Gray's heart gave a leap of rapture. Her boy had a companion—a human comrade other than herself. It had come at last! The dream had come true! She watched Pearl, fascinated, fearful. Was it a dream, or was there really a human being, and such a lovely one, a guest at her fireside?

With a quick movement she flung open the door, James ran to his mother with a welcoming shout. Then Pearl stood up, and the two women shook hands without a word. They looked long into each other's eyes; then with a quick impulse, and a sudden illumination, Pearl put her arms around the older woman and kissed her.

Annie Gray held her away from her, so she could look at her again. Then with a laugh that was half a sob, she said:

"Prayers—are—sometimes—answered," and without any warning, surprising herself even more than she did the others—she began to cry. "Three years is a long time."

CHAPTER XIX

WHEN Pearl opened her eyes the next morning it was with a delicious sense of well-being, which increased as she looked about her. It may have been the satiny smoothness of the sheets, the silk eiderdown quilt, with its plumy yellow chrysanthemums, the pale yellow scrim curtains, across whose lower borders young brown ducks followed each other in stately procession; the home-made table with its gray linen runner, across which a few larger ducks paraded, and which held a large lamp, with a well-flounced shade; the soft buff walls, with their border of yellow autumn woods, sunsweet and cool, with leaf-strewn paths that would be springy to walk on. It may have been these, for Pearl's heart could easily be set tingling by a flash of color that pleased her. But there is no doubt the room had a presence, a strong, buoyant, cheerful presence. It had been furnished to defy loneliness. Who could be lonely looking down at a thick plushy rug of woolly white sheep, shading into yellow, lying on the very greenest of grass, beside a whimsical little twisting stream that you were just sure had speckled trout in it, darting over its gravelly bottom, if your eyes were only quick enough to catch the flash of them; and who wouldn't be glad to wash in a basin that was just lined with yellow roses, with a few of them falling out over

the sides; and who wouldn't accept the gift of a
towel from a hospitable oak hand, which held out
a whole bouquet of them—one on each finger;
towels with all sorts of edgings and insertions and
baskets of flowers and monograms on them just
begging you to take your choice. And if anything else were needed to keep the heart from dull
gray loneliness, or ugly black fear, on the wall over
the bed was a big gilt-framed picture of an amber-
eyed, white-collared, blessed collie dog, with the
faintest showing of his red tongue, big and strong
and faithful, just to remind you that though changes
befall and friends betray and hopes grow cold,
faithfulness and affection have not entirely vanished
from the earth.

Pearl's sense of freedom, of power, of comfort,
seemed to increase as she lay watching the spot of
sunshine which fell on the rug with its flock of
sheep and seemed to bring them alive. The whole
room seemed to fit around her, the ceiling bent over
her like a kind face, the walls, pictures, and furniture were like a group of friends encouraging her,
inspiring her, soothing her.

Pearl searched her mind for a word to describe
it. "It feels like—Saturday—" she said at last,
"—freedom, rest, plans, ambitions—it has them all,
and it has something deeper still in it—it is like
a section of a tree, in which history can be read,
storms and winds and sunshine," for Pearl knew
instinctively that it was a tower-room that Annie
Gray had made for an armor for her soul, so it
would not be pierced by the injustice and unkindness
of the world."

'They do not understand," Pearl said again, "that's all—they do not mean to be so horrid to her—it's queer how badly people can treat each other and their conscience let them get away with it. Even if Mrs. Gray had been all they said, she had not done any wrong to them—why should they feel called upon to punish her? Well, I can tell them a few things now."

A fire burned in the fireplace, and the breakfast-table was set in front of it. Mrs. Gray, in an attractive mauve house-gown, came in from the kitchen. She was a tall woman, with steel gray eyes, with pebblings of green—the eyes of courage and high resolve. Her features were classical in their regularity, and reminded Pearl of the faces in her history reproduced from the Greek coins, lacking only the laurel wreath. Her hair was beginning to turn gray, and showed a streak at each side, over her temples. A big black braid was rolled around her perfectly round head; a large green jade brooch, with a braided silver edge, fastened her dress. Her hands were brown and hard, but long, shapely and capable looking.

The boy was sleeping late, so Pearl and her hostess ate their breakfast alone.

"Will you let me stay with you, Mrs. Gray?" Pearl asked, when breakfast was over. "I will make my own bed, keep my things tidy, try not to spill my tea. I will wipe my feet, close the screen door, and get up for breakfast."

Mrs. Gray looked across the table, with her clear eyes fastened on her guest. Suddenly they began to grow dim with tears.

"Pearl," she said, laughing, "I don't know what there is about you that makes me want to cry. I've gone through some rough places in life without a tear, but you seem to have a way all your own to start me off."

"But I don't hurt you, do I?" Pearl asked, in distress. "Surely I don't—I wouldn't do that for the world."

"Not a bit of it," laughed her hostess, as she wiped her eyes, and then, blinking hard to clear away the last traces of grief, she said·

"Pearl, before you come to board with me you should know something about me; you have no doubt heard some strange things."

Pearl did not deny it.

"And you should know the whole story, and then judge for yourself whether you consider I am a fit person to live with."

"But I do already," said Pearl. "I consider you a very proper and delightful person to live with. I don't want to know a thing about you unless you care to tell me. You don't know anything about me either—we both have to take a chance— and I am willing if you are."

"But there will be an insurrection in the neighborhood. They won't let you, Pearl. They can't forgive me for coming here without reference or character, and with a child, too."

"Well, he's a pretty fine child," said Pearl, "and, I should say, a sort of certificate for his mother."

"Well, no matter how fine a child he is—no

matter what care a mother has taken in his training—nothing can atone, in the eyes of society
for the failure of conforming to some of their laws.
Society's laws, not God's laws. Society is no friend
to women, Pearl."

"But it is just because people do not think,"
said Pearl, "They have made certain laws—and
women have not made any protest, so the men
think they are all right."

"And do you know why, Pearl?" she asked.
"Women who are caught in the tangle of these
laws, as I was, cannot say a word—their lips are
dumb. The others won't say a word for fear of
spoiling their matrimonial market. The worst
thing that can be said of a woman is that she's
queer and strong-minded—and defies custom. If
you want to be happy, Pearl, be self-centered,
virtuous, obey the law, and care nothing for others."

"You don't mean that," said Pearl. "You've
been hard hit some way I do not want to know
until you want to tell me. But I am going to stay
with you if you will keep me. I am determined to
stay."

Annie Gray's steely eyes clouded over again,
like a sun-kissed lake when a cloud passes over it.
They grew deeper, grayer, and of misty tenderness.

"You are doing something for me, Pearl, that
I thought could never be done; you are restoring
my faith. Remember, I have not been as unhappy
as you may think. I had my happiness—that's
more than some women can say. I have had the
rapture, the blessedness of love—I've had it all—

the rapture of holding and the agony of loss—I'm only thirty-one, but I've lived a thousand years. But, Pearl, you've done something for me already; you have set my feet again on something solid, and I am a different woman from yesterday. Some day I'll tell you a strange story, until then, you'll trust me?"

"Until then—and far beyond it—forever," said Pearl. "I'll trust you—I have an idea you and I are going to stick together for a long time."

Pearl went back to the school and found her letter of acceptance in the desk. She tore it up and wrote another, thanking the department for their kindness in offering her such a splendid position, but explaining that she had decided to stay at the school at Purple Springs. She made her decision without any difficulty. There was a deep conviction that the threads of destiny were weaving together her life and Annie Gray's, and she knew, from some hidden source in her soul, that she must stand by. What she could do, was vague and unformed in her mind, but she knew it would be revealed to her.

Pearl, child of the prairie, never could think as clearly when her vision was bounded by walls. She had to have blue distance—the great, long look that swept away the little petty, trifling, hampering things, which so slavishly dominate our lives, if we will let them. So she took her way to a little lake behind the school, where with the school axe she had already made a seat for herself under two big poplar trees, and cut the lower branches of some of the smaller ones, giving them a neat and tidy appearance, like well-gartered children dressed for a picnic.

There were a few white birches mixed with the poplars, so delicately formed and dainty in their slender branches and lacey leaves, they looked like nice little girls with flowing hair, coming down to bathe in the blue lake, timidly trying out the water with their white feet. The trees formed a semi-circle around the east side of the lake, leaving one side open to view, and she could see the prairie falling away to the river, which made a wide detour at this point.

Pearl settled herself in her rustic seat, putting the newspaper, which she had left for the purpose, behind her back as she leaned against the tree, to keep the powdery bark from marking her blue coat, and leaning back contentedly, she drank in the spring sounds.

The sun, which stood almost at noon, seemed to draw the leaves out like a magnet; she could almost believe she saw them unfolding; above her head there was a perfect riot of bird song, and a blue-bird, like a burst of music, went flashing across the water. A gray squirrel chattered as he ran up a tree behind her, and a rabbit, padding over the dead leaves on his way to the lake, made a sound like a bear.

Up through the tree tops there had climbed a few blue rags of smoke, for behind her a sleepy prairie fire was eating backward toward a ploughed fire-guard, and the delightful acrid smell brought back the memory of past prairie fires, pleasant enough to think of, as life's battles are, if they end victoriously. Not a breath stirred in the trees, and the prairie fire that smouldered so indolently was surely the gentlest of its race.

Suddenly there came a gust of wind through the trees, which set them creaking and crackling with vague apprehension, for the wind is always the mischief maker—the tattler—the brawler who starts the trouble—and the peaceful, slumbering absent-minded prairie fire, nibbling away at a few dead roots and grass, had been too much for it. Here was a perfectly good chance to make trouble which no wind could resist.

A big black cloud went over the sun, and all in a minute the placid waters of the lake were rasped into a pattern like the soles of new rubbers—the trees were bending—crows cawing excitedly, and the fire, spurred by the wind, went racing through the lake bottom and on its way up the bank toward the open country. The cattle, which had been feeding at the east side of the lake, sniffing danger, turned galloping home to furnish an alibi in case of trouble.

But the excitement was short-lived owing to a circumstance which the wind had overlooked. The wind had made a mistake in its direction, and so the fire had one wild, glorious race up the bank only to find its nose run right into a freshly ploughed fire-guard, steaming damp and richly brown. The fire sputtered, choked and died down, black and disappointed, leaving only a few smoking clumps of willows.

Then the wind, seeing no further chance of trouble, went crackling away over the tree tops, and the sun came back, brilliant and warm as ever, and there was nothing to show that there had been any excitement, save only the waves on the lake. The wind was gone, laughing and unrepentant, over the tree-tops; the sun had come back as genially as if it had never been away—but the lake could not forget, and it fretted and complained, in a perfectly human way, pounding the bank in a futile attempt to get back at some one. The bank had not been to blame, but it had to take the lake's repinings, while the real culprit went free and unreproached.

Pearl could tell what the lake was saying, as it lashed itself foaming and pounding just below her feet. It called to the world to listen.

"Look how I'm used," it sobbed, "and abused— and confused."

Pearl put her hands in the silk-lined pockets of her coat, and thought about what she had just seen.

"Life is like this," she said at last, "human nature is full of mischief. It loves to start trouble and fan a fire into a destructive mood; and there's only one way to stop it—plough a fire-guard. I wish there had been some one here to plough a fire-guard when the fires of gossip began to run here three years ago."

"I'll go now and dress up, and break the news to the neighborhood that I am going to the house at Purple Springs to board. There will be a row—

there will be a large row—unless I can make the people understand, and in a row there is nothing so sustaining as good clothes—next to the consciousness of being right, of course," she added after a pause.

An hour later, 'Pearl Watson, in her best dress of brown silk, with her high brown boots well polished, and her small brown hat, made by herself, with a band of crushed burnt orange poppies around the crown, safely anchored and softened by a messaline drape; with her hair drawn over the tops of her ears, and a smart fawn summer coat, with buttons which showed a spot of red like a pigeon-blood ruby. Pearl looked at herself critically in the glass:

"These things should not count," she said, as she fastened a thin veil over her face and made it very neat at the back with a hairpin, "but they do."

CHAPTER XX

The Purple Springs district was going through a period of intense excitement. Housework languished, dough ran over, dish-water cooled. The news which paralyzed household operations came shortly after one o'clock, when Mrs. Cowan phoned to Mrs. Brownlees that the teacher had just been in, and said she was going to board with the woman who lived alone. The teacher had said it, according to Mrs. Cowan, in the "most off-hand manner, just as if she said she had found her jackknife or her other rubber—just as easy as that, she said she had found a boarding house. Mrs. Howser could not take her, but Mrs. Gray could, and she was moving over right away."

Mrs. Cowan, according to her own testimony, nearly dropped. She did not really drop, but any one could easily have knocked her down; she could have been knocked down with a pin feather. She could not speak—she just stared. She went all "through other," and felt queer.

"Do you know that woman has a child?" she managed to say at last, and the teacher said, "Sure —one of the nicest I've ever seen—a perfect beauty."

Mrs. Cowan admitted to Mrs. Brownlees, who sympathized with her, that she did not know what to say then.

At last she said, "But she has no right to have a child," and the teacher said:

"Why not if she wants to. She's good to him, dresses him well and trains him well. My mother had nine—and got away with it—and likes them all. Having a child is nothing against her." Now, wasn't that an awful way for her to talk?

Mrs. Brownlees said it certainly was fierce! and the other listeners on the phone, for the audience had been augmented as the conversation proceeded, politely said nothing, but hung up their receivers with haste, and acquainted the members of their household with the disquieting news.

Mrs. Switzer threw her apron over her head and ran out to the pump, where Bill was watering his three-horse team. Bill received the news in that exasperating silence which is so hard to bear. When urged for an opinion, he said crustily: "Well, what's the girl goin' to do? None of you women would take her—she can't starve—and she can't sleep in the school woodpile. Mrs. Gray won't bite—she's a fine lookin' woman, drives a binder like a man, pays her debts, minds her own business. I don't see why it wouldn't be a good boardin' place."

In telling about it afterwards to Mrs. Howser, Mrs. Switzer said, "You know what men are like; in some ways they are hardly human—they take things so easy."

Pearl was surprised at the storm that burst, but soon realized the futility of further speech. They would not listen—they were so intent on proving the woman's guilt, they would hear no defence. From what they said, Pearl gathered

that they knew nothing about Mrs. Gray except
what the sewing-machine agent had told them,
and even he had not claimed that he had any
definite knowledge. The worst count against her
was that she would not tell anything about herself.
That she would not tell anything about herself,
could only have one explanation! There must be
nothing good to tell!

On Sunday, at the little stone church in the
valley of the river Pearl took her place among
the worshippers. The attendance was unusually
large. A new bond of interest was binding the
neighborhood together, and they spoke of it as
they congregated in the church-yard before the
service. Pearl sat inside and watched them as they
talked together excitedly. Snatches of their conversation came to her. "Well-behaved people
should stay with well-behaved people, I say"—
this was from Mrs. Switzer.

The men did not join in the conversation, but
stood around, ill at ease in their stiff collars, and
made an attempt to talk about summer fallowing
and other harmless topics. Their attitude to the
whole affair was one of aloofness. Let the women
settle it among themselves.

From the window where she sat Pearl could see
far down the valley. The river pursued its way,
happily, unperturbed by the wrongs or sorrows
of the people who lived beside it. Sometimes
it had reached out and drowned a couple of them
as it had done last year—but no one held it against
the river at all.

The rejuvenation of nature was to be seen everywhere, in springing grass and leafing tree. Everything could begin life over again. Why were the
people so hard on Annie Gray, even if all they believed about her were true? Pearl wondered about
the religion of people like the group who were
so busily talking just outside the window. Did
it not teach them to be charitable? The Good
Shepherd, in the picture above the altar, had
gone out to find the wandering sheep, even leaving
all the others, to bring back the lost one, sorry
that it had been wayward, not angry—but only
sorry—Pearl hoped that they would look at it
when they came in. She hoped too, that they would
look at the few scattered tombstones in the church-
yard, over which the birds were darting and skim-
ming, and be reminded of the shortness of life,
and their own need of mercy—and she hoped that
some of the dead, who lay there so peacefully now,
might have been sinners who redeemed the past
and died respected, and that they might plead now
with these just persons who needed no repentance.

But when the service was over, and a brief sermon
on Amos and his good deeds, the congregation
separated, and Pearl went back to the brown house
with a heavy heart, and the cry of her soul was
that God would show her a way of making the
people understand. "Plough a fire-guard, O Lord,"
she prayed, as she walked, "and let these deadly
fires of gossip run their noses square into it and
be smothered. Use me if you can—I am here—
ready to help—but the big thing is to get it done."

Around the open grate-fire that night, after
James had gone to bed, Pearl and Mrs. Gray sat
long before the pleasant wood fire For the first
time Annie Gray felt she had found some one to
whom she could talk and tell what was in her
heart, and the story of the last eleven years was
revealed, from the time that pretty Annie Simmons,
fresh from Scotland, arrived at the Hudson's Bay
post at Fort Resolution coming by dog-train the
last two hundred miles to her cousin, the factor's
wife—the thin-lipped daughter of the Covenanters—
who kept the pretty young cousin closely at work
in the kitchen with her pots and pans when the
traders came in, for Mrs. McPherson had no intention of losing Annie and her capable help after
bringing her all the way from the Isle of Skye.

After a year of hard work, and some lonesome
times, too, in the long, dark winter, there came to
the Post a young trapper and prospector, Jim Gray.

"When I saw him," said the woman, with the
silver bands of gray encircling her hapely head,
"I knew him for my own man. He was tall and
dark, with a boyish laugh that I loved, and a way
of suddenly becoming very serious in the middle
of his fun—a sort of clouding over of his face as
if the sun had gone under for a minute."

She spoke haltingly, but Pearl knew what was
in her heart, and her quick imagination painted in
the details of each picture. She could see the homesick Scotch girl, in the far Northern post, hungry
for admiration and love, and trying to make herself as comely as she could. She could sense all

the dreams and longings, the hopes and thrills.

"Tell me more about him," Pearl urged.

"He had the out-of-doors look," said Mrs. Gray, "big, gentle, fearless. I knew as soon as I looked in his eyes that I would go with him if he asked me—anywhere. I would dare anything, suffer anything for him. Nothing mattered; you will know it some time, Pearl, I hope. It brings sorrow, maybe, but it is the greatest thing in life. Even now, looking back down these black years, I would do the same—I would go with my man.

My cousin and her husband, the factor, forbade him the house when they saw what was happening. They had nothing against him. Every trapper said Jim Gray was straight as a gun-barrel. It was just that they would not let me go—they wanted my work, but I had already worked out my passage money, and considered myself free. They locked me in my room at night, and treated me like a prisoner. They said abominable things."

One night a tapping came at the little square window It was a heavy, dark night in July, with thunder rolling in great shaking billows. It was Jim, and he asked me if I would come with him. He had spoken to the missionary at the post, who would marry us. Would I come? I did not know whether he had a house, or even a blanket. I only knew I loved him."

"Under cover of the storm Jim took out the window-frame, lifted me out, and we were off through the rain and the storm. But when we got to the missionary's he would not marry us—the factor had

forbidden him. Jim would have taken me back but
I was afraid. The factor had said he would shoot
him if he ever came for me. He was a high-tempered
man and ruled the post and every one in it with
his terrible rages. What would you have done,
Pearl?"

"Was there no one else?" said Pearl, "no magis-
trate—no other missionary or priest ?"

"There was a missionary at the next post, sixty
miles away. We could reach him in two days.
What would you have done, Pearl?"

Pearl was living with her every detail, every
sensation, every thrill.

"What would I have done?" she said, trembling
with the excitement of a great decision. "I would
have gone!"

Annie Gray's hand tightened on hers.

"I went," she said, "and I was never sorry. Jim
was a man of the big woods; he loved me. The rain,
which fell in torrents, did not seem to wet us—
we were so happy."

"At the missionary's house at Hay River we
were married, and the wife of the missionary gave
me her clothes until mine dried. We stayed there
three days and then we went on. Jim had a cabin
in a wonderful hot springs valley, and it was there
we were going. It would take us a month, but the
weather was at its best, hazy blue days, continuous
daylight, only a little dimming of the sun's light
when it disappeared behind the mountains. We
had pack-dogs from the post—Jim had left them
there—and lots of provisions. I dream of those

campfires and the frying bacon, and the blue smoke lifting itself up to the tree-tops."

She sat a long time silent, in a happy maze of memory.

"I had as much happiness as most women, but mine came all at once—and left me all at once. We reached the valley in September. I was wild with the beauty of it! Set in the mountains, which arched around it, was this wonderful square of fertile land, about six miles one way and seven the other. The foliage is like the tropics, for the hot springs keep off frost. The creeks which run through it come out of the rocks boiling hot—but cool enough to bathe in as they run on through the meadows. Their waters have a peculiar purplish tinge, which passes away after it stands a while, and a delicate aroma like a fragrant toilet water. I called it the 'valley of purple springs.' "

"Our house was of logs, and built on a rock floor, which was always warm. There were skins on the floor worth fortunes, for the animals came to the valley in winter by the hundreds, black foxes and silver, martins and bear. They came in, stayed a few days and passed out again. The ferns in the valley stood seven feet high, and the stalks were delicious when boiled and salted.

"Jim had planted a garden before he left, and we had everything, cabbages, cauliflower, beets, mushrooms. Jim got the skins he wanted—he didn't kill many—and we tanned them in the Indian way.

"At first the Indians had been afraid to come.

They called it 'The Devil's Valley,' and though the young bucks might come in and spend a night, just as a bit of bravado, they were frightened of it; but after I came they took courage and came in.

"We found out that the water in the streams had healing power, and made one's skin feel soft as velvet, especially one stream which had the deepest color. One old squaw, whose eyes had been sore for years, was healed in three weeks and went back to her people with her wonderful tales of the valley. After that we had Indians with us all the time. They brought their sick children and their old people, and the results were marvelous. I never knew the stream to fail. Even the tubercular people soon began to grow rosy and well. The food seemed to have healing power, too, and some who came hollow-cheeked, feverish, choking with their cruel paroxysms of coughing, soon began to grow fat and healthy. At first the sick people just slept and slept on the warm rocks, and then came the desire to bathe in the stream, and after that they went searching for the herbs they needed.

"We lived there three years. At the end of the first year little Jim was born—my precious Jim, with his wonderful eyes, reflecting the beauty of the valley. The Indian women tanned the softest buckskin for his little things, and he had the most elaborately beaded garments. No little prince was ever more richly dressed. He grew lovlier every day."

Pearl could refrain no longer: "Why did you ever leave?" she asked breathlessly.

"Conscience," said Annie Gray, after a pause. "We couldn't keep it all to ourselves and be happy over it. We couldn't forget all the sick people to whom our purple springs would bring healing. Mind you, we tried to deaden our consciences; tried to make ourselves believe it was not our duty to give it to the world. We fought off these spells of conscience—we tried to forget that there was a world outside. But we couldn't—we owed a duty, which we had to pay.

"One day, with our winter catch of furs packed on the dogs, we came out. The Indians could not understand why we were leaving, and stood sorrowfully watching us as far as we could see them— there was a heaviness on our spirits that day, as if we knew what was coming.

"On the Judah Hill, at Peace River, came the accident. The train went over the bank. When I came to I was in the Irene Hospital there, with little Jim beside me quite unhurt. But I knew— I knew. I saw in the nurse's face—my Jim had been killed."

All the color had gone from her voice, and she spoke as mechanically as a deaf person.

"He was instantly killed—they did not let me see him.

"I went on. I knew what I should do. I would carry out as far as possible what Jim and I had started out to do. We had filed on the land, and I had the papers—I have them still. In Peace River we had sold the furs, and I had quite a lot of money, for furs were high that year.

"Jim had told me a lot about his father, a domineering but kindly old fellow, the local member of Parliament in a little Eastern town—a man who had had his own way all his life. Jim had not got along well with him, and had left home at eighteen.

"I remembered Jim had said that he wouldn't tell his father about the valley until he had talked it over with a lawyer and got everything settled, for the old man would run the whole thing. So when I went to his home I said little about our valley, except to tell them of the beauty of it.

"I was very unhappy. He raged about Jim and his wild ways. I could not bear it. He knew nothing of the real Jim that I knew, the tender, loving, sweet-souled Jim. I could see how he had raised the devil in the boy with his high-handed ways.

"He was passionately fond of the little Jim, and foolishly indulgent. He would give the child a dollar for a kiss, but if he did not come running to him the very moment he called he would be angry. Yet I could see that he adored the little fellow, and was very proud of his clever ways.

"One day he told me he was going to send Jim to a boys' school in England as soon as he was nine. I told him it could not be. Jim had said to me that we would bring up our boy in the wild, new country, where men are honorable and life is simple. I would follow Jim's wishes—our boy would not go to England. I defied him. I saw his temper then. He told me I had nothing to say about it, he was his grandson's guardian. Jim had made a will before he left home, making his father executor of his

estate. He told me the father was the only parent
the child had in the eyes of the law, and I had no
claim on my boy.

"I had no one to turn to. Jim's mother was one
of those sweet, yielding women, who said 'Yes,
dear,' to everything he said. She followed him
around, picking up the things he scattered and the
chairs he kicked over in his fits of temper. Sometimes when he swore she dabbed her eyes with a
daintily trimmed handkerchief. That was her
only protest. She advised me to say nothing, but
just do whatever 'father' told me, and I said I
would see him in hell first, and at that she ran
out with her fingers in her ears.

"Then a strange thing happened. McPherson,
my cousin's husband, the factor from Fort Resolution, met Jim's father at a lodge meeting, and told
him Jim and I had gone away without being married
—the missionary had refused to marry us—and we
had gone away. I think he knew better, for in the
north country every one knows everyone else, and
it was well known that Jim and I were married at
Hay River. He came home raging and called me
names. I'll never forget how they went crashing
through my brain. He was a proud man, and this
'disgrace' of Jim's, as he said, was the finishing
touch. But when he began to abuse Jim I raged too.
I said things to him which perhaps had better been
left unsaid. I was sorry afterwards, for Jim was
fond of his father for all his blustering ways. I did
not tell him that Jim and I were legally married,
for the fear was on me that he could take little

Jim from me, and it did not matter to me what they thought of me. I had one thought—and that was to keep my boy and bring him up myself— bring him up to be a man like his father.

"That night I left. I was proud, too, and I left money to pay for the time I had been with them. I had a few hundred dollars left, not enough to take me back to Purple Springs. My first plan was to get a housekeeper's position, but I soon found I could not do that—the work was hard, and Jim was not wanted. I worked as waitress in a restaurant, and as saleslady in a country store, but Jim was not getting the care he should have.

"One day I saw an advertisement in a paper. A prospector, crippled with rheumatism, wanted a housekeeper. It said 'a woman with sense and understanding,' and I liked the tone of it. It was blunt and honest.

"When I went to see him I found a grizzled old fellow of about sixty, who had been most of his life in the north, and when I found he had known Jim, and had trapped with him on the Liard River, and knew what a splendid fellow he was, I just begged him to let us stay. He was as glad to get me, as I was to find a home.

"I cared for him until he died. He was a good man, a man of the big woods, whose life was simple, honest and kindly.

"In the little town where we lived the people gossiped when I came to him. They wanted to know where I had come from, and all about me. I told them nothing. I was afraid. I had changed my name, but still I was afraid Jim's father might find me. Mr. Bowen thought it would be better if we were married, just to stop their tongues, but I couldn't marry him. Jim has always been just as real to me as when he was with me. Mr. Bowen was kind and gentlemanly always, and many a happy hour we spent talking of the big country with its untold riches. If I could have taken him to Purple Springs he could have been cured, but we knew he could not stand the journey, for his heart was weak.

"I went to night school while I was with him, and learned all I could for Jim's sake. But he died at last, and left me very lonely, for I had grown fond o him.

"By his will he left me all he had, and the deed of this farm was part of his estate. So, after his death, Jim and I came here. Mr. Bowen had advised me to stay on this farm—he had taken it because there were indications of oil, and he believed there would be a big strike here some day. He also left me four thousand dollars, and I have added to it every year. Sometimes I've been tempted to sell out and get back north, but Jim is too young yet, I think, I should go somewhere and let him go to school. I thought when I came he could go here. I have only one thought, one care, one ambition—I've lived my life—I've had my one good, glorious day, and now I want to see that Jim gets his.

"It's a queer story, isn't it, Pearl? I ran away and got married, and then I ran away from marriage to keep my boy. I could prove in a moment that my marriage was legal, of course, the certificate is here, and the marriage was registered by the missionary, who has come back now and lives in the city. But I dare not tell who I am—Jim does not know who his grandfather is."

"He surely couldn't take your boy," cried Pearl. "There is no justice in that."

"Only the unmarried mother has the absolute right to her child," said Annie Gray, as one who quotes from a legal document. "I talked to a lawyer whom Mr. Bowen sent for. He showed it to me in the law."

"Peter Neelands was right," said Pearl after a while, "it is exactly the sort of a law he said the other one was."

The two women sat by the fire, which by this time was reduced to one tiny red coal. There was not a sound in the house except the regular breathing of little Jim from the adjoining room. A night wind stirred the big tree in front of the house, and its branches touched the shingles softly, like a kind hand.

"I'll tell you the rest of it, Pearl, and why I am so frightened. Perhaps I grow fearful, living here alone, and my mind conjures up dreadful things. Jim's grandfather has moved to this Province from the East. I read about him in the papers. He is a powerful man—who gets his own way. He might be able to get doctors to pronounce me insane—we read such things. He has such influence."

"Who is he?" asked Pearl wonderingly.

"He is the Premier of this Province," said Annie Gray. "Now do you wonder at my fear?"

Pearl sat a long time silent. "A way will be found," she said.

CHAPTER XXI

THE OPENING OF THE WAY

"I WONDER where they are," Pearl said to herself, as she looked anxiously out of the window of the school on Monday morning. The roads leading from the Purple Springs school lay like twisted brown ribbons on the tender green fields, but not a child, not a straw hat, red sweater, sun-bonnet; not a glint of a dinner-pail broke the monotony of the bright spring morning.

The farm-houses seemed to be enjoying their usual activity. The spielers among the hens were announcing that the day's business was off to a good start, with prospects never brighter, dogs barked, calves bawled, cow-bells jangled—there was even a murmur of talking.

"They are not dead," said Pearl, as she listened, bareheaded, at the gate, "not dead, except to me— but they are not going to let the children come! They have turned me down!"

At nine o'clock, a flash of hope lighted up the gloom that had settled on her heart. The Snider twins, two tiny black dots, side by side like quotation marks, appeared distinctly against the vivid green of their father's wheat field and continued to advance upon the school-house, until they were but half a mile away. Then, noticing that no one else was abroad, they turned about and retraced their steps in haste, believing it must be Sunday, or a holiday—or something.

They were quite right on the last guess. It was something. But not even the teacher knew just what. The school room was clammily, reproachfully silent, every tick of the elm clock which told off the time without prejudice, seemed to pile up evidence of a hostile nature.

Pearl's brows were knitted in deep thought, as she looked in vain down the sparkling roads. What was back of it all? What had she done, or failed to do? Why did no one want to give her board and shelter? This latest development—the boycott of the school—was of course a protest against her association with the woman of Purple Springs.

Pearl squared her shoulders and threw back her head. She remembered the advice she had given her young brothers, "Don't pick a fight. Don't hit harder than you need to—but when trouble comes, be facing the right way." She would try to keep her face in the right direction. Here was prejudice, narrowness, suspicion, downright injustice and cruelty—of this she was sure— there were other elements, other complications of which she had no knowledge. Peter Neelands had told her the Government was watching her, but she had not taken it seriously.

She began to wonder if the invitation to work in the Educational Department might not be a plan to get her safely out of the way until after the election. It seemed too absurd.

Life was not so simple and easy as she had thought, or was it true that the element of trouble was in her own mind. Did she attract trouble by some quality of heart or brain. But what else could she have done? Hadn't she told the truth and done what seemed right all the way? But to be turned down in her school—left alone—boycotted.

Pearl's depression, poignant and deep though it was, did not last long. There would be a way out— there was always a way out! She would be shown the way!

"They that are with us," said Pearl solemnly, struggling with a wave of self pity, "are greater than they that are against us. I wish I could get them all lined up and talk to them. There is no use in talking to them one by one—they won't listen—they're too busy trying to think of something to say back. But if I had them all together, I could make them see things—they would have to see it. They are positively cruel to Mrs. Gray, and the dear little Jim—and without cause—and they should be told. Nobody would be so mean—if they knew—even the old grandfather would feel sorry."

When ten o'clock came, and not one pupil had arrived, Pearl decided she would go over to the post-office for her mail. There would be a letter from home, and never before had she so much needed the loving assurance that she had a home where a welcome awaited her, even if the world had gone wrong. The Watson family would stand by her, no matter what the verdict of Purple Springs.

In addition to the home letter, with its reassuring news that four hens were set and the red cow had come in, and the boys had earned three dollars and fifteen cents for their gopher tails, and the "twenty-fourth" being a holiday Jimmy would come over for her—in addition to this, there was a large square envelope from the city. The letter was from the Women's Club, telling her that they were preparing a political play and wanted her to come at once to the city to take an important part. They had heard of her ability from Mr. Neelands. Would she please let them know at once?

A smile scattered the gloom on Pearl's face. Here was a way out. Would she go? To play an important part in a play? Would she go?

Pearl went down the road on light feet, to where Mr. Cowan, the Secretary, was ploughing stubble. Mr. Cowan was expecting a call, and dreading it, for in spite of careful rehearsing, he had been unable to make out a good case. He was an awkward conspirator, without enthusiasm, and his plain country conscience reminded him that it was a mean way to treat a teacher whom he—himself—had selected. But why hadn't she accepted the offer to go to the city, and get away from a neighborhood where she could not be comfortable. Naturally, he could not urge it—that would give away the whole game. But he could hardly keep from asking her.

He resolved to say as little as possible, when he saw her coming. There was no trace of either gloom or resentment in her face when she greeted him. Mr. Cowan was equally friendly.

"I want to ask you something, Mr. Cowan," said Pearl. "What is wrong with me? Why don't the people like me? What have I done?"

Mr. Cowan had stopped his team, and lifting the lines from behind his back, he wound them deliberately around the handles of the plow before speaking. His manner indicated that it was a long story.

"Well, you know what women are like. No one can reason with women, and they won't stand for you boarding with Mrs. Gray. They're sore on her—and don't think she's just what she should be—and—"

Pearl interrupted him:

"But, Mr. Cowan, even before I went there, there was something wrong. Why wouldn't they give me a boarding place? You thought that I could get a boarding place when you hired me. Come on, Mr. Cowan, you may just as well tell me—it's the easiest way in the end—just to speak out—it saves time. If you ask me not to tell—I won't."

George Cowan did not expect to be cornered up so closely, and in desperation he said what was uppermost in his mind:

"Why don't you take the offer to go to the city? That's a great chance."

He had forgotten to be discreet.

"I am going to," said Pearl quickly, "that's what I came over to tell you—I want to go. I wanted to ask you if it would be all right."

"Now you're talking," cried her trustee gladly—a great burden had been lifted from his heart. "Sure you can go—it would be a shame for you to miss a chance like this."

In his excitement he hardly knew what he was

saying. This was just what he had been hoping would happen. Wouldn't George Steadman be pleased! He had given out a delicate piece of work to be done, and it had been successfully managed.

"You were just fooling us by pretending you were going to board at Mrs. Gray's—weren't you? You knew all the time you were going to the city; You were just playing a joke on us—I know. Well the joke's on us all right, as the cowboys said when they hanged the wrong man."

George Cowan rubbed his hands; the whole world had grown brighter. The political machine was the thing—real team-play—that's what it was. It's hard to beat the machine—and the best of it all was, there was no harm done, and nobody hurt. She would be as safe as a church when she was in the employ of the Government—and in a good job too—away ahead of teaching. No government employee could mention politics. Some people thought women were hard to manage, but it just required a little brains—that was all. Diplomacy was the thing.

"You are sure you don't mind my going," said Pearl, "without notice?"

"Not a bit—and we'll be glad to have you back, say for the Fall term. I'll fix the salary too and make out your cheque for the full month. It wouldn't be right for us to stand in your way—of course you may not want to come back—but if you do just drop me a line. I suppose you will want to go home before you go into the city. I can take you over this afternoon in the car."

"Thank you, Mr. Cowan,   Pearl said, "you are very kind. I'll be ready at one o'clock. But tell me— how did you know I had an invitation to the city? That was pretty clever of you."

Mr. Cowan was untwisting the lines from the plow handles preparatory to making another round. He suddenly remembered to be discreet, and winked one eye with indescribable slyness.

"A little bird whispered to me," he laughed.

At noon, when he told Mrs. Cowan about it, he said it was queer how that answer of his seemed to hit the teacher. She went away laughing, and he could hear her for fully a quarter of a mile kind of chuckling to herself.

CHAPTER XXII

THE PLAY

"SORRY, sir," said the man in the box-office of the Grand, "but the house has been sold out for two days now. The standing room has gone too."

'Can you tell me what this is all about, that every one is so crazy to see it?" the man at the wicket asked, with studied carelessness. He was a thick-set man, with dark glasses, and wore a battered hat, and a much bedraggled waterproof.

'The women here have got up a Parliament, and are showing tonight," said the ticket-seller. "They pretend that only women vote, and women only sit in Parliament. The men will come, asking for the vote, and they'll get turned down good and plenty, just like the old man turned them down."

"Did the Premier turn them down?" asked the stranger. "I didn't hear about it."

"Did he? I guess, yes—he ripped into them in his own sweet way. Did you ever hear the old man rage? Boy! Well, the women have a girl here who is going to do his speech. She's the woman Premier, you understand, and she can talk just like him. She does everything except chew the dead cigar. The fellows in behind say it's the richest thing they ever heard. The old boy will have her shot at sunrise, for sure.

"He won't hear her," said the man in the waterproof, with sudden energy. "He won't know anything about it."

"Sure he will. The old man is an old blunder-buss, but he's too good a sport to stay away. They're decorating a box for him, and have his name on it. He can't stay away."

"He can if he wants to," snapped the other man. "What does he care about this tommyrot—he'll take no notice of it."

"Well," said the man behind the wicket, "I believe he'll come. But say, he sure started something when he got these women after him. They're the sharpest-tongued things you ever listened to, and they have their speeches all ready. The big show opens tonight, and every seat is sold. You may get a ticket though at the last minute, from some one who cannot come. There are always some who fail to show up at the last. I can save you a ticket if this happens. What name?"

"Jones," said the gentleman in the waterproof. No doubt the irritation in his voice was caused by having to confess to such a common name. "Robertson Jones. Be sure you have it right," and he passed along the rail to make room for two women who also asked for tickets.

The directors of the Women's Parliament knew the advertising value of a mystery, being students of humanity, and its odd little ways. They knew that people are attracted by the unknown; so in their advance notices they gave the names of all the women taking part in the play, but one. The part of the Premier—the star part—would be taken by a woman whose identity they were "not at liberty to reveal." Well-known press women were taking the other parts, and their pictures appeared on the posters, but no clue was given out as to the identity of the woman Premier.

Long before sundown, the people gathered at the theatre door, for the top gallery would open for rush seats at seven. Even the ticket holders had been warned that no seat would be held after eight o'clock.

Through the crowd came the burly and aggressive form of Robertson Jones, still wearing his dark glasses, and with a disfiguring strip of court plaster across his cheek. At the wicket he made inquiry for his ticket, and was told to stand back and wait. Tickets were held until eight o'clock.

In the lobby, flattening himself against the marble wall, he waited, with his hat well down over his face. Crowds of people, mostly women, surged past him, laughing, chattering, feeling in their ridiculous bags for their tickets, or the price of a box of chocolates at the counter, where two red-gold blondes presided.

Inside, as the doors swung open, he saw a young fellow in evening dress, giving out handbills, and an exclamation almost escaped him. He had forgotten all about Peter Neelands!

Robertson Jones, caught in the eddies of women, buffeted by them, his toes stepped upon, elbowed, crowded, grew more and more scornful of their intelligence, and would probably have worked his way out—if he could, but the impact of the crowd worked him forward.

"A silly, cackling hen-party," he muttered to

himself. "I'll get out of this—it's no place for a
man—Lord deliver me from a mob like this, with
their crazy tittering. There ought to be a way
to stop these things. It's demoralizing—it's un-
seemly."

It was impossible to turn back, however, and he
found himself swept inside. He thought of the side
door as a way of escape, but to his surprise, he
saw the whole Cabinet arriving there and filing
into the boxes over which the colors of the Province
were draped; every last one of them, in evening
dress.

That was the first blow of the evening! Every
one of them had said they would not go—quite
scornfully—and spoke of it as "The Old Maids'
Convention"—Yet they came!

He wedged his way back to the box office, only
to find that there was no ticket for him. Every
one had been lifted. But he determined to stay.

Getting in again, he approached a man in a
shabby suit, sitting in the last row.

"I'll give you five dollars for your seat," he
whispered.

"Holy smoke!" broke from the astonished seat-
holder, and then, recovering from his surprise, he
said, "Make it ten."

"Shut up then, and get out—here's your money,"
said Mr. Jones harshly, and in the hurriedly vacated
seat, he sat down heavily.

Behind the scenes, the leader of the Women's
Party gave Pearl her parting words:

"Don't spare him, Pearl," she said, with her hand

around the girl's shoulder, "it is the only way. We have coaxed, argued, reasoned, we have shown him actual cases where the laws have worked great injustice to women. He is blind in his own conceit, and cannot be moved. This is the only way—we can break his power by ridicule—you can do it, Pearl. You can break down a wall of prejudice to-night that would take long years to wear away. Think of cases you know, Pearl, and strike hard. Better to hurt one, and save many! This is a play—but a deadly serious one! I must go now and make the curtain speech."

"This is not the sort of Parliament we think should exist," she said, before the curtain, "this is the sort of Parliament we have at the present time—one sex making all the laws. We have a Parliament of women tonight, instead of men, just to show you how it looks from the other side. People seem to see a joke better sometimes when it is turned around."

Robertson Jones shrugged his shoulders in disgust. What did they hope to gain, these freaks of women, with their little plays and set little speeches. Who listened or noticed? No one, positively no one.

Then the lights went out in the house, and the asbestos curtain came slowly down and slowly crept into the ceiling again, to re-assure the timorous, and the beautiful French garden, with its white statuary, and fountain, against the green trees, followed its plain asbestos sister, and the Women's Parliament was revealed in session.

The Speaker, in purple velvet, with a sweeping plume in her three-cornered hat, sat on the throne; pages in uniform answered the many calls of the members, who, on the Government side were showing every sign of being bored, for the Opposition had the floor, and the honorable member from Mountain was again introducing her bill to give the father equal guardianship rights with the mother. She pleaded eloquently that two parents were not any too many for children to have. She readily granted that if there were to be but one parent, it would of course be the mother, but why skimp the child on parents? Let him have both. It was nature's way. She cited instances of grave injustice done to fathers from having no claim on their offspring.

The Government members gave her little attention. They read their papers, one of the Cabinet Ministers tatted, some of the younger members powdered their noses, many ate chocolates. Those who listened, did so to sneer at the honorable member from Mountain, insinuating she took this stand so she might stand well with the men. This brought a hearty laugh, and a great pounding of the desks.

When the vote was taken, the House divided along party lines. Yawningly the Government members cried "No!"

Robertson Jones sniffed contemptuously; evidently this was a sort of Friday afternoon dialogue, popular at Snookum's Corners, but not likely to cause much of a flutter in the city.

There was a bill read to give dower rights to men, and the leader of the Opposition made a heated defence of the working man who devotes his life to his wife and family, and yet has no voice in the disposition of his property. His wife can sell it over his head, or will it away, as had sometimes been done.

The Attorney General, in a deeply sarcastic vein, asked the honorable lady if she thought the wife and mother would not deal fairly—even generously with her husband Would she have the iron hand of the law intrude itself into the sacred precincts of the home, where little cherub faces gather round the hearth, under the glow of the glass-fringed hanging lamp. Would she dare to insinuate that love had to be buttressed by the law? Did not a man at the altar, in the sight of God and witnesses, endow his wife with all his goods? Well then—were those sacred words to be blasphemed by an unholy law which compelled her to give back what he had so lovingly given? When a man marries, cried the honorable Attorney General, he gives his wife his name—and his heart—and he gives them unconditionally. Are not these infinitely more than his property? The greater includes the less—the tail goes with the hide! The honorable leader of the Opposition was guilty of a gross offense against good taste, in opening this question again. Last session, the session before, and now this session, she has harped on this disagreeable theme. It has become positively indecent.

The honorable leader of the Opposition begged

leave to withdraw her motion, which was reluctantly
granted, and the business of the House went on.

A page brought in the word that a delegation of
men were waiting to be heard.

Even the Opposition laughed. A delegation of
men, seemed to be an old and never-failing joke.

Some one moved that the delegation be heard,
and the House was resolved into a committee of the
whole, with the First Minister in the chair.

The First Minister rose to take the chair, and was
greeted with a round of applause. Opera glasses
came suddenly to many eyes, but the face they saw
was not familiar. It was a young face, under iron
gray hair, large dark eyes, and a genial and pleasant
countenance.

For the first time in the evening, Mr. Robertson
Jones experienced a thrill of pleasure. At least the
woman Premier was reasonably good looking. He
looked harder at her. He decided she was certainly
handsome, and evidently the youngest of the
company.

The delegation of men was introduced and received—the House settled down to be courteous,
and listen. Listening to delegations was part of
the day's work, and had to be patiently borne.

The delegation presented its case through the
leader, who urged that men be given the right
to vote and sit in Parliament. The members of
the Government smiled tolerantly. The First
Minister shook her head slowly and absent-mindedly
forgot to stop. But the leader of the delegation
went on.

The man who sat in the third seat from the back found the phrasing strangely familiar. He seemed to know what was coming. Sure enough, it was almost word for word the arguments the women had used when they came before the House. The audience was in a pleasant mood, and laughed at every point. It really did not seem to take much to amuse them.

When the delegation leader had finished, and the applause was over, there was a moment of intense silence. Every one leaned forward, edging over in their seats to get the best possible look.

The Woman Premier had risen. So intent was the audience in their study of her face, they forgot to applaud. What they saw was a tall, slight girl whose naturally brilliant coloring needed no make-up; brilliant dark eyes, set in a face whose coloring was vivid as a rose, a straight mouth with a whimsical smile. She gave the audience one friendly smile, and then turned to address the delegation.

She put her hands in front of her, locking her fingers with the thumbs straight up, gently moving them up and down, before she spoke.

The gesture was familiar. It was the Premier's own, and a howl of recognition came from the audience, beginning in the Cabinet Ministers' box.

She tenderly teetered on her heels, waiting for them to quiet down, but that was the occasion for another outburst.

"Gentlemen of the Delegation," she said, when she could be heard, "I am glad to see you!"

The voice, a throaty contralto, had in it a cordia

paternalism that was as familiar as the Premier's face.

"Glad to see you—come any time, and ask for anything you like. You are just as welcome this time as you were the last time! We like delegations —and I congratulate this delegation on their splendid, gentlemanly manners. If the men in England had come before their Parliament with the frank courtesy you have shown, they might still have been enjoying the privilege of meeting their representatives in this friendly way.

"But, gentlemen, you are your own answer to the question; you are the product of an age which has not seen fit to bestow the gift you ask, and who can say that you are not splendid specimens of mankind? No! No! Any system which can produce the virile, splendid type of men we have before us today, is good enough for me, and," she added, drawing up her shoulders in perfect imitation of the Premier when he was about to be facetious, "if it is good enough for me—it is good enough for anybody."

The people gasped with the audacity of it! The impersonation was so good—it was weird—it was uncanny. Yet there was no word of disrespect. The Premier's nearest friends could not resent it.

Word for word, she proceeded with his speech, while the theatre rocked with laughter. She was in the Premier's most playful, God-bless-you mood, and simply radiated favors and goodwill. The delegation was flattered, complimented, patted on the head, as she dilated on their manly beauty and charm.

In the third seat from the back, Mr. Robertson Jones had removed his dark glasses, and was breathing like a man with double pneumonia. A dull, red rage burned in his heart, not so much at anything the girl was saying, as the perfectly idiotic way the people laughed.

"I shouldn't laugh," a woman ahead of him said, as she wiped her eyes, "for my husband has a Government job and he may lose it if the Government members see me but if I don't laugh, I'll choke. Better lose a job than choke."

"But my dear young friends," the Premier was saying, "I am convinced you do not know what you are asking me to do;" her tone was didactic now; she was a patient Sunday School teacher, laboring with a class of erring boys, charitable to their many failings and frailties, hopeful of their ultimate destiny, "you do not know what you ask. You have not thought of it, of course, with the natural thoughtlessness of your sex. You ask for something which may disrupt the whole course of civilization. Man's place is to provide for his family, a hard enough task in these strenuous days. We hear of women leaving home, and we hear it with deepest sorrow. Do you know why women leave home? There is a reason. Home is not made sufficiently attractive. Would letting politics enter the home help matters. Ah no! Politics would unsettle our men. Unsettled men mean unsettled bills—unsettled bills mean broken homes—broken vows—and then divorce."

Her voice was heavy with sorrow, and full of

apology for having mentioned anything so unpleasant.

Many of the audience had heard the Premier's
speech, and almost all had read it, so not a point was
lost.

An exalted mood was on her now—a mood that
they all knew well. It had carried elections. It
was the Premier's highest card. His friends called
it his magnetic appeal.

"Man has a higher destiny than politics," she
cried, with the ring in her voice that they had heard
so often, "what is home without a bank account?
The man who pays the grocer rules the world. Shall
I call men away from the useful plow and harrow, to
talk loud on street corners about things which do
not concern them. Ah, no, I love the farm and the
hallowed associations—the dear old farm, with the
drowsy tinkle of cow-bells at eventide. There I see
my father's kindly smile so full of blessing, hard-
working, rough-handed man he was, maybe, but
able to look the whole world in the face. . . . You
ask me to change all this."

Her voice shook with emotion, and drawing a huge
white linen handkerchief from the folds of her gown,
she cracked it by the corner like a whip, and blew
her nose like a trumpet.

The last and most dignified member of the Cabinet,
caved in at this, and the house shook with screams
of laughter. They were in the mood now to laugh
at anything she said.

"I wonder will she give us one of his rages,"
whispered the Provincial Secretary to the Treasurer.

"I'm glad he's not here," said the Minister of Municipalities, "I'm afraid he would burst a blood vessel; I'm not sure but I will myself."

"I am the chosen representative of the people, elected to the highest office this fair land has to offer. I must guard well its interests. No upsetting influence must mar our peaceful firesides. Do you never read, gentlemen?" she asked the delegation, with biting sarcasm, "do you not know of the disgraceful happenings in countries cursed by manhood suffrage? Do you not know the fearful odium into which the polls have fallen—is it possible you do not know the origin of that offensive word 'Poll-cat'; do you not know that men are creatures of habit —give them an inch—and they will steal the whole sub-division, and although it is quite true, as you say, the polls are only open once in four years—when men once get the habit—who knows where it will end—it is hard enough to keep them at home now! No, history is full of unhappy examples of men in public life; Nero, Herod, King John—you ask me to set these names before your young people. Politics has a blighting, demoralizing influence on men. It dominates them, hypnotizes them, pursues them even after their earthly career is over. Time and again it has been proven that men came back and voted— even after they were dead."

The audience gasped at that—for in the Premier's own riding, there were names on the voters' lists, taken, it was alleged, from the tomb-stones.

"Do you ask me to disturb the sacred calm of our cemeteries?" she asked, in an awe-striken tone—her big eyes filled with the horror of it. "We are doing very well just as we are, very well indeed. Women are the best students of economy. Every woman is a student of political economy. We look very closely at every dollar of public money, to see if we couldn't make a better use of it ourselves, before we spend it. We run our elections as cheaply as they are run anywhere. We always endeavor to get the greatest number of votes for the least possible amount of money. That is political economy."

There was an interruption then from the Opposition benches, a feeble protest from one of the private members.

The Premier's face darkened; her eyebrows came down suddenly; the veins in her neck swelled, and a perfect fury of words broke from her lips. She advanced threateningly on the unhappy member.

"You think you can instruct a person older than yourself, do you—you, with the brains of a butterfly, the acumen of a bat; the backbone of a jelly-fish. You can tell me something, can you? I was managing governments when you were sitting in your high chair, drumming on a tin plate with a spoon." Her voice boomed like a gun. "You dare to tell me how a government should be conducted."

The man in the third seat from the back held to the arm of the seat, with hands that were clammy with sweat. He wanted to get up and scream. The words, the voice, the gestures were as familiar as his own face in the glass.

Walking up and down, with her hands at right angles to her body, she stormed and blustered, turning eyes of rage on the audience, who rolled in their seats with delight.

"Who is she, Oh Lord. Who is she?" the Cabinet ministers asked each other for the hundredth time.

"But I must not lose my temper," she said, calming herself and letting her voice drop, "and I never do—never—except when I feel like it—and am pretty sure I can get away with it. I have studied self-control, as you all know—I have had to, in order that I may be a leader. If it were not for this fatal modesty, which on more than one occasion has almost blighted my political career, I would say I believe I have been a leader, a factor in building up this fair province; I would say that I believe I have written my name large across the face of this Province."

The government supporters applauded loudly.

"But gentlemen," turning again to the delegation, "I am still of the opinion even after listening to your cleverly worded speeches, that I will go on just as I have been doing, without the help you so generously offer. My wish for this fair, flower-decked land is that I may long be spared to guide its destiny in world affairs. I know there is no one but me—I tremble when I think of what might happen these leaderless lambs—but I will go forward confidently, hoping that the good ship may come safely into port, with the same old skipper on the bridge. We are not worrying about the coming election, as you may think. We rest in confidence of the result, and will proudly unfurl, as we have these many years, the same old banner of the grand old party that had gone down many times to disgrace, but thank God, never to defeat."

The curtain fell, as the last word was spoken, but rose again to show the "House" standing, in their evening gowns. A bouquet of American beauty roses was handed up over the foot-lights to the Premier, who buried her face in them, with a sudden flood of loneliness. But the crowd was applauding, and again and again she was called forward.

The people came flocking in through the wings, pleading to be introduced to the "Premier," but she was gone.

In the crowd that ebbed slowly from the exits, no one noticed the stout gentleman with the dark glasses, who put his hat on before he reached the street, and seemed to be in great haste.

The comments of the people around him, jabbed him like poisoned arrows, and seared his heart like flame.

"I wonder was the Premier there," one man asked, wiping the traces of merriment from his glasses, "I've laughed till I'm sore—but I'm afraid he wouldn't see the same fun in it as I do."

"Well, if he's sport enough to laugh at this, I'll say he's some man," said another.

"That girl sure has her nerve—there isn't a man in this city would dare do it."

"She'll get his goat—if he ever hears her—I'd advise the old man to stay away."

"That's holding a mirror up to public life all right."

"But who is she?"

"The government will be well advised to pension that girl and get her out of the country—a few more sessions of the Women's Parliament, and the government can quit."

He hurried out into the brilliantly lighted street, stung by the laughter and idle words. His heart was bursting with rage, blind, bitter choking. He had been laughed at, ridiculed, insulted—and the men, whom he had made—had sat by applauding.

John Graham had, all his life, dominated his family circle, his friends, his party, and for the last five years had ruled the Province. Success, applause, wealth, had come easily to him, and he had taken them as naturally as he accepted the breath of his nostrils. They were his. But on this bright night in May, as he went angrily down the back street, unconsciously striking the pavement with his cane, with angry blows, the echo of the people's laughter in his ears was bitter as the pains of death.

CHAPTER XXIII

COMPENSATION

The next day the Premier kept to his room, and refused to look at the papers. The cabinet ministers telephoned in vain; he was out, the maid said. He hated them, every one—for their insane laughter their idiotic applause—this disloyal attendance at such a place! He could not speak to them or see them.

When his wife spoke to him, he snapped back at her like an angry rattlesnake, and asked her why she had never tried to develop a mind of her own. Her patience, submissiveness, the abject way she deferred to him and tried to please him—the very qualities he had demanded of her, now infuriated him beyond words. He began to despise her for her spiritless submission.

Fortunately for her, the days that followed took him away from home, and the household breathed easier each time he departed.

"This settles it," said Rosie, the housemaid, when he went out angrily slamming the front door. "I will never marry a member of Parliament, no, not though he goes on his bended knee to ask me. I may not have wealth or fame—but I'll have peace."

"Don't be too sure," said the cook, who was Scotch, and a Presbyterian. "You can't be sure of any of them—they are all queer. You never know what a man will do till he's dead."

The Women's Parliament held sessions for three nights in the city before it began its tour of the country with every night an audience that packed the theatre to the roof. Each night the woman "Premier" took her curtain calls and received the bouquets which came showering in, but not a word could the public find out about her. The papers said her identity would remain a mystery until all the engagements were filled.

On the last night, when Pearl went to her room— she was staying with the President of the Women's Club—a box of flowers was on her table. When she opened it, she found an armful of American Beauty roses, and a letter. Pearl's face went suddenly aflame like the roses, and a jagged flash of lightning tore her heart. He had not forgotten her!

Hastily locking her door, for no one must interrupt her, Pearl read her letter. She had faced three thousand people two hours before, but her hand trembled now as she read:

"I have been in your audience, Pearl, drinking in every word you say, rejoicing over you, loving you—but glad every minute that I played the game fair. You have won the election—of that I am sure— for you have set the whole Province laughing at the old-style politician. It is easy going for the rest of us now. Our old friend George Steadman has had the ground torn from under his feet. They all think you left Purple Springs to take some gentle and safe job in the Department of Education, and are breathing curses on this mysterious stranger who has upset the foundations of the Government. Driggs suspected as soon as he heard about the play, and he and I came into the city to see for ourselves—we held hands to keep from disgracing ourselves last night when you got up to speak.

"The leader of the Opposition, who seems to be a solid sort of chap, would like to meet you when it is all over—he is well pleased with the women's activities, and especially your part, and wants to meet you personally.

"I do not need to tell you, dear, what I think. I believe you know. I am in a mellow and pleasant state of being able to say 'I told you so.'

"I am not sending you roses because I think you are short of bouquets, but just because there are certain things a red rose can say, that I can not. H. C."

"And why can't you say it?" Pearl whispered, "and why don't you say it, and me hungry for it. Who is stopping you from saying it—I'm sure it's not me."

She threw aside her pride, and going to the phone, called the hotel where she knew he stayed.

"Is Dr. Clay of Millford there?" she asked, trembling with eagerness.

"Just a minute," said the clerk.

Pearl's heart was pounding in her throat, her ears sang, her mouth was dry with excitement. She wanted to hear his voice—she wanted to see him.

It seemed a long, long time—then the clerk's voice, mechanical and dull as the click of an adding machine: "No, Dr. Clay checked out tonight."

Pearl hung up the receiver listlessly. The ripple of laughter and waves of voices came from the drawing-room below. A company of people had come over from the theatre, some one was calling to her outside her door, asking her if she would come down.

Suddenly it had all become distasteful to her, hollow—useless—vain—what was there in it?—a heavy sense of disappointment was on her. After all, was life going to disappoint her, cheat her— giving her so much, and yet witholding the greatest joy of all?

She caught the roses in her arms, and kissed them fiercely. "I love you—red roses," she said, "but you are not enough. You do not say much either, but I wish you would tell me why he is so stingy with me!"

In a week, the election was over, and the Government defeated. The newspapers, in red headlines, gave the women the credit, and declared it to be the most sensational campaign the country had ever seen. "The barbed arrows of ridicule had pierced the strong man's armor," one editorial said, "and accomplished something that the heaviest blows of the Opposition had been powerless to achieve." Dr. Clay had defeated George Steadman by a large majority, and the Millford "Mercury" was free to express itself editorially, and did so with great vigor.

The Premier had fought valiantly to the last,

but his power was gone—the spell broken—he could no longer rouse an audience with his old-time eloquence. His impassioned passages had lost their punch, for the bitterness, the rage which filled his heart, showed in his words and weakened them; and the audiences who before had been kindled with his phrases, showed a disposition now to laugh in the wrong place.

The week of the campaign had been to him a week of agony, for he knew he was failing as a leader, and only his stern pride kept him going. He would let no one say he was a "welsher." The machine worked night and day, and money was freely spent, and until the last, he hoped his party would be returned, and then he could resign and retire honorably. He did not believe the machine could be defeated. They had too many ways of controlling the vote.

When the news of the Government's defeat began to come in from the country places—the city seats having all gone to the Opposition—the old man went quietly home, with a set face of ashy pallor. He walked slowly, with sagging shoulders, and the cane which he used, did not beat the pavement in rage, but gropingly felt its way, uncertainly, as if the hand which guided it was hesitant and weak.

In his house on Water Street, a big, square, brick house, with plain verandahs, the ex-Premier sat alone that night. A few of his followers—the close-in favorites—had called to see him, but had been denied. His wife, flutteringly made excuses. He

sat in his big black leather chair, looking into the
fireplace, where no fire was kindled, and when one
of the maids had come in to build the fire, he had
gently told her he liked it better as it was, dull,
bleak and dead, it suited the occasion—and she
had gone out hurriedly, and in the kitchen burst
into tears.

"It ain't natural for him to be mild like that,"
she sobbed to the cook. "I'd rather have him damn
me up and down. The old man's heart is broken,
that's what it is. He's sittin' there so calm and
quiet—it would make any one cry that has known
him in his good days. I don't believe we'll ever
hear him rip and tear again—the blessed old dear."

"Well indeed, I'll be glad if we don't," said the
cook grimly. "He's raised enough hell in his time
for one man, if he never does another turn at it.
I've put up with him for over fifteen years. I saw
him drive out Master Jim, and Jim's poor wife,
with the dearest little pet of a grandson any man
ever had. He was sorry enough after, but that
didn't bring them back. I hope he will sit still
for a while and think it all over, and give the poor
missis a rest. She's been bawled at, and sworn
at enough too, and her that gentle and pleasant."

"She's cryin' in her room now," said the housemaid, dabbin' her eyes with her handkerchief and
wishin' he'd come up and rage over anything.

"O, is she?" said the cook. "I'll bet she's not.
The house is so quiet it makes her nervous—that's
all! But she'll get used to it. O no, Rosie dear, he's
got his, and it's about time. I ain't worryin' over

him, for all I like the old man—but I believe the day
of judgment begins here. He's reapin' what he
sowed—and all I wonder at is that the harvest has
been so late."

"That's all right for you—you're a Presbyterian,"
said Rosie tearfully, "but I belong to the Army.
You know God's side of it better'n I do, but we're
all for the sinner, and I can't bear to see him so
quiet and mild. It's just like havin' a corpse in
the house to see him there in front of the dead fire;
I wouldn't wonder if the morning light will find
him cold and stiff in death." Rosie's tears gushed
forth anew at this sad picture.

"No chance," said the cook, "I haven't cooked
breakfast for him for fifteen years without knowin'
him better than that. He'll come back."

But the Presbyterian cook, so sure of her theology
and her knowledge of human nature, had no breakfast to cook for him the next day, for the ex-Premier
kept his bed, and declined to see any one except
his wife, whom he did not let out of his sight. His
gentleness was terrible—he was even pleasant.
When Rosie brought the mail to the door, he actu-
ally thanked her, which brought on another par-
oxysm of tears, and made even the cook shake
her head doubtfully.

He spoke little, and made no complaint. He
was only tired, he said—just a little weary. No,
he would not see a doctor—it was not a doctor he
needed.

Beside him sat his wife, the quiet, self-effacing
little woman who had had no thought or ambition

apart from him. Under half-closed eyes, he watched her, wonderingly. What were the thoughts of her heart—this gentle-faced woman who had so tenderly cared for him, and put up with him all these years. Many a time he had made her cry— he had driven away her son—and her grandson— and yet she had offered no word of remonstrance. How old and sad she looked when her face was in repose. It was a face of deep lines and great sadness—a wistful, troubled, hungry face, but dominated by a self-control of iron power. She sat beside the bed, without moving; waiting, watchful.

"You've been good to me, Jessie," he said at last, as he stroked her hand.

She started nervously.

"Better than I have been to you—but I am going to be better—it is not too late yet."

With eyes of alarm, growing wider every moment —she watched him as he spoke.

"I guess I needed a set-back," he said, "and I got it—and I've learned a lot in a short time. One thing was that you are more to me than I thought. My friends—in politics—were everything to me—but they valued me only for what I could do for them. I could harangue the crowd— gather in the votes—keep things going. I remembered every one, slapped every one on the back, called them by their first name—and it went. But they laughed at me behind my back. Their only interest in me was that I could carry elections. With you, it has been different. I don't know why you stuck to me. Why did you, Jessie?"

Without replying, she hastily left the room—
and phoned for the doctor.

The papers that night reported the ex-Premier's
condition as "causing grave apprehension to his
friends."

When Pearl read it in the evening papers, she
made a quick resolve. A letter must be sent to
Purple Springs.

When Annie Gray and Jim went to the post-
office for the mail, two days after the election,
they were not disappointed, for Pearl had written.

"It is all over," wrote Pearl, "and the Government has gone down to defeat. The new Government will make good its promises too. But I am
sure from what I have heard and seen of your
father-in-law, you have nothing to fear from him.
He would not take little Jim away from you even
if he could. You can tell the people of Purple
Springs all about yourself now, and wouldn't I
like to see Mrs. Cowan's face when she hears who
your father-in-law is?

"Tonight's paper says he is not well, and I am
wondering if you hadn't better come in to the
city, you and Jim. You will know best about this.
I feel sorry for Mr. Graham. He is a domineering old man, full of prejudice and narrow
ways. There could be no progress so long as he
was at the head of affairs—so he had to be removed.
He held the door shut just as long as he could,
and when the crash came, quite naturally he was
trampled on, and that is never a pleasant experience.
But the whole thing has a pathetic side. I wish
it could have been settled without this.

"The night of the election, women paraded the streets, singing and cheering, mad with joy, it made my eyes blur to see them. I am sorry it had to come to a show-down, for it seems to set men and women against each other—at least, I know some men feel that way. Of course we had lots of men helping us—we could not have got far without them. Peter Neelands has been one of the best. He was elected in one of the city seats, and we are all so glad.

"Here are some stamps and two balloons for Jim. I do hope you will come—. Lovingly, Pearl."

The winds of June, which whipped the dust of Water Street into miniature whirlwinds under the noses of the horses, were heavy with the unmistakable perfume of wild roses. The delivery man, sniffing the air, decided he would go that night to the Beach, just to see the fields of roses; the street-car conductor went suddenly homesick for a sight of the poplar trees, with the roses on the headlands, and the plushy touch of green grass under his feet, and the wizened little Scotch milliner across the road took what she called a "scunner" at the silk and muslin flowers, with their odious starchy, stuffy smell, and wondered where the farmer was, who two years ago had asked her to marry him. The wind—heavy with the perfume that stirred so many hearts with longing, eddied carelessly into the garden of the big brick house with the plain verandas, doubling round to the garden at the back, where, in an old-fashioned rocking chair with chintz cushions, sat the ex-Premier.

The wind, still charged with wild roses, stirred the lilac trees and mountain ash, and circled noiselessly around the chair where he sat, and played queer tricks with his memory, for all of us are young in June, when the pageant of summer is passing by.

"I like to see you knitting, Jessie," he said gently, "it is a peaceful art, untouched by worldly cares. I wish I could hear hens cackling, and the drowsy sounds of a farmyard, all set in nature's honest key. I'm tired of people and machinery and telephones and committees, and all these other inventions of the devil."

Rosie, scrubbing the veranda, hearing the last part of the sentence, piously thanked God for the master's returning health of body and mind, and flattened her head against the veranda post, to catch more.

"The things I have given my life to," he said sadly, "have fallen away from me—I built on a foundation of sand, and when the rains descended and the floods came, my house fell and left me by the ruins, groping in the ashes."

"It isn't so bad as that, James," his wife said timidly. "You are a respected man still, you know you are— you have plenty of friends, if you would only let them come. It's no disgrace for a public man to be defeated."

"It's not that, Jessie," he said. "It doesn't matter to me now what the world thinks, it can't think any worse of me than I think of it. No, the bitterest part of all this to me is that I have none of my own. I want some one of my own. I was too harsh—too hasty."

"If Jim had lived," she began, wistfully—

The front veranda bell pealed loudly, and Rosie hastily wiped her hands on her petticoat, and went to answer it, sorry to miss any part of the conversation.

"I won't see any one," said the ex-Premier, again. "She knows—I won't. Go and tell her I won't."

When Rosie opened the door, a card was put in her hand, and the visitor, a young lady, asked her if she would be good enough to give it to the ex-Premier.

"He won't see you," said Rosie quickly. "He won't see any one. I am turning them away by the dozens."

The visitor took the card from Rosie's hand, and hastily wrote a few words on it. Rosie told the cook about it afterwards.

"She had eyes like a fairy princess, lips like cherries, and the nicest clothes, but you could tell she wasn't thinkin' about them. I just wanted her to stay and talk to me. 'Will you give this to him,' she said to me, 'I'll wait here, and if he doesn't want to see me—it is all right—I will go away— but I think he will want to see me,' says she, with a smile at me that made me want him to see her too, and she sat down on one of the veranda chairs.

"When I gave him the card, he read it out loud— ain't he the nicest ever? Lots of people wouldn't have read it out. 'Miss Pearl Watson,' says he,

and what's this, 'teacher at Purple Springs,' and
he nearly jumped out of his chair.

"'My God!' he says, and he reached for his cane,
like as if he was going somewhere. 'Bring her here,'
he said, and his voice was more natural than it has
been since—it made me all prickle," said Rosie.

When Pearl was taken around to the back garden,
Rosie retired to a point of vantage on the sleeping-
porch above, and got most of the conversation,
by abandoning all scrubbing operations, and sitting
very still.

The ex-Premier's wife arose as if to leave, but
he motioned her to stay.

"This concerns you too, Jessie," he said.

For a moment a silence fell on them, as the wind
gently stirred the lilacs in front of them and a humming
bird on silken wings went. flashing past, like a
flower that had come alive.

"You are a teacher, your card says, at Purple
Springs. Is that in the far North?" The ex-Premier
endeavored to speak calmly.

"No," said Pearl, "it is only a hundred miles
from here."

His face clouded with disappointment.

"But it was named for the valley in the far
North, by a woman who came from there."

"Where is the woman now," he asked, with a
fine attempt to make his question casual.

"I came to tell you about her," said Pearl, with
evasion. "That is, of course, if you would like
to hear. It is an interesting story."

He motioned to her to begin, trembling with
excitement.

Pearl told the story that had been told to her the night she and Annie Gray had sat by the dying fire, told it, with many a touch of pathos and realism, which made it live before him. His eyes never left her face, though he could not discover how much she knew, and yet the very fact of her coming to him seemed to prove that she knew everything.

The old man's face twitched painfully when she spoke of the young widow's quarrel with her husband's father.

"He was not accustomed to having his wishes thwarted," said Pearl simply. "He was a man whose word was law in his own household and among his friends. But she had the freedom of the wilderness in her blood, and they quarrelled violently. He was determined to send the boy to England for his education."

"He only said that—he wouldn't have done it— he loved the boy too well," he burst in, impatiently.

"Well, of course, the young mother did not know that—not being a mind-reader, she had no way of telling—and besides, he threatened to take the child from her altogether. He was his son's heir, and he was therefore the guardian of the child. The law was with him, I believe, in that. That is one of the laws that have roused the women to take a hand in public matters.

"So, to save her boy, to keep him for her very own—she allowed her father-in-law to think she had not been legally married. She gave up her good name, to keep her boy. She went away—with only her two hands to make a living for them both."

"Where is she?" cried the old man, with something of his old imperiousness.

Pearl did not at once reply. He should hear all of the story. She did not minimize the hard struggle that Annie Gray had had in her attempts at self support, even when she saw the old man wince. He got it all.

"When she came to the farm on the Souris, she could not tell her story—the fear was on her night and day that she might be discovered, and the child taken from her."

"No judge in the country would do that," he cried stormily. "She had nothing to fear even if—if—"

"Unfortunately," said Pearl quietly, "she did not know that. She believed her father-in-law. She thought it was true, because he had said so, and she knew that the illegitimate child belongs to the mother, and to her alone. so she chose to let it stand at that.

"The people at Purple Springs adopted the name she had put upon her gate—but ostracized her. The fact that she did not tell them anything of her past, was proof to them she was not a good woman, and a man from Ontario, who knew something about the case, fed the curiosity of her neighbors with gossip which confirmed their suspicions."

"For three years she has lived alone, not a neighbor has come to her door—and she has kept herself and little Jim; has worked the farm, educated her boy, for the trustees would not let him come to school—kept sweet and sane in spite of it all.

"When I went to see her, she cried with joy to see a human being of kindly intention in her house. But the neighbors cut me dead, and kept the children home from school because I went to live with her."

A groan broke from him. "Poor girl!" he said brokenly, "Poor girl, she didn't deserve that."

Pearl's heart was softening, so she hurried on.

"The little fellow got into a fight at school, because a boy said things about his mother. He is the sweetest tempered child I ever knew, but he knew when to fight, and thrashed a boy a head taller than himself; and the trustees turned him out."

"What kind of people are they?" he stormed. "It was a brave thing for the boy to defend his mother—a brave thing I tell you. The other boy should have been expelled—you are the teacher— why did you let them?"

Pearl let him rage, then very quietly she said, "It happened three years before I knew them— but you should not blame the boy, Mr. Graham, or even the trustees. They were under no obligation to protect the woman or her boy. The boy's own grandfather had said much worse things about her than the boy at the school. He not only insulted her, but his own son as well—when the rage was on him. So why should strangers spare her?"

"Go on," he said hoarsely, "let me hear it all."

She was standing in front of him now, and her eyes were driving the truth deep into his soul. Something about her eyes, or her voice with its rich mellowness, caused him to start and exclaim.

"Who are you, girl—tell me, who you are—I have heard your voice somewhere! My God! was it you? was it you?"

"Yes," said Pearl, "it was me; and when the women of the city here, who had come to you and tried to break down your stubborn prejudices, tried to reason with you, but found it all in vain; when they told me that first night to think of some sad case that I had known of women who had suffered from the injustice of the law and men's prejudice, and strike without mercy, I thought of your daughter-in-law and all that she had suffered. I saw again the hungry look in her sweet face, when I went to see her. I saw the gray hairs and the lines of sorrow; I saw again the heroic efforts she makes to give her boy everything that the world is bent on denying him—I thought of these things—and the rest was easy. There was no other way, sir; you would not listen; you would not move an inch—you had to be broken!"

Speechless, almost breathless, he looked at her— all the fight had gone out of him.

"I am going now, sir," she said. "I have delivered her message. She only wanted to clear your son's memory. She will tell the people now who she is, and prove her marriage, for little Jim's sake."

"Don't go, girl," he cried, "sit down—tell me more. Tell me what the boy is like—how big is he?" "The boy is like you," said Pearl, "a tall lad for ten; clever far beyond his years."

"Does he know about me—does he hate me—

has she told him?" His voice was pitiful in its eagerness.

"Not a word—the boy has a heart of love, and as sunny a disposition as any child could have. She has made his life a dream of happiness, in spite of all."

The old man's face began to quiver, and a sob tore its way upward from his heart. His face was hidden in his hands.

"Would she ever forgive me?" he said, at last, lifting his head. "Would she believe me if I said I was sorry—would she have pity on a broken old man, who sees the evil he has done—would the boy let me love him—and try to make it up to him and his mother? You know her—why don't you answer me, girl? Is there no hope that she might forgive me?"

Pearl stepped back without a word, as Annie Gray came quickly across the lawn. She had been standing in the shade of a maple tree, waiting for Pearl's signal.

A cry broke from Mrs. Graham, Jim's mother, a welcoming cry of joy.

The old man rose to his feet, uncertainly holding out both his hands.

"My girl," he cried "I don't deserve it—but can you forgive me?"

And Annie Gray, who had suffered so bravely, so tearlessly, found her heart swept clean of resentment or bitter memory as she looked at him, for it was Jim's father, old, sad and broken, who called to her, and to Jim's father's arms she went with a glad cry.

"Dad!" she said, "Oh Dad! Little Jim and I are very tired of being orphans!"

And on the back veranda behind them, where she had been crouching with her ear to the paling, Rosie came out of hiding and burst out like a whole hallelujah chorus, and with the empty scrub pail in one hand, and the brush in the other, beat the cymbals as she sang:

> "O that will be glory for me,
> Glory for you and glory for me,
> When by His grace I shall look on His face,
> That will be glory for me!"

CHAPTER XXIV

"Quit your whistlin' Jimmy, and hold your whist—all of you—don't you know your poor sister is dead for sleep. Hasn't she been up hill and down dale this last six weeks. I never saw the like of it, and it's a God's mercy she ever lived through it—and then last night when she drove over from her school nothing would do your pa but she must talk half the night, when she should have been in bed. So now clear out you lads, and let's keep the house quiet, for Pearl is a light sleeper and always was."

"And a light stepper too, ma, for here I am—up and dressed, and hungry as a bear." It was Pearl herself who opened the stairs' door.

A shout of joy arose from the assembly in the kitchen, dearer to Pearl than any burst of hand-clapping she had ever heard in a theatre, and there was a rush for the first kiss, which Danny landed neatly, though we must admit it was done by racing over his brother Patsey, who sat on the floor tying his boot, and Patsey's ruffled feelings did not subside until Pearl opened her valise, which stood inside the "room" door, and brought out jack-knives for the youngest four boys. Patsey declared, still smarting over the indignity of being run over, and stood upon, that Danny should not get a knife at all, but Mrs. Watson interposed for her latest born by saying:

"O Patsey, dear, don't be hard on him. He was just that overjoyed at seein' Pearl, he never noticed what he was standin' on; anything would ha' done him just as well as you."

"I'll overjoy him, you bet," grumbled Patsey—tenderly feeling the back of his neck, "when I get him outside. I'll show him what it feels like to have some one stand on your neck, with heavy boots."

Danny made no defence, but gazed rapturously on his sister, and expectantly at the valise, whose bulging sides gave forth promise of greater treasures yet to come.

"I have some things here for broken hearts and rainy days," said Pearl, "that Ma and Mary will be placed in charge of. I believe a skinned neck should qualify, so if Patsey Watson will dry his tears and iron out his face and step back against the wall, close his eyes—and smile—he will get a pleasant surprise."

Patsey complied with all the conditions. Indeed, he not only smiled, he grinned, showing a gaping expanse in the front of his mouth from which the middle tooth had gone, like a missing gate in a neat white fence.

When Pearl placed a box in his hands, which contained the makings and full directions for setting up a red and black box-kite, a picture of which in full flight adorned the cover, a war-whoop of joy rent the air.

"Ain't you the luckiest kid!" cried Tommy enviously, as he crowded to get another look. "If there's anything goin', you get it."

"Now clear out, all you boys, and let Pearl get her breakfast," said Mary. "I haven't had a chance to speak to her yet, and I want to know how the girls are wearing their hair and how long a girl of sixteen should wear her skirts, and lots of things."

The boys departed to make whistles with the new knives, Pearl offering a prize for the shrillest and farthest reaching; to be tried at twelve o'clock noon, and silence settled once more on the kitchen.

"It's sort of too bad you came home on Saturday, Pearl," said her mother anxiously, as she toasted a slice of bread over the glowing wood coals. "The boys will pester you to death today and tomorrow—though of course I know you have no other time."

"I like to be pestered, ma," said Pearl, as she began on a generous helping of bacon and eggs. "Home is the best place, ma, and I never knew just how good it was to have home and folks of my own, as the day I went to school and found no children there. Isn't it queer, ma, how hard people can be on each other. It makes me afraid God must be disappointed lots of times, and feel like pulling down another flood and getting away to a fresh start again.

"But I am not going to talk about anything—until I get back to feeling the way I did when I went away. I want to see the hens and the cows and the new pigs. I want to get out in the honest, freckly sunshine. Do the potatoes need hoeing, ma? All right, pa and I will go at them. I like people, and all that, but I have to mix in lots of blue sky and plants, and a few good, honest horses, cows, dogs and cats—who have no underlying motives and are never suspicious or jealous, and have no regrets over anything they've done."

"But don't you like the city, Pearl?" Mary asked. "Don't you wish we all lived there? I do, you bet."

"I am glad my people live right here, Mary, out in the open, where there's room to breathe and time to think. O, I like the city, with its street cars weaving the streets together like shuttles; I love their flashing blue and red and green lights, as they slide past the streets, clanging their bells, and with faces looking out of the windows, and every one of the people knowing where they are going. I like the crowds that surge along the streets at night, and the good times they are having. I like it—for a visit. It's a great place to go to—if you have your own folks with you—I think I'd like it —on a wedding trip—or the like of that.

"But I want to see everything 'round home," said Pearl quickly. "Is the garden all up, and what did you sow, and where are the hens set, and did the cabbage plants catch?"

"You bet they did," said Mary proudly. "I transplanted them, and I put them in close. Pa said I would need to take out every second one, but I said we'd try them this way for once. You know the way cabbages sprawl and straggle all over the place—all gone to leaves. Well, mine won't, you bet, they'll heart up, because there's nothing else for them to do. Pa admits now its the best way.

They've got no room to grow spraddly and they're just a fine sight already. Cabbages are just like any one else; it doesn't do to give them too much of their own way, and let them think they own the earth."

When breakfast was over, Pearl, Mary and Mrs. Watson went out into the hazy blue sunshine. The ravine below the house was musical with thrushes and meadow-larks. The blossoms had gone, and already the wild cherries and plums were forming their fruit. Cattle fed peacefully on the river banks, and some were cropping the volunteer growth of oats that had come on the summer fallow. The grain was just high enough to run ripples of light, as the gentlest of breezes lazily passed.

Pearl remembered the hopes and visions that had come to her the first day she and her father had come to the farm, and through all its dilapidation and neglect, she had seen that it could be made into a home of comfort and prosperity, and now the dream had come true. The Watson family were thriving; their farm had not failed them; comforts, and even a few luxuries were theirs, and Pearl's heart grew very soft and tender with a sense of gratitude.

It was not too good to be true, she thought, as she looked at the comfortable home, the new barn and the populous farmyard spread out under the quivering sunshine.

"It was not too good to be true," thought Pearl. "I can't complain, even if some of my dreams have failed me—and maybe—who knows?"

"It's got to come right," she thought it so hard, she looked up to see if Mary or her mother noticed. But they were busy with a hidden-away nest, just found in the willow windbreak.

The news of the neighborhood was given to her by Mary.

"The Paines are putting up a new house, Pearl, and Mrs. Paine has some real nice clothes, and they seem to be getting on far better."

'That's good," said Pearl, and then added, with such deep conviction, as if she were trying to convince some one, she said:

"There's nothing too good to be true."

At noon, when all the family had been fed, and the horses were resting in the well-bedded stalls—John Watson gave himself and his horses a two hours' rest in the heat of the day—when every one was present, Pearl told them something of her adventures on the six weeks of her absence. Especially did she tell the young brothers of the lonesome little boy who had no playmates, but who loved his mother so much he would not let her know that he was lonely.

Patsey had a solution of the difficulty:

"Take me back, when you go, Pearl, and I'll play with him, and let him fly my kite n' everything."

"O, he isn't lonely now," Pearl said, "thank you all the same—but I'm going to bring him over in the holidays, for he needs to play with boys of his own age."

"Danny better not run over him, and stand on

his neck, though—he ain't used to it—the way we are," Patsy said, but was promptly advised to forget it, and let Pearl go on with the story, by Danny himself, to whom the subject was growing painful.

"His grandfather and grandmother came out when we did," Pearl said, "and they're staying at Purple Springs, and Jim and his grandfather are together all the time. Mrs. Gray—her real name is Mrs. Graham now—doesn't want her boy brought up in the city, and his grandfather is tired of the city too, so they're all living in the brown house, and every day's a picnic day."

"But oh!, say we did have one of the grandest picnics a week after we got home from the city. On Mrs. Graham's farm there's a little stream which runs down to the river, and we got it cleaned out, and a big, long table made, and seats and all. Jim and his grandfather did the work—he was brought up on a farm, and can do anything. And the two women cooked for days, and I went round and asked every one to come to the picnic—and I told them who Mrs. Gray was, and all about it."

"Told each one in a secret, I suppose, and told them not to tell," said her father, smiling.

"I hope you rubbed it in, good and plenty," said Mary, "about them bein' so mean and full of bad thoughts."

"I did my best," said Pearl, "especially with some of them who had had so much to say, and they were keen to come, I tell you, to meet the Premier. That's what he'll always be called, too, and he

sure looked it that day when he sat at the head of
the table, with the sunshine dappling the long
table, with its salads and jellies and plates of sliced
ham, and all the people sitting around kind of
humble and sheepish. He wore his Prince Albert
coat and his silk hat. He didn't want to—he thought
it wasn't the thing for a picnic, but I held him up
to it, for I didn't want the people to see him in
his corduroy hunting suit. I knew how impressed
they would be with the fine clothes, and I was
determined they should have every thrill.

"So he put on all his good clothes, even to his
gray spats. I had to argue a long time to get them
on him. He said they looked foppish, but I just
got the button-hook and put them on him while
he was arguing, and asked him who thought of
this picnic anyway! and he just laughed and said
he guessed he had to pass under the rod.

"And after all the people had been introduced,
and the men were standing back, pretty hot and
uncomfortable in their white shirts, he got up and
asked every one to have a seat at the table, for
he wanted to say a few words before we began
to eat.

"You could have heard a leaf fall, it was so still,
and then he told them all about his son, and how
he didn't understand him, and never made a chum
of him, and how he was so taken up with politics
he forgot to be a father to his own boy. And he
told about his son's marriage, and the whole story,
right up to the time I went to see him in the city."

" 'It's not easy telling this,' he said, 'but I put

my daughter-in-law in wrong in this neighborhood, and I am going to make it right if I can. She is a noble, brave woman,' he said, 'and I am proud of her. I lost the election,' he continued, 'but I am glad of it, for in losing it, I found a daughter and a grandson,' and then he put his hand on my shoulder and said, 'and here's the deepest conspirator in the country, who managed the whole thing. This is the girl who made fun of me, and lambasted me, but who brought my daughter-in-law and me together, and when she runs for the Legislature, I promise I will get out and campaign for her.'

"Every one laughed then, and the people crowded up around him, and Annie, and you never saw so many people laughing and crying at the one time in your life.

"We had a big boiler of coffee on the little tin stove in the trees, I grabbed off the white pitchers, the biggest girls from the school helped serve, and we got the people all started in to eat, for it doesn't do to let people's feelings go too far.

"When they had quieted down a little, and were nearly through eating, the minister, who was at the other end of the table, got up and said he had an idea he wanted to pass on.

" 'I'm ashamed,' he said—and I know he was—'of the way this community has treated Mrs. Gray and Jimmy— he didn't seem able to call her anything else either. 'On behalf of the district of Purple Springs, I apologize. We'll show our apology in something better than words, too, I hope,' he said, kind of swallowing his Adam's apple. 'We denied her child the right to play with our children, through our stupid and cruel thoughtlessness, now let us apologize by doing something for all the children of this neighborhood. This is a beautiful spot, a natural park; let us make it the Jim Gray Playgrounds, with swings, and sand-pile and acting bars and swimming pool, with a baseball ground up on the hill; where all our children, young people and old people too, can gather and be young and human and sociable together.'

"The people broke out into cheers and cries of 'We'll do it!' It seemed to relieve them.

"'And let us hold our church service here on Sundays, too, when the weather is fine. Our religion has been too stuffy, too mouldy, too damp, too narrow. It needs the sunshine and the clear air of heaven to sweeten it and revive it. I feel it today, that God is in the sunshine more than in the narrow limits we have tried to set upon Him.'

"'We sometimes deplore the tendency of our young people to go to the city,' he continued, 'but I don't know as I blame them. We've been living dull, drab lives for sure. Let us liven things up a bit, and give our people something to look forward to during the week, and something pleasant to remember. It's the utter dreariness of life that kills people—not hard work.'

"And then," said Pearl, "I could see the people wanted to sing or cry, or dance, or something, to work off their emotions; so I signalled to Bessie Cowan, who is one of our best singers, to start a

hymn that the children sing every morning. They
knew it well, and the people had learned it from
them. I never heard anything like it. It flashed
up through the highest branches of the trees, into
the blue air. I am sure God heard it, and was
pleased:

> 'God is in His temple
> Let the earth keep silent.'

"Little Jim knew it too, and his voice was sweeter
than all the rest. It seemed easy for every one to
talk or sing or laugh—or do whatever they wanted
to do. It was wonderful to see people come out of
their hard brown husks and be natural and neigh-
borly."

"Sure, and it was more like a revival meetin'
than a picnic, Pearlie," said her father, laughing.

"It was that, pa," she answered, "and like a
term in a reform school for some of them. There
had been a big quarrel among them about a road-
scraper, and the next day every one was offering
to wait, instead of grabbing at it the way they
had been; and the women who had fallen out over
a sleeve pattern and fought rings round, and called
each other everything they could name, made it
up right there.

"Before they parted, they agreed to have the
services there on Sunday—that's tomorrow, and
the ex-Premier is going to speak after the service
on 'How to Build a Community.' All the women
are baking, and everybody will bring their visitors,
instead of staying home from church the way they've

been doing, and the children can play in the sand-pile, and sail their boats on the little creek, and it looks as if Purple Springs has experienced a change of heart."

"Don't you think there's a danger of leadin' them to thinkin' too light of the Lord's day, Pearlie, picnicing that way," asked her mother anxiously, "and maybe makin' them lose their religion?"

"O, I'm not worried about that neighborhood losing its religion, ma," said Pearl. "Any neighborhood that could treat a stranger the way they did! But I do believe the sunshine and blue sky, the flowers and birds, and the getting together, along with the words of the sermon and the hymns they'll sing, will make them a lot more human. I never can think it would hurt God's feelings a bit to see children playing, and neighbors happy together on His day.

"They want us all to come; if you don't think it's too far to drive with the whole family, and I've been training the children all week to sing—it looks like a good time."

"We'll go!" cried Danny and Patsey, with one voice, and with brotherly unity prevailing—for once.

CHAPTER XXV

"O don't touch it—it hurts," Danny wailed, when Pearl examined his grimy little foot, from which a trickle of blood was showing through the murk of prairie soil.

"Just let me wash it, dear," said Pearl soothingly. "We cannot tell how badly you are hurt until we get the dirt off. It may not be so bad at all."

This was the afternoon of the same day.

Danny's tears came in torrents. "It is bad," he sobbed. "It's the worst sliver there's ever been in this family—or maybe in these parts."

"Well now, maybe it is. I wouldn't wonder if we'll have to send for the doctor," said Pearl, "and that will be one on Patsey—he never had a doctor in his life—and maybe never will. Just let me see how serious it is—and I'll promise you if I can't pull it out with my fingers—the doctor will be phoned for at once, and told to hurry."

With this promise to sustain him, Danny bravely submitted to a thoroughly good washing of the afflicted member, and even the cleansing of the other, for Pearl explained to him that feet came in pairs, and had to be treated alike in matters of washing.

But the sliver refused to move, though Pearl appeared to try to pull it out.

"Send for the doctor, Pearl," Danny gasped. "I'm getting weaker every minute, and everything is goin' from me—and now its gettin' dark—can't some of yez light a lamp?"

Danny had heard his mother tell so many times the story of his grandfather's last moments—it came easily to him now, and he revelled in the sensation he was making.

"Rouse yourself, Danny dear," his mother cried tearfully, "speak to us, darlin' and don't let yourself go to sleep—I'm feart it's gone to his heart."

"It couldn't ,ma," said Pearl, "it's only a sliver—it's not a telephone pole—a dash of cold water in the face will bring him back."

Danny suddenly returned to the earth, that his young soul seemed about to spurn, and the look he gave his sister was at once an appeal and a reproach.

"Haven't you anything in your rainy-day box that's good for slivers?" he asked.

"Sure there is," said Pearl, "I think in a case of this kind, an accident that calls for medical treatment entitles its owner to a very substantial donation from the emergency chest. Mary, will you please make a selection, while I go and phone, and remember, your youngest brother is grievously wounded; do your best for him."

Pearl went to the phone, with a curiously lightened heart. At least she would hear him speak—she would see him. Not once had she seen him since the day she had been in his office. Not once—and that was three months ago. Three months, which seemed like three years!

"Give me twenty-one, please Central," she said steadily.

She knew the way he took off the receiver.

"Dr. Clay, this is Pearl speaking," she hurried on, without giving him time for reply. "Danny has a sliver in his foot, and we want you to come out. Can you come?"

"Right away," he answered. "I'll be there in twenty minutes. Is it very bad, Pearl?"

"No, not very—I nearly got it out myself."

"Well, I'm glad you didn't,"—his voice was eager.

"But he wanted you—"

"Good for Danny—he was always a wise child."

When the patient was made comfortable in a rocking-chair, with a package of Japanese water "Flowers" and a cup of water in which to expand them, as a means of keeping his mind from despair, Pearl made a hurried survey of herself in the mirror, and pulled her brown hair into curls over her ears.

"Ears are not good this year, Mary," she laughed. "They must not be seen."

A roar of pain from Danny brought her flying back to him.

"Stay with me, Pearl," he shouted, "I'm a sick man, and tell the kids to keep quiet—it jars me— I can't stand it—it makes me all go cold!"

Pearl sat down beside him, making a rather unsuccessful effort to be becomingly solemn. Mary hushed the shouts of the others, who were quite ready to be thrilled by their brother's precarious condition—and when the doctor came in, the Watson brothers assembled to hear the verdict.

"He will recover," said the doctor. "Not only recover, but regain the full use of the injured member. But it's a bad, bad sliver just the same, and some boys would cry if they had it."

Danny set his lips tightly together, as one who was determined to endure to the end.

Very tenderly the doctor took him on his knee, and examined the little foot. "I'll have a basin of water, Pearl, please," he said.

"It has been washed," Danny cried, with indignation. "Pearl washed both of them."

"Sure enough," the doctor said, "but you just watch and see what I am going to do."

The doctor opened his black bag to get out a lance, the sight of which was too much for Danny's reserve of courage, and in spite of his brave efforts, the tears burst forth.

The doctor laid the lance back in the bag, and said, "Now Danny, I am going to tell you a real true story, and we won't touch your foot at all, unless you ask me to.

"There's a bad, bold sliver about this long, that ran into Danny Watson's foot. No one asked the sliver to go in—no one wanted it—but it went. Danny's foot does not like it—and every nerve is crying 'Pull it out—pull it out,' and the blood has gathered round to see what's wrong, just like a crowd of people on the street, growing bigger every minute, so Danny's foot is beginning to swell and get red and hot.

"Now, if we leave the sliver alone, the foot will get it out its own way, but it will take a long time.

The foot will get redder, hotter, sorer. It will be very stiff, and Danny will not be able to walk on it. And even after the sliver works out, it will take quite a while to heal, and there may be an ugly mark here for a long time. Still, that's one way to get rid of slivers.

"There's another way. It is to let me cut the skin with this sharp knife—sharp like a razor-blade —and then take these little tweezers, catch the end of the sliver, and give one quick jerk. Then we'll put your foot in the warm water and let all the blood that has been gathering to see what was wrong, run away, and then we'll put on something nice and soft, and some absorbent cotton, and make a fine bandage, and about tomorrow it will be as good as the other one.

"Which way will we do it, Danny?"

Danny had followed every word of the story, his eyes meeting the doctor's calmly.

"Which way, Danny?" the doctor repeated.

Danny buried his head in the doctor's shoulder, and said one word:

"Jerk!"

In a few minutes it was all over, and Danny, looking a little pale, with his foot resting on a pillow, was taken for a ride in the new wheelbarrow, well padded with fresh hay by his thoroughly concerned and solicitous young brothers. Danny, knowing the transitory nature of his popularity, was not too overcome by his recent operation to accept promptly the presents his brothers offered, and did so with a sweetly wan and patient smile which kindled a noble rivalry in the matter of gifts. Patsey, now very repentant, brought his catapult, Bugsey his alleys, his loveliest "pure," and the recumbent lamb set in a ball of clear glass; Tommy surrendered his pair of knobbies. Their mother, watching the procession leaving the gate, was moved almost to tears by these expressions of brotherly love.

"They fight and squabble and jander at each other, but when trouble comes, they cling together. That's what the psalmist means when he says 'A brother is born for adversity.' It's the day of trouble that proves what your own mean to you."

Mary and her mother were at the kitchen door, having come out to get the patient properly started for his ride.

"I never knew it meant that, ma," said Mary, "but that's a nice meaning anyway."

She looked into the living-room, where Pearl and the doctor sat without speaking, and just as her mother was about to go to join them, she said:

"I believe there's cream for a churnin', ma, it will be too sour before Monday. If you come out and stay with me, I'll do it, but I hate to work alone."

As she flung the cream from end to end of the barrel-churn, while her mother sat beside her mending the boys' shirts for the Sabbath, Mary said to herself:

"A sister is born for adversity, too—you bet."

Meanwhile, the doctor and Pearl, left alone, had broken the silence which fell upon them at first.

"Come out for a ride, Pearl," he said at last. "Saturday is the teacher's happy day, and I haven't seen you for months—not to speak to you—and I want to hear all about what you've been doing. You haven't told me yet that you are glad I was elected."

"But I wrote you a note, didn't I?"

"Oh yes indeed, you did," he agreed, "but you know even the best notes in the world lack color— or something."

"Even roses," said Pearl, "lack something too, though it isn't color."

"You will come, won't you, Pearl?" he urged.

Pearl sat on the flowered lounge, looking at him intently.

"Just wait a minute, doctor," she said, "your explanation of slivers and their treatment interests me very much. I think I had better consult you now as my physician. I have never had a physician, but it would no doubt be you if I should need one."

"Thank you, Miss Watson," he said, quite gravely, "I appreciate the compliment," and waited for her to speak.

"I have a sliver, too," she said at last. "No, not in my foot. It is in my heart, and I am afraid I have been trying the foolish way of letting it work out. You are quite right in saying it is slow, and painful—and attracts attention to itself. It does. Now that day, the second day of March, you and I had some serious conversation. I didn't understand why you said what you did. I don't yet. I am sure you said what you thought you should say. You may have been telling the truth—or if not, something you considered better than the truth, easier, more comfortable, less painful."

"Sometimes a very bitter thought comes to me—a sore thought—it is the sliver. I am not trying to be tactful now, just truthful. Tact and truth do not always combine naturally. This is one of the times. I am going to ask you something—but, don't speak until I am all done."

Here Pearl straightened her fine young shoulders, and her eyes grew very dark and luminous.

"Was it really because you think I am too young to know my own mind, that you spoke as you did, or is there another reason?"

She was looking into his eyes with such intensity, with such directness, that he knew he was going to tell her everything. It seemed as if she must read whatever was in his heart.

"My people are common, working people," she went on—and her head was held very high now, and her voice, all silver as it was, had an inner foundation of steel, like the famous silverware. "My people have always worked for a living. They are honest, kindly, honorable people, but they are what the vulgar would call—and do call—people who have no 'class.' My father eats with his knife; my mother does not know anything about having her subject and predicate agree in certain fine points in which subjects and predicates are supposed to agree. She knows how to work in harmony with her family and her neighbors, but her adjectives, verbs and nouns do sometimes tangle. I don't mind. These are small matters to me. I love my own people—admire and honor them."

Pearl's cheeks were flaming now.

"If you care greatly for these things—I know many do—and feel they are too serious, I want you to do something for me as my physician. You can do it with one word. It will hurt, but not for long. It will heal quickly. I will wash out the place with pride, and put on a bandage of the love I bear my own people. It will just be the first shock—there will be no after effects. Tell me the one word. Was it because—my father eats with his knife? Danny buried his face in your shoulder so he could not see. I will use a pillow—it is— more seemly. All right! Ready! Jerk!"

The pillow was thrown across the room, and Pearl found herself looking into his eyes, as he held her close.

"No, Pearl," he cried, "it is not that. I love you—more than all the world. I would marry you—if every relative you ever had had been hanged on the highest hill   There are no two people I know, to whom I would rather be related, than your father and mother. But there is a gap between us. I did not tell you the truth that day, because I felt it was more honorable to hide it. But I will tell you everything now."

When he was done, Pearl's eyes were soft and tender, and her arms tightened around him.

"Is that all?" she said happily. "Is that all?"

"You don't understand, dear, how serious it is," he said, "I couldn't ask you to marry a sick man."

"But you love me?" she said, "You want me— you have been miserable trying to give me up."

"It has been a bitter fight," he said, "a miserable, lonesome fight."

Pearl stood up suddenly, and he thought he had never seen her so beautiful, so queenly or so compelling. He knew he was going to do whatever she said. The weight of responsibility seemed to he lifted.

"Come out," she said quickly, "we are too happy to stay inside. I must breathe the sunshine and look up at the sky. My heart is too full for a house."

They drove to the river bank, a mile away, and sat on a fallen log at the head of a ravine, which fell sharply to the river below. Through the opening in the trees, they could see the slow running Souris, on which the sunshine glinted, making its easy way to join its elder brother, the Assiniboine, on the long, long march to the sea. Across the river plumy willows, pale green and tremulous, grew paler still as a wind passed over them.

The afternoon sun was sinking in a sea of wine-red mist, throwing streamers of light into the upper sky, like a giant's fan.

"I know now," said Pearl, "why I was led to Purple Springs, and why I felt when I met Annie Gray that my life would be knit with hers;" and then as they sat, hand-in-hand, with the glory of the sunset transfiguring the every-day world, she told him of the wonder valley of hot springs

in the far North, whose streams have magical
powers of healing. The valley of Purple Springs—
away beyond the sunset.

"We'll go over tomorrow," said Pearl, "and
Annie will tell you all about it, with its arch of
mountains, its tropical flowers, the size of the
vegetables and grains which grow there, and the
delight of the Indians when they find their sick
people growing well again. Annie has been longing
to go, and I told her yesterday I would go with
her, and we can still get there before the cold
weather."

The doctor made one last effort to hold to his
original intention:

"Pearl, I cannot let you bind yourself to me until
I am well again. I am holding my own, Dr. Brander
says. He thought the election would pull me down,
but it didn't. My case is a hopeful one. It's too
much like taking advantage of your romantic way
of looking at this. To marry a sick man is a serious
affair, and I cannot ask a girl like you, so full of
promise, so splendid in every way, to do it."

"You won't need to," she laughed, slipping her
arm through his. "It's all settled—I'll just marry
you without being asked. The covenant between
you and me was made before the foundations of
the world. You're my man. I knew you the moment
I saw you. So when I say, 'I, Pearl, take you,
Horace,' it's not a new contract—it's just a rati-
fication of the old. It's just the way we have of
letting the world know. You see, dear, you just
can't help it—it's settled."

"But are you sure, Pearl; you are so young in years; I mean—are you sure you will not be sorry? I love you, Pearl—I want you, but I desire still more to see you get the most out of life."

"I'm sure," she said steadily. "If I can't have you, life has fooled me—cheated me—and I do not believe God ever intended that. Peter Neelands said I was in love with life, with romance; that because you were the nearest hero I had selected you and hung a halo around you, and that maybe I was mistaken."

"What does he know about it?" asked the doctor sharply.

"I told him," said Pearl. "He was the only person I could talk to, and when there came not a word from you—and Mrs. Crocks told me you went quite often to the city to see Miss Keith, I began to wonder if I could be mistaken—so I tried to forget you."

"You did!"

"Yes. I worked two weeks on it, when I was in the city."

"How did you go about it?" he asked, after a pause.

"Peter said most girls were so romantic and ready to fall in love, they often loved a man who cared nothing for them, but who married them rather than break their hearts, and that's what causes so many unhappy homes. Of course, it works the other way too, and he said the way to tell if it were a real true, undying love, was to try the 'expulsive power of a new love.' That's a fine phrase, isn't it?"

"Well, Peter was willing to be experimented on. He said if he had come to Millford about the same time you did, I might have selected him instead of you, and made a hero of him."

"He has his nerve," exclaimed the doctor.

"O, I don't know," she said. "I mean I didn't know. I was willing to see. So Peter stuck around all the time, and he drove me everywhere, and always saw me home. I like him—all right—but you see I couldn't make my heart beat when he came into the room, and there was no rainbow in the sky, or music in the air, when he came to see me, and every day I got more lonesome for you, until it just seemed as if I couldn't go on. The three years when I thought you loved me, I saved up a lot of happiness—sort of money in the bank— and I used it every day and told myself you would tell me everything some day—and it would all come right. I got that mixed in with my prayers every night. But when you didn't come—and didn't come—my balance in the bank grew less and less— and I got panicky, and afraid I had been mistaken. So just to be sure, I did try to like Peter—not because I wanted to, but just to see if it could be done— in the interest of scientific research, Peter said it was."

"But I couldn't get accustomed to having him with me—he tired me sometimes—he talked too much, and I never could let him pay for my lunch, when we had lunch together. I could not let him spend a cent on me—not even the price of a movie."

"I'm glad you didn't, Pearl," the doctor said

quickly. "You were quite right about that, but you won't feel that way about me, will you, dear? These new women can get to be so independent— they are uncomfortable to live with."

Pearl rubbed her cheek against his shoulder, like a well-pleased kitten.

"No chance!" she said. "I'll let you pay every time—I'll just love spending your money—I won't ever know it from mine."

"O won't you?" laughed the doctor. "Well now, I am glad to be warned, and I am glad there are some laws to protect poor simple-minded men like me. I'll speak to Driggs about it as soon as I go back, and you may expect to see on the front page of the 'Mercury' something like this: 'I, Horace Clay, physician of the village of Millford, hereby warn the public I will not be responsible for my wife's debts.'"

At that, they laughed so much that the woodpecker in the tree above them stopped drumming, to listen, and when he found out how matters stood, he turned the whole story into telegraphic code and sent it up and down the valley; and a brown squirrel looked at them through a tangle of cranberry leaves, and when he got the drift of their conversation, he raced to the top of the highest tree and chee - chee - chee-d the news to all the other squirrels in the woods; and old silver-spot, the crow, scenting a piece of gossip, came circling over the trees and made a landing on a stump quite near them, and with his head on one side, listened for a few minutes, and then, with an insufferable smirk, rose cautiously and, circling high over the trees, made a rapid flight up the river, without uttering a sound.

The doctor watched him as he disappeared around the bend. "Do you know where he's off to, Pearl?" he said. "He's going to tell Mrs. Crocks. She understands Crow, of course—it's left over from her last re-incarnation. This will save an announcement!"

All afternoon, a black cloud, thick and thunderous, had huddled over the hills to the north, but before the sun went down, there came across its shoulder, a shining ribbon of rainbow.

THE   END